PRA

'An entertaining debut with an all-too-believable ending' *Sunday Telegraph*

'A rattling good yarn' *Irish Independent*

'An insider's account of the pleasure and pain associated with playing with vast amounts of other people's money . . . Kilduff writes with authority . . . He handles the world of high finance and soft-top BMWs with aplomb' *Irish Times*

'An attractively written first novel, whose strength lies in the creation of the bank's atmosphere, and the detailed analysis of financial jiggery-pokery' *Evening Standard*

THE DEALER

'A cleverly crafted and gripping financial thriller' *Belfast Telegraph*

'Plenty of insight into the murkier side of the financial world, a sprinkling of corruption, a soupcon of intrigue, not to mention a smattering of sex' *Publishing News*

'On the evidence of this, his second pacy insider-dealing thriller, he could soon be in a position to give Grisham a run for his money' *Dublin Evening Herald*

By the same author

SQUARE MILE
THE DEALER

THE FRONTRUNNER

Paul Kilduff

CORONET BOOKS

Hodder & Stoughton

Copyright © 2001 by Paul Kilduff

First published in paperback in 2002 by Hodder and Stoughton
A division of Hodder Headline

The right of Paul Kilduff to be identified as the Author
of the Work has been asserted by him in accordance with the
Copyright, Designs and Patents Act 1988.

2 4 6 8 10 9 7 5 3 1

All characters in this publication are fictitious
and any resemblance to real persons, living or dead,
is purely concidental.

A CIP catalogue record for this title is
available from the British Library

ISBN 0 340 81928 6

Typeset in Centaur by Palimpsest Book Production Limited,
Polmont, Stirlingshire
Printed and bound in Great Britain by
Mackays of Chatham PLC, Chatham, Kent

Hodder and Stoughton
A division of Hodder Headline
338 Euston Road
London NW1 3BH

For Linda

In Memory of colleagues David Brady, Robert McIlvaine and Michael Packer, 11th September 2001, New York City.

ACKNOWLEDGMENTS

I should like to thank my literary agent Patrick Walsh and editor Wayne Brookes for their expert advice. Thanks are also due to Kate Lyall-Grant and Lynn Curtis for their incisive feedback, and to Judith Chilcote for her encouragement. Audrey McNair, Colm McDermott, Docia Lin and Mak Vartholomis keep me in touch with life in the City of London. My former colleagues, Guy Kelly in Hamilton and John Porter in Amsterdam, added local knowledge. Tony and Mira Rocca at the Podere Collelungo estate and the team at the Surfside Beach Club provided great hospitality, as did Sheila in London W9. Finally, I should like to thank those colleagues at Merrill Lynch & Co. who suffer an author in their midst.

Fed Chairman Flies to Secret European Meeting

New York, July 12th – Federal Reserve Board Chairman Walter P. Sayers left JFK airport last night on a government jet to discuss the continuing global crisis with his international peers.

Sayers will shortly commence several days of high-level meetings with the Governor of the Bank of England, the President of the European Central Bank, the Chief Executive of the Hong Kong Monetary Authority and the Governor of the Bank of Japan. His exact destination has not been disclosed but insider Fed sources indicated to the *Journal* that the parties would likely rendezvous in a private luxury holiday retreat near the Mediterranean Sea.

The only topic on the agenda will be the continuing precipitous slide in world stock and bond markets. Global market indices have fallen by up to 35 per cent this month, with no apparent floor in sight. The panic has been underlined by the flight by major institutional investors to the traditional safe havens of the US currency, gold and other precious metals.

Some observers trace the root cause back to the death of a rogue futures dealer at his downtown

Manhattan apartment and the subsequent collapse of the giant hedge fund Alpha Beta Capital Inc. Other market insiders believe that global markets first became unstable when Hong Kong authorities ruthlessly crushed escalating civil unrest, following the assassination of the Chinese premier on a visit to the former British colony three weeks ago.

The Wall Street Journal

THE EVE OF DESTRUCTION

Was it the summit meeting that saved the world from Armageddon? Or was it the night on which Wall Street's crony capitalists, backed by the taxpayer, looked after their own? Whatever the interpretation, there wasn't much time to philosophise. Apart from festive occasions, the fortress-like Federal Reserve Bank of New York has seldom hosted such an illustrious gathering of Wall Street heavy-hitters. This time the mood was far from festive. 'I sensed a lot of fear in that room,' recalls one participant. We report on five days that shook the world.

Euromoney

PROLOGUE
CENTRAL
HONG KONG – 9.50 A.M.

The last moments in the life of the Chinese premier were captured on live television. Newscopters fought each other among the skyscrapers of downtown Central for the best panoramic shot as, far below, pairs of fluorescent-clad police outriders flanked the single-line convoy of black Mercedes S-class saloons. The first gleaming Merc was for the minor players. The second was bulletproof and bombproof, a customised import from the exclusive Brabus engineers in Germany. The other cars with pennants were mere decoys. Nothing but the best would do for Premier Zhiang on his latest visit to his most prized possession.

Cut to camera two located at street level along the carefully chosen route. Close-up shots of exuberant locals with Red Star flags behind rows of metal crash barriers. Enthusiastic waves as the blur of darkened windows passed them by at necessary speed. The personal Airbus

A320 had touched down at the flagship Chek Lap Kok airport on Lantau at 9.04 a.m. The entourage had effortlessly crossed the six-lane Tsing Ma bridge and emerged from the Western Harbour tunnel in Sheung Won, but by then was still running four minutes behind schedule.

Cut to camera four located outside the harbourside Exhibition Centre in Wanchai. The cavalcade stopped on cue. The door of the second Merc was perfectly positioned by the edge of the red carpet. Touchy state bodyguards gave the scene the once-over, with one eye on the crowd and one on their employer. One ear for the cheers and one for the earpiece humming with constant intelligence from their rooftop colleagues. The eyeball was satisfactory. A mutually assured nod to each other. A right hand was placed on the nearside car door. Zhiang gingerly alighted from the safety of the interior.

Cut to camera six for a side shot of the seventy-three-year-old premier as he commenced his twenty-yard marathon up the carpeted steps. He teetered, wobbled, swayed, stumbled – everything except a confident stride. Stiff upper-body movements, like a robot running low on juice. The arc limelight today, as ever, was his alone. The party hacks followed behind at a respectful distance and prayed that this relative youngster wouldn't falter in public. Welcoming hands reached out over the barriers and between the rows of edgy policemen who had their instructions from the omniscient event organisers. Die-hard voters threw multicoloured paper petals in the direction of their leader from the old country. Others watched silently from the back rows, their enthusiasm as genuine as the petals overhead.

A small object sailed high over the crowd. All five million viewers in the residential high-rise tenements of Kowloon and Sha Tin saw it. The egg missed its target but splattered on to the red carpet in an ugly ochre stain. Some definitely didn't share the collective enthusiasm. The clutch of bodyguards moved closer to their charge. A plainclothes officer identified a lone student in the crowd as he tried to melt away. He was lifted off his feet and dragged away, rough hands drowning out his vehement protest. A solitary elderly lady moved forward into the recently vacated space, one frail hand inside an almost empty shopping bag.

Cut to camera seven. Zhiang was on the conference podium, milking the sea of fawning applause. Much mutual bowing and nodding with the welcome committee headed by the Chief Executive. Camera seven zoomed in on his boxy navy suit, patently too large, with ridiculous shoulder pads as if in a nostalgic scene from *Dallas*. Sleeves so long they almost hid his tightly clenched fists. The monotone speech was mercifully short and apolitical. One Country. Two Systems. Same old story.

Then shock, horror; the close-up view on screen was too much. Pixel TV at its worst. A square head topped by oiled jet-black hair evidently well acquainted with dye. A pasty face with too much make-up. Thick bifocal glasses that were the height of fashion in downtown Beijing but not the norm in trendy Honkers. A pair of dead eyes, drugged to the hilt after a week of 'recuperation' at a private sanatorium. A fixed yet meaningless smile. A façade as genuine as his sentiments of goodwill to the local expatriate community. The cameraman obliged the Star TV viewers and panned back to a respectful distance; a good career move on his part. The attendees choked back the yawns, politely stood, clapped their leader from the hall and looked discreetly at their wristwatches.

Cut back to camera four outside in the humid air. Zhiang exited the entourage now eight minutes behind schedule. The crowds surged forward for their last chance to enthuse or to rebel. The elderly lady with the shopping bag in the front row was crushed against the metal barriers. A police officer in green HKPD uniform, peaked black cap, belt and holster ignored her plight. The officer forgot the strict instructions given at this morning's 7 a.m. briefing at the Central station. Instead, he turned away from the massed rabble to catch a quick glimpse of the main man.

The final scene was played back in slow motion from Sky to FOX, from CNN to BBC, from Channel 9 to TFL. The old woman's hand dipped into the shopping bag and emerged almost immediately holding something grey. The freeze-frame shots later clearly showed the standard-issue Smith & Wesson 0.38 revolver, weighing approximately six pounds, six rounds plus another six in a speedloader, worn usually with a straight-draw side holster and without a lanyard while on duty, the long gunmetal barrel suddenly shockingly visible beside the guilty police officer with the limited attention span. One round was enough from close range. The baying crowd, the revving Merc engines and the overhead helicopters drowned the sudden explosion of noise as the small-calibre bullet exited the chamber and instantly entered an already dying brain.

Camera four was live to the world as Zhiang lost his footing on the carpet and stumbled forward. His aides rushed to forestall political embarrassment of international proportions. Old age or something worse? They held his leaden arms and brought him back to his feet but it wasn't working as it usually did. Zhiang slumped forward again. One of the bodyguards felt the warm trickle of blood on his sweaty palm.

They closed ranks in mutual protection, dodged the blaze of TV lights and camera flashbulbs, and carried him on the longest journey of their lives. They stretched him out on the rear seat of the car. He didn't move against the black leather. The pool of blood widened. They looked at each other, silently acknowledging the awful truth. They were out of a job. Cut back to camera two as the sirens screamed and the convoy took off for the University Hospital. Beyond the neat rows of utterly useless crash barriers, the blood of the late Chinese premier seeped into the red carpet.

A scuffle broke out in the crowd as loyal party members pointed accusing fingers at an elderly lady with a smoking shopping bag and one less bullet. The authorities dragged her off in an eight-wheel truck to the main barracks. They sat her at a rusted metal table in a holding cell that stank of fear. They didn't know what to do. If she were forty years younger and male, they would have bounced her around the pitted concrete walls of the cell for a few hours for the sheer enjoyment factor alone.

Instead they asked her about the gun. She said it came from her eldest son's wardrobe. He was a policeman in the local force, off duty on this day of days. They didn't need to beat a confession out of her. I did it, she admitted. They knew that, they advised. It was on television. She asked to see a replay. They refused her request.

Next morning, the assassin was christened 'The Shopping Bag Killer' by the *Hong Kong Express*. The *South China Morning Post* was as ever more factually accurate, naming her Elouise Grace Pang, a sixty-six-year-old widow from a council estate in deepest Mongkok, near the old airport.

She talked freely in the barracks to release the pent-up hatred of her shattered life. Her younger son had been arrested while protesting in Beijing eight years ago – a trivial enough crime yet it earned him a five-year labour camp sentence in northern China. The winters in the draughty wooden cabins behind the razor wire were brutal. A weak twenty-three-year-old with asthma stood little chance without expert local medical assistance. Her son had died on the first day of the October snows.

Zhiang was the then Minister of Internal Affairs who'd twice refused the doctors' requests for clemency on medical grounds. Today had been sweet and worth the long wait, she declared. Charge me, she insisted, and get it over with as soon as possible.

*　　*　　*

Scott Chapman admired the views of the serene Hudson from the twenty-eighth-floor balcony of his Battery Park apartment in downtown Manhattan, before switching on NBC for the early morning news. The first TV advert always made him wince. 'If you have five hundred dollars, you can open a cash account at E*Trade. If not, get back to work.' If only it were that easy.

The sound of the power shower and the electric razor almost drowned out the breaking news in the bedroom, but Scott realised immediately that he was in trouble. He slumped down on the edge of the bed, soap and foam dampening the sheets, as he watched white smoke emerge from the barrel of the gun over and over, wishing he could rewind the videotape.

Scott checked his Bloomberg. The same grim news was on the screens. The markets were closed for the weekend. He needed political turmoil at this particular time like a hole in the head. His fiancée Kim surfaced from sleep and slid an inquisitive hand around his towelled midriff. He brushed her away, his mind fixed on the billions of naked dollars he had riding on the local markets and how many millions more he might lose when trading opened on Monday.

He was in deep at Alpha Beta Capital on Wall Street and no one else, including the proprietor, Art Greenbaum, knew that Scott had busted his dealing limits a long time ago.

CHAPTER ONE

VIGO STREET, LONDON, W1 – 8.10 A.M.

Jonathon Maynard alighted from the rush-hour Victoria line at Green Park station and followed the throng up the steps to the welcome sunlight and relative fresh air of Piccadilly. He glanced again into the windows of the Mercedes-Benz showroom, safe in the knowledge that Jack and Imogen would trash the leather seats in that CLK 320 Kompressor Coupé, and anyway he and Eva wouldn't have enough space for the weekly trip to Safeway's. He walked on automatic through the side streets, past moribund art galleries and awakening Italian delis, nodded to the doorman and entered the discreet offices of Richemont et Cie. The red voice-mail light on his telephone console flashed. Someone else was in early today. He played the message, left at the ungodly hour of 7 a.m., as he threw his suit jacket over the back of his chair.

'Jon, see me as soon as you get in.'

No need even to leave a name. Jonathon knew that

13

distinctive Switzer-Deutsch accent. He rode up to the fifth floor. Jackie, the middle-aged PA who almost doubled as private security, let him pass immediately. He knocked once on the door out of tradition rather than respect, but didn't wait to be asked in. The floor-to-ceiling window with its view of St James's Park below framed his boss.

'Just arrived, Jon?'

He moved nearer, aware that physical proximity often inhibited the Managing Partner's power play. Just for effect he stood closer, ran his right hand through his conservative haircut then along his jawline, painfully encountering the nick from this morning's shave after the mad rush for the bathroom.

'Just played my voice mail,' he countered.

They stood side by side. His boss needed to make his own seniority felt and took the easy option.

'Take a seat.'

Olivier Richemont was fifty something, slight, tanned, manicured, pedicured, silver haired with a very precise parting, and wearing a light continental suit cut too sharply for London. Jonathon wondered how his boss's skin always managed to be in such good condition, with never a blemish or a razor gash, always moisturised and pampered like that of some actor about to appear on a movie set. Richemont sat down opposite him.

'I've been here since seven o'clock, Jon.'

Evidently still on Central European Time. He needed to get a life outside his beloved personal fiefdom.

'So I gather.'

Richemont rested his elbows on the edge of the desk, then joined his hands and steepled his long fingers together in the ultimate display of confidence and power. Jonathon could read the body language but did his best to relax anyway, reclining indolently.

'Are we busy these days?' asked the Managing Partner as he subjected his cuticles to close scrutiny.

Jonathon assumed that the question did not include the entire staff of the management consultancy, but was rather addressed to him alone. As a director of four years' standing, he knew it was important always to tell the largest single shareholder that here was a loyal consultant who worked flat out and contributed the maximum amount to the firm's bottom line.

'I've got two assignments on the go. One is a suspected fraud at a Dutch broker in Moorgate and the other a large emerging market loan loss at a Japanese bank in Canary Wharf.'

'Forget them.'

Jonathon didn't think he could reply in the negative but he gave it a shot.

'I've got four consultants working on those assignments. I need to keep an eye on their progress.'

'This matters more.' Richemont paused. 'How are things at home these days, Jon?'

Suddenly his boss was being too sociable, softening Jonathon up for something worse. He appreciated the personal interest but knew he hadn't been asked up here for a chat about the home front. The truth about Jack and Imogen? Unmitigated chaos. Eva just barely kept them in check.

'We're managing.'

Richemont sat back in his seat and raised his eyebrows.

'Really?'

Jonathon had only just survived today's scrum at the breakfast table in the basement kitchen. Wholesome cereals discarded in favour of choco-coated flakes of gunge containing more plastic dinosaurs and lethal toys than calcium and folic acid. Freshly squeezed orange juice loaded with Vitamin C discarded in favour of bottles of industrial chemicals which had never been near a Californian orange grove and contained more sugar than an entire can of regular Coke. A fight over the two identical lunch boxes as Jack and Imogen decided whether the distribution of assorted goodies by Eva was equitable.

'Yes.'

'Good. Then you can take on this new assignment immediately. Delegate the other jobs to another director or else wrap them up by this Friday.'

'What's the assignment?'

Richemont wasn't going to be rushed in the palatial office he occupied for a few days every month as he parachuted in via LHR to annoy his directors. Jonathon knew the routine and waited. In his own time Richemont patted a closed manila file on the desk.

'It's for a very prominent client. You've been impressing the right people of late, Jon. They asked for you by name.'

'The Bank of England again?' he guessed. Jonathon recalled other assignments he had undertaken for the Bank in recent years. They had all been high profile and were well received. He'd done work on the copper trading scandal and an exotic-options black hole, his covert consultancy work performed in conjunction with the Bank's own investigation department. The ageing civil servants needed a cutting-edge expert who knew the darker recesses of investment banking from the inside. The fees had been huge. Richemont had been delighted that their firm had been appointed, but then he knew the Governor well.

'No. Our next-best client. They received a terse letter from a regulator last week regarding very large futures trades of one of their institutional clients. I don't know who. That letter is here, with records of trading activity and other relevant papers. I'm sure you'll know how to proceed. Their New York head office wants to know what's going on, and some independent assurance that all is well.'

There were enough clues there. Jonathon went for the biggest investment banking name of all.

'Mitchell's?'

'Your old firm.' Richemont nodded. 'They obviously appreciate your inside knowledge of their workings. You must have been an inquisitive burrowing mole when you worked there.'

'I was a bond trader. Big difference.'

'Not really. Living in the dark, surviving on scraps and rubbish, constantly wondering when you'll get caught?

Sounds like a mole to me. It's always puzzled me why they fired you.'

Jonathon shook his head.

'They didn't fire me. We compromised on my resignation. On a point of principle, actually.'

Richemont leant back and smiled, his carefully polished molars in full view.

'In investment banking?'

'If you have any concerns about me then you could always lose me.'

Jonathon knew that he held all the cards. Experienced management consultants with inside knowledge of bulge-bracket banks were in short supply. Two other directors had been headhunted by bigger firms last month. Richemont needed Jonathon as much as Jonathon needed a well-paid job to pay off his mortgage and finance the school fees.

'Maybe Mitchell's want you back on a trading desk. Ever thought about it?'

'I wouldn't touch them with a bargepole.'

'Even for a large pay cheque?'

'Even for a golden hello, a guaranteed bonus, a lock-up contract and a blank pay cheque signed by old Norman Newman himself. When I worked there, management told us we were the cream of the investment banking world and almost everyone else agreed. Traders at Mitchell's were notorious for being rich and thick.' Richemont didn't react to the old joke. 'Which Mitchell's office is it?'

'Does it matter?'

'You know it does.' Jonathon thought of the recent sleepless nights with the kids jumping up on the bed at 6 a.m. A short trip would be bearable provided he could sell it to Eva. Somewhere local like Paris, Frankfurt or Amsterdam would be fine. Out of sight and out of earshot for five days but still only an hour away by plane if he were needed at short notice. 'I can't do a long-haul overseas trip. I need to stay close to home and to be with the kids at weekends. That's the only time they get to spend with me these days. So where's the assignment?'

Richemont nodded.

'It's somewhere, that has just . . . how should I say it? . . . become topical.'

Richemont didn't have the balls to tell him to his face, but Jonathon wasn't playing guessing games today. The Managing Partner made it clear that their meeting was over by standing up and returning to the view.

'I've told Mitchell's you'll be there next Monday morning. Show me a draft report when you get back. That is all.' Richemont's limited attention span was shot. 'Good luck. Enjoy the trip.'

Jonathon left for the elevator bank. He opened the miserly file as he descended through the glass atrium. A letter fell out on to the deep dove-grey carpet. He picked it up and read the heading. He had failed to interpret Richemont's subtle clue. Jonathon would indeed be far away from the kids and Eva. The headed notepaper was in the name of Mitchell's Hong Kong. Too far by seven thousand bloody miles. How was he to break the news at home?

Lauren Trent's disastrous boyfriend had downed a heady succession of imported beers, neat vodkas, tequila slammers and assorted liquor shots. She rescued him at midnight from the smoky recesses of the retrospectively named Bar 1997 in hilly Lan Kwai Fong, placed him in the front seat of her Golf and carefully drove him back to Repulse Bay on the other side of Victoria Island, where he crashed out on her bed among the plump pastel cushions and the fine oriental sheets.

He looked horrendous in the unflattering light of her 7 a.m. alarm call, courtesy of the chrome Dream-Machine, as he sprawled beside her like unwanted baggage, hung over beyond all hope. He stank. BO, Marlboro, dubious weed and much alcohol. Stubble had appeared overnight. She prodded him.

'James? You awake?'

He was a reject from the playing fields of Eton or Harrow, meandering through the Far East to join his pater at some remote embassy outpost in Jakarta. They had been together for a month as suddenly his need to travel onward had diminished. He said he liked to be with a local. After nine years working in Asia, Lauren too liked to think of herself as a local. Her spacious home and lucrative career proved the fact, memories of her folks back in Manhattan kept comfortably at bay.

'Uhhhhhh?'

'C'mon, James. Time to get up.'

Lauren made for the shower, banging as many doors as possible, rolling up all the blinds. She showered methodically for five minutes, trying simultaneously to erase memories of a wasted Monday night. She always left her shoulder-length auburn hair wet, not wishing to damage it with a savage drier, knowing that the commute to work would sort the informal central parting and flyaway fringe. A hint of Givenchy *parfum*, but definitely not enough to interest Big Mac, Brad or any others on the floor. A slim gold chain around her throat. A quick dusting of powder and a hint of grey eyeliner and the morning transformation was complete. Pity it wasn't so easy to transform James.

She stepped into the walk-in wardrobe and chose appropriate clothes for work – a pair of navy culottes and a peach blouse with a faint check. Then the pair of well-worn Nike Air sneakers. Hardly appropriate for work yet essential for the early morning commute. Driving in heels was an impossibility. She pulled on a cardigan, and last of all her Yankees baseball cap, a classic design icon of the twentieth century as well as a reminder of younger days at Yankee Stadium, she'd do breakfast later. Now for the excess baggage amidst the sheets. Time to dump it in left luggage.

'Let's go, James.'

He hadn't the stamina of the well-spoken suits in the Ritz Carlton and Hilton bars or in the Jump or Joe Bananas. He couldn't compete with the Mitchell's big shots who visited the Hong Kong office, nor with the fund managers who came over from the States to see

Lauren at the sales desk. Most of all he couldn't compete with that handsome hedge fund trader from New York, her star client at the futures desk and her biggest source of commission. Such a pity he had mentioned a fiancée during their first working lunch at Fans by the harbour. She only ever seemed to meet traders on the make and men still struggling to get past puberty. Guys were like bar stools in Bar 1997. All the best ones were already taken.

'Let's go.'

James hadn't yet taken the hint. He rolled over, held his throbbing head and moaned about the damage done. Phat Cat appeared behind Lauren, brushed past her legs and jumped up on to the bed, as was his custom. This was the only reliable male in her life, a previously emaciated two-year-old stray Ginger Tom that had finally found a loving home with a reliable owner. Her guest wasn't so convinced. He swung out wildly with one hand.

'I hate bloody cats!'

Yes, James was history. Lauren was leaving and he wasn't staying any longer. She picked up his cheesy clothes — striped boxers, a dank fake YSL shirt, creased chinos and ten-buck M&S navy canvas deck shoes.

'Let's go, James. Now. I mean it.'

He slowly opened his bloodshot eyes and ran his hand through greasy hair standing up on end.

'Oh, now, come on . . .'

He was struggling to remember something, she knew. Probably her name.

'Outside. C'mon.'

The urgency in her voice alarmed him. That and the way she was bundling up his meagre possessions. She rolled him off the sheets and on to the floor. He hit the cold tiles with a painful thud.

'Wait! I need my stuff.'

Lauren threw him the disgusting boxers and he hopped, skipped and jumped into them on one leg. Some semblance of decency was required as she shut the apartment door behind them. He foolishly followed her down the stairs and out into the residents' carpark. The Brit expat from next door was already at his car. He worked for a major bank too. He smiled back at the odd couple, James still hopping about on one foot.

'What's happening here, Lauren?'

His memory had evidently returned.

'I'm going to work.'

Boxer Man instinctively stepped behind the inadequate cover of a blooming rhododendron. Lauren hit the remote control and the doors of her silver Golf opened to the touch. She relaxed into the front seat while Boxer Man looked on, puzzled but admiring. She knew the company car came with bucket leather Recaro sports seats, alloy wheels, air-conditioning, two litres of turbo injection power, tinted windows, soft top, metallic paint and sports pack suspension, whatever that was. The sad thing was that these sorts of petty auto details really seemed to matter to the guys at work.

James's innate survival instinct took over. He looked back at the locked apartment and made for the passenger door, but Lauren beat him to it, activating the central locking. As always the VW engine roared into life with the first turn of the key. She reversed back towards the main road and executed a perfect three-point turn and spin on the gravel. He shouted at her, clothes still in hand.

'When will I see you again?'

She rolled back the soft top while the car was stationary.

'Never.'

Then his true colours shone through.

'Fuck you, bitch! How do I get back to my hotel in TST?'

'Best to hitch a ride. The main road is over there. Put some clothes on first. It'll be so much easier.'

She left him in a cloud of dust as the Michelins spat out the loose stones. She passed the triangle of green of the prestigious nine-hole Royal Hong Kong Golf Club on Deepwater Bay and hit fourth gear on the almost deserted gradients as she snaked towards the Wong Nai Chung Gap. As she waited in the queues before the booths at Aberdeen Tunnel to pay her five-buck toll, she took off the baseball cap and ran her hands through her almost dry hair, one eye on the rear-view mirror where she could see the expat Brit on his way also to Central still smiling at the way she'd handled herself back there.

The dashboard clock showed 7.42 as she turned on the eight-speaker radio. They were playing some Sounds of the Eighties, Laura Brannigan and 'Self Control'. It reminded her of growing up in New York, of weekends spent with friends on the beaches of Long Island, of shopping with her mother on Fifth, of evenings spent in the cosmopolitan restaurants and bars off Columbus Circle, of nights going back to her father at home alone. She shuddered and turned off the radio, dismissing the past.

Hong Kong came into view after thirty minutes. All looked the same as last Friday, but it was an illusion. Monday had been a day of national mourning at the request of sombre government types. The local markets had been closed. Today was their first day back at their desks. The Hang Seng index would lose hundreds of points today. Perhaps even thousands. It wasn't every weekend that some old woman bagged the Chinese premier.

Lauren slowed down in Central, hung a smooth right into the rear of the bank's carpark and stopped before her usual space, number eighteen on the upper level. Brad had parked his muddied BMW 5 series in it. Must have done it deliberately. After all, he was crap with numbers. She stopped near by and killed the engine dead, one among many corporate metallic symbols parked up for the next ten hours of international cut and thrust. Big Mac's Jaguar XJ6 was here already too. She was last in today. Blame James.

Another day in the global financial markets beckoned once she had retrieved her modest heels from under the financial futures and options sales desk at the leading US investment bank of Mitchell Leonberg & Co. Inc. Or the FF&O desk, as they all called it. She trudged to the elevators. Yes, another day, another dollar. Or a few million. Maybe even a billion, if she was lucky.

Scott Chapman was exhausted. They had done twelve fast minutes to the end of the Battery, then faster back. Now Kim wanted to do one more return circuit of the traffic-free boardwalk they both knew so well. It was too much. His straining lungs and tired muscles could take no more. He spent too much time at work, not enough in the gym. Sweat ran down his matted dark hair and on to his aching body. He wiped the beads off his face with the sleeve of a Russell Athletic sweatshirt. He trailed in her wake along the esplanade of old pitted railroad sleepers. Kim saw the hollowed eyes and pale skin and knew he was in worse shape than ever.

'You okay, Scott?'

'Yeah.'

'So how many should we invite?'

'You tell me.'

'Mother says four hundred.'

'Jeez! That's too many.'

'Mother says it's the socially accepted norm these days. Joel and Stacey had four hundred.'

'So what?'

Scott hated all socially accepted norms. Hated all social functions in fact. Hated weddings. Specifically a wedding where he was to be the joint host and the main centre of attention. Kim wasn't convinced.

'That would be two hundred from your side and two hundred from my side ...'

'I can do basic math. It's my goddamn job! I'm a trader.'

'So that's okay, then?'

'I don't know two hundred people. I'd have to invite total strangers.'

Kim jogged past their favourite local restaurant, Steamers Landing, without a glance. Scott felt his head spin with fatigue. He could do with a monster burger, fries – hold the salad – and a couple of iced Buds. It would be the perfect end to the weekend. No such luck with Kim and her health binge which kept her perfect body the object of every man's desire. They overtook an old woman walking a pampered coiffured dog on a red lead. Kim was pulling away from him again, almost gloating at him from several feet ahead.

'You can invite your colleagues from that bank you work at.'

Wishful thinking. Scott had no real friends there, and they'd hate him all the more if they knew what he was doing, knew about the hole he was in. The wedding would have been more appropriate a year ago when everything was still okay. Now he was barely hanging on by his fingertips. Damn Chinese premier kicking the bucket like that . . .

'Alpha's not a bank, it's a hedge fund. I've told you that before.'

'You think I care what a hedge fund is? Sounds like something to do with horticulture to me. Mother says we should visit her in California to finalise all the arrangements. Take a few days off work.'

Scott was almost yelling at her now, across the gap widening between them.

'I'd prefer tying the knot somewhere quiet. How about the Caribbean? With four guests.'

Kim didn't look back. She was way out ahead.

'Mother wants a real big party and so do I, you know that. Take some time off work. You need a break. You never take any vacation at that bank.'

Scott let it go. Kim was more observant than Art and the others at Alpha, who hadn't noticed that he hadn't taken a single day in twelve months. Even when he had been almost dying with some lethal viral infection, he had gone in to sit by Dieter. It was too dangerous otherwise. Scott couldn't risk the chance of discovery while he was away. No one cared enough to notice at Alpha, not even Art. All they were interested in was his dealing profits.

'Have you booked a week's vacation for the honey-moon like I asked?'

Scott was almost out of breath, his heart racing dangerously. He'd have to cut back on the coke at work next week.

'Don't you know what the hell happened this week-end? Someone shot the Chinese premier. That will send shock waves through the stock markets. I can't book a vacation when that sort of uncertainty is out there.'

'Someone else can do your job for a while. Mother needs to see you more often. She told me that she's been checking out that website you built with our photographs. It's supposed to be for our friends and your parents upstate, but she uses it more than anyone. It's the only chance she has to see you.'

Two reckless rollerbladers in baggy grunge sped by in the opposite direction and cut them up.

'You can get a two-hundred-buck fine for doing that round here,' called Kim.

One of the guys heard her, leered back at her tight sports top and running shorts and raised a finger at Scott.

'Gotta catch us first, asshole.'

Kim bit her lip.

'Do something, Scott!'

'What exactly? I'm wasted,' he panted.

Kim finally halted by the boardwalk within sight of the new hotels and the Jewish Museum of Heritage, near Scott's old Athletic Club on Washington which he used to frequent before he started taking daily lines of pure coke with the other jaded traders in the powder room at work.

'Scott, I'm worried about you,' she said, frowning in concern. 'You still go to the gym at lunch-time or are you too busy for that now?'

'Sure I still go. I'm okay.'

Kim grasped the metal rail that ran along the bank of the Hudson, stretching her calf muscles and shoulders in her habitual wind-down. She unravelled and then regathered her long natural blond hair into a neat ponytail. Adjusted her wraparound Oakleys. There was hardly a trace of perspiration on her lightly tanned skin. She looked exactly what she was, a successful yoga teacher who was about to make life complete for a Wall Street star. Scott's eyes lingered on her orange Adidas halter-neck top which left nothing to the imagination, but still he remained anxious. He glanced at his watch.

'Let's get back to the apartment. I need to check the screen.'

'That goddamn screen is ruining our sex life!'

'It's a necessity.'

'It's a pain in the ass. You should be staring at me in bed, not the screen.'

'I have to monitor the situation in the Far East. If panic spreads from Hong Kong to the other markets then we're all screwed and I mightn't be able to pay for our fancy apartment or the wedding your mother reckons you should have.'

Kim stopped stretching and leaned against the rail beside him. They stared out across the still water. Scott watched the two-bucks NY Waterway ferry off to the right. Kim watched the steaming Staten Island ferry plying its ceaseless passage over to the left.

'Okay, take it easy. I was just kidding about the horticulture thing. Explain it to me again now. What exactly do you do?'

'Not now, Kim.'

'Yes. Now. You trade securities?'

He always did his best to glamorise his job at Alpha to her. The jargon about leverage, indices, variation margin calls, butterfly spreads and ratchets impressed his fiancée, his own parents and hers out on the West Coast. He had told Kim once in bed that he was engaged in riskless principal index arbitrage. She had smiled as if he were talking a foreign language. Now he was desperate for her to really understand.

'No. I trade derivatives.'

'What's the difference?'

He needed to make this as simple as he could, so he used the analogy Art used for idiots.

'The difference between dealing in securities and derivatives is the same as the difference between driving a Ford and a Ferrari. Securities guys buy and sell listed securities of blue-chip companies, take some modest capital gains and dividends and look for an annual return to beat the Dow. They park their new Ford automobiles with great care, wash the gleaming bodywork by hand every weekend and worry about how much they will lose when they trade up in three years' time. And at worst a forty mph Ford driver can only injure a pedestrian or prang a fellow motorist and worry about the effect on their no-claims bonus.'

'And derivatives?'

'They are an entirely different ball-game. Derivatives guys like me deal in billions, try single-handedly to corner the markets, fight the Fed and national governments on a daily basis, look for tiny percentage profits on giant-sized positions. We gun our red Ferraris down the East Side's FDR on a Monday morning at seven a.m., don't give a fuck about the potholes on NYC's decaying streets, burn rubber on the warm asphalt as often as we do between the sheets, and trade up after six months when the auto's ashtray is full. A reckless Ferrari driver at ninety mph can wipe out a party of schoolchildren and nuns, entire financial markets, global competitors, sometimes themselves too. The money is huge, billions every day. That's why I'm putting in these fucking crazy hours at Alpha at the moment. And why I cannot book a week off solely because it suits your mother.'

Kim was silent. The monologue had been too much. He looked over at the barren New Jersey shore, safe in the knowledge that they lived and worked on the right side of the river. He stared at the tremendous vista before them – the lush greenery of the Frank F. Wagner Park, the helicopters hovering overhead on their way to the downtown heliport, the Statue of Liberty and Ellis Island off in the distance. Then back towards their high-rise apartment in Hudson Tower near the WFC. The Colgate Pier clock showed almost six o'clock. Definitely time to check the overseas markets on Bloomberg. Kim suddenly straightened up and set off at speed in the direction of the apartment, yelling back at him.

'Sorry I asked.'

She was gone. Scott was dead on his feet. He could only manage to stagger back by sticking close to the dense undergrowth along the boardwalk, so as not to impede runners with more stamina. It wasn't supposed to be like this for a hotshot trader. He was about to marry the most gorgeous girl in Manhattan, if not in the entire state. He should be feeling on top of the world. But he'd grown addicted to this trading game, taken too many risks, too many lines. He'd doubled up when he should have cut his losses.

Life for Scott had become a dead end, a one-way street towards the day of reckoning with Art and the SEC at the other end. He couldn't stand to make small talk about wedding arrangements when he was up to his neck in millions of hidden losses at Alpha. Couldn't risk working days away from the desk, even for a dream honeymoon and tantric sex with Kim. He wasn't sleeping. He wasn't exercising. He wasn't eating. He wasn't living. He was no longer climaxing. And the lines of excellent coke from Rico were slowly frying his jaded brain.

The Chinese cleaning lady had established a set daily routine after ten years of work. Arrive at 6 a.m., hail, rain or shine, and get the buckets of steaming hot soapy water lined up. Select the scrubbing brushes and the old cloths. Enter the 1960s latrine block at 6.15 a.m., immediately after reveille in the vehicle park that doubled as a parade ground at the rear of the Central complex.

There had been a well-publicised change of tenant, but essentially her work hadn't changed. Five years spent working under the benign instructions of a friendly kilted sergeant-major from the Aberdeen Highlanders, then five less pleasant years under the aggressive stares of various captains in the Chinese Popular Army who seemed to come and go. She often wondered how popular the army actually was.

First she cleaned the still-warm shower stalls, removing the foaming pubic hair from the congealed drains. She washed the row of eight cracked washbasins, scrubbing away the remnants of stubble at the waterline. Then into the six narrow toilet cubicles. Don't ask. She always put the worst off till last and tried completely to empty her mind as she tackled the ten urinals by the high row of windows at head height. No job for a sixty-year-old with a bad back and no pension, but ultimately urine was still urine, British or Chinese.

Today was no different — one eye on the sodden cigarette butts that she extracted delicately by hand and one eye through the dirty panes of glass and rusted metal grilles on the awakening world. It was busier than usual outside, but she knew that was to be expected. Life in the walled barracks had changed since the untimely death of their glorious septuagenarian commander-in-chief. The much-publicised shopping-bag killer was being held in a cell near by and everyone inside and outside the barracks knew it.

The cleaner watched as soldiers clambered into the cabs of high-axle trucks parked along the rear wall. They cranked up diesel engines, and plumes of exhaust clouded the scene as they unnecessarily pumped the gas. Others moved Jeeps and an APC to the other end of the vehicle park. A few oil drums were rolled away. A space had been created by the back wall. An officer pointed a rattan cane as a group of soldiers moved to stand near by. All six carried rifles.

The cleaner's tired eyes turned towards the grey concrete detention block off to the right. A party of three emerged: two gaunt surly soldiers in ill-fitting khaki uniforms with a frail elderly woman between them, the latter clad in dirty black trousers and a torn white top.

Her bare dusty feet were lifted off the pitted concrete of the yard by the youths goose-stepping on either side. The cleaner recognised that harrowed face from the stills on the week's evening news broadcasts. The truck engines were still revving. She guessed that the prime suspect was on the move.

The soldiers took their charge past the windows of the latrine block. The cleaner could see that the prisoner's hands were tied behind her back with coarse rope. Her feet were also bound together. The soldiers ignored the waiting vehicles, but stopped by the twelve-foot-high wall topped by strands of barbed wire. More shouting, this time more rapid and authoritative. Orders were barked at the six with rifles. The cleaner saw their set expressions. This prisoner was travelling nowhere.

The cleaner dropped her brush on the tiled floor as she comprehended the scene. The escort stood their bound charge against the wall. The six soldiers lined up less than twenty feet away. Others standing in the yard watched but did nothing. No blindfold was offered. The prisoner knew what was about to happen and collapsed on to the concrete. More orders were barked. A chair appeared. They sat her in it.

A hand was raised. The soldiers took aim. The truck engines roared in unison, the noise deafening, the fumes wafting over the yard. The cleaner didn't hear the volley of fire until it echoed around the concrete walls, over and over. The shooting party couldn't miss. The body slumped down to ground level again, dissolving into a tiny pile of soiled clothes and a pool of blood. The engines fell silent.

The officer turned and yelled some more orders. The escort took the crumpled body back into their care and disappeared inside the detention block. The door slammed behind them. Some of the trucks were reversed back into their original parking spaces, as if nothing had happened. Yet one space remained, the blood upon it visible for all to see. The officer turned towards the latrine block.

He saw the cleaner watching the scene. She knew. He summoned her outside. She fell down on her knees but didn't need to plead. He didn't seem to care that she had seen it all. He pointed at the pool of blood, then at her bucket and brush, and barked instructions in an aggressive Chinese dialect. She understood.

Ultimately it was like no other morning on cleaning duty inside the barracks. She'd never forget scrubbing warm blood off oiled concrete. It took her less than five minutes to remove but the stain would last much longer. Her radical grandson in university would soon see to that.

CHAPTER TWO

VIGO STREET, LONDON, W1 – 9.05 A.M.

Jonathon returned downstairs. Nikki, his loyal PA for the past two years, had arrived. She put a pound coin down on his desk in preparation for their Monday morning ritual.

'Ready?' she asked.

Nikki had been up West all weekend. She wore a new low-cut top in shocking pink, jewellery dangling from all parts and chunky platform shoes that might have needed local planning permission. He noticed the subtle difference in the new tint in her cropped hair. There was enough Egyptian Dust air-brushed on to her face to rouse any dormant pharaoh. She was more than ready. He took out his pound coin.

'So how was your weekend, Jon? Any key project deliverables achieved?' she asked.

Jonathon often reminded himself that he was eleven years older than Nikki, and any perceived flirtation was surely an illusion on his part, though some in the office still talked about the two of them at Richemont's twentieth anniversary bash at the Café Royal a few months ago. Nikki's little black number with the dangerous slit up the side, her elongated silver feather boa and her goggle-eyed boss all featured in the photographic evidence. But he knew he wouldn't dare have another relationship so soon. He wasn't always sure that Nikki was of the same opinion. He took a deep breath.

'I had many high-level networking opportunities. A big win-win scenario playing one-on-one soccer with young Jack on Saturday. Ball-park figures and no one moved the goalposts this time. Then the heavens opened and we took a raincheck with Playstation. One dispute with Jack but we took it off-line and touched base amicably later. Imogen was difficult on Saturday but I made her think outside the box and she hit the ground running on Sunday morning. She saw the big picture with me in the Odeon, Leicester Square. She knows I am one of the movers and shakers because I too appreciate Pokémon. The bottom line took a bit of a hit in IKEA, Brent Cross, on Sunday afternoon. Otherwise a value-added weekend with plenty of synergy, some lessons learned and minimal reinventing of the wheel. And your weekend?'

Fortunately Nikki had rehearsed during the Tube ride on the Victoria line from Stockwell.

'Eddie, my latest, didn't know the whole game plan. I was more proactive than reactive. I ran an idea up the flagpole and he saluted. We met several key milestones at exactly the same time with no quick wins and the occasional cherry-picking on our part. We are a good strategic fit. I'm impressed with his core competencies and best practice. By Sunday morning we were both singing from the same hymn sheet. There were no show-stoppers, no playing hardball. What we enjoyed wasn't rocket science, it was good old-fashioned touchy-feely stuff with plenty of knowledge-sharing. We'll revisit it next weekend, do some more gap analysis, see if we can find some more bandwidth for the extra mile.'

Nikki caught her breath. No further words were needed. She was the winner all right. She gathered the two coins into her hand and sat down in the corner couch by the window. Jonathon exhaled.

'You know more consultancy jargon than I do.'

'I see it in all your reports, don't I? Maybe you and I need to put all this jargon to bed?'

He made eye contact, recalled events at the Café Royal and resisted the temptation.

'We need the jargon to be real consultants. It stops others understanding what we're talking about.'

'Including the clients?'

Jonathon was momentarily distracted by his list of unread e-mails as he powered up his PC.

'Especially the clients.'

'So what's happening?' asked Nikki.

'I've got to go away next week.'

'Have you cleared it with the boss?'

'He gave me the assignment personally.'

Nikki gave Jonathon a wry grin.

'I meant the dreaded Eva. The real boss.'

He let it pass.

'Who's the client this time?'

'Mitchell's.'

'They always ask for you. Jackie told me the other day that you used to work there but they fired you. What happened?'

Richemont's PA was an overhead who inhabited the rarefied zone that was the Adminisphere. Nikki talked to her at smoking breaks and thus gleaned what was really happening at the firm. Jonathon frequently found it useful, but not today.

'I worked on a bond trading desk,' he explained. 'Mitchell's sold a junk TMT bond issue to a bunch of investors who had no idea what they were buying from us. The price went from ninety to sixty bucks in two months. The investors were livid. The desk head told me to buy back some of the bonds at cost, take a loss-making position from some investors in Tokyo, hold it over their financial year end in March and sell it back to them at the same price in the new tax year. No loss to Mitchell's, the investors' profits weren't dented, and in fact they were going to pay us half a million bucks under the table for the trade.'

'What's wrong with that?' asked Nikki.

'It's illegal. It's rigging the books of the investors. I could have got done for it, so I said no way. The desk head, some arrogant American, went bloody ballistic. We had stand-up fights about it. He dragged me down to see FVPs and CFOs but I stood my ground. Mitchell's sent me on six months' gardening leave.'

'Which is ... ?'

'I sat at home, still an employee but with no job to do, on full pay, unable to work elsewhere.'

'Sounds ideal. How do I get a job like that?'

'You don't want it. You go senile watching daytime TV and reading newspapers. All your friends are at work. You end up doing the laundry because there's nothing else to do. Mitchell's finally gave me a nominal pay-off which I spent on legal fees. I resigned and signed a ridiculous contract written by a bunch of anxious lawyers in New York headquarters agreeing to say nothing to anyone in public.'

'So why come here?'

Nikki's natural curiosity always impressed Jonathon. She would make a good management consultant.

'Because Richemont heard I had resigned and wanted someone to take the banking assignments here.'

'Why do Mitchell's give us all these consultancy assignments, then?'

Jonathon was again distracted as more junk e-mail arrived on his screen. He'd let it wait in his inbox.

'They want someone else to do their dirty work. What do consultants really do for clients? We borrow their watch, tell them the time and then charge them royally for the privilege. Anyone with two red pens in their inside suit pocket is a management consultant these days. The lifestyle is the worst part. I live on room service in hotel rooms. I rack up air miles I don't want. A two-pager in the *Economist* suddenly makes me an industry expert. I hyphenate-words-that-don't-need-to-be-hyphenated. I coin three-letter acronyms of my very own. TLAs, you know? I advise friends on everything. I almost live life in a series of bold bullet points. I begin to think that some case study matters more than real life.' He paused and looked at the family photograph framed on his desk. 'Worst of all I spend too many days away from Jack and Imogen. What's the point of it all?'

Nikki recalled more pearls of wisdom from her chats upstairs.

'But it's better here than at one of the bigger firms, isn't it? Jackie says we're different from McKinsey or Booz Allen or Accenture. Richemont is a different type of consultancy.'

Another falsehood propagated by the Managing Partner. Richemont et Cie was a private unlimited partnership which didn't like others knowing that last year they had earned six million dollars' profit on fee revenue of twenty million. Good margins. Richemont had only five offices and didn't want any more. The head office was in Geneva, where the reclusive Richemont orchestrated global operations, inherited ten years ago from his father, who in truth had done all the hard work in the boom of the eighties. Jonathon had visited the other offices in New York, Tokyo and Sydney. The big-name competition by contrast had letterheads with a list of cities at the foot of the page that read like an atlas.

'Don't believe all you read about this firm, Nikki. Richemont makes the rules and calls the shots.'

She made for the door.

'One last question about Mitchell's. What exactly is the difference between an investment banker there and the dishy Scottish guy who works behind the counter at Barclays on Piccadilly?'

Jonathon gave her the full benefit of his inside knowledge.

'About a hundred K a year minimum, I'd say.'

The FF&O sales team, located on the dizzy heights of the twenty-first floor of Century Plaza, sat in the most prized location, alongside the sheer smoked-glass windows with their panoramic view of the harbour and the Kowloon side. Lesser mortals in Mitchell's selling plain vanilla products like listed securities and fixed income bonds sat in the inner well of the building and dialled up the FF&O team to ask what the weather was like outside. Lauren's boss called over to her.

'Someone pick up.'

They called him Big Mac but not to his face, because it sure pissed him off. He had never been seen in a restaurant with emaciated French fries, triple-decker gherkin-infested burgers or tepid E-numbered milk shakes.

'I got it, Mac.'

Her boss, Alan McFarland, wasn't even big, just five nine and a bit. He was a stocky expat with gelled-back ginger hair and a multitude of freckles on his pale face, born forty years ago somewhere near Edinburgh. He had been in Hong Kong almost longer than the Chinese, and wasn't tempted to leave at the time of the handover.

The line was dead. Someone had beaten her to it. Brad, wearing a stupid pair of braces over an excessively formal shirt and tie, yelled over at Lauren from the other end of the sales desk.

'Some crappy client called Alpha on line two, Lauren. Pick up the goddamn call.'

She felt the immediate rush of energy. Her biggest client was calling all the way from NYC. His orders were lucrative and kept her afloat each month end. She knew that more decent sales commission was on the way. Big Mac would have the numbers that mattered. She might even make pole position in the commission rankings this month. Brad would be but a distant second and would lose the smarmy grin.

'I got it, Brad.'

Averting her gaze from the windows, she turned to the screens, slid her chair in close to the desk, checked the latest Hang Seng Index futures prices and hit the flashing green light on the telephone board.

'Mitchell's.'

'Scott here.'

The resonance of his voice certainly worked for her. His deep sensual accent always reminded her of home. Big Mac said it was right to make a client feel good. Might help to get a bigger order too. She always remembered the words of Dale Carnegie and loved to let her callers hear their own name.

'You're on late today, Scott.'

'Don't remind me. Say, anyone else been shot recently in Hong Kong?'

'Only the premier, Scott.'

He usually liked banter but she sensed that today was different. He was under pressure. They both knew the opening prices. The HSI was down seven hundred points since the opening bell thirty minutes ago, almost 6 per cent down from last Friday's close before the assassination. The bears were running the bulls out of town.

'Lauren, the market looks real bad from where I'm sitting.'

She glanced at the array of wall clocks at the far end of the sales floor – 9 a.m. Twelve hours' time difference.

'And where are you sitting, Scott?'

'At the end of my bed.'

She remembered his last visit to Hong Kong. She'd spent a day in the office with him, enjoying the admiring glances from the other girls on the floor. A few drinks in that same bar on the hill where she'd first met James, although that time she had found a bar stool without any trouble. They'd had a meal in a quiet Vietnamese place with sweet wine, bamboo canes and polite waiters. Then came the downside from an engaged man. He'd put her in an impossible situation. She needed him as a client but he came on too strong. She had avoided an embarrassing refusal by asking for the details of his forthcoming wedding. He took the necessary guilt trip, finally made his excuses and returned alone to the Mandarin top-floor suite to call Kim long distance.

'It's the worst I've seen the markets here for a while.'

'Perfect.'

She was puzzled. Scott must be seriously long the market. He had bought thousands of Hang Seng futures contracts this month alone which were now on the down tick thanks to that widow and her revolver.

'Perfect for what, Scott?'

'Perfect for buying real cheap, Lauren. It can't go any lower, know what I mean?'

She knew he was ready to trade. The FF&O sales team did their best to complicate the inner workings of the desk but in reality their role was simple. The institutional clients in London, Singapore, Frankfurt or New York phoned them up from dawn to dusk. The sales staff chatted them up, added some sexual innuendo, gave them the local patter on the Hang Seng index and plagiarised the latest research produced by the Mitchell's Extel-rated analysts. The clients eventually placed their orders to buy or sell futures or options.

'So how much are you in for today?'

Scott was in at the deep end and she knew it. Keep him relaxed. He was definitely teasing her.

'Tell that floor team to be fast today. They were damn slow last time with the execution.'

Did he suspect something? She hoped not.

'Will do.'

Lauren relayed orders to Charlie the Geek on the floor of the Hong Kong Futures Exchange. His team ran into the heaving trading pit, did thirty seconds of frantic waving and almost obscene hand signals and filled the order with other local brokers. The floor team was fast. Too fast sometimes for Lauren to act.

'Buy a thousand HSI September contracts at market. Do the very best you can for me.'

Lauren was always ready for a huge order. This was real size and, as every girl knew, size mattered. This Alpha order would move the futures market in one way only. The futures market would in turn drive the cash market higher. Constituent stocks of the index would immediately rise. Big Mac was away in a director's office. Brad was working the bank of telephones with some guy in Fidelity back in the States. No one else about.

Lauren glanced around the sales floor. No one could see her PC screen. She clicked her mouse on the MS toolbar and brought up www.schwab.hk. It was her personal account with the best local on-line stockbroker, run out of a giant warehouse dangerously near the old Chinese border. She had enough Honkie dollars in cash in the account to deal right now in maximum size. She needed to find thirty more seconds.

'Good call, Scott. I'll put the order through immediately.'

She hit the mute switch on the handset and clicked on the drop-down menus. The required text was already there, always typed in first thing every morning by Lauren. 'Buy ten thousand shares in Hong Kong & Shanghai Bank at best.' That was her usual trade. In and out of HSBC. She hit 'Deal'. The screen flashed back. She spoke through the squawk box to her omnipresent floor trader on the HKFE.

'Charlie, buy a thousand September HSI for Alpha at best. Do it in smaller lots.'

Charlie the Geek silently swore back at her. He had nine years' experience and knew how to deal these mammoth orders for Alpha. It was crazy to try to do it in one fell swoop, spook the market and force the near-month futures price to spike up. Best to buy in small amounts, say 250 lots at a time, before the others on the floor knew that there was a buyer in size out there today. Lauren took the phone off mute.

'Scott, your order has been placed on the floor.'

The HSI index was showing at 12,550 on-screen and was flashing green. It was on the up tick. She looked at her own personal stock order. This was all happening too slowly. Time was against her. Her own order had to be executed before Charlie started to deal. Otherwise there was no point in dealing. The word 'Dealt' flashed back at her. The screen was instantly updated. She had bought HSBC stock at HK$124. Just in time. Settlement was due in five days. No way. She was selling this position today.

'Working the order now,' advised the Geek. Suddenly he screamed back at her on the PA over the din of the floor. 'Two-fifty done at 12,550.'

She relayed the price to Scott. He did not deduce that Lauren had taken vital time out of the normal dealing process. He was too brain-fried to notice, too anxious about the performance of his overall portfolio, too terrified about the market falling back farther. Charlie came back again.

'Two-fifty done at 12,560.'

The screen was flashing again. The price was on

the up. A big buyer was in the market. The others knew.

'Two-fifty done at 12,570.'

Lauren gave the prices back to Scott. He wasn't so happy. This was getting expensive.

'Last two-fifty done at 12,580. All done,' advised Charlie.

The order had moved the market. There were few other buyers out there today. They were all thinking about state funerals, crackdowns, martial law, public show trials and worst-case scenarios. She immediately knew the average execution price in her gifted mathematical brain and confirmed it to Scott.

'All done, Scott. You averaged at 12,565.'

'Guess it'll have to do. See ya.'

Lauren looked around again. No one about. She couldn't afford to hold the stock in her account and couldn't contemplate having a loss-making trade. She avoided eye contact with Big Mac across the floor. It was an art she had acquired over five years at Mitchell's. The farther he was from her the better. Brad had gone walkabout. She reopened the Schwab dealing screen and picked the sell option at best price. Her Bloomberg showed the futures price was still on the up tick. The HSI cash market was up fifty points. She knew that the recovery might not last. HSBC was up three bucks. She clicked on 'Deal' and sold all.

She did the numbers in her head. Ten thousand shares at three dollars' profit each. Thirty thousand local Honkie bucks, divided by seven point eight, the pegged HK dollar rate to the US dollar. She logged the profit in her spreadsheet. She had made four thousand US bucks for ten minutes work with absolutely minimal downside. But it was another dangerous profit. She'd stop this practice soon. Once she had made enough. After all, it wasn't addictive.

Jonathon stood by the granite kitchen worktop, still in his work shirt, sleeves rolled up, stainless-steel knife in one hand, clump of fresh basil leaves in the other. He had seen it on TV. He needed only a few slices of buffalo mozzarella on crisp leaves, green olives with pimiento, sliced Santa tomatoes and the herb, but it didn't look like it did on TV. Something was missing. Virgin olive oil. He knew how much was required. It was a technical term – a drizzle. That's what the celebrity chef always said. Eva returned from upstairs.

'They're asleep now. Jack took a while to calm down. He's excited about Sunday. That looks good.'

Evenings in the Maynard household were so much better when Eva stayed late to eat.

'It's essentially a salad in a bowl.'

'You've become a good cook since I've known you.' She instantly regretted the comment.

'Out of necessity, I guess,' he replied.

She redirected the conversation. 'What else is there?'

'All I can do. Pasta. This is our Italian evening together.'

Eva inspected his modest preparations and moved to lay the pine table with two sets of cutlery.

'I'll get a bottle of red.'

He watched his Scandinavian nanny search the wine rack. His colleagues at Richemont, particularly Nikki, had begged him many times to tell them about Eva. Was she lithe, blonde, twenty years old, somewhat homesick and possessed of a wonderful husky accent as in those cool vodka adverts in the snow? Jonathon dissuaded them but they needed proof. Nikki wanted a holiday snap from last year's nightmare in the Provence rain-trapped in a run-down gite. Then one afternoon Eva had suddenly appeared at Richemont's offices, looking for Jonathon's set of house keys after Jack had chucked her own set down the drain. That had stopped the chatter. Eva was fifty-plus, resilient, reliable, substantial, and as physically imposing as any historic double-fronted residence in Chester Row. She chose a Cab Sauv. 'Talk it up to me, Jon.'

'It's no spag bol. It's fresh angel-hair pasta dropped into salted boiling water for a few minutes. Then the *al mare* sauce. A few Norwegian prawns cooked in oil, strips of smoked salmon, and at the last minute some mussels and clams. A pinch of seasoning, garlic and pulped tomatoes, and it's done.'

'You been watching BBC2 again?' She smiled.

'Yep. Eight-thirty last night. Sad, isn't it?'

'You need to get out more often during the week. You need to find someone.'

He didn't think that the time was yet right, it was too soon, but Eva was close to the truth. Jonathon needed someone to crawl close to in a warm bed on a lazy

Sunday morning in deepest winter, someone to share birthday and Christmas gifts, someone to telephone from Richemont to say he'd be late home, someone to share his inner thoughts, his fortunes and misfortunes, someone to expand his horizons with, someone to share his interests, someone to love and be loved by, someone to help carry the precious burden of parenthood of an eight-year-old son and a four-year-old daughter.

'All in good time, Eva.'

'You're becoming old before you need to,' she said.

The warning signs were there. Jack had caught him watching Channel 4's *Time Team* archaeology programme last week. Capital Gold played better music than Capital FM in his opinion. He was growing interested in garden sheds and hanging baskets. He was powerless to resist the lure of self-assembly furniture. He always had skimmed milk in the fridge. He never went out in the FWD unless he knew where to park. He worried about his parents' health up in York. He had plenty of disposable income but everything he needed cost hundreds. He remembered when there were only three TV channels. And Tony Blair was not forty-eight, he was only forty-eight.

'I am old,' he contradicted her.

The pasta was ready. Eva sat down and ate hungrily. She did everything for Jack and Imogen but she didn't cook. Couldn't, so she said. She knew how to open M&S precooked meals and how to order a Domino's pizza or a Chinese takeaway by numbers but that was it. Jonathon duly obliged. They ate without saying much, Jonathon waiting for the right time to break the news. It didn't come. When she'd downed a cup of lemon tea, Eva rose from the table, glancing at her watch. It was 9 p.m.

'My bus leaves in five minutes. Today's Wednesday.'

He had almost forgotten. He took out the cheque and handed it over in a Richemont envelope nicked from work. Every six months they renegotiated Eva's weekly rate, though there was never much negotiation in truth. Eva named her revised price for caring for Jack and Imogen from seven to seven, including occasional weekends, and Jonathon acquiesced. He was convinced that she was a significant cause of wage inflation in the UK economy. He wished she would agree to move in permanently but she said she needed her own space for her sanity. She folded the envelope into her bag. Now was the time to broach his request.

'I may have to go away on business next week.'

There was no choice in the matter. Richemont had spoken. Jonathon was fully committed.

'All week?' she enquired.

'It's long-haul. I can't be here in the evenings. Can you oblige?'

Eva never explicitly agreed to anything. 'I must remember to launder enough shirts for you by the weekend,' was sufficient confirmation for Jonathon. 'You will be here on Sunday morning though, won't you?'

'Wouldn't miss it. I fly Sunday evening.'

Eva left. He sat alone in the peaceful kitchen, reading the remains of the *Standard* and nursing a lukewarm second cup of lemon tea, listening to the wall clock remorselessly tick towards ten o'clock. The silence in the house was otherwise deafening. Closing the newspaper, he looked at the empty beech chair at the head of the table. He lowered his head, closed his eyes, dreamed about the past, then raised his head and half hoped Rebecca would still be there as he opened his eyes.

He glanced over at his favourite framed picture of their last trip together, a weekend in Florence. Life had been so wonderful with Rebecca. Now there was too much time on his hands and no one to share it with. No one had seen the disaster coming. A routine screening and pelvic examination by the family GP led to the identification of malignant tumours in both ovaries. The diagnosis came too late. Radiation therapy and chemotherapy proved futile. Surgery proved ineffective. Ovarian cancer had taken hold of his wife.

Rebecca had died just before Christmas. From a thirty-six-year-old wife and mother of two to a terminal patient in a depressing Middlesex hospice in less than four months. The last few weeks watching her inner beauty deteriorate were the worst. He'd seen his wife suffer with abdominal pains, vaginal bleeding, nausea and vomiting. He'd sat with her by her bedside until the very last day.

Ever since, he had done his best for his children. He ensured they all enjoyed at least one meal together each day, he gave them more hugs than they knew what to do with, he helped with their easy homework, he aimlessly kicked a ball around with Jack, he watched Imogen tentatively tread the boards as a fairy at the school play, he knew all their teachers' names, knew their schoolfriends on the street and their parents too, he encouraged, praised, listened and talked. It was hard work. Jonathon knew that Jack and Imogen didn't understand what had really happened to their mother. He wasn't sure he did either.

Scott resisted the allure of the steaming bathtub and instead focused his strained eyes on the real-time prices on Bloomberg. He was certain his 20/20 vision was rapidly disappearing. He rubbed his reddened eyes again and stared at the ever-changing numbers that mattered. It had been Art's idea to install the screens at the traders' homes. He said it would help them make even more money for Alpha. If only it were that easy. There were too many decisions to make and no one to help.

'Scott, come on. I'm tired of waiting. The water's getting cold.'

Kim was lying among the soapsuds, wet all over, waiting for him to dive in. On the other hand the Hang Seng index was still shot at 12,570 and he was as far under water as Kim. This was hard work. Unsociable too. Almost midnight on a balmy Tuesday evening in NYC. Twelve hours away it was nearly time for a lunch break on a Wednesday morning in the raging futures pits on the floor of the HKFE. He needed a long communal soak, some serious foreplay and climactic sex with his fiancée before any sleep tonight. But he couldn't perform to the max until he had unloaded this huge futures position he had regrettably taken on twenty-four hours ago. He shouted back to Kim from the bedroom.

'Gimme a minute.'

The September HSI futures price was stuck in the same tight trading range it had been in since he had got into the market in size. It had seemed such a good idea at the time. Lauren had thought so too, but then she always agreed with him. He had bought at 12,565 in the sure knowledge that all the bad news about the stiff Chinese premier was now out there in the market. The political news could never be as bad again. This had to be an all-time low for the index. The price had to go north. Some time soon.

'I've got the Jacuzzi on,' implored Kim.

Dream on. A slimy realtor had sold them the apartment a year ago with many such false inducements. It wasn't a real Jacuzzi and they both knew it. More like a cheap oversized plastic tub with a few holes along the rim for very scarce bubbles. Scott got more visible tidal action in the bath after an excessive night of green Thai curries and Singha long-necks in SoHo with the guys from the trading desk.

'Are you coming in or not?'

But he could not perform with Kim tonight with this huge dealing position stifling his libido. He was as naked out in the Far East as she was next door. He had to sell up now, otherwise there would be a margin call to Alpha for millions of Honkie dollars tomorrow. He couldn't plead for any more loot from the ugly bean-counters in Finance. Romero, the overbearing CFO in the grey suit and teased hair, was already asking him too many loaded questions. He could sell and break even on this trade or hope for a profit. He hadn't yet increased his huge losses year to date. What to do? Sex or sell?

'Okay. I'm coming now, Kim.'

No, there it was! Some market action. The Bloomberg flashed green and the HSI price moved up five, then ten points. There were actually some other buyers out there in the big bad world. Some other poor bastards who also thought that this was real cheap today. Too cheap to ignore from where they sat in London or Frankfurt or Toronto or Bahrain. Then another five points' increase. Way to go!

'Hang on . . .'

But Kim's enthusiasm was dwindling as fast as the meagre bubbles.

'Jeez, Scott!'

Up another ten points. A definite trend was emerging. The revised trade volume proved it. Big trades. Some buyers in size were out there. Bloomberg was flashing green again. Scott sat and then knelt down on the carpet, implicitly praying that the screen would deliver manna from heaven. It did. The market was technically oversold. The bears had been caught as short as a guy looking in vain to take a leak at the break in Madison Square Garden on a sell-out Knicks night. They were covering their short positions.

He wasn't listening to Kim in the bathroom. His attention was elsewhere as the HSI rose to top the 12,610 mark. Scott was already working out his unrealised dealing profits as Kim let the bath water escape down the drainage pipe of the world's smallest Jacuzzi and out into the black depths of the Hudson. He lay back on the bed, admired the interior of an apartment fit only for a star trader, reached for the telephone, hit the first speed-dial button, which he knew so well, and waited for the tone to ring so very far away. The response was as immediate as ever. Time costs money in the business world and this particular investment bank wanted to keep their reputation for being the quickest on the draw.

'Mitchell's.'

'Lauren?'

'Yeah, Scott. What's happening?'

'Sell the thousand lots from yesterday at market now. All to go.'

'Will do.'

He waited, one eye on the Bloomberg. So far so good. A minute ticked by. Sometimes these orders took so long to fill. He must talk to Lauren about it again. But it was difficult to vent verbal crap on the one person who may already have deduced how much he had lost but said nothing about it. Sales staff always looked for the upside and gave their clients the ego massage they deserved.

'You're all done, Scott. Average price was 12,610. Any more today?'

'Nope.'

Talk was cheap on any sales desk. Big Mac always told them that. Keep the clients talking.

'So, Scott, was this a good trade?'

'Sure was.'

Lauren had done the mathematics that mattered to them all.

'I reckon you must have made about one hundred and forty thousand bucks on that trade in one day.'

'Looks like it.'

'Are you celebrating?'

Scott cast his eye back to the half-open door of the bathroom.

'In about five minutes' time.'

'You must be a shit-hot trader.'

If only. Today was one of those crazy do-or-die bets of epic proportions that he had to wager to stay alive. Scott was like any other greedy speculator, like any optimistic punter at the Kentucky Derby dirt track, like any red-eyed Vegas junkie drooling over the green baize at midnight. One hundred K plus today was a tiny reward in comparison to the risk he had already run. It was pissing in the wind with a Midwest typhoon coming in the opposite direction. The underlying notional value of a thousand HSI contracts at 12,610 a shot was close to 140 million US bucks. The profit was almost immaterial.

'Sure, I'm hot. See ya.'

He hung up the telephone and leaned back against the stacked pillows. The bathroom door opened fully and his fiancée dripped her way towards him, wearing a dangerously loose peach towel and not much else. Her long hair hung over strong bare shoulders. Hers was truly a body to die for. Kim stared back.

'You find the prices on that screen more interesting than me.'

He sat up on the bed and cradled her in his arms as she sat beside him.

'You know I don't. These late hours are just a hazard of trading in the Far East. I want to make enough bucks for you go wild in Saks on Fifth. And on that honeymoon we'll take. Hawaii? Rio? Acapulco? Anywhere you say, baby. How about we have a little rehearsal, right now?'

Kim lay down on the bed, pulled the sheet up to her neck and turned away from him.

'Forget it.'

CHAPTER THREE

VIGO STREET, LONDON, WI – 10.50 A.M.

Jonathon sat in awe as he paged through the Mitchell's file, making rough scribbled notes as he went. The client which Richemont had missed was the giant US hedge fund Alpha Beta Capital Inc., the product was tens of thousands of HSI futures contracts, the money was huge, the stakes were high, the report was eagerly awaited, the Head of Financial Futures & Options was an Alan McFarland, and the relevant account executive was a Lauren Trent.

Richemont bustled into Jonathon's office in the late morning and commanded his attention.

'I need you to do lunch upstairs today, Jon.'

'I can't make lunch today.'

'We have the CEO and CFO from a German commercial bank in town. It's a chance to pitch for some new consultancy business and grease their palms. It's a three-line party whip.'

Jonathon shook his head.

'Not for me it isn't.'

'It's going to be the full works. Five courses. Good wine from the cellar. Cigar box. Port. The lot.'

Last time they'd lunched upstairs, Richemont had asked Jonathon to recommend a good port. On the spur of the moment he'd suggested Southampton. Richemont had glared at him. Everyone else had laughed.

'I have another appointment today.'

'Is it long arranged?'

'Months in the making.'

'It's not in your Outlook diary on the network.'

Jonathon swivelled to view his largely vacant diary on-screen.

'I never use Outlook.' He didn't mind using the software but he was damned if Microsoft was going to run every minute of his working life. He wondered how anyone had designed software that required him to use the 'Start' button every time he wished to shut down his PC. 'I'll stick with my desk diary.'

'I'm not impressed. I'll have to find someone else.'

Richemont was about to leave. Jonathon held up an airline ticket.

'Nikki is changing the ticket Jackie sent down earlier.'

'You're going to Hong Kong and that's final.'

'I can't do Saturday. I've got a prior engagement. I'm moving the flight to Sunday.'

'You'll lose a day out East. You know, Jonathon, you need to develop a better attitude to work . . .'

'Or what? What are you going to do about me? Kill

the fatted calf that brings in the best assignments from Mitchell's and the Bank of England? I doubt it. I'll get the job done in the four days, trust me.'

Richemont gave up and left. Jonathon worked on his notes until Nikki came back from an early lunch break. She bounded in and produced the latest technology from her pocket.

'I got a new mobile phone.'

'You get one of those every few weeks,' he observed.

'It's a WAP phone. Flip-top too. Look.' Jonathon's face was blank. 'Eddie can send e-mails to my phone.'

'The day I get a flip-top phone is the day I watch *Star Trek*. And does Eddie have a PC or a WAP phone?'

Nikki looked away. 'He's getting one soon. You're out of date. A mobile is a fashion statement. Right now, the smaller the better.'

'Unlike everything else in life, then.'

'What do you have? Let me see.'

'I leave mine in the car in case of emergency.'

'What if Richemont wants to contact you urgently?'

'I rest my case.'

She left and he read on. At a quarter to one Jonathon retrieved his suit jacket and briefcase and left the office. He was thankful that Richemont preferred a third-floor sixties office on Vigo Street behind the Royal Academy to more glamorous locations as he took the short cut through Burlington Arcade, first opened in 1815, which, as Nikki always said, was too late in the evening for shopping. He marvelled at the goods displayed in the tiny shop windows in this oasis of tranquillity. Varieties of hand-made soaps in the Savonerie. Antique maps of Olde England at two grand a shot. Silverware, jewellery and cuff links. He remembered the old days when he used to come here to buy spur-of-the-moment gifts for Rebecca.

First stop this time was the Prêt-à-Manger on the corner. He bought a BLT on low-calorie brown bread, a fresh orange juice, hand-made vegetable chips and the largest red apple available. Next stop was the enormous flagship Waterstone's bookshop near Piccadilly Circus. He bought two books in the children's section downstairs, as was his custom. Jack and Imogen expected something whenever he left them. It helped Eva with the bedtime process. His children might not have the most visible father, but they were well read.

Next stop was the Tower Records store at Piccadilly – full-length posters and displays for tiny teen artists he had never heard of. Blazing spotlights inside attracted the tourists and students like flies to a kitchen exterminator. One window announced the arrival of the chart-busting *Now That's What I Call Music* 49. Jonathon winced. He remembered the ads for *Now* 1 and 2 many years ago. He bought a CD.

Last stop was Green Park. The sun shone down on a vista of rolling grass and rows of deckchairs. Jonathon found a quiet space, sat down, opened his lunch and downed it in five minutes. He rolled his suit jacket up and laid it on the grass, loosened his top button and tie, took off his black shoes and socks and enjoyed the sensation of mown grass on his bare soles.

Finally he opened his briefcase, ignored the few business papers and magnetic disks and took out the slim Sony Discman. He inserted today's purchase, slipped on the stereo headphones, lay back on his folded jacket, closed his eyes and took in the Dublin lads' three years' hard work: *All That You Can't Leave Behind.*

Once or twice he opened his eyes to check the time on his silver Tissot. He could see the distinctive brickwork of the top of Richemont's office from his vantage point. His boss would be inside, stuffed to the gills with rich food and richer red wine, inhaling his odious cigar smoke and fawning over the assembled suits. Lunch in the park with Bono, the Edge, Adam and Larry was infinitely preferable until he listened to the lyrics of track ten, 'New York', and remembered Rebecca. Something about hitting an iceberg in your life, but knowing you're still afloat. Something about losing your balance, losing your wife, in the queue for the lifeboat. Heavy lyrics, Bono, as ever.

Lauren arrived on the sales floor. Every male eye glanced in her direction as she walked alone towards the pole position at the FF&O desk. They had stared at her like this every day for six years as she came into work. Surely they were aware of what she looked like by now? She knew most of them; she'd even had a few drinks with the more intelligent specimens, mixed with them socially, but never much more than that.

'You're late. Today of all days. Where were you?' observed Brad.

She'd made it clear she wasn't interested in Brad the week he joined the firm. His inherited Latin features and tall frame didn't fool her. Brad serviced the long-term blue-chip client base of Boston fund managers and Connecticut mutual funds. It was a clientèle much like himself: affluent, well educated, polished, with a New England twang ... and too squeaky clean by far.

'I don't owe you an explanation because I don't work for you. We're colleagues. Live with it.'

'You get some action between the sheets last night?'

'Get a life.'

She sometimes wondered what she had to do to escape the jibes on the sales floor. Leaving her parents in New York immediately after graduate school and surviving three years' solo backpacking and odd-jobbing in Oz and South-East Asia was surely an achievement in itself. She didn't return home except for Thanksgiving, when her parents demanded the attendance of their only daughter around the familial table as her father carved. The temp PA job at Mitchell's became permanent after three months, and then there was a gradual elevation to the sales desk. Others left for Goldman's and Deutsche. She stayed and worked towards a six-figure salary and a lifestyle that even her dad now liked to drop into his conversations with the others at his Citibank office in Midtown. 'My gal sells index futures out East.' They hadn't spoken since last December.

'Did you meet up with James last night?'

Someday she'd sue Mitchell's for harassment. She and a few others in the office would take a class action in the States. The media would love it. Mitchell's would settle for a million bucks each out of court rather than go into the gory workplace details in open court. She had spent last night alone with Phat Cat on the sofa, James a distant memory in the rear-view mirror of the Golf. Next time she'd choose more carefully.

'James who?'

The desk head arrived. It was that time of the month. Big Mac had the stats that mattered.

'I've got the numbers from Finance. It's now official. Only one winner today. You guys ready?'

Lauren and Brad vied for the top slot in the monthly commissions table. Last month he had garnered fifty K more in commission than his female adversary. Lauren must be closer this month. Big Mac liked the rivalry. It made each of them strive to do better for the firm. He stood between them both, smiling at Brad, mentally undressing Lauren, enjoying the attention that he commanded.

'And the winner is . . .'

Others near by stopped working to listen in. Lauren had a chance this month. She had the client contacts that generated the lucrative order flow. She had the energy to work twelve hours a day, to party, to skip sleep, to come to work the next day at seven. She had the IQ to work out spreads, prices, profits, volumes and FX rates without a fifteen-digit Casio. She had the inside track to give the best advice to clients. She had the personality to entice hedge fund clients to deal when they had only called up for a social chat.

'... Brad. Again. Seven thousand bucks ahead in commission.'

Lauren could see Brad's fear. Seven grand was nothing. Just one good trade and they both knew it. Sometimes she thought Big Mac rigged the numbers to keep them both chomping at the bit. Brad stood up and took a bow by the desk. A few other expat Yanks on the floor gave him some modest applause. Lauren worried what they'd do when she won. Maybe next month? Big Mac moved on.

'The market is fast today. Talk to some punters. Keep the clients on the phone. Get those orders in. Let's make even more commission in all this turmoil. Next month's numbers are only twenty working days away. That's if we even have a stock market at the end of next month.'

The market was down again. The clients were worried about being left with long positions. Brad said that his clients were selling in size. Lauren needed a call from Scott soon. She swivelled her leather chair towards the harbour view to look down at the hordes of commuters and tourists boarding the bobbing Star Ferry at the twin piers. The scene seemed more frantic than usual. Fear and pessimism were abroad on the streets too. Brad seized another negative opportunity but Big Mac was already out of earshot.

'Lauren's gone window-shopping again.'

She turned back and looked at the ever-present Schwab icon on her PC, small enough for no one else to see unless they sat in her very seat and stared hard. She blamed her current predicament on the persuasive realtor who'd sold her that millstone apartment in Repulse Bay for close to ten million Honkie dollars plus property taxes. Just weeks later the local property market had crashed. Prices were down 60 per cent since 1997. Her negative equity with HSBC was still in the millions of dollars. Her very financial independence was threatened. She couldn't live the rest of her life in debt. Couldn't let her father know about it and call her a failure.

Every time Lauren traded with Schwab, she placed her entire career on the line. But once the bulk of the HSBC mortgage was paid off, she promised herself, she'd stop the intra-day trading. The external account breached all of Mitchell's internal law and compliance rules. Big Mac would go ballistic if he ever found out about it, while Brad would ensure everyone else on the sales floor knew. Every major regulator in every global financial centre outlawed the practice of executing your own personal order ahead of a large client order. It was a sure thing. A one-way ride. The technical term for the strategy was frontrunning.

Scott leaned over the washstand, opened the small foil packet on to the marble, emptied the magic white dust on the gleaming surface, used his Amex card to sweep the powder into a perfectly straight line, lowered his putrefying nasal passage to the coke and inhaled in one smooth breath. He stood up, rolled his head back, exhaled deeply, examined his bloodshot eyes in the mirror and shook his head.

'Who's selling you that shit?'

Dieter, the hotshot honcho from Hamburg, who dealt the European index business like the FTSE, CAC and the DAX, exited the first cubicle after a very obvious dump. Scott didn't bother to hide the effect the drug was having; the rush of pure euphoria, however temporary, filled him with crazy confidence.

'Go ask Rico over at Lehman's. He's making a market daily. Has a real-time bid-offer spread. Says he's making more in coke than his crappy day job punting in Brady bonds. Want some?'

'No.'

'Shouldn't that be *nein*?'

Dieter didn't wash his hands but stood next to Scott and pointed one germ-ridden accusing finger.

'You must have taken a hammering in Hong Kong last night, Scott.'

'Think again, wise guy.'

'You shitting me?'

Dieter's command of the English language was rapidly improving, though irony was obviously still a foreign concept. Scott tossed the spent foil in the trashcan with the others. Who cared? He wiped down the marble with the palm of his hand and then ran his tongue along his palm. Tasted good too. A particularly good score from Rico.

'I'm as serious as cancer. I did a day trade that made Art four hundred K plus. Bought and sold a thousand

HSI lots without ever putting up a damn cent of margin. Beat that.'

Dieter knew the established trading strategy at Alpha, in fact at any hedge fund.

'So while you ran the long position in Hong Kong, you also had a short position somewhere else?'

Scott knew that lying was easier. Art told them the rules often enough. He made for the door.

'Who'd be stupid enough to go naked out there with the Chinese PM shot to hell?'

Dieter wasn't convinced as they left the powder room.

'You better be right. We don't want a big hit at our desk before bonus time.'

Our desk? Art had hired a cautious German who only did coke if it came with 99 per cent sugar in red aluminium ring-pull cans. Scott, the acknowledged star, had earned half a million bucks last year for his efforts. They went back to work. The dealing floor at Alpha was pitifully small for a hedge fund with billions of dollars of positions. The seven traders occupied a corner of the floor space, with a huddle of operations, finance and administration staff taking up the remainder.

'What's the story in the Far East today?'

Art Greenbaum had emerged from his glass-walled office to perform his early morning inspection, making straight for an inquisition with Scott, who gave the boss the news he wanted to hear.

'The Hong Kong market's bottomed out. I made some good money last night, Art.'

For once Scott spoke the truth.

'How much?' Greenbaum never asked how he did it, just how much. Scott told him. It put a smile on Art's face. 'What else should I know about today, Scott? Anything you want to tell me?'

Scott's attention had been focused on events elsewhere. He wondered whether the boss knew more about his Far East dealing than he was letting on. He said nothing. Dieter and he stared blankly at their boss.

'Come on, guys.'

The German suddenly obliged.

'NFPs?'

Scott had missed a trick. Greenbaum stated the obvious.

'Non-Farm Payroll worker numbers are the most important monthly data from the government. They undoubtedly move the markets. Good low numbers help the bond and securities market. So what's your forecast today, guys?'

Dieter was first to cut in.

'NFPs up three hundred thousand. Unemployment at say four per cent. Average hourly earnings up two cents.'

Jeez, this guy was good. Scott had lost the plot. That coke ... His boss gave him a piercing stare.

'And you, Scott? What's your expert estimate?'

He hadn't a clue. He hadn't read the research. He hadn't trawled the screens. He took a long shot.

'NFPs up three hundred and fifty thousand. Unemployment under four per cent. Average hourly earnings up three cents.'

Utter crap. Greenbaum knew it. He shook his head.

'That's a very bearish forecast. No one thinks average hourly earnings will rise by that much. Let's have a hundred bucks on that, guys. We'll know in a few minutes' time. Watch the S&P futures price go.'

The two traders each placed a hundred-buck bill on the dealing desk, as was the custom. Greenbaum switched over to the CNBC squawk box and looked at the prices trailing across the foot of the screen.

'S&P futures are now up four point three points. Two minutes to go to half-past eight. Watch this space.'

The TV screen cut to a sweltering balding reporter in a nasty tan suit outside a federal building, logo mike in hand. He checked his watch, took a single page in his hand and read out the latest numbers.

'The Federal Reserve announces that Non-Farm Payrolls were up three hundred and ten thousand in June. The unemployment rate was four point one per cent. Average hourly earnings were up one cent to thirteen dollars sixty cents, that's one cent less than the consensus forecast. All in all, it's a benign set of numbers that should provide some relief for the markets today in contrast to the huge overnight sell-off in the Far East. No wage pressures out there and no cost-push inflation. I'd call the data tame. The bond markets will love it.'

Greenbaum killed the sound, handed the two bills over to the German and smiled back at Scott.

'Tough luck, Scott. You were only a cent out but, as we know, a cent matters a lot in this biz.' His boss looked at him up close, as if he could read the signs. 'You okay? You still taking that shit?'

'Nope, Art. No way.'

'Good.'

The reaction was instantaneous. The S&P futures price climbed rapidly on-screen in minutes. The long bond yield on the thirty-year treasury fell. The Dow would open up much stronger. The German placed his own one-hundred-buck bill back in his Gucci wallet. He pinned the other bill up on the wall so that Scott would get a good long look at it during the dealing day.

'You wanna take less coke and read the *Journal* instead in the powder room.'

An hour later the DJI rose 190 points in the first few minutes of trading at 9.30 a.m. The tech-ridden NASDAQ index rose a couple of hundred easy points. S&P futures took off like a runaway train. The troubles in the Far East had been forgotten in NYC. All was well again.

The others left early. Scott sat alone at the desk and contemplated his hidden losses further. He hated the instrument of his demise in his right hand, a perfectly sculpted handset with a mute switch essential for all dealing rooms. Balancing the stellar example of twenty-first-century technology in his open palm, he felt the smooth black plastic against his sweaty skin. In one movement he gripped it and slammed the earpiece end hard against the desk, anticipating the shattered plastic remains. Not so. The telephone remained undamaged. The bevelled edge of his veneer desk was destroyed.

*　　*　　*

The three tickets had been stuck to the door of the chrome kitchen fridge with a purple Barney magnet for the past two weeks. Well worth £8.50 each. Every other eager child in school had been up at least once while a lucky few had been twice. Jack could take no more peer pressure from his vociferous classmates. The flight to Hong Kong could wait a day. Sunday morning had at last arrived.

'You two brushed your teeth?' asked Jonathon.

'Yes,' they responded in unison.

'Then let's go.'

Jack put on his jumper, pulled a cap over his tousled hair and took his Boots throwaway camera for the views. Jonathon thought his son looked pale, with flushed cheeks. He hoped he wasn't coming down with a bug just before this long-haul trip. Jack ran up and down the stairs, hyperactive in anticipation. Imogen needed some help with her coat, her unnecessary gloves dangling from the sleeves on elastic, before they closed the hall door.

One-way Chester Row in the Borough of Westminster presented a tranquil scene. Jonathon and Rebecca had bought the home together at the end of the nineties property slump, though at the time it put them up to the hilt in debt. The Maynard family, now minus one, lived at the less ritzy end of the street. Their two-storey over-basement terraced residence with loft conversion was overlooked by three-storey neighbours. Rebecca had all the good ideas, adding polished brassware to the front door, tiling the hall with white marble, painting the exterior brickwork cream and displaying two terracotta pots with topiary upon the stone steps. Jonathon knew that he would never sell up. Rebecca had loved her home too much.

'Wait! Mind that car. Now, let's cross together. Slowly.'

He searched for his motor amidst the rows of parked abbreviations – BMWs, VWs, CLKs, Z3s, SLKs, MPVs, FWDs. He strapped the children into the rear seats of the two-litre Freelander, as much out of convenience as for safety. They had chosen the car together three years ago one weekend on a St John's Wood forecourt. He didn't want the oppressive set of chrome bullbars on US imports, while Rebecca wanted anything in British racing green. Now he always left the front passenger seat vacant.

The drive took twenty minutes owing to random Transco roadworks and a Barbour jacket and green wellies aka Countryfile mass demonstration near Parliament. Jack saw it first and pointed upward.

'There it is, Dad!' A gleaming white monstrosity perched like a wheel on an upturned kid's trike. Sixteen hundred tonnes of metal. Four miles of cable. 'It's moving.'

Jonathon buried the car in an extortionate NCP basement carpark. The Maynards were early. Their tickets said 11.15 a.m. They had ice creams and watched the others get their thirty minutes of aerial awe 420 feet above the London skyline. Jack didn't finish his ice cream and said little. Imogen gazed skyward and smeared her face and coat with Häagen-Dazs. They walked with the assembling crowds towards the orderly queues.

They took the compulsory red-eye photo opportunity in a darkened communal booth, then passed the Wordsworth platitude extolling the virtues of London and boarded the glass pod. The revolution had begun, albeit at a mere half mile per hour. A cheery freckled girl in a blue uniform stood before them.

'Welcome to your flight today on the British Airways London Eye. We have fifteen thousand passengers every day. Twenty-four per capsule. We hope you enjoy your trip with us. I am your host.'

Jonathon wondered whether perhaps there would be in-flight service. Chilled Chardonnay? Even air miles?

The pod gained height as it moved in an anticlockwise direction. Soon there was a view of sorts. Jonathon wished he had tickets for a better day. London looked grey and the horizon was hazy. The BA girl did her best at the hard sell.

'You can see for twenty-five miles. Usually. Ask me any questions you like.'

Jack sat down on the only wooden bench in the centre and watched the floor. Imogen leaned against the glass windows and peered downward, waving at passing river traffic on the Thames.

The hype was true, this was actually enjoyable. It was better than Disneyland. Better than the Dome had been. Better than the swaying Millennium Bridge below. Up close, Jonathon noticed the small logo on the glass door of the pod. Made in France. German engineering visible on the outside too. No wonder it worked. The idyll was shattered as a mobile telephone went off. A woman dug the latest chrome Nokia out of her bulging carrier bag.

'All right. Yeah, I know. I'm in the Eye ... ya know? ... the wheel thing ... yeah, that's right.'

Jonathon kept a watchful eye on Jack, who looked subdued and even paler than before.

'You okay, Jack?' He wasn't. Up close he was white. Gasping for air. Almost hyperventilating. Refusing to look around. 'What is it?' Jonathon asked anxiously.

'It's too high. I'm scared. Can we go back down? Now?' pleaded his son.

There were twenty minutes left. They hadn't even reached the zenith.

'I'll soon have you back safe on the ground. Don't worry,' Jonathon reassured him, and scooped him up to sit on his knee. Usually Jack resisted this manoeuvre. Today he mutely slid his head under Jonathon's chin and closed his eyes with a tired sigh. The cheery BA girl approached them.

'Is the little fellow all right?'

'We need to get back down again. Fast.'

'Sorry, but I don't drive this. I only work here.'

Jonathon wondered what an eighteen-year-old East Ender on a summer job knew about vertigo, wondered how his son got it and whether it would stay with him for life. And why he himself had never made this discovery before. Rebecca would have known about it, he was sure, would perhaps have first taken an exploratory trip on top of a double-decker with Jack instead. If she'd still been here. He saw no more of London, concentrating on his tight-faced, shivering son. Imogen saw it all, giving them a running commentary from the Dome to Battersea power station, Buck Palace to Lambeth Palace. Towards the end Jack lay horizontally on the wooden bench, inhaling and exhaling rapidly, while Jonathon cradled his head. It was the longest twenty minutes of his life, trapped inside this swaying, airless goldfish bowl.

When the doors finally opened he carried his weakened son out into the fresh air. He strode past those queuing for their souvenir photograph, overlaid on a backdrop of the river courtesy of a bank of incessant and hyperactive Sony DVDs, sat Jack on a stone wall on *terra firma* and waited ten minutes for his colour to return. He sourced a large Pepsi from the McDonald's in the old County Hall, now owned by the Japanese and converted into an aquarium. The caffeine shot did the trick.

They walked back to the car together twenty minutes later. Jonathon wondered what sort of peer pressure Jack was under, and whether he felt different at school from the other eight-year-olds. He was the odd one out after all, the sad child, the one without a mother to come home to. His son seemed to have recovered. Jonathon was sure that his classmates would get a different version of the trip on Monday. Jack took one last look back.

'Dad, did we get the photograph? I need to show them all at school.'

CHAPTER FOUR

CHESTER ROW, LONDON, SW1 –
4.50 P.M.

Jonathon liked to be on time. The children had other ideas. Imogen had unpacked the suit bag several times, playing with the assorted zips and locks, while Jack followed him around the house, old enough to know the significance of the luggage by the radiator in the hallway.

'Will you be home tomorrow night, Dad?'

'Don't think so, Jack.'

'I have homework to do. Maths. You always help me.'

'Eva will help you.'

'Of course I will.' She gave Jonathon a grim-faced look, but she had saved the day yet again, packing the Samsonite bag with five well-ironed shirts, two dark suits, five silk ties, boxers, socks and shaving kit. He had taken care of the tickets, passport, Honkie dollars and, most importantly, of all the confidential papers on Mitchell's futures problem out East. Jack saw the open front door. The black cab was in view. The cabbie honked again. Waste of time in truth. The meter was running and Richemont were paying.

'Bring me some presents, Dad. I like presents from airports.'

As they waved him off from the steps by the hall door, Eva shouted, 'Send us all a postcard.'

'No point, Eva. I'll be home before it arrives.'

'You'd better be.'

The tailbacks on the Hammersmith flyover were horrendous. Then roadworks on the M4. Terminal 4 was manic. Long queues at the Club World counter, as bad as the beaches at Dunkirk. Some problem with the check-in computers. Others jumped ahead of Jonathon, claiming to be on earlier flights. Wallies in dark blazers and ridiculously pressed chinos, with manicured hair and beer bellies, flashed BA Gold cards at wonderfully unimpressed counter staff. They argued over aisle and window seats and went a shade of pale whenever middle seats were mentioned. They insisted on three or more pieces of hand luggage. Blood pressure rose. Beads of sweat rolled. Jonathon observed from afar until his turn came.

'Any baggage, sir?'

He pushed his Samsonite through.

'Mr Maynard, do you have an air miles card?'

He did, but not today. He had last seen the blue card in the bathroom, and didn't think the pieces could ever be recovered from the depths of the toilet bowl, where

Jack had dropped them. It didn't matter. What was the point of racking up air miles over years of unwanted corporate travel when all you earned was more bloody flights? Not much fun any more without Rebecca. He shrugged at the Indian girl called Pritt.

'There are more important things in life than air miles.'

'Quite a change from our passengers' usual attitude. Seat 15G, sir.'

The BA terrace lounge was grim. Dozens of solo suits in their forties and fifties guarded their four chairs and laptop PCs with their lives. The larder was almost empty. The buckets of ice had melted. The sarnies were cold and wet. There were rows of terracotta coffee cups that even the Reject Shop wouldn't touch, while yesterday's newspapers lay on the pastel cushion chairs. Guilty masochists looked for furtive smoking zones. Eurosport blared from the corner Panasonic wide-screen. Fake tapes of jungle birds and running waterfalls played. The central water feature was an embarrassment to any self-respecting TV gardener. The overhead screens now showed a one-hour delay for BA7. Jonathon left for a quieter corner of T4. He called Eva from a pay-phone for the last time to satisfy himself that all was well at home.

Another queue at departure gate fourteen, parties of ten tourists with guide, attached as if by invisible umbilical cords to each other. The harassed BA staff fed computers that in turn spewed back the remnants of the shredded boarding cards to eager recipients.

Jonathon didn't push forward. Why bother? BA weren't going without him. His turn came eventually.

'Have a nice flight, Mr Maynard.' He almost had his boarding card. 'One moment, please.'

A quick glance at an invisible screen below the counter, a look of recognition, a single stroke of a black pen on his boarding card and then he was past. He looked down. Seat 15G was now 5A. He was thinking, why bother? And thinking too that row five was very near the front. He turned left on to the 747.

'This way, Mr Maynard.'

Surely some mistake. This cabin interior was opulent. Cream orchids on tables. Acres of space. Tranquillity personified. Seats with enough pitch to form a horizontal bed. Four windows by one seat for his use alone. A menu, wine list, headphones, sleeper suit and personal amenities kit lay on the ample shelf space. The drop-down table was big enough to contain a meal and the Mitchell's file at the same time, while the partitions meant he could see only one other passenger inside the cabin. Such privacy was unprecedented. He was in the first-class cabin, right in the very nose of the 747.

'There's a mistake. I'm not in First.' He smiled at a senior purser with many years' service, who looked at his boarding card.

'You are, as we say, SUG?' Jonathon looked blank. 'It's jargon. Suitable for upgrade.'

Another new TLA to tell Nikki about.

'Why me?'

'Who knows? Perhaps First is empty today. Perhaps

BA want to get to know you better. Perhaps our check-in staff thought you were good-looking or were impressed with your immaculately ironed shirt. Enjoy.'

After dinner was cleared away, Jonathon opened his file. There was a badly copied fax of a letter sent from the Hong Kong Futures Exchange Market Regulation Department to Mitchell's New York office dated early last month. Mitchell's had bided their time before they decided to call in Richemont. The Exchange wished to 'make Mitchell's aware of the trading volumes of their clients and sought clarification of their clients' trading strategy'. No names were mentioned but the file notes said Alpha Beta Capital Inc. was the culprit. The Exchange had passed the buck to the investment bank.

He ran his eyes over some print-outs from the mammoth Mitchell's futures system in New York showing trading activity in the single Alpha account for the past few months. The volume trend was definitely upward. A thousand contracts every few days some months ago. Now it was often thousands every day. In and out of the market on a daily basis. Incredibly speculative trading, in Jonathon's professional opinion.

Then some statistics courtesy of the HKFE showing total daily trading volumes on the Exchange. Jonathon did the calculations in his head. He never needed to use a calculator. Alpha's trading was up to thirty per cent of the total daily market volume. Some funds boasted that they could move markets unilaterally. Others scorned that opinion and held the view that greater global forces were always at work. These numbers were the proof.

Alpha could toy with the Hong Kong market whenever it felt the urge. Jonathon knew their buy orders would boost the market, their sell orders hammer it.

The assignment fee was US $50,000 plus incurred expenses. Jonathon's standard charge-out rate was three thousand a day, and few clients complained. The expected duration of the assignment was one week on-site and one week back in London working on the report with Nikki. He deduced that Richemont had added on an extra twenty grand. Nice work if you could get away with it. But fifty grand was pissing in a tin can to a billion-dollar bulge-bracket bank like Mitchell's.

Lastly, he saw the standard two-page engagement letter signed by both Richemont and Mitchell's CEO, Norman Newman, himself. The scope of the assignment was suitably vague. 'Investigate and report on recent HSI futures dealing by Alpha Corp. via Mitchell's Hong Kong office.' He was to maintain complete assignment confidentiality, exercise maximum discretion. He would speak to only two named employees: Alan McFarland and Lauren Trent.

The University of Hong Kong Student Union president and secretary at the campus office didn't believe the news of the summary execution at dawn in the barracks until the lone student persuaded them to visit his grandmother in her tiny flat in one of the high-rise tenements of Mongkok. The aged cleaner spoke passionately, sometimes in tears. The students were convinced. They joined with other activists and went to Central by MTR.

Lauren, Brad and Big Mac didn't take many futures orders as they looked out of the smoked glass at the developing chaos below. They saw sixty of the more dedicated students standing outside the main gates of the barracks. They carried home-made placards reading 'Fair Trials For All'; 'Justice For All'; 'No Army Law'; 'Show Us She's Alive'. The latter placard annoyed the squaddies behind the steel gate. Word spread around the campus over the lunch break. Three hundred students turned up in the early afternoon to join the first group. Lauren was curious and went out to find the traffic at a standstill in Central. She called her clients but took no decent-sized orders, left work early and drove home to Repulse Bay with other anxious drivers.

TV crews and reporters gathered by the barracks. It was media circus time. The soldiers erected crash barriers on the pavements and stood behind them in sullen rows, eyeing up the troublesome students. The more adventurous protesters hung their placards on the railings. Candles guttered and died amidst molten wax on the roadside. Periodically the soldiers tore down the signs of protest and decisively quenched the flames with their hobnailed boots.

When lectures ended, two thousand students massed by the gates. The campus was deserted except for loyal party members. Evening lectures were cancelled. The academic staff joined the students. Tension rose downtown in the evening, with no formal denial by the authorities. Rumours spread about the fate of the elderly prisoner inside. The army fought back the crowds as reinforcements and machines moved inside the barracks at increasingly frequent intervals.

Lauren saw the deaths live on Star TV. In the poor light of dusk, five undergraduates dared to sit in front of a late convoy arriving at the barracks. Some later said the lead driver never saw the students. Others said he did but wanted to make an example of them. Friends dragged one away in time but not the others. The huge tyres rolled over them at speed and extinguished four young lives. The crowd bayed. Unnecessary ambulances arrived at the scene. Crash barriers were toppled. Shots were fired in the air. The army retreated behind the gates. Four young martyrs were born.

Lauren watched the news at nine. A solemn local newsreader announced that a summary trial had been held *in camera*, an admission of guilt had been made, and that the sentence of the army court had been passed and carried out immediately. That was all the puppet said but the populace got the drift. One elderly life for another. The deaths of the four students were somehow omitted from the news bulletin, but mobiles and text messages spread the word. Thousands switched off the TV in their high-rises and took the MTR downtown to show their solidarity with the students. Lauren sat alone at home with Phat Cat, too scared to venture outside alone, too uncertain of what was unfolding in the city she called home.

The night was long and ugly. The gates of the barracks were broken down. Only the lines of armed soldiers inside prevented entry. Baying crowds roamed the streets of Central looking for anything genuinely Chinese. The China Airlines office was burned to the ground; the new statues in Chater Square were defaced; the CITIC building was looted and diplomatic offices were attacked. Petrol bombs were hurled, cars hijacked and set alight, flames fanned by the humid night air. Gunshots were heard periodically. In six hours of bloody unrest, nineteen civilians, three police officers and two soldiers died.

At 2 a.m. a noise outside woke Phat Cat, who stirred alongside Lauren on the bed. She heard a noise too and pulled back the edge of a rear curtain. Nothing at first, only a view of a deserted carpark with rows of parked motors, her own car directly outside. Then she saw a group of youths on the other side of the low boundary fence. They wore scarves to partly cover their faces. They saw her and reacted. Stones flew over the fence. One hit the Golf, and shattered the side window. They yelled in approval.

The tallest youth jumped over the fence and smashed two more stones through the other tinted side window. There was more vocal encouragement from the roadside. The youth was close to her apartment. She hid behind the curtain. Phat Cat was hissing, standing with his back arched and feline hair erect. Lauren dialled the police. The number was engaged. She hit redial. Still engaged. The glass in her own window cracked.

Then shouting in English accents. Some swear words. She dared to look outside. The burly English expats from the other end of the apartment complex had appeared.

The solo youth turned and ran. The last cries of rebellion against the affluent foreigners dwindled into the dark night. Anarchy and rage had turned to jealousy and greed in a single day as the very fabric of life in Hong Kong crumbled.

Lauren lay awake in bed for most of the night. She had no one to take care of her and no one to protect her. She was alone in the world, thousands of miles from home and her parents. She knew that she couldn't live in Hong Kong for ever; something irresistible was drawing her back to the US. She would have to return to Manhattan eventually, but only when the time was right.

Olivier Richemont shaved twice every morning. First he used a Braun battery razor to remove most of the grey overnight stubble, then a wet shave with a cut-throat Wilkinson blade to erase every last offending follicle. He polished his teeth, still all his own, with an electric toothbrush, and used half a metre of dental floss. Sometimes he ran the floss back and forth until his gums bled raw red. He used copious amounts of anti-ageing Clinique moisturiser on his tanned skin and then sufficient hair oil to ensure a linear parting. As the years went by, he grew more convinced that his perfect skin belied his middle age.

Downstairs, Richemont's driver, Max, scratched his goatee beard and two-day stubble, still indulging in the mistaken belief that his shaven head made him look hard. Sometimes he wished he had been blessed with the Teutonic gift of natural blond hair. He eyeballed the immediate vicinity in the *strasse*, then escorted Richemont down the steps into the rear seat of the Audi A8 4.2 Quattro, his charge partly shaded from the early morning sun by Max's six-foot-two bulk. Richemont had fallen five years ago for the age-old belief that a bigger bodyguard is a better bodyguard. Max drove as Richemont relaxed behind the darkened windows. He opened the *Wall Street Journal* but was distracted by the dismal state of his fingernails. He took out his black Swiss Army Huntsman penknife, opened the nail scissors but decided the risk was too great in motion. His damaged cuticles would soon revive with a manicure from Helga at the health club.

Seven years spent in the German traffic police had taught Max the basics. He always checked the rear of the car before Richemont sat inside it. He utilised the central locking from the inside. He knew his optimal route but used four alternate well-travelled roads to get into Geneva. He'd sourced a wide-lens rear view mirror for improved visibility. He never tailgated and left enough space in stationary traffic for any necessary evasive manoeuvres. Sometimes he missed the adrenal rush of high-speed chases along the autobahns and always regretted the day he was cashiered for beating the crap out of three Turkish immigrants after they ran from a routine traffic stop near Munich. He'd been forced to leave the force after one had died later in hospital.

The journey to the Aldstadt took fifteen minutes. Richemont sat in the car outside while another ten minutes ticked by. It was important to keep others waiting, particularly when they had summoned him into town. That telephone message received at home from Mitchell's had insisted he show up in person; this time the attendance of his local accountant would not suffice. Once inside, the two of them were ushered into the exclusive private-client wing of Mitchell Leonberg Privée Banque Suisse SA. Max sat outside the small office. A young man in spectacles greeted Richemont inside.

'Good morning, Mr Richemont. I'm Todd Liebowitz.' Like it mattered or something? Richemont didn't immediately sit down, requiring an explanation. 'Mr Werner has moved to another position in the bank. One where he can't authorise any new loans to customers.'

'He's my account manager.'

'I have taken over his loan portfolio. I'm your new account manager. Take a seat.'

They sat across a traditional desk that had seen many more years of service than its present incumbent. Richemont ignored the coffee, thinking, Todd who? Wondering whether it had one 'd' or two and whether it was short for a more normal forename. His answer came when Liebowitz handed over a pristine business card with a Mitchell's logo. It was two 'd's. Todd as in Toddler, perhaps? Richemont wondered whether he was a WASP from the States, hopefully without the sting in the tail.

'Are you properly qualified to be my account manager?' he asked loftily.

'I have a Masters in Finance from Penn State and seven years in private banking at Citibank and Mitchell's. I handled high-net-worth clients for many years in the States before moving to Europe. And to be honest, back in the States I would never have opened an account for someone like you.' Richemont knew exactly where this was going and he was sorely tempted to leave. 'You're late. I expected you at ten.'

'Heavy traffic on the way.'

Toddler cast a withering look through the window at genteel Geneva street life below. He let it pass.

'We have a problem, Mr Richemont.' Richemont didn't agree. If you owed the bank a hundred K, then you had a problem. If, however, you owed them several million, then the bank had the problem. Toddler shifted in his seat. He was about thirty yet still had bad pockmarked skin. 'There's no easy way to put this. You are in a bizarre position. You are very wealthy but unfortunately have no cash at your disposal.'

Richemont was going to make this as difficult as possible.

'That's the way it's always been. Ask Werner. I own a large piece of Richemont et Cie. The rest of the family, a few senior partners in Geneva and some venture capitalists own the remainder. You have my stake in the business and other investments as security for the loans you have made to me.'

Toddler was looking at a screen which faced towards him, and him alone.

'You haven't made any repayments. And because Richemont et Cie is an unlisted company we can never realise any of our security. Do you intend to list your company on a stock exchange soon?'

'No.'

'Then you must do what any other customer of this bank would have to do.'

Richemont folded his arms in a suitably defensive move.

'I am not any other customer of the bank. I am Olivier Richemont, a customer of many years' standing with an impeccable credit record with this institution. Check your files.'

Toddler pushed a buff file a few inches to the left on his desk.

'I have checked the files. The evidence is all here in hard dollars. Mitchell's can't go on like this.'

'Meaning?'

'You'll have to live within your means.'

Toddler almost spat out the words with glee. And a smirk too. Richemont wondered whether he'd suffered bad acne as a child and whether the condition had adversely affected his formative years. He hoped so.

'You've lost me.'

'You must liquidate some assets for cash.'

'Liquidate what?'

'Sell some property. That vacation villa in Nerja perhaps?'

'No. I need to take holidays.'

'Some of the luxury cars you own, then. Like that Audi you arrived in. Or the Porsche.'

'No. I need to be mobile and I need a choice.'

'Sell your large investment in the Alpha hedge fund. You have made good profits in the past few years.'

'No. I don't sell successful investments.'

'Then you will have to reduce your monthly expenditure.'

'It's already pared to the bone.'

Toddler smiled again and pulled out from the files a single page with a Visa logo on top.

'Your wife spent four thousand dollars on her credit card last month.'

Richemont had a go at mimicking that smirk.

'I got off lightly. You want to see her on a good month. She once lost that card and I didn't report it to you for a few weeks. The thief was spending less than she did.'

There was no reaction from Toddler.

'Perhaps you could reduce staff expenses. Such as the wages of that gentleman sitting outside in the hall.'

'Max is no gentleman, he's my protection. He arranges things. I need him for security. And I don't pay him wages, I pay him a salary because he is a professional.'

Toddler shifted in his squeaky seat.

'You have recently instigated a large regular dollar payment to one Carla Gambino via BCI in Milan.'

'There's no law against that, is there?'

'May I ask who she is?'

'You may not.'

'Is the payment necessary?'

Surely a man's sexual cravings deserved to be satisfied by someone under twenty and looking even younger?

'Most necessary.'

Toddler wouldn't let go.

'You are withdrawing large amounts of US dollars in cash at regular intervals.'

'It's petty cash. Miscellaneous disbursements and the like.'

'And large amounts of traveller's cheques too.'

'A man's got to travel. You don't expect me to spend the entire year somewhere like Switzerland?'

Toddler threw the file on the desk.

'Let's cut to the chase. We need you to repay part of the loan.'

This was enough for one day. Richemont stood up and straightened his tie.

'I want to deal with someone more senior.'

Toddler stood up too. He suddenly looked so much taller. Richemont wished he had Max alongside him.

'Don't bother. I report to the board on delinquent loans, like yours. We need to see a sizeable repayment of the accumulated loans. The board will need five million dollars.'

'That will take me some time.'

'The next board meeting is in six weeks. We want to see the money by then.'

'If I don't pay up?'

'I'll leak the story to the local gossip rags. They'll love an inside tip on a bankrupt tycoon.'

'You wouldn't dare!'

'It worked back in the States on several occasions. Try me.'

They didn't shake hands. Richemont followed Max down the long tiled corridor, through the main banking hall for the unwashed masses and back into the womb of the Audi. He placed one hand in his pocket and fingered the surfaces of his penknife, which he knew intimately. He'd like to have run the longest, sharpest blade over the acne-ridden face of one particular account manager.

Scott knew that discovery was closer than ever. The facts on Bloomberg were inescapable. The Chinese authorities wanted life to go on as normal and insisted that the Hong Kong Stock Exchange open for business as usual at 9 a.m. There were few sales staff on the floor and even less interest among the financial community. Brokers dared not leave their homes to travel to work. Martial law had been declared. Soldiers shot looters on sight. Trading volumes were minuscule, the first prices dealt scary.

Scott watched the blue-chips tumble. Hong Kong Telecom fell five dollars. Cheung Kong fell seven bucks. Hutchinson Whampoa lost eleven. The second-line stocks took a bigger hammering. The red-chips, stocks listed in Hong Kong but with mainland Chinese exposure, fared worse. CITIC lost almost a quarter of its value. Guangdong Investment Corporation met the same fate. The HSI was down 9 per cent by midday. Many traders in investment banks went home – there didn't seem much point in carrying on. The evening newspaper called it Meltdown Tuesday. It made a change from Black Monday.

South-East Asian markets couldn't escape the ripple

effect. Stock markets far less robust than their neighbour in Hong Kong were also ravaged. Jakarta lost 8 per cent. Singapore lost 10 per cent by their close. Manila, Taiwan and Bangkok were wiped out too. Tokyo was still open and needed no excuse to follow the trend. The Nikkei 250 lost one thousand points in late trading. The Osaka Stock Exchange mirrored their larger northern counterpart. The government in Malaysia suspended trading at the KLSE mid-morning, their Prime Minister as ever blaming the evil influences of international capitalism. He was wrong. Fear of the unknown was the reason.

When the markets in time zones to the west opened for business, there was no avoiding the grim facts from overseas. There were no buyers. Screens were red, international blue-chips caught in the vicious downward spiral. Dieter at Alpha watched Paris and Frankfurt open 5 per cent lower in the biggest market correction for years. Everyone knew in theory that anarchy out East shouldn't affect the value of a Deutsche Telekom or an Elf Aquitaine share but it did. Sentiment had changed.

The FTSE lost three hundred points at the opening. The investment managers and pension funds sold in volume. Hardest hit were FTSE 100 stocks with Far East exposure. Billions of pounds were wiped off the market value of HSBC Holdings, Cable & Wireless, and Standard Chartered. The market makers and traders stared at the negative price changes flashing across their screens and felt impotent.

The Alpha traders saw the panic close up on the other

side of the pond. Word had spread early by telephone and pagers to those who mattered. The players arrived at their desks in Wall Street in the early hours of the morning to watch the carnage in Europe. They feared the worst for New York and were not proved wrong. The DJI opened six hundred points lower while the weaker NASDAQ lost 6 per cent of its value by the close. Greenbaum asked them all to work late but it was to no avail.

Later in his apartment in Battery Park, Scott sat alone on his bed. Kim was out with friends. He could recall the precise day when Greenbaum had had a stand-up row with the risk manager and fired him on the spot over some erroneous risk report he had produced. Greenbaum said they would save a few hundred K a year by doing without a risk manager. All change after that – no one monitored Scott's trading positions. He had ignored Art's strategy with impunity. The Hong Kong market became a one-way bet. Scott bought HSI futures and watched them go up in value. He never took any short positions in other Far East markets as directed. Greenbaum walked over once a day to his desk and asked him how he was doing. Fine, said Scott. Finance never found the phantom profits. And was he perfectly hedged with no risk? Sure, said Scott. Not.

He had never known a bear market like this in his life. He stared at the final HSI futures price on Bloomberg, reliving the nightmare of only a few days ago, knowing that he was somehow going to have to find tens of millions of dollars tomorrow to meet the next huge margin call from Mitchell's as his HSI position headed south. He was running out of cash. And time. And confidence. And hope too.

CHAPTER FIVE

CENTURY PLAZA, CENTRAL,
HONG KONG – 8.40 A.M.

Mitchell's main reception was vast but poorly policed. Jonathon waited alone while a confused gofer tried to contact the Head of Financial Futures & Options on the sales floor. There was no answer from his extension. Jonathon deduced the director was too busy with panicky clients or too wary to meet an intrusive visitor with an unknown agenda and a file courtesy of head office in NYC. He waited, downed a complimentary cup of weak Chinese tea and examined the framed tombstones on the walls extolling Mitchell's undoubted prowess in the local equity and debt IPO markets.

Reading the glossy corporate mission statement, Jonathon remembered the same buzz words on the walls when he'd worked in Mitchell's London. The more cynical traders knew what the PR meant. 'Sharing' meant never having to take all the blame themselves.

'Aspiration' meant aiming low, reaching your goals and avoiding disappointment. Eagles soared but weasels never got sucked into jet engines. 'Progress' meant that if at first you didn't succeed, then you tried management or you shredded the evidence. Screwing up a job continually led to real job security. You never did tomorrow what could be avoided entirely. Indecision was the key to flexibility. When the going got tough, you went for coffee. Anyone who smiled in the face of adversity already had a scapegoat lined up. And retirement was always only thirty years away.

Alan McFarland appeared from behind a double door with numeric keypads at 9.03 a.m. He wore the uniform of the new casual era: khaki chinos, loafers, blue cotton Oxford shirt with button-down collar, open neck, and no tie. His sleeves were rolled up, with damp patches under the armpits. Jonathon formally introduced himself and was offered a reciprocal sweaty handshake and a grunt.

'Air-con sucks today. And can we get a fucking guy in to fix it?' observed McFarland. He took a look at Jonathon. 'No one told you it's casual now in Mitchell's? What's with the suit and tie?'

'We still wear suits on client visits.'

'You want to move with the times. I didn't think you'd show here today, with the trouble on the streets.'

'I was in the air somewhere over China when it happened.'

McFarland looked out at the city, apparently in no hurry to talk shop.

'I spent the weekend holed up watching the locals

trash the streets on live TV. I saw some kid with a Molotov cocktail shot in the head. Great shot. This city is finished. I'm half thinking of catching a plane back to London. You planning on staying here long?'

'As long as it takes.'

McFarland turned and wiped some of the sweat from his brow.

'This is the worst possible day to visit. I can't spare you any time this morning.' Jonathon caught his drift. McFarland clearly didn't want an independent outside expert reviewing the activity of his FF&O desk. 'I've reserved a conference room for you for as long as you dare stay this week.'

Another message received loud and clear as McFarland ushered him towards a windowless room miles from sales and dealing. The farther this visitor was from the pulsing heart of the FF&O team, the better for all concerned in this bank. Jonathon didn't enter the room.

'I need to be near the sales desk.'

McFarland frowned.

'This will do you.'

The final coup de grâce was required. Jonathon delivered. 'I'm sure Norman Newman would have a different view. We can check with his office if you like.'

To swan in here and name-drop as if he and the Mitchell's CEO were best buddies ... McFarland shrugged and walked Jonathon to that part of the office he called home in his waking hours.

'Don't complain to me about the bloody noise and the lack of privacy. Or the air-con.'

Jonathon took in the vast sales and dealing floor — rows of screens, miles of cables and copper, hundreds of frantic staff shouting orders and executions at each other. The ticker on the wall showed local stock prices with big red negative signs. McFarland pointed at the FF&O desk. Jonathon took the only free seat by the window, looked out from on high and wondered again why Jack suffered from vertigo. It certainly wasn't heriditary.

'When can we talk?'

McFarland was miles away already, looking at screens like some couch potato hooked on soaps.

'It could be hours until this market finds a support level.'

Jonathon took the hint, opened his briefcase and perused his miserably thin file for the first hour. He encountered diminishing returns by mid-morning and went over to McFarland.

'You got some time now?'

McFarland sat with a handset hung on his shoulder and hardly took his eyes off the screens.

'Do you really know Newman in New York or was that some bullshit for my benefit?'

Jonathon hedged like any good futures trader would.

'My instructions for this assignment come directly from your CEO.'

Perfect answer after years of management consultancy. A one hundred per cent truthful response, but he never actually answered the question. McFarland shrugged.

'And what is your assignment? To crawl all over my FF&O desk like a bad rash?'

'To answer the enquiry from the HKFE. To understand Alpha's trades.' Neither of them mentioned the hidden agendas on both sides. To see whether the consultant from London knew anything. To see whether McFarland and Trent were managing the account relationship correctly. Jonathon took out a pad and pen. 'I need some answers on Alpha first.'

'Shoot.'

Jonathon thought he meant it.

'What sort of client is Alpha? What is their strategy?'

'Don't you know how hedge funds operate?'

'Sure. When do they buy and sell? Do they day-trade? Are they using other investment banks? Do they meet margin calls? Are they in control? Are they net long or short? Are they in the red today?'

McFarland was out of his depth.

'How do I know, for fuck's sake?'

'You know the guys at Alpha?'

'Yeah. Art Greenbaum and Scott Chapman have both been out here. We took 'em out on the town.'

'Do you talk to Chapman every day?'

McFarland shook his head in disappointment at the lost opportunity.

'I'd love to. Alpha has grown exponentially in the past few years. But try to talk to Chapman without Lauren on the line and she'd break your balls. She had a great working relationship with the trader.'

Jonathon looked around. There didn't seem to be any spare seats.

'Where is she?'

'She's out today.'

'Sick? Holidays?'

'I told her to stay at home.'

'Because I was coming here?'

'You're not that important. I didn't want a girl driving alone to work through these streets.'

'She'll be in tomorrow?'

'Maybe.'

Jonathon knew this was one of those Salmon Days that every management consultant experiences. You spend all day swimming upstream and still get nowhere. He needed to meet this Lauren. McFarland's attention was gone. He looked out past Jonathon and spoke to no one in particular.

'The guys in Mitchell's London said they fired you because you lost a shitload for us on a bond desk.'

'No. I resigned.'

'I heard you met your wife at the firm and that she was very ill. She's better now, I hope?'

The best place to wake up in the world in Arthur Greenbaum's opinion was in a 5.3-million-dollar penthouse apartment on 77th and Fifth. He had seen the glossy advert in the back pages of the Bloomberg magazine on one of the trader's desks in Alpha. The others gazed in awe at the shots of the interior in the Greenthals on Madison residential brochure and joked about the ridiculous prices for prime real estate on the Upper East Side. Greenbaum looked at the advert, thought about how much liquid cash he had over at Chase private banking, gave it the once-over on a rushed lunch-time visit with Victoria and paid cash via his attorney within ten days. It was the sort of residence made for a Wall Street player.

He loved the hardwood floors, the eleven-foot-high ceilings, the wraparound planted terrace and west-facing roof deck, the ample six thousand square feet of space, the renovated kitchen and three bathrooms, the Jacuzzi and adjacent steam room, the exercise gym which he rarely had time for, the oils in gilt frames and the constantly replenished fruit in the bowls which they never seemed to eat. Most of all he loved the views of Central Park, lake and all. The Latino maids' quarters were bigger than entire apartments elsewhere in this city; the maintenance costs were more than a month's rent elsewhere. Greenbaum didn't mind. He was a man of substantial means. Always had been, and always would be.

The apartment gave out the right signal to the wealthy who had invested in his Hedgling Alpha fund just five years ago. They liked to visit and see that the awning featuring the number of the prime address reached right out to the sidewalk, that a welcoming doorman in gold piping and peaked cap met them with an open umbrella in the rain, that the private elevator went direct to the sixth floor, and that the marble was as genuinely Italian as the Mafia. Art also liked to socialise with his investors, meet up with them when he went abroad or play a round of golf. Victoria liked the investors who lived in New York to attend her lavish private dinner parties, or to swan around at her charity bashes for a thousand bucks a plate.

'Are you all right for tonight, dear?' his wife asked from one of the curved staircases.

Art was bemused.

'What's on tonight?'

'Art, I told you last weekend! It's in the diary. It's a benefit for those poor little orphans in some part of eastern Europe where there was a war. There are fifty coming at seven.'

'Orphans?'

'Our guests. Black tie.'

Greenbaum pondered his wife's request while he threw on his suit jacket.

'Dunno. This Far East market trouble might get worse. There's some real heavy stuff going down there per CNN. I need to see how we're positioned. I'll try to make it. No guarantees, though.'

'Be there. You're the host. And don't forget the UJA dinner later this week. You spend too much time at that damn firm.'

Greenbaum owed it all to Alpha Beta Capital Inc., his own creation. He had grown bored after years of stitching up clients at Salomon's muni desk, where he would give them chapter and verse on bond yields, coupon stripping, bullet repayments, deep discounting and treasury spreads. The clients agreed knowingly, placed their orders and paid the prices on the screens. He had made so much loot in his last year at Solly's that the preppy summer interns christened him Art Greenback. So he had taken his accumulated millions of salary, bonus and stock options, booked some optimistically long-lease space within sight of the NYSE and set up shop with a new title, a brass nameplate and a glamorous receptionist. It wasn't often that a thirty-nine-year-old could retire from a firm like Salomon's and better himself.

Greenbaum had lured Scott, Dieter and the others from desks at Morgan's, Wasserstein, DLJ, Goldman and Solly's. Scouring the campus of MIT, he had taken the best economics researchers and mathematicians in exchange for hard cash. He'd added some academic types from Harvard and Yale and nailed a Nobel prize-winner who was at the cutting edge of stock options pricing models.

Sourcing enough money from investors was thus never a problem with the list of star CVs he used for presentations and marketing. His ex-colleagues chipped in a few million for starters – the great and good from his old days on the Street. He even interested the Fed Chairman and his UK counterpart, the CEOs of top-tier firms and some high-net-worth Europeans with excess cash to burn. Some former clients, mutual funds and offshore money managers gave him tens of millions each. The three hundred million bucks equity capital was enough to get the show on the road.

'Your car is outside, Mr Greenbaum.' The doorman at street level nodded politely. 'Have a nice day.'

Said with all the conviction of a serial liar.

'You too.'

Greenbaum stepped out into the world. He carried

no briefcase, being unconvinced of the merits of ever bringing work home. He carried no overcoat, being wholly reliant on his car service. He still believed that a dark Boss suit with a white shirt and muted designer tie from Madison sent a more reassuring signal to clients than the crazy world of dress-down in Wall Street boilerhouses. He didn't go to a barber; rather the barber came to him bi-weekly. His shoes were polished by a keen youth from the ghetto for five bucks daily while he sat at his desk. He was confident that he was worth, and looked, a million bucks. Minimum.

He stopped at the door to let a fortysomething blonde in black culottes with dark sunglasses pass in front. Two minuscule yapping poodles trailed reluctantly in tow. One of the canines stopped to take a leak by a pitiful hedgerow, right beside a sign that urged local residents to 'Curb Your Dog'. The blonde saw him watching the urinary pursuits and was almost embarrassed. He made eye contact with the shades.

'Thanks for watering our plants. It's much appreciated.'

She scowled back but the exchange gave him some early adrenaline. Perhaps next time he'd give her a ride home at speed with the two crapping poodles tied to the rear fender. There was no sign of his car. Seventy-seventh was chaos, wall to wall with black limos and sedans. It was a problem living in an area where every other building was an overseas consulate or embassy. The local residents had never set foot on the subway or on an MTA bus in their insulated lives. The place was crawling with NYPD officers to keep the diplomats safe who considered enforcement of the city traffic regulations to be well below their elevated CD status. Zero tolerance hadn't yet reached the Upper East Side. Plumbers' and electricians' Dodge vans were double-parked by hydrants and private garages. The unseen residents had a deep desire for incessant remodelling work in their prized homes, provided the blue-collar classes were never seen in person and always used the discreet side entrance.

'Mr Greenbaum, over here.'

He nodded to his regular driver, originally from the Bombay slums. His car was parked down near the stores at the Madison end, past the Mark Hotel, one of Victoria's favourite eating spots. They turned left on to Fifth and drove downhill with the awakening Park on the right-hand side. The traffic was gridlocked near Trump Tower. Greenbaum eyed the front page of the *Journal* and read the overnight comments about turmoil in world markets, assured that his own giant hedge fund was indeed hedged and he was fully aware of the strategy that all his traders were pursuing. He put the newspaper to one side. Way down below, past the peaked cap of the driver and between the canyons of buildings that lined Fifth, he could make out the glittering skyscrapers of Downtown. This was the only way to commute to work in New York.

Jonathon was in early next morning, having had little sleep overnight. He'd called Eva in the dead of night as he sat alone by the hotel window watching far-off plumes of smoke meshing with neon signs. Jack and Imogen were well. Eva had asked whether he was safe. She'd seen the sensational ITN news, all blood on the streets. He reassured her. Now he sat at the FF&O desk and wondered whether his quarry would show up today.

'You're in my seat.'

Turning around, he was immediately impressed. A girl in a white cotton blouse and dark herringbone pencil skirt stood beside him. Medium-length auburn hair. Maybe thirty. Her accent was American. McFarland was out of sight at the far end of the sales floor. She offered no other information. Jonathon stood up awkwardly. She sat down and then immediately swivelled so that her legs were unfortunately completely hidden under the desk. Jonathon stood beside her, feeling surplus to requirements.

'Where do I sit?'

'That's your problem. I work here. You don't.'

'I'm Jonathon from Richemont in London.'

'So I heard.'

Suddenly he deduced who she was. He was sure that McFarland would have briefed her on what to say. Probably as little as possible.

'You must be Lauren.'

She turned towards him. Her complexion was perfect, her eye contact unfaltering, her voice alluring. Jonathon suddenly thought that Scott Chapman at Alpha was a lucky guy. He got to talk to her every day.

'I am. How are your other psychic powers today? Which way is the damn market going?'

Fortunately he'd read the *South China Morning Post* over room service breakfast.

'Down, I'd say. More shootings overnight. Martial law extended. A weak Wall Street close. Bearish sentiment. Large stock overhang.'

Jonathon sensed she was vaguely impressed but she did her best to disguise any reaction.

'You know it all?'

'Not quite. I'm here to look at Alpha. McFarland says you know most about them.'

'He would say that.'

'We need to talk.'

'No distractions before the market opens. Period. Later.'

The morning dragged on. Lauren came and went several times. Jonathon looked through the same pages as yesterday and almost lost his patience. He glanced over at the row of wall clocks and checked European time. Richemont would soon be in the Geneva office. He could call him and expedite the matter. Richemont could call Newman at home. By late morning, Jonathon didn't feel like wasting any more time. Day two of a four-day week was disappearing rapidly. He approached Lauren.

'I need to see your records of Alpha's trades in the past three months.'

She turned and placed her hand under her chin, holding the pose.

'Mac told me you have that information from our systems people in New York.'

Jonathon wondered how much they knew about what he was here to do.

'I need to see who wrote the sales tickets, what times the calls came in, the order time stamps, any errors or corrections on the tickets, who executed the orders, what the average prices were like.'

Lauren smiled for the first time that day. Jonathon hoped that it might even be genuine.

'You must think I have some sort of full-time admin assistant here?'

Reaching under the desk, she produced a large cardboard box stuffed with bundles of grubby sales tickets bound with rubber bands and bulldog clips, and threw it over to Jonathon.

'I'm off to lunch.'

No invitation to join her. Stopping only for a beef salad sandwich and a Sprite from downstairs, he spent a working lunch alone looking at sales tickets and entering some salient details into an Excel on his laptop. He finished the box by early afternoon and checked the down tots. He reckoned Alpha had lost tens of millions in the past month. He wondered who exactly knew about it at Mitchell's and at Alpha.

Lauren and McFarland returned together at two o'clock. After speaking to her boss out of earshot, Lauren approached and pulled up a chair close to Jonathon. She looked wonderful and maintained steady eye contact with him.

'I got some time now. What do you need to know?'

She had changed her tune over lunch. He held

her gaze and wondered why she was insisting on such prolonged eye contact. He pointed at the pile of tickets.

'These trade tickets confirm the computer records. It's as I feared.'

'Feared what?'

'Alpha have lost millions in the past few months. There are so many loss-making trades.'

'I don't think so. You're way off base.'

She was holding his gaze for too long. It was almost uncomfortable. She had radiant eyes.

'What makes you so sure?'

'I asked Scott about this. Alpha use a few other investment banks to deal in Hong Kong. What they buy through us they can sell through another bank. We never know if they've made or lost money. They might make a loss with us and a profit elsewhere. They keep us guessing.'

She was edgy. Jonathon watched her eyes and saw that her pupils were dilated. He persevered and noticed that she blinked repeatedly. He made it about a hundred blinks per second. She was unconvincing.

'Alpha show all the signs of classic over-trading, pure speculation, even desperation.'

'No. Chapman knows what he's doing. He made a hundred K plus one day last week.'

'That isn't much when he has millions of losses. His gross positions are huge.'

He knew he was sowing some doubts in her mind. She shifted uncomfortably. He saw her hands on the desk.

One of them was tightly clenched. He pushed his luck while she was still responsive.

'Does anyone other than Chapman give you futures orders for Alpha?'

'No.'

'What about when Chapman is away on holiday?'

'No.'

These answers were useless. She was obviously avoiding going into any detail.

'Can you expand on that? Does he telephone orders in from some holiday location?'

'He never takes vacation time. Not since I've known him.'

'Doesn't that strike you as unusual?'

She stared back at him. They were thinking the same thing. Traders who never took holidays were a worry, maybe covering up some black hole in their complex trading books, afraid to leave it to others more honest to mind the shop in their absence.

'I never thought of it like that,' she said. The pitch of her voice was oscillating.

'What happened when Chapman came here?'

What did he mean? Some trading, research, lunch, dinner, junkets and cocktails. No sex.

'It was business. He met the faces behind the telephone. We were marketing our services.'

'How long was he here for?'

'Two days.'

'And he gave you orders while he sat here in this office?'

'Yes.'

'And outside work?'

'He hung out with us. We showed him the nightlife. A junk trip to Lamma Island.'

'That's it. He knows no one else here. Chapman doesn't use other investment banks. He has no other relationships. He has no profits elsewhere. His losses here are real.'

This line of deduction was too much. Lauren broke off eye contact and turned to McFarland at the top of the desk. He knew what the signal meant. She needed help immediately. He wandered over.

'Lauren,' he shouted. 'Come over here and look at this price trend.'

She stood up. Eyes near by looked at her and once again Jonathon was aware that she had presence.

'I gotta go.'

He watched McFarland and Lauren talking, unsure what the topic was. She was animated, then defensive. When she returned alone, Jonathon saw her examine his face up close.

'Maybe we can meet up later?'

He almost choked.

'Sure.'

'Where are you staying?

'The Ritz Carlton.'

'Be in the hotel bar at eight. I'll be finished here by then. I'll need a stiff drink with a market like this.'

It was the best offer Jonathon had got from anyone in Mitchell's.

* * *

Scott was dragged into the early morning meeting and sat near the head of the conference table, being one of the longest-serving traders at Alpha. His boss stood in front of the assembled trading staff.

'Guys, I've seen this all before,' advised Greenbaum. 'We had it in '87, in '98 and in 2001.'

'This is one serious nosedive that we ain't gonna pull out of. It's crash and burn time'. Interjected Dieter.

'I disagree. The Nikkei plunged overnight, the FTSE took a hammering this morning and the Dow is fucked. There's an Armageddon scenario out there but in three months' time we'll look back and laugh about this week. The US economy hasn't somehow changed overnight. The NFP's from last week don't change. This vicious circle will only last until one market in the world bucks the trend, when everything looks too goddamn cheap to ignore, and then Hong Kong or Frankfurt or Tokyo will bounce back and we'll be off again on this magic roundabout we call capitalism. That's why we love this business so much. It's a chance to make some serious loot.'

One or two faces relaxed at the politically incorrect comments of their founding father.

'This is different, Art,' observed Dieter, apparently intent on making career-limiting moves.

'No. Wise up to what happens. Our research gurus have the historic evidence. The markets always rise and fall. They roll on without a care until someone inadvertently coughs in the corridors of power in the

Fed or the ECB. Then there's panic and the virus spreads down the telephone lines to all the world's financial capitals like a bad case of the shits. It's the herd mentality. This time the only difference is the catalyst. It's down to some senile Chinkie politician being shot in Hong Kong, a few students run over by the Red Army tanks and some peasants looting designer boutiques for new gear.'

Greenbaum had rolled up his shirtsleeves, a reminder of his old days at Solly's.

'We follow the proven Alpha trading strategy, known as the futures spread trade. There is no risk, only reward. It doesn't matter whether world markets go up or down. We know that the markets move together. We have long positions in many markets and short positions in others. We buy a future on one market index and we sell a future on another market index. We look for those differentials. We don't have naked positions. On a net basis we are always flat. Square. Ain't that the truth?'

Greenbaum unfortunately turned to Scott at this point with his accusing finger. Scott nodded. The younger traders in the room visibly relaxed. Scott tried to hide his guilt. Greenbaum was so good at this PR that Scott could almost believe some of his wishful sentiments. Greenbaum continued.

'This is good news for hedge funds like ours. We want, we need, big market movements. We like volatility. We need big up and down swings. It gives us the opportunity for bigger profits. That's why we like the volatility of emerging markets so much. London or Tokyo may change by a few percentage points but the Bovespa could soar or plunge by five times that much and KL or Jakarta can leave Brazil in the fucking shade on a good day.'

Greenbaum walked over to Scott and put his hand on his shoulder.

'Look at our star trader.' He wished they wouldn't. 'Scott buys Hong Kong futures like they are going out of fashion but sells Malaysian futures on the KLSE and Indonesian futures in Jakarta. Markets like Hong Kong are mature, with well-managed economies, stable governments, pegged currencies and a tradition of hard grind. There's limited upside but limited downside also. The new tigers like Indonesia and Malaysia are light years behind, with quango governments, political risk, banana economies and too much downside. Tuesday is either election day, revolution day or stone-the-riot-police day with a free water-cannon shower on the side. Scott's long position in Hong Kong will be worth relatively more in the future and his short positions in Malaysia and Indonesia will be worth relatively less. Alpha works. Shit, Scott made four hundred K one day last week just by sitting here and making two phone calls to some hot babe out East. Yeah?'

'Sure did, Art,' said Scott.

Greenbaum stated the obvious for those who managed the fund's billions.

'Damn right. Hedge funds are the ultimate capitalist creation, a wonderfully high-geared risk-averse investment vehicle that employs minimal amounts of expensive capital in return for maximum amounts of reward. Alpha is okay in this market, but others will not fare as well as us. So don't gloat to others on the Street.'

Dieter went for a high five with another trader. Greenbaum cut off the premature celebrations.

'If I ever catch someone who isn't following the agreed strategy, then their balls are mine in a vice. Ain't that so?' He made eye contact with Scott again. Lying was now an eminently more convenient way of life.

'Sure thing, Art.'

CHAPTER SIX

THE RITZ CARLTON, CENTRAL,
HONG KONG – 7.50 P.M.

Jonathon made it back to the hotel through streets patrolled by soldiers. He left his room on cue, not knowing whether he was going to a business meeting or on a hot date. He sat alone in the downstairs bar for fifteen minutes, playing with the remnants of his G&T. Reality dawned. This must be some sort of joke at his expense. McFarland and Lauren would still be in the office planning their next move to disrupt his work. She'd say tomorrow that she forgot or that the markets called her away. But at 8.20 Lauren appeared on her own and wrapped her long legs around the adjacent bar stool.

She had evidently had time to go home. She wore a loose silk blouse and slim-fitting trousers. All black. She placed a silver lamé evening bag on the counter and nodded to the barman, who produced a double vodka and white instantaneously. A dangerous drink for a dangerous girl. The barman seemed to know her. Jonathon was about to ask whether Art Greenbaum or Scott Chapman had sat on this bar stool. Other sad solo business travellers in the bar eyed him from afar and wondered who the lucky guy in such great company was. Jonathon still wondered whether this rendezvous was business or pleasure. She ordered a second G&T for him without asking. He watched her hold a glass in her hand, no ring evident on the finger that mattered.

'Hungry?' she asked.

There was nothing to lose. He needed to get to know her. It might help his work. He was starving.

'Where will we go?'

'The restaurant here is good. I already booked a table.'

They sat at the best table in Jardin Chinois, a place with a posh name so that some French chef could take local ingredients, give them lisping French explanations on the menu, serve up a Chablis or any old plonk and charge the earth to corporate locals on expenses. The maître d' greeted Lauren like lost family. Jonathon guessed it was a hazard of working on a sales desk in the biggest investment bank in town. An older guy at the next table started on a vile cigarette. Lauren turned and gave him the look of death. He stubbed it out.

'Disgusting habit,' she opined.

Two kir royales arrived on a silver tray, both fizzing with effervescence. Lauren downed hers. Jonathon followed suit, not a fan particularly, but willing to accept the convention. He noticed an after taste. The menu was enormous. He ordered the four set courses and chose from an expensive wine list. When the salmon and caviare starter was placed in front of him, he momentarily stopped to select something from the wide cutlery display. Lauren leaned forward and placed her hand on his. She lowered her voice.

'Selecting the right knife is like foreplay. It's best to start on the outside and work inwards.' He almost choked on the first wafer-thin slice of wild salmon. 'You worked with Richemont for long?'

'Four years. Before that I was with Mitchell's.'

'You glad you left Mitchell's?'

'Yes.'

Lauren leaned closer. Her perfume worked for Jonathon. 'Tell me why, Jon.'

She had used his first name. He wondered what was happening here.

'You know why. US investment banks work you to death. They have breakfast research meetings at seven a.m. and conference calls to head office at nine p.m. You take a sandwich at your desk and never see the light of day. They give you free cabs home after eight p.m. purely to encourage you to work late. The only break you get is to go to the gym and work out your frustrations on some Stairmaster or punch-bag. You can be a star at a trading desk one day and the next you can be out the door with no warning. They cancel your holiday and make you work instead. You get loads of loot and bonuses but you have no time to spend or enjoy it. You never get enough time to be at home with your family. Most of the bankers I knew got divorced. It's a Faustian pact with the Devil himself, only in reverse. Thirty years of hell followed by eventual retirement and pleasure. You agree?'

'Almost. You forgot the leering oversexed males with the big egos and the bigger appendages.'

'I wasn't one.'

Too much rich food and alcohol followed in the next two hours. The aperitifs, a white wine, red, liqueurs ... Jonathon felt his impulse to question her slipping away.

'You live in London?' she asked. He nodded. 'You travel much?'

'Too much.'

'Your wife must be very understanding.'

Evidently Lauren too did not have on all the salient facts.

'My wife died last year. Rebecca. Cancer.'

Lauren's facial expression dropped, her shock clearly apparent.

'I'm sorry, I didn't know. You have kids at home?'

'Two great kids. Jack and Imogen. They're eight and four. I don't think they really understand what happened with Rebecca.'

'No one could understand something like that. You must miss them.'

'I had an agreement with Richemont not to travel. Until this trip.'

It was late. Jonathon felt heady, almost dizzy. Lauren must be feeling the same. Then he noticed an empty litre bottle of still Evian on the side and realised she'd been on the water for ages. He found the room claustrophobic and hot. Loosening the collar of his shirt, he wondered why he was sweating so profusely, what time it was back in SW1 and whether Jack and Imogen were in bed. He wished he was. The bill arrived on another silver tray, discreetly folded over so they couldn't see the ransom demanded.

'I'll charge it to my room. A gentleman always pays.'

He could hardly hold the pen. Lauren helped him.

'What room are you in?'

Jonathon struggled to remember, even to get the words out.

'1818.'

She wrote down the room number and he signed for the bill. They hadn't mentioned Alpha all evening. He had gleaned no information. Grabbing her lamé bag, Lauren leaned towards her dinner companion.

'I have to go, Jonathon. Are you okay?'

The room was a blur. His head truly ached. How much had he drunk? Hard to believe.

'I don't feel so great.'

'I'll take you upstairs to your room.'

He had difficulty standing up. Lauren cajoled him to the elevators in the lobby and upstairs to 1818. He couldn't open the door with the plastic credit card key. Again, she assisted him. He fell on to the covers of the double bed. Her job was done. She made to leave, then looked around and debated. McFarland might find out that she went to the room. But this visitor needed help and it was her fault.

She sat beside him and removed his damp shirt, running her fingers over his chest, around his nipples and through the few respectable strands of chest hair. She undid his belt with ease and slid his trousers off and on to the floor. She left his boxers. He stared back at her, head spinning, the air clammy on his skin. He was unsure of the vision before him, wondering how he had fallen into this stupor. She folded a cotton sheet over him and shifted his aching head on to a pillow.

'God, I feel awful. What's happening?'

'Don't worry, Jon. You'll be okay.'

Delirium had taken control. He could only make out a beautiful face close to his.

'Is that you, Rebecca? What's happening to me?'

'Try to sleep.'

Lauren took a hand towel from the bathroom and ran it under the cold tap, then folded it in half and placed it on his sweating forehead. She let it lie there a moment and turned it over, trying to cool him down. She watched him up close, studiously examining his profile, his jawline, the few wispy grey hairs in an otherwise dark head of hair, his bare square shoulders and the pale chest which slowly moved up and down as sleep eventually overcame her trusting dinner companion. She thought about what had made her stay with him, why she hadn't left the room earlier, about the dark empty millstone apartment she would soon return to in Repulse Bay; wondered what it was like to live with somebody you really cared for.

In another ten minutes the first light snores emanated from her victim. Her mission had been accomplished.

McFarland would be content tomorrow. She pulled the door to 1818 closed behind her, having turned off the lights and pulled the duvet up over her sleeping adversary.

Scott knew he would throw up if he tried to digest anything. He skipped lunch. The HSI closed at 9,150. Down 7 per cent in one day. He sweated profusely despite the air-conditioning. Avoided Dieter and his desk colleagues. He felt his gut tightening. His palms were constantly wet with the tension. This was hell on earth.

By late afternoon his hopes had risen. He had made it through another day. He could regroup overnight, phone Lauren for some ego massage, watch the Bloomberg altar at home, say his prayers in his bedroom tonight, have sex with Kim, maybe twice if she let him, and hope that somehow this market would turn tomorrow. He thought about doubling up on his long futures positions but decided against it. That strategy had ruined too many alleged star traders. Instead, he went to the john and did an excellent line of coke on the marble. Dieter called over to him on his return.

'Art's looking for you. You gotta see him right away.'

'Are you winding me up?'

'He's sure pissed about something and it looks like you're in the frame.'

Scott swivelled around and saw Greenbaum on the telephone. Best to leave the visit until later. Greenbaum would probably forget about it as usual. They made eye contact momentarily. Greenbaum held up a hand and pointed downward to his desk. As Scott entered, he slammed the office door, sat behind his desk and held up a single page as evidence for the prosecution.

'Romero in Finance has just given me this P&L spreadsheet for our Far East dealing. She says you're down forty-three million bucks in the past twenty-four hours. That can't be fucking right, can it?'

'No way.'

The Finance staff at Alpha were absolute crap and they all knew it, particularly Julia Romero. If any of them had a modicum of intelligence or ambition, they would get a better job at a real institution, one with customers, capital, liquidity and a reputation to cherish. Romero signed the monthly payroll cheques. She knew that millionaires worked in Alpha but none would ever be in her finance department. Greenbaum threw the page on to the desk. Scott eyeballed the damning columns of negative dollar numbers. Romero was close enough to the truth this time. Scott said nothing. Greenbaum pushed him.

'Is this spreadsheet correct?'

Scott sensed the implicit meaning. Greenbaum didn't know the truth. He was as blind as the rest of them, caught up in the memory of the good years when they had made more bucks than they knew what to do with, when markets never plummeted, when assassins didn't stalk the streets of a former Far East colony, when the Chinese PM wouldn't even have had the political neck to visit Central on a junket.

'It's way off base.'

'Good. I might fire Romero. She gave me some fucking scare.'

Forty odd million bucks lost in a single day? It was way off. More like twice that. Scott bluffed.

'This is a one-page Excel spreadsheet which she prepared manually. We can't be sure that the positions are the same as on our dealing system, nor can we be sure that her valuation market prices are the same as Bloomberg. This is all fiction. I don't rely on Romero's expertise much.'

Greenbaum had second thoughts. He frowned. He wasn't giving up so easily.

'I checked it. All the positions are here and they seem to be correctly valued. And it adds up.'

This was getting more difficult. Greenbaum had slogged away with the HP calculator on the desk. He studiously examined the page while Scott simultaneously dreamed up better excuses.

'I see what's wrong. I'm long and short in different stock markets. Romero's shown all my positions as long. There should be some short positions. Everything in the Far East is down and the prices are falling, but I am also short some index futures. I can buy them all back for less real soon.'

Greenbaum was thinking about his personal fortune in Alpha and Victoria's charitable spending habits.

'There's only one way to solve this discrepancy.'

'Yeah?'

Greenbaum hit the hands-free button on his speaker-phone. He searched for an extension in Finance.

'I'll get Romero down here. We can give her a good going over and tell her this page is a pile of crap.'

Jeez! No way. Scott needed more time. He threw an obvious glance at his watch.

'Hang on, Art. This will take some time. I need to get some print-outs and prepare the right numbers for her. We have to convince her once and for all. We can't have her making the same mistake again.'

'I've got the time. Let's do it right now.' Greenbaum was dialling Romero's line.

'I haven't got time, Art. I gotta leave soon.'

'What's so important all of a sudden?'

Scott was thinking on his feet, lying as only he could. The telephone was ringing.

'I'm meeting Kim uptown. We're having a meal out with her parents.'

'That can wait. But this worries me greatly.'

So many lies required to buy even more time to lie again. The telephone was still ringing.

'We're fixing the details of the wedding. I gotta be there. Kim would go mad otherwise.'

''Bout time you got hitched. 'Bout bloody time. Okay. Go for it.'

Greenbaum paused, the call was answered and a female voice boomed back. Shit.

'Julia Romero.'

'Art here. We think that your Far East desk P&L is all wrong.' He smiled over at Scott. 'You come down here at nine a.m. tomorrow and we'll show you how to value long and short positions in index futures and how to make forty-three million bucks of phantom losses disappear in one fell swoop.'

Greenbaum hung up. The shit was sure going to hit the fan tomorrow morning. Time was running out. The boss slapped Scott on the back as they both stood up. Scott couldn't get out of there fast enough.

'Romero is wrong, isn't she?'

'Sure thing, Art. You have my word.'

'Good. Enjoy the evening. Marriage is big step. Life will never be the same.'

Sir Charles Cavendish could stare down a presenter on Channel 4 news, tackle a heavyweight CEO in the boardroom, handle an international conference call with his peers, give rib-tickling after-dinner speeches or toy with a hostile House parliamentary committee across their baize-covered table in Westminster, but mere culinary matters were beyond his capability. He had no desire to play with a vicious tin-opener, ignite a lethal gas jet with a single match, pour out a bowl of Alpen or fight a Tetra Pak carton of real OJ with bits. Consequently he had given up on eggs Benedict on rye toast or warm oatmeal. At home, Marjorie had never let him near the kitchen. So now he left for work without breakfast.

He looked out past the dirty windows, the decrepit balcony with the dead plants, the turquoise-painted handrails, and through the lead oxide saw that he needed no coat today. He left the grim Barbican rented apartment, his temporary home for the past five months, and walked through the shaded alleyways of the towering concrete disaster left over from the 1960s. The official black Rover Sterling collected him at the usual location on the double yellow lines. He could have walked the short distance but a man in his elevated position didn't walk to work as a matter of principle.

The new apartment was closer to work but he missed Kensington. He missed home. He even missed Marjorie sometimes. He hadn't seen her in months, and the last meeting in a solicitor's office off Chancery Lane had been too acrimonious even to contemplate a repeat performance. His lawyer would speak to hers in future. Colleagues told him that half the marriages in the UK ended in divorce. Now Marjorie was going to take him for half of everything he owned – the house in Kensington, the Italian place, maybe even that lucrative investment in Alpha made courtesy of his trusted peer in the USA.

They drove down Beech and Chiswell Street, busy even at this early hour, then a quick right on to Moorgate, the street densely packed with combative buses and cabs. South along Moorgate and past the peace and tranquillity of Finsbury Circus, where the bankers still played lunch-time bowls on the immaculate lawns at this time of year. Past London Wall and on to Princes Street. Here was the old heart of the City. Left again down a narrow street adjacent to Bank Junction. The aged doormen in the pink livery and top hat always opened the main door when they saw their boss arrive in the style to which he was accustomed.

The Bank of England generously provided a free breakfast to all before 8.30 a.m. Their Governor always dined with the staff. It was democracy in action, his chance to meet the people, assess the mood of his several hundred staff, but there were unspoken rules. The Governor had the best table by the window. Only a select few dared to sit and make small talk with their boss.

Others watched Cavendish from afar, wondering whether he was as intelligent as he looked, with his owlish features, deceptively small eyes, a carefully combed greying balding pate with a high forehead, an often sombre expression and heavy-rimmed glasses which all served to lend extra intellectual credibility. Others watched to see what he ate. Bacon, egg, sausage, fried tomato, grilled mushrooms, bubble and squeak, fried potatoes. No baked beans ever. Titled gentry didn't seem to do beans, the nearby staff surmised. He would ingest every last morsel. Some had seen him discreetly use the last slice of toast to mop up the remnants of egg on the plate with the Bank's gold crest.

Sometimes Pamela came downstairs on his behalf and they watched her move gracefully among the self-service counters. Opinion was equally divided as to whether she had a serious thing going with the Governor. Some said she was too young, her suits and skirts too conservative, her make-up too subtle, her tousled hair too unkempt, and her IQ and confidence too high to contemplate such a relationship. But all agreed that she was hyperactive and thus must have a high sex drive.

Cavendish himself had not been seen in the canteen since the Chinese premier was unceremoniously bagged. Today the table by the window was unused. No one else dared to sit there. Instead, his junior staff came down to gather the necessary daily provisions. Of late, orders for coffee and toast for ten were delivered upstairs on silver trays to the specially convened crisis room on the top floor. Cavendish's senior colleagues were missing too, digesting so much more upstairs than cold toast. Global events. Panic trading. Short selling. Plunging stock prices. One of the staff asked how the Governor was? Hungry, came the reply.

Scott was sick of the good wishes. Dieter wished him well on his hot date with the in-laws-to-be. The others were making jibes about Kim, unaware of the one big story that was sure to break tomorrow morning at 9 a.m. in Greenbaum's office. If tomorrow ever came. Kim wouldn't marry a criminal doing time in the state pen.

Scott took two frantic telephone calls from Lauren in Hong Kong. Soldiers had shot more civilians. The HSI was down another 6 per cent. She faxed over an account statement. She wanted him to pay some huge margin calls the next day. He lied and said the money was already on its way from Alpha's account at Chase. He took his cellphone in his pocket and left the trading desk soon afterwards. He needed to be home before Kim tonight.

Walking the few blocks on autopilot, he crossed the

intersections with pedestrian lights glowing red. Cab drivers honked horns at the distracted jaywalker. He barged into deli runners and FedEx drivers. Couriers on bikes turned to swear at him. He ignored the greeting from the concierge in the basement lobby. He hit floor twenty-eight inside the elevator without really knowing how he had made it to a sanctuary of sorts. Throwing off his suit jacket, he collapsed on to the bed. He couldn't exist like this.

The Bloomberg screen was still displaying the HSI page. The price chart today looked like the edge of a cliff. He knew how it felt to stand at the edge. The buoyant months of the past were a lifetime away. He went to turn off the screen that ran his life, but couldn't find the power-down switch on the back of the hot monitor. He had never switched it off, he realised. He grabbed the bundle of grey cabling and yanked all the plugs out of the wall. Sparks flew from the socket towards the curtains and a burning odour hung temporarily in the bedroom. The screen crackled as life ceased to pulse.

Millions of bucks in losses always looked better through a haze courtesy of Rico. He searched at the back of the bottom drawer on his side of the bed. No joy. Then in the washroom cabinet, as he stared momentarily into the mirror but didn't recognise the sunken face he saw. No joy there either. He went through other drawers, old coats, wallets, everything. He needed one last line to sate his craving. Reality dawned. He had no decent shit in the apartment save for a can of diet shit in the humming GE fridge.

He tried the bottom drawer on Kim's side of the bed. His hands rested on the piece in the corner under a pile of carefully folded garments. She had bought it last year after that crack-crazed mugger on Second took her cash, her leather wallet, her jewellery and nearly so much more. He felt the steel in his shaking hand. He needed closure. Kim would be home soon. She would be first at the scene. She'd find the blood splattered across the walls, on the carpet and over the cotton sheets they had shared so often. There had to be a better way. He closed the drawer and got a last Bud out of the cooler.

He walked back through the bedroom and opened the French doors on to the well-planted balcony. He heard the all-pervasive hum of New York river life below. He stepped out and dared to look down from twenty-eight floors. Distant figures scurried back and forth, small, cosseted children and their anxious minders played on the riverside boardwalk, lost tourists ambled along with open downtown maps, pairs of posing yuppie joggers passed in Lycra gear and Walkman earphones. Directly below he could see the dense bushes where the NYC Parks groundsmen carefully plied their daily trade.

The remains of the sun shone low across the Hudson. He took in the view of the urban sprawl of Hoboken set amidst the polluted haze of industrial New Jersey. He eyed the wisp of diesel fumes from the Staten Island ferry as it took early commuters home to their own little piece of the American Dream. He took a lingering slug from the iced Bud long-neck. He knew that the Dream had a bitter aftertaste.

Manhattan was where it all happened. It was where the players lived, dined, drank, dealt, spent, screwed and made a killing on Wall Street. It was where wealth, power and success spoke volumes. This was no place for a compulsive liar who had lied once too often, no place for a failed trader at a bankrupt hedge fund in the midst of a global financial meltdown, no place for one of life's dead-beat losers. He had no desire to do time for a billion-dollar corporate crime with no victim but himself.

Scott took one look at the vista before him, committed it to memory for an eternity to be spent in hell, and took his last drink of the cold Dream. He leaned against the low metal railing.

CHAPTER SEVEN
CENTURY PLAZA, CENTRAL, HONG KONG – 8.15 A.M.

After twenty-four hours spent recovering from the worst bout of food poisoning he could remember, Jonathon appeared early on the sales floor, apparently much to the surprise of McFarland.

'Where were you yesterday? We thought you'd gone chicken and flown home.'

The worst place to be when you were seriously ill was alone, seven thousand miles away from home and family. Jonathon had spent the early phase on his knees over the toilet bowl in the bathroom, reliving the fine food of the Jardin Chinois. He had called down to reception in the early hours and a doctor appeared as quickly as room service. The hotel manager had appeared soon afterwards to apologise for the unprecedented event at the Ritz Carlton. Jonathon's body was still racked with aches and pains. He felt lethargic and dehydrated, but McFarland didn't need to know all the grim details. Best to bluff it.

'I had others to meet as part of my investigation.'

McFarland smiled a knowing smile, his best attempt at a counter-bluff.

'The situation's getting worse here. A lot of arson and looting last night.'

'So I hear.'

'So you're flying home tonight?'

'No. I need a few more words with Lauren.'

McFarland threw a cautious glance over at his colleague's empty desk.

'She's in and around somewhere. Take a seat. Maybe she'll show again.'

McFarland walked off. Jonathon knew this was all a game to them. Lauren was nowhere in sight. He needed her co-operation before he could leave. This investigation was getting to him. He scribbled some notes and then watched the screens, sad in the knowledge that all world markets were following the lead of the Far East. Confidence was shot to hell. He looked at Lauren's PC screen. The FTSE down 328 points yesterday. He thought of Eva and the kids in London. He hadn't seen an English newspaper in days.

He looked at the icons displayed on the toolbar at the bottom of her PC screen. He was sure Lauren would have the Internet on her PC. They all had access at Mitchell's in London. He'd check out *The Times* website. He never used the Web at home or at Richemont et Cie, remaining convinced that it was primarily used by young single men to surf porn sites or suicidal day-traders to churn NASDAQ stocks. He looked at the tiny font. One icon was for the compulsory Bloomberg. Another for Datastream for research purposes. Another for Reuters TV through a PC. Another was some Excel file called trading.xls. Then the Web. He looked again at the truncated web display: www.schwab.hk.

His curiosity was aroused. Mitchell's hated Ameritrade, TD Waterhouse Schwab E* Trade and all the on-line new boys. On-line dealing was still the rage, even after the well-publicised calamities of those day-traders who lost six-figure sums and the lunatic shoot-outs in the USA. Where else? A site like this was primarily for personal dealing. Why would Lauren want to look at the website of a competing on-line broker when she could deal personally through Mitchell's if she desired? Once, of course, McFarland approved her own trade prior to dealing.

Checking there was no one else near by, he moved the mouse to the bottom of the toolbar and maximised the view. The screen showed details of share dealing in the past month. Jonathon saw the pattern: intra-day buys and sells, immediate profits of thousands of Honkie dollars, no losses whatsoever. He scrolled back up to the top. The name on the account was Ms Lauren Trent and the address was shown as an apartment in Repulse Bay. No doubt about it, this was her personal dealing account.

Jonathon thought laterally and clicked back to the left on the Excel file. A list of HSBC stock purchases and sales opened up, all in neat chronological order. There was a new trade almost every weekday. He scrolled down to the foot of the spreadsheet. Profits of three hundred thousand local dollars in the past month. Close to forty K US. Easy money. No losses at all. It was an outside account which was consistently profitable. He checked the recent trade times on Schwab versus the times of the Alpha HSI tickets he had seen earlier and found the two to be very closely correlated. He knew what he was seeing. He had seen colleagues fired for doing this in Mitchell's before. This was frontrunning at its most effective.

He dumped the web screen on to a nearby printer and then printed the one-page Excel file. He placed the still-warm pages in his briefcase and closed it. He wondered whether there was more to the Chapman–Lauren relationship, whether there was some scam on the side, whether kickbacks were in play here and how wide-ranging his report on Alpha was going to be.

He was still alone at the desk. He looked for more evidence, sifted the pages near by and noticed a photocopy of a Mitchell's futures account statement. He assumed that it was Lauren who had circled the figure of $60 million plus small change. The narrative confirmed that it was a variation margin call, the amount of additional funds that a client must deposit with a bank to continue to run a loss-making futures position. Alpha's name appeared on the statement, care of a 212 fax number in New York. Alpha had owed the money for the past three days. More worrying signs.

'Enjoy scavenging around? Found anything interesting?'

McFarland suddenly stood beside him. Jonathon held up the Mitchell's statement.

'Just the fact that Alpha haven't paid sixty million in margin for three days. But you already know that.'

From the look on McFarland's face, Jonathon deduced that this at least was news to him.

Walter P. Sayers II, the most powerful unelected government official in Washington, DC, always prepared meticulously for one critical day each quarter, knowing that the eyes of the world would be on him more than ever. The first draft was penned in the bath at 6 a.m. when he knew that his IQ was twenty points higher than at 6 p.m. The thirty-minute hot soak also eased the pain in his lower vertebrae that the best MDs couldn't assuage. He chose his words carefully, endeavouring to emphasise the positive and eliminate the negative. He reworked the monologue several times in the rear of the limo stuck in the traffic of Manhattan's Midtown tunnel before catching the early Delta shuttle from La Guardia to Washington National Airport. The government car then took him directly to Capitol Hill.

Some snappers photographed him as he climbed the tiers of steps. The better photographs would be front-page news in tomorrow's papers. Sayers was once again conscious of what he carried under his arm. The infamous Briefcase Theory was still out there. The size of his briefcase was an indicator of the US's policy. The watchers opined that if Sayers were about to announce a major policy change, he would bring plenty of supporting documentation with him to DC. If there was to be no change then he travelled light. The Chairman of the Federal Reserve Board liked to keep them guessing.

As he entered the public room shortly before four, Sayers was reminded why he had given up a post in fundamental research at Salomon's seven years ago to take this job at a mere 133k per annum. He was now in his second four-year term. There were many more cameras, flashlights and microphones than last time. His speech was to be broadcast live. He wondered how he'd look, how much grey hair he had shed and how many pounds he had gained since last time. He stood at the table, held his open right hand raised as required and took the oath. The world's traders and bankers sat at their desks, waiting on his every word, watching every nuance, every pause, every blink of an eye, every expression, every hesitation, every stare. Sayers could unilaterally send the markets to heaven or to hell in less than a minute of perfect diction.

The old Republican from Texas with a hairpiece and a penchant for older married women spoke first. Then came the formal invitation for the Chairman of the Federal Reserve Board to make his contribution. Sayers took a drink from a glass of disgustingly flat tepid water. Now the limelight was his and the House of Representatives Committee on Banking and Financial Services took a back seat.

Sayers wondered what exactly would happen if he said something stupid or flippant. Would he crack a joke about those who thought the Federal Reserve was a national bird sanctuary? Would the markets collapse before he got to the end of the first sentence? He recalled that occasion when he had warned of 'irrational exuberance in the markets' in the midst of a bull run and the Dow tanked thirty minutes later. He coughed once merely for effect. He was no orator in truth, but nonetheless there was complete silence.

'Mr Chairman and other members of the Committee, I appreciate this opportunity to present the Federal Reserve's report on monetary policy.'

Sayers stopped after his usual introduction. He could assume all was well and dive into the minutiae. He could speak about annual consumption, labour markets, household wealth, durable assets, manufacturing inventories, hourly productivity, housing starts, GDP forecasts, inflationary pressures, current deficits, liquidity growth and all that jazz. But he'd read the editorial in the *Journal*. He needed to confront the issues of the day. The media wanted their soundbite. The investment gurus needed the comfort factor.

'Before I review our economic performance, I wish to comment on the recent falls in global equity and bond markets. We have seen the value of some investments fall by up to twenty per cent. It is clear to me that this fall was originally triggered by political unrest in Asia and has had a domino effect on other Asian and European markets. I do not believe that the economic fundamentals in the United States have changed and I believe that a sustainable recovery in these markets is both possible and probable.'

The faces at the top table relaxed. No wonder. Sayers was sure all the tanned Reps up there were millionaires because it was the only way to finance a trip to run for Congress. They had stock market investments going south and had lost as much as any John Doe in the past few weeks.

He was finished twenty minutes later. The morning headlines were penned. The Dow rose a hundred points when he started speaking but fell back sharply in the final minutes before the closing bell. Sayers wondered why his words did not have the desired effect, wondered whether this market slide was something more fundamental, and whether Alicia was waiting in that room at the Hilton.

McFarland came over to Lauren as she eyed the grim dealing screens. There was still panic selling out there in the big bad world. There were now deaths on the streets in daylight, according to the midday news on the TVs suspended over the FF&O desk. Two expats in a flash car had been attacked over on the Kowloon side while stuck in gridlock. Driving to work was almost too dangerous for a Yank. McFarland ensured that Jonathon was out of earshot, placed a single fax page on her desk and glared at her.

'You tell me everything that happens here?'

'Sure do, Mac.'

'Anything I should know about Alpha?'

'Like what?'

'Like the fact that they haven't paid any margin for the past three days. Their huge HSI position is way down the money. All their T-bond and cash collateral has been posted and used. They owe us sixty-three million US bucks in variation margin as of yesterday. The credit department is livid. So why didn't you tell me about this?

How come I hear it first from that smarmy consultant from London?'

Lauren swivelled her chair around to face her boss.

'I didn't want to worry you.'

'Have we got cash yet?' She shook her head. 'What have you done about it?'

'I called Scott. He says the funds will be with us asap.'

'Saying he'll send funds and actually seeing a credit in our bank account are light years apart.'

'I'm sure Alpha will pay.'

McFarland pointed at the numbers on the statement page.

'You need to call Chapman right now and find out what the hell is going on.'

Lauren made a mental note to steer clear of Big Mac. This bear market was taking its toll.

'It's very early in New York.'

'I know the time in New York. It's on the fucking wall behind us. You need to sort this today.'

'Scott isn't at work right now.'

'You got his home number?'

'Mac, it's five a.m. there.'

'So what? Call him at home. We gotta get margin off them. The Alpha account is frozen until they pay up. No more trading unless it's a sell order. Otherwise we start enforced liquidation of their positions. Operations and Credit upstairs are getting itchy. We need to keep them sweet at times like this.'

McFarland left her and walked over to another director's office. She watched him through the glass. He looked highly animated, hands everywhere, clenched fists, finger pointing in the director's face. Lauren assumed they were talking about Alpha. The other director threw a deadly glance in Lauren's direction. They were.

She refocused, reached for her Palm Pilot organiser, found Scott's 212 home number and dialled. It rang and rang for an eternity. C'mon, pick up, Scott, damn you. An answering machine kicked in and she heard Scott. It was a tape. Then someone did pick up. She heard a girl's distant sleepy voice.

'Scott?'

It must be the girlfriend. Kim? she thought.

'Hi. Is Scott there?'

'Who is this?'

'It's Lauren from Hong Kong.'

'Do you know the time here?'

'I need to speak to Scott urgently.'

'So do I.'

'What do you mean?'

There was a long pause. Lauren heard Kim inhale and exhale a few times. Heavy sighs.

'I know Scott came home after work but he went out somewhere. There was a half-finished beer on the balcony and the doors were open but he didn't come back last night. I don't know where the hell he is. I've tried his folks. I've tried everyone we know. I tried every place we go. Nothing.'

Lauren needed to make contact with the man who had her sixty-three million dollars.

'Did you try his cellphone?'

'It just rings and rings. No one answers.'

'Is he at work? Can I call him there?'

'I tried all last night. He isn't there either. Do you know where he is?'

'How would I know? I'm thousands of miles away.'

'Then don't ring here again. Leave me alone. He could call me any moment.'

Kim hung up abruptly. Lauren was puzzled. McFarland saw her hang up and rushed back over.

'Did you get through to his home number?'

Big Mac was all over her, right up close, in her face, leaning into her, pressurising her.

'Yeah, I did.' Not strictly a lie.

'And has the fucker paid the margin?'

So close to her. Overpowering. She wilted and gave Mac the answer that he so desperately needed.

'Yeah. No problem, he says.'

The attendant from the NYC Parks Department manoeuvred the white electric three-wheeler van out of the overnight garage and began his rounds along the landscaped verges of the boardwalk that ran south from the World Financial Centre to the Battery itself. A few joggers passed him by. He eyed the panting females and knew that his wife would disapprove. Heck, you can look at a menu without having to order anything.

He parked up near Hudson Tower and admired his perfectly cut turf and pruned standard rose bushes. He tended all this as if it were his own garden. He lit a Marlboro, took in the rays and eventually began the work he put off until the latter part of each week. He thought that he could hear a cellphone ringing not too far way, but then it went quiet all of sudden. He liked these early summertime starts. His eldest son had a Little League game in the Bronx at five tonight and he'd be there to see the first pitch thrown in anger at East Tremont.

He foraged alone amidst the urban rubbish that was funnelled between the towering blocks and deposited in this sheltered undergrowth, using a rusted rake to extract flattened Sprite and Coors cans, McDonald's Styrofoam cartons, lurid *Post* newspapers, Wrigley's gum wrappers and even the occasional used rubber with remnants of bodily fluids inside. The things these loaded residents got up to at times . . . His rake hit something he couldn't move. He stopped and parted the undergrowth with his left hand, saw a person, some bum, a wino, some wasted dropout high on glue or speed.

'Hey, let's move on out. Time to rise and shine, fella.'

He saw the shoes first with their fine Italian leather. Then the shirt. What sort of bum wears cuff links and a loosely knotted tie? None that he had seen before. The form was still, its weight flat against the baked earth, crushed vegetation and sharp stones. He looked up through the trees and saw the light. A few branches had been parted from trees. He saw the white exposed bark, sap running like blood. No one survives a fall from that height. Not even a Battery Park resident. This was a corpse. He called the NYPD.

He heard the siren minutes later. A local precinct car drove at speed along the narrow boardwalk. A lone jogger took evasive action. The tyres stopped on the patch of grass mown yesterday. The earth flew as the carpet of turf was disturbed. The passenger door swung open and decapitated two of his prized rose bushes.

A beanpole cop with a tight ginger crew cut emerged from the car and crossed the wooden boardwalk. His name badge proclaimed O'Neill. He looked about twenty years old. Jeez, they sent kids to check out deaths these days. O'Neill had been in early morning combat with a Gillette razor blade and come away a poor second with significant loss of blood. Could have been Assault with a Deadly Weapon. He was apparently excited to be at the scene of his first decent crime in the NYPD.

'So who's in charge here?' asked the grunt.

'You are.'

'We heard you got a stiff. Whatcha know about him?'

The parks officer recognised a distant brogue. He obliged with the necessary minimum.

'Nothing. I haven't touched him. He's all yours. Good luck.'

O'Neill seemed to have forgotten the procedure they'd taught him at boot camp seven weeks ago upstate. He turned for help as his experienced buddy slowly emerged from the driver's seat, slipped a long, lethal nightstick down by his belt, loosened the clip on his handgun, looked lazily around the scene and placed a peaked cap upon his swarthy Italian head. He threw a roll of regulation yellow tape at Junior.

'You do the easy bit, Joe. Tape off the area. Leave

twenty feet all around. I'll do the ID. Then let homicide take over.'

The unnecessary siren of the NYPD car had roused rubber-neckers from the nearby apartments. Several dressing-robe-clad inhabitants appeared to stare down at the scene below. The parks attendant took one last look at the distressing scene. He walked twenty feet to the right, standing directly in the visible path of the body's fall. He raised his eyes up towards the balconies, scanning them one by one. They were all deserted. People had already left for work or were not missing any loved ones at home.

Up and up his eyes went, counting off floor by floor until he reached twenty-eight. A single small figure hung over the edge, a girl with long tresses dressed only in an oversized white T-shirt with a visible Adidas logo. Her head slowly shook from side to side in disbelief. Their eyes met. She implored, begged him for an easy answer. There was none. She collapsed out of sight. He turned to leave. O'Neill was still experiencing difficulty with the simple task of knotting fluttering tape to nearby trees and boardwalk rails.

'Hey, we need to talk to you.'

'You don't.'

'Is that so?'

'If I was you, I'd talk to the girl living on this side of the twenty-eighth floor of this block.'

The grunt looked up for the first time and scratched his head.

'How d'ya know that?'

'Call it experience. You'll know what that is some day.'

CHAPTER EIGHT

CENTURY PLAZA, CENTRAL,
HONG KONG – 2.40 P.M.

Jonathon saw Lauren during the morning on the sales floor but they didn't speak. She sat at other desks in the near vicinity, chatted to dour colleagues, even spoke to McFarland for a while. He watched her from afar, admired her form, liked the way she stood by the desk, how she held the telephone, how she arched her back, and ultimately realised she was the first person he had lusted after for almost a year. The memories of that night ill in bed at the Ritz Carlton were vague but she had been there to care for him.

It was an impossible situation. He knew what was going on. She was frontrunning, dealing on the side as often as she could and making as much as she could. It was such a pity. Her career was in jeopardy. He sensed she knew he was watching. They exchanged brief glances. Part of him felt sad that he would be leaving on Friday, probably never to see her again. He cornered her after lunch.

'Were you ill after that meal?'

'I was okay.'

'I was up all night. I woke with a head like someone had taken a sledgehammer to it.'

'Too much alcohol?'

'Food poisoning. No. It was more than that. I felt drugged. Still do. I can hardly concentrate on my work. I have no recollection of going back to my hotel room. It's all a total blur after I signed the bill.'

'I helped you upstairs to your room. Remember that?'

Jonathon didn't wish to pursue this line of questioning. Lauren pointed at the badly scribbled yellow Post-It note on her desk.

'There was a message for you. Something's up at home. You need to call Eva urgently. Is she your other half?'

'Not quite.'

Jonathon moved to a quiet corner and dialled home. Lauren watched him pick a line from the mass of lights on the dealer board. He could still work the telephones in Mitchell's. The telephone rang many times.

'Jon here. Is everything okay, Eva?'

The line was good from London. No time delay at all. Mitchell's leased tie-lines were the best.

'Jack's watching TV. He's seen all the shootings and burning buildings out there. Knows where you are. He thinks you're in danger. He won't sleep. Won't eat. Won't go out. He needs to see you.'

Jonathon knew what was most important in life. He looked at his watch and realised he could leave today.

'I'll be at home seven a.m. tomorrow morning. Tell Jack. 'Bye.'

Lauren studied his face as he put the handset down.

'Everything all right?'

'Should be. I'm going home. Today. Now.'

She thought for a moment and took a business card from a pile on her desk.

'If you need to know anything else, then call me.'

He wondered why she had offered the card, whether there was some ulterior motive or whether she was genuine. McFarland had obviously seen enough sociable chat and brushed between them both, arriving late into the conversation.

'You still here?'

'Apparently so.'

'The FO is advising all their nationals who can do so to leave Hong Kong. It's all over the BBC at home. I wish I could leave as easily as you can but I have a wife and three kids up in the Mid-Levels. Mitchell's are providing security for us expats at home from tonight onwards, and buses to and from work. It might even be safer here in the office. A French tourist and a Korean businessman were killed in Kowloon. One of them got it with a meat cleaver in the back of the neck. Know what I mean? If you'll take my advice, you'll finish this investigation and get the hell out of here.'

Jonathon had all the evidence he needed about Alpha,

the over-trading, the huge losses, the unpaid margin calls. Eva's phone call was the decisive factor.

'I've got all I need.'

'Good. There's no point hanging around here any longer. We can deal with this without you. We are in full control of the situation. So what are you going to say in your report?'

Jonathon stood his ground and faced off his adversary.

'My numbers show that in the past month Alpha bought about two billion dollars of futures, sold some for about one billion, and what they have left are worth a mere two hundred million. That's eight hundred million thrown away by the one-man show that is Scott Chapman.'

'Impossible. They use other local brokers too,' noted McFarland.

'They don't. Chapman visited no one else when he was here. You see all the order flow.'

McFarland turned to Lauren.

'Is that true?'

She nodded. Jonathon cut in.

'You should monitor your clients more closely. Alpha still owes you millions in unpaid margin.'

'Lauren spoke to Chapman yesterday. Alpha are paying up today.'

'Have you seen any of that money?'

McFarland again turned to Lauren.

'Not yet,' she admitted after a suitable pause.

Shortly afterwards Jonathon gathered his papers.

Lauren watched him leave while McFarland walked him to the lifts and stood beside him, obviously hoping that one would arrive soon to rid him of this intruder for good. He took a step closer.

'You're a fucking seagull. You fly in here, make a lot of noise, spend days living off us and crap all over us from a great height. The Romans didn't create an empire by having meetings and writing reports and memos. They did it by killing everyone who opposed them. Be very careful what you say in your report to the States.'

Jonathon let this pass. The lift arrived. McFarland delivered his parting shot. 'Have a safe flight. Mind the peasants on the way to the airport. Don't run over too many of 'em. See you on *News at Ten*.' McFarland was so close that Jonathon could smell bad aftershave, BO, a hint of fear, and a curried lunch of some sort. 'A blow-in consultant like you will never know as much as I do.'

Jonathon put his foot in the way of the closing lift doors and stared back at McFarland.

'I know everything I need to know about the FF&O desk.'

'You know fuck-all, mate.'

McFarland was goading him. Memories of that night spent throwing up in the bathroom came back to Jonathon. He recalled the Schwab web page on Lauren's PC. He was still unsure whether this was wholly relevant to his report. McFarland must know about it if he sat beside her all day. They must all be at it.

'I know you're all frontrunning client HSI orders by day-trading local stocks on the Web.'

The lift door was trying to close again. This time McFarland put his foot in the way. 'Who the hell do you think is doing that? Because I know for a fact that they wouldn't dare do it on my desk.'

'You are.'

'No, I'm not.'

The words just came out.

'Well, Lauren is.'

'No, she's not.'

'She frontruns Alpha's big orders. She makes good money day-trading HSBC shares with Schwab.'

Jonathon only just got to see the look on McFarland's face. The doors closed and then the lift descended. He was left alone with an awful feeling that he had just made a serious mistake.

Greenbaum sat with Romero. He was of the view that his token Chief Financial Officer had deteriorated of late. Her dyed teased hair had too much volume and too much length for her narrow painted face. Crude chunky rings sat on all her bony fingers except on the one that mattered, looking more like a set of knuckledusters, while her heavy-rimmed glasses gave his CFO an air of intelligence she simply didn't possess. Romero ran her pen nervously over the rows of numbers on the incriminating spreadsheet.

'Mr Greenbaum, my schedule is correct. My numbers today show the losses are now significantly greater than they were yesterday. I believe we are almost eight hundred million dollars in the red in HSI futures. That's more than our capital base. We can't afford losses like that, we'd be bust.'

Greenbaum had no idea from where this glorified bean-counter had got these numbers. It was embarrassing.

'I'm not convinced. As soon as Scott arrives, we'll prove it to you.'

He got up and yelled at his harassed PA outside, who was still tackling her morning doughnut.

'Where the hell is Scott? He's hours late. Did you call him?'

She spoke through a mouthful of sticky dough, red jam and sugar crystals.

'There is no answer from his home.'

'Use your IQ. And don't talk to me again until you find him.'

Ten minutes later Greenbaum gave Romero her marching orders and fumed alone. He needed Scott today of all days. The longer the uncertainty went on, the more worried he became. Scott was never late like this. Never took a day off. What had happened last night with Kim? Had the evening meal with his future in-laws been a disaster?

He continued to pace the room alone, staring at screens full of red prices and downing gallons of vile black coffee. The markets were still falling out of bed out East. More overnight rioting. Government offices attacked. CS gas and pepper spray deployed by troops. The Hang Seng was down another 6 per cent. The Far East desk at Alpha had remained unmanned for way too long. His PA came in with a puzzled expression on her face. He jumped up from his seat.

'You got Scott? Where is he?'

'There are two officers here to see you. Police.'

'Get them to talk to someone else. I'm too busy today.'

'They need to talk to you.'

'Stall them, goddamn it! That's what I pay you to do.'

But his PA couldn't take no for an answer. The two men hove into view behind her.

'They're Homicide. Here about a member of staff.'

Greenbaum's mind was racing. Two guys in faded brown suits with visible holster bulges and NYPD badges worn on their belts joined him uninvited. One sat on a low chair by the wall and surveyed the contents of the office, taking mental notes. That seemed to be his sole function. The other stood before Greenbaum and leaned on the desk.

'I'm Detective Hamill. You know a guy called Scott Chapman?'

They had found him at last. What had he done? Some last bachelor stunt?

'He's a trader who works for me.'

The detective placed his nail-bitten hands upon the very edge of Greenbaum's desk.

'Used to work for you. We found him this morning below his apartment.'

Greenbaum was still lost. Scott had to sort out this Far East futures mess.

'I don't understand. Is he okay?'

The guy in the chair looked at his colleague, then surveyed the dealing room outside and spoke slowly and clearly.

'He fell twenty-eight floors to mother earth. He's a jumper. Massive internal injuries. Shattered spinal cord. Immediate death say the coroner's office. He's gone to the big dealing room in the sky.'

Greenbaum slumped back into his chair, held his head in his hands and practically sobbed.

'Fuck!'

'Sorry,' said the cop sardonically. 'Thought he just worked here. Didn't know he meant that much to you.'

'He didn't. It's his damn dealing that matters to me.'

'Do you know of any reason why he might have jumped? Pressure at work maybe?'

Greenbaum thought about eight hundred million bucks of undisclosed losses. He needed to check his facts first.

'There's always pressure here. It's the job.'

The quiet guy in the chair stood up and spoke.

'We need you to ID the body.'

But Greenbaum's mind was on far more important matters.

'Get his girlfriend to do it. Kim?'

'She's real cut up about this. Under sedation uptown. We need you to do it. That's why we came.'

'I'm too busy.'

'The NYPD don't take no for an answer. Sure you can do it.'

'Dieter worked with Chapman. He can do the ID. Tell him to do it. If not, he's fired.'

The detectives shrugged, gave Greenbaum a contemptuous stare and left reluctantly. He hit the speakerphone.

'Romero, get yourself down here immediately!'

Through the glass he watched the detectives hassle the unfortunate German until he took his jacket and left. He saw the reaction outside as word spread. The others near by knew what had happened. Romero brushed past the curious onlookers and into his office. Greenbaum closed the door and dropped the rows of black Venetian blinds in one single movement. Suddenly Romero was his saviour.

'Chapman is dead. Killed himself last night jumping from his apartment.'

'God, that's awful.'

'Sure is.'

'Poor Kim. The wedding.'

'Forget about her. I'm wondering what sort of shit he's left us. Let's look at your numbers again. This time I won't interrupt you. You tell me how much you think the Far East futures desk has lost up to now. No one else at Alpha is to know about this until we are both in agreement.'

They spent over six hours together. Lunch was ordered in after three o'clock. Greenbaum ignored his cream cheese bagel. The final calculations at six o'clock showed losses of over a billion dollars.

'Jeez! How can one guy have done this to us? If I had Chapman here now, I'd fucking kill him myself.'

He ignored all telephone calls. His PA dared to enter before she left for the evening.

'I told you, no interruptions.'

'Victoria is on the line.'

'Tell her I can't talk now.'

'Tell her yourself. You don't pay me enough to sort out your home life.'

His wife came through on his direct line, at her most insistent.

'Art, I'm reminding you again. Eight o'clock this evening at the Hilton. See you there.'

'What?'

'The UJA dinner. You're getting that presentation for your philanthropic work.'

'Can't be there. I've too much to do here.'

'But you're vice-chairman of the board.'

'We're not going. Period.'

'Give me one good reason why.'

'Because I can't show my goddamn face at any Wall Street hotshot event ever again. That do you?'

He hung up, let Romero leave and made a telephone call to the one man who maybe could help him.

The first ominous signs were two sixteen-wheeler APCs parked up on the verge in front of the entrance to the Ritz Carlton. The huge ridges of their rubber tyres had ploughed through the painstaking patchwork of manicured rose bushes and a low rockery. The surly crew-cut drivers in grubby battle fatigues didn't care. They twitched nervously every time some distant shots became audible, trying to determine whether they were CS gas, rubber bullets or live rounds, machineguns cocked aggressively. Jonathon wondered whether their purpose was to deter the locals or to keep the guests inside. Whatever, he was leaving fast.

The hotel lobby was like the backdrop to a TV news bulletin. Journalists and reporters hovered in clusters, comparing notes and discussing rumours. Mobile and satellite telephones pulsed. CNN and NBC logos abounded. Late arrivals checked in with mountains of broadcasting gear in rows of chrome containers. Heated arguments developed at reception. Rooms in this developing war zone were at a premium. Every newshound wanted a rooftop room with a balcony view to the killing zone way below. No one was checking out of the biggest news story on the globe except Jonathon. He waylaid a harassed porter.

'I have a BA car due. Is it here yet?'

'No.'

'You sure?'

The aged porter shrugged, apparently more interested in the mounting collection of luggage.

'No airport cars. Drivers are too scared. They got attacked. Anyone in expensive car is a target.'

Jonathon was thinking about Jack and Imogen. Eva too. She'd be livid if he didn't make it home.

'Call me a taxi.'

'No taxis either.'

'How do I get to the airport?' The porter shrugged and said nothing. 'How did all these media people get here?' Jonathon pressed him.

'On bus.'

'Which bus?'

'Hotel staff bus around side of building. Manager's idea. It goes to airport to collect more journalists in one hour. You can ride in bus if you like but dangerous, I think. You decide.'

Jonathon would take his chances. The BA flight was scheduled to leave in a few hours time. The bus was an ancient rusted white Toyota Hi-Ace van with four bald tyres. There was no glossy Ritz Carlton logo on the exterior. Think of the shame. The six seats inside were made of cheap rotten plastic. His luggage was stowed in a hold that smelled of beer. Jonathon got inside without a word of protest. Word had obviously spread. An elderly German husband and wife joined him. The driver, aged about eighteen, was sweating profusely and seemed extremely agitated.

'No one knows it's hotel bus. You get down,' he advised his three dubious passengers.

The youth drove off at speed down through Central, past the Olympic centre and the new MTR line. Jonathon and the others did as he suggested and crouched amidst the rubbish on the floor, daring occasionally to peer outside. It was worse farther out, nearer the container port and the highways on reclaimed land. They passed burning cars, smoking tyres, shuttered shops, daubed and blackened walls. The bus's windows were closed as the air-con pumped, but still the stench of a city under siege permeated the interior of the vehicle. Hitting queues of traffic, they waited. Some locals glared over at the stalled vehicles, looking for trouble. The German raised his head and was seen immediately. Shouts rang out.

'*Gweilo!*'

Jonathon shouted at the driver. 'Let's go. Fast!'

'Too much traffic.'

Fists pummelled the sides of the bus. Hands appeared at the plate glass.

'Pull out. Overtake. Do it. Now!'

The youth panicked and made to leap out of the driver's side on to the street, preferring his chances on foot. Jonathon caught him by the scruff of the neck and dragged him back inside, across the front seats, hit the central locking and jumped into the driver's seat. A long metal bar appeared at eye level. The nearside window shattered instantly, shards of glass falling on Jonathon as he scrambled for the pedals on the floor.

'Get down.' Animated faces filled the windscreen, dark with anger, shouting threats he instantly understood even though the words were meaningless to him. 'Hold on tight.'

He swung the steering wheel to the right, swerving out of the hold-up and across the median as he pumped the accelerator to the floor. Oncoming traffic screeched out of the way, the drivers swearing at him. Jonathon snatched a glance back at the furious mob in their wake. The Germans got up from the floor and thanked him in fluent and effusive English. The youth shook his head gravely and settled back in a passenger seat.

'No more stop at traffic lights,' he instructed. 'Too fookin' dangerous.'

They got to the airport at speed and without further trouble. The Germans insisted on shaking Jonathon's hand profusely, the husband simultaneously trying to present him with a pile of Hong Kong dollars in an expression of their sincere gratitude. Jonathon refused and instead got their luggage out of the bus. He threw the set of keys into the hands of the driver, who sat on the pavement, still in a daze, shaking so much that he could hardly connect a plastic lighter with a cigarette drooping from his mouth.

Airport security inside and outside was unprecedented. Soldiers relished their task of checking every passport and ID in sight, while panic reigned at the BA ticket counter as hopefuls realised there were only a finite 410 seats on the departing Boeing 747-400. The staff couldn't squeeze any more on despite the pleading and offer of cash bribes.

'I'm in club class. Get me on this plane tonight. Jesus, I'll even go economy!'

Jonathon sat in the lounge in his dirty, dishevelled suit, his grubby shirt sticking to him. It was impossible to look less SUG, but he didn't mind at all. He dialled Eva for an update, spoke with Jack and then listened to his newest and fave CD on the Discman. Bono, for once, was entirely wrong. It wasn't a 'Beautiful Day' Jonathon had seen the world in green and blue; he'd seen China right in front of him, and it was too near for comfort. But he didn't care. He was going home to his family.

They boarded an hour late. The jumbo taxied past ominous military aircraft sporting red stars, parked farther out on the outskirts of the apron. The smoothly enunciated announcement from the BA captain over the intercom immediately after takeoff was different from the norm.

'Ladies and gentlemen, I hope you enjoy your flight with us tonight on what is the last BA flight from Hong Kong. London has advised that we are today discontinuing our service on advice from the Foreign Office.'

In the late afternoon Lauren walked downstairs to the money transfer team in Operations.

'Do we have the funds yet from Alpha?'

'No,' replied the bespectacled supervisor who monitored the dollar receipts in Mitchell's main bank account.

Lauren hadn't spoke to Scott in two days. She went back to her desk and looked at the wall clock. She'd have to call his home and annoy Kim again. She dialled. The telephone rang twice.

'Hello.'

A deep New York accent. At last she had found him.

'Scott, where have you been?'

'Who is this calling?'

It was someone else on the line, she realised.

'Who are you?'

'Detective Don Hamill. NYPD.'

'Is Scott there?'

'Who is calling?'

'Sorry, I think I misdialled.'

She hung up. She knew she hadn't misdialled. The police were answering Scott's home telephone.

Lauren sat alone with her thoughts for much of the remainder of the day, wondering where Scott was and who she could call and when McFarland would be back to hassle her. In the late afternoon she looked out of the window at the acrid black smoke, wire-meshed police vans and running crowds below, which she interspersed occasionally with live coverage on the TV screens. You could almost bottle the smell of fear in the frantic sales desk as clients sold all at any price. Noise levels were unprecedented. Still Alpha didn't call.

In the early evening she grazed the various local channels on the floor until she came to rest on the incessant CNBC screen, an ever-present reminder of life back in the States. The expats liked CNBC. An anchor shot cut suddenly to a black-and-white high-school photograph of a good-looking guy in a suit and tie. It looked like a younger version of Scott. A glossy caption appeared below. She stood up.

'Quiet, guys. Turn up the sound on CNBC. Now,' she implored.

One of the recent six-foot-three beefcake new hires on the bond syndicate desk obliged with an unseen remote control. A few heads turned to Lauren and then to watch the TV. The floor went quiet. They saw shots of Battery Park, the smashed undergrowth, a lens zooming up twenty-eight floors to a balcony. Brad saw it too.

'That's the end of Lauren's best account. In fact, Chapman was her only account.'

Lauren bit her lip and suppressed her shock. Scott and Alpha were dead in the water. Massive futures positions heading south. Unpaid millions in margin calls. McFarland heard the noise levels drop and appeared at the far end of the room. He strode up to the FF&O desk. Lauren turned away to the outside view, then watched his expression in the gleaming plate glass and the reflected harbour view. He scowled.

'What's on TV? Someone else shot?'

She lowered her voice.

'Scott Chapman is dead. We have a problem.'

McFarland turned away as if the very act distanced him from the news.

'This is your account. You have the problem.'

CHAPTER NINE
VIGO STREET, LONDON, W1 – 9.20 A.M.

Jonathon stared at the eighty-seven e-mails he had received while he was away. This e-mail lark was a bloody curse. Most of it was junk or unnecessary cc mails. There were a few good jokes forwarded by Nikki. Some communications were even work-related. The only three that mattered were from Richemont. The first requested an immediate update on Mitchell's Hong Kong, the second instructed him to update his CV for any future assignments, and the third concerned the relaxation of the suit-and-tie dress code in the London office.

Nikki seemed to be ahead of the game and arrived in a tight orange T-shirt that left nothing to the imagination. She sat down, displaying a miniskirt and a pair of brown boots, her relaxed posture an obvious sign that she was here to stay. Catch-up quality time today instead of buzz-word bingo. He held up an ashtray.

'This yours?'

'I had a few in here while you were away.' She took the offending article and assumed he had missed the regular banter. 'I see the Japanese banking crisis is getting worse.'

He fell for it. 'Really?'

'Sure.' Nikki smiled. 'Origami Bank has folded. Sumo Bank went belly up. Bonsai Bank plans to cut some branches. Karaoke Bank is for sale and is going for a song.

Unfortunately he wasn't ready to counter today. 'Did I miss anything last week? What about Richemont? Is he around?'

'No. Away in Geneva last week. Jackie says he's at his holiday pad now. It was so quiet I took a few days off.'

'What did you do?'

'Nothing much. Hung around. Took Eddie to Texas. He loved it.'

Jonathon was wondering if Nikki had a secret life when he was out of the country.

'Texas? Really?'

'Texas in Romford. The DIY store. Next week we're going to Iceland.' Nikki shouldn't have been a PA. She should have been on a stage somewhere. 'How about you? I'd love to go to Hong Kong on expenses. Would you ever need an assistant to carry your bags? I need a proper holiday.'

'It wasn't a holiday destination. It was bloody dangerous.'

'It looked bad on TV. I was worried about you.'

Jonathon had thirteen hours to think on the flight. McFarland was welcome to rough it out there. With a bit of luck some trigger-happy squaddie would nail him. Lauren was an entirely different matter.

'It's tough if you have to stay there.'

'How are the kids?'

'Jack didn't think I'd make it back in one piece. He wouldn't let me out of his sight all weekend. I don't think I can ever go away again. Not unless he comes with me.'

'You worry too much.'

'It's called parenthood. You'll understand what comes with it someday.'

Nikki stared back. Jonathon regretted his choice of words. She refocused.

'Have you some work for me? It was too quiet last week.'

Nikki was one of the few members of staff who could decipher Jonathon's handwriting. She said he should have been a doctor. Somehow she could combine a Word file of his random manic thoughts and a few Excel files of numbers into a bound colour report with perfect headings, font, pagination, justification, bar charts, pie charts, an accurate contents page and a logical process flow. Her end product was always a revelation to him. They made a good team. He was lucky to have her. He held up some pages of notes.

'Mitchell's New York won't like much of it, but such is life. I'll give you my hieroglyphics and you can magically convert them into a stunning glossy report. One with everything, as in those lusty bodice-rippers you read on the Tube. Greed, money, conflict and treachery.'

Nikki took some of the pages and print-outs from him and scanned them. She flashed her eyes and tilted her head to one side. 'Is there a dashing hero?'

'There is. Wealthy too, I guess, once upon a time.'

'Can I meet him?'

'Only if you move to New York.'

'So no happy ending. What about the heroine? Is there one of those?'

Jonathon thought back to the close encounters. The meal, the hotel room, the vague memories.

'There might be. There was this girl ...'

He paused, curtailing his inner emotions. Nikki sat up, somewhat less relaxed now.

'It's a long time since I heard you say that.'

'It's not like it sounds. She works for Mitchell's out there.'

'Similar interests. What exactly does she do?'

'She's a futures sales executive.'

Nikki dared to push the boundaries, to discuss topics not broached in many months.

'You've been out of this game far too long. Go on? What's she like?'

'She's maybe thirty, tall, auburn hair, alluring, dresses well, feisty, independent, American.'

'Name?'

'Lauren.'

'Posh too.' Nikki let her lurid imagination run riot. 'As in Hutton?'

'You wish.'

Nikki was wondering whether this conversation had therapeutic undertones for Jonathon.

'Is she available?'

He thought back to the meal for two and recalled some salient facts.

'She doesn't wear a wedding ring.'

'So you looked for one. What about a boyfriend?'

'None that she mentioned when we had dinner.'

Nikki pulled her chair closer and persevered.

'You saw her outside of work? Socially? One on one?' He nodded. 'Who asked who out?'

'She asked me.'

'Did you talk shop the whole time?'

'We discussed how we both hated working for Mitchell's. No work talk otherwise.'

'Then what?'

He decided to indulge Nikki's burgeoning fantasy temporarily.

'We went back up to my hotel room.' Nikki was on the edge of her seat. 'She put me to bed . . .'

'Funny! Seriously, though?'

'Seriously. I was ill. Worst case of food poisoning ever. Gastroenteritis, said the doc.'

'Is she okay?'

'I thought so.'

'I mean, is she safe? With all the rioting. You gotta call her. You do care, don't you?'

He did. But he was thinking about what he'd said to McFarland and whether Lauren still had a job at Mitchell's.

'She won't talk to me,' he said, heart sinking at the thought.

'Of course she will. You're an eligible guy. Good looking, available, solvent, nice home, great kids . . .'

Jonathon would have loved to have made contact with Lauren, but not yet.

'Let's finish my report first. Anyway, I bet she hates me by now. You see, I caught her frontrunning.' He ignored Nikki's blank reaction. 'Mentioned it in a conversation with her boss because I thought he knew about it. If I was right, I'd say I've destroyed her career.'

Walter Sayers walked alone through the revolving doors of the World Financial Centre Marriott, stopping momentarily amidst the thick-pile carpets and polished brass of the lobby area. He had somehow found the time in a packed schedule to meet with an old friend from his days on the Street. Art Greenbaum wanted to discuss a problem at Alpha but hadn't said much else during their short late night telephone call.

He had been to enough munificent PR, investment bank and corporate functions in this very venue to find his way to the agreed venue. Eschewing the elevators, he strode up the circular slated steps to the mezzanine level and into the relatively tranquil surroundings of the Glasshouse Café. A few of the world's wealthiest tourist families sat in fours before embarking on an early assault on NYC's sights. The maître d' offered him an immaculately presented table at the rear, surrounded by tall plants. Sayers eyeballed the others in the room. No press types. No one he knew. No one to recognise him. Perfect for a private breakfast meeting.

'Morning, Walt. Long time no see.'

Sayers rose to greet Greenbaum, who looked to have aged considerably since the annual black-tie Salomon's reunion at the Waldorf last fall. Sayers was immediately concerned.

'Art, you okay?'

'Could be better.'

'Couldn't we all? These are difficult times. Hungry?'

'No. My stomach's churning up. You attack the buffet.'

Sayers eyed the buffet from afar. It was a sumptuous spread, manned by a team of proud and jovial Hispanic chefs. He didn't wish to be seen by others raiding the buffet. Instead he took a sip of chilled OJ with real pith and perused the à la carte menu instead. Cranberry juice, fresh cantaloupe, oat-bran raisin muffin, seasonal berries, eggs served a million different ways, skimmed this and decaff that. Greenbaum ran his finger curiously over the Wellness Breakfast with wholewheat toast and salt-free seasonings. Sayers took the All-American Breakfast. Two eggs over easy, herbed sausages, thick Canadian smokehouse bacon, griddle pancakes on the side, extra maple syrup.

'What will you have, Art?'

'Nothing.'

'I'll order you the Wellness Breakfast. Looks like you could do with it.' The waiter left them. 'I'm not that keen on late night phone calls at home unless it's an emergency, Art.'

He leaned forward.

'It is an emergency. You and me go back a long way, Walt. We had some good times together at Salomon's. Good days indeed. Shit, they seem like a long time ago now!'

'What are you trying to tell me, Art?'

Greenbaum paused while the waiter hovered. 'What I gotta tell you about Alpha can't go farther than the two of us.'

Sayers nodded. Twin silver pots of regular coffee arrived. Taken as read. Sayers faked a smile.

'It's not too serious, is it? I'm a big investor in your hedge fund.'

Greenbaum was about to break the news when the waiter interrupted again to top up the OJ. He was starting to annoy Art.

'A guy called Scott Chapman killed himself last week. He jumped from his apartment in Battery Park City.'

'I saw that on NY1.'

'The bad news is he worked for me.'

Sayers wasn't getting the message. He seemed more interested in the maple syrup.

'You weren't working him too hard, were you?'

Greenbaum dropped his voice to a mere whisper.

'The guy lost us some money.'

'This has been the worst few weeks in the markets

that I can recall. Everyone lost money. But you're a hedge fund. Your problems can't be any worse than your competitors'.'

The waiter arrived with the orders. Was he doing this deliberately? Greenbaum waited a moment.

'I lost a lot.'

'How much?'

'I can't say yet.'

'You can't say?' Sayers was incredulous.

'I can't quantify it yet but it's big.'

The hot breakfasts looked good. Surprisingly Greenbaum started to eat. Sayers didn't.

'Define the word big.'

'We've been through Chapman's futures positions. He lost millions trading in the Far East in the past few months and much more in the past few weeks. Ever since that damn Chinese premier was shot in Hong Kong. He should have followed our in-house dealing strategy but he wasn't hedged, he had huge long Hang Seng Index futures positions. He was selling our bonds and securities to meet massive margin calls from brokers and investment banks.'

Sayers hadn't even lifted his knife and fork. Greenbaum was making steady progress, downing his food so fast that he couldn't even taste it.

'Didn't you know what Chapman was doing? Don't you monitor and control your dealers?'

'He hid it from me for months. Then he cracked under the pressure and jumped. He was still doing a lot of coke. So said the cops after the autopsy.'

'You had a trader doing drugs?'

'They all do it.'

The waiter bobbed up again but vanished at a glare from Sayers.

'So what's the damage? Bottom line. Tens of millions?'

'Billions. I've had my CFO looking at this for the past twenty-four hours. Could be two billion bucks. Maybe more. Our capital is gone. We're bust. Alpha is finished. I'm finished.'

'And my own investment?'

'Sorry, Walt, we might get five cents on the dollar back. That's all.'

Sayers looked distraught.

'I invested more than three million with you four years ago . . . my retirement fund.'

Greenbaum could offer no solution. He changed tack.

'I'm not telling you this as an investor, nor as a friend. I'm telling you this as a regulator. Alpha has huge exposure with other banks and brokers. I'm worried about the damage we are going to do to the system. We will fail them this week and then the whole house of cards will come down. I'm talking about systemic risk here. Banks failing other banks. Brokers failing other brokers. You'll know what to do, Walt.'

Sayers suddenly took from his pocket a series of papers stapled together, handwritten comments scribbled down the margins. He looked at his watch and sighed heavily as he put them down.

'This is a speech that I'm about to give to the world's

media on the Street in one hour's time. It will be shown live on every network. I was about to remind the world that this global crisis is attributable solely to events in the Far East. I just told the House in DC that this meltdown wouldn't impact the US. I can't say that now with a rogue trader and a multibillion dollar hole in a giant US hedge fund. I gotta leave and rewrite this in the car in the next sixty minutes. Then I gotta sort out Alpha. Tell no one else about this yet. And thanks for breakfast, Art. You're paying the tab, if you can still afford it.'

Lauren sat on a teeming sales floor, but she was utterly alone. The entire floor knew about the unpaid margin calls. The word was out and the word was trouble. She was none the wiser about Alpha, being stuck in the wrong time zone. Greenbaum wasn't returning her calls and she had no answers to the questions that were sure to follow. She hadn't seen McFarland for hours. Rumour had it on the squawk box that he was upstairs with the Chief Operating Officer, and had been spotted in the compliance department. Shortly after three o'clock, an unknown Chinese secretary approached her.

'The COO and Mr McFarland want to see you.'

She took the elevator and entered the COO's salubrious office for the very first time. The atmosphere was cool. No easy pleasantries. She pre-empted the two men, who sat close together.

'I'm still trying to find out more about Alpha ...'

'Close the door, Lauren,' ordered McFarland.

She sat down. The Chief Operations Officer, a

middle-aged bull of a man with thick jowls and an enormous intimidating build, looked at her hard. She hardly knew him. He had been sent over recently from head office, like some unwanted FedEx parcel. COO was a big title but the old guy did zilch except pose for press pics, attend launches, go walkabout, authorise expenses and eat well on the firm. He also hired and fired staff, and of course signed the bonus cheques at year end. Today he said nothing but deferred to McFarland.

'For your information, we did talk to Art Greenbaum at home,' Big Mac announced. 'He says that Alpha can't pay any margin. They have serious cash flow problems. The Alpha account is frozen and you are to have no more contact with Greenbaum. Understand?'

She nodded.

'What can I do to help?'

McFarland waited a suitable length of time and gave her a withering look.

'Let us take care of Alpha. It's now a client relationship issue for the firm. But we are here to discuss a far more serious issue than that.'

Lauren was puzzled.

'What can be more serious?'

McFarland nodded to the COO, who finally made his contribution. She noticed he was perspiring.

'Our IT department monitors the usage of the Internet by staff to ensure compliance with firm guidelines on electronic communications? They check for anyone surfing pornographic, sexist or racist sites, for example. We keep a master file of the user IDs, the sites they access and when they access them.' The COO paused to let the information sink in. Lauren was considering the ramifications, thinking about one particular site. 'Is there anything you wish to tell us, Ms Trent?'

He was being way too formal. She didn't like the negative vibes.

'Like what?'

'Like do you operate a personal dealing account outside the firm?'

Lauren hedged. Like her best clients, she thought.

'What do you mean?'

'It's a simple question. It requires a yes-or-no answer. Which is it?' Still she deliberated. The COO produced a page of data. Lauren could see the local Schwab website address printed all the way down one side. He knew. It was there in black and white. The page showed every time she had logged on to the website, how much time she had spent on-line and when she'd moved to other sites. Reluctantly, she nodded.

'Yes.'

The COO was in her face.

'Do you know the procedure at this firm for operating outside dealing accounts?'

'Yes.'

'Spell it out for any benefit.'

'I need pre-trade approval from compliance and I must give copies of monthly account statements to Mac.'

'And have you done that?' Lauren shook her head. 'So offence one is established. Offence two is somewhat more serious. What do you trade with Schwab?'

The COO was asking all the right questions. He already had the answers. She wondered how. This was a show trial.

'I trade HSBC stocks.'

The COO fingered a bunch of papers.

'Our compliance department contacted Schwab's compliance department. They faxed over your account statements. You buy and sell once a day, always before the large Alpha orders are time-stamped at the desk. You make a quick profit every single time you day-trade. That's not luck, that's frontrunning.'

Lauren still wondered if the IT guys had told management or whether someone else had sunk her. Her very livelihood was disappearing before her eyes. She wished she had never opened the Schwab account. All she'd wanted was a way to pay off her mortgage. The COO dialled a number without meeting her eye. An HR manager appeared moments later with a one-page letter of some sort. Damp patches had now appeared under the COO's arms.

'We could talk about this for weeks and involve the local regulators and the SFC but that's bad publicity Mitchell's doesn't need. Neither do you, Ms Trent. There is an easier way. This is a letter of resignation. Your name is at the bottom. It's effective today.' He pushed a fountain pen towards her. 'Sign it now.'

Lauren refused to grasp the pen and instead folded her arms.

'Who really told you about this?'

'Let's just say a visitor helped us'.

'I need time to think. This is happening too fast.'

'You don't get any time to think. Sign the letter, dear.'

Lauren knew she had no choice. She scribbled an untidy signature at the foot of the page. The COO called Security and a uniformed guard appeared outside in nanoseconds. He had been waiting, she thought. This had been carefully prearranged. He was a local, slight and puny, much smaller than Lauren in her heels. She could have knocked him to the ground if she felt like it, but all her usual energy had deserted her. She turned to her boss.

'What's happening here, Mac?'

He looked away, either unwilling or unable to lend her any support. The COO stood up.

'Security will escort you from the building.'

'I need to get some things from my desk first.'

The COO guided her firmly to the open door.

'We'll courier them to you tomorrow.'

She resisted his arm and stood her ground.

'Take your hands off me. I need my house keys. They're on my desk.'

He gave an instruction to the guard, who soon reappeared from the far side of the sales floor with a set of keys. McFarland stepped forward, eyed the key-ring, removed one and handed the rest over to Lauren.

'We'll take the key to the Golf. It belongs to the firm. You'd better get home some other way.'

'But it's crazy outside! It's dangerous. People are dying in the streets, Mac.'

'You should have thought of that first.'

They watched her leave. Afterwards McFarland stood by the door and looked at the COO.

'Do I tell the guys on the desk that we fired Lauren because of personal account trading violations?'

'Tell them we fired her because of Alpha. That'll make them collect their margin calls in future.'

Charles Cavendish awoke in the best guest room, left Pamela to sleep on alone, showered, shaved, dressed in a pair of light trousers and polo shirt and descended for breakfast. The maid met him downstairs.

'*Hola*. Señor Richemont is outside.'

Cavendish never grew tired of the vista at the rear of the villa. The pool was of almost Olympic proportions with ample space around it for taking the sun in style. Pink geraniums and red salvias hung from adjacent walls while floribunda roses grew from cross-beams and pastel awnings that extended from the house. Small patches of grass did their best to survive irregular irrigation in the extreme heat. The concrete underfoot was already sizzling to the touch, such was the oppressive heat at 9 a.m. in the hills of Nerja overlooking the Costa del Sol.

'Morning, Charles. You're just in time.'

Richemont lounged with a bunch of assorted newspapers strewn around, a tall vitamin drink and a mobile telephone alongside. His silver hair was combed back, still wet after a recent plunge. He wore fashionable shades, a pair of well-pressed navy shorts, a loose open floral shirt and no shoes.

'I'm never late for the tee-off,' countered Cavendish.

'Ever wished you'd bought your holiday place here too? Better golf here than in Italy.'

'Better wine where I am. Anyway, Marjorie insisted on Tuscany. It was all the rage at the time.'

They sat at the cluster of white wrought-iron tables and chairs sheltered by bright canvas parasols near the deep end, a continental breakfast close to hand. Richemont pushed some plates towards Cavendish.

'Eat up. You'll need it. What's your handicap now?'

'Golf itself. I don't know which exact golf course I'm playing, until I drive off from the first tee.'

'You play very well,' enthused Richemont as his mind drifted away, safe in the knowledge that Cavendish was a keen, yet appalling, self-taught golfer who was irresistibly attracted to the fairway rough and the sand traps, labouring under the common delusion that his game would improve merely because he had left grey skies and winter rules behind in the UK. On each such previous occasion, Richemont had felt obliged to hook, shank, slice and three-putt a few just to make Cavendish last the full eighteen. The norms of corporate hospitality demanded such uncharacteristically unselfish behaviour from the host.

Cavendish looked around and tried to read bold German headlines upside down. Richemont wondered how to break the bad news to him. Reluctantly he broached the topic.

'It's all gloom and doom. Asian markets falling farther. Europe too. You'll have to take some action soon.'

Cavendish shrugged, his thoughts already miles away on the eighteenth hole.

'The work is for my peers out East. I play golf in the sun. They sweat it out in Hong Kong.'

'What if the meltdown continues in Europe? Then you would act?'

'That'll never happen. The recovery is underway. Markets in Europe were steady last week.'

Richemont leaned over the table, took off his shades and smiled.

'Charles, Richemont et Cie is always there to help the Bank. You know we're the best in our niche.'

'Is the sales pitch part of today's itinerary?'

'All I'm saying is that we have some good consultants.'

Cavendish downed the last almond croissant and gulped a glass of chilled low-fat milk.

'Is that guy Maynard still with you?'

Richemont nodded. 'He's always available for the Bank.' Richemont looked again at the newspaper. The time was right. 'There's something in the paper about Alpha.'

'Doesn't surprise me much. It's big in Asia.'

'Not that. One of their traders died in New York. Suicide. This paper says that Art Greenbaum has gone to ground and can't be contacted.'

Both men thought about the large personal investments they had in Alpha. Cavendish had Sayers to thank for telling him four years ago about the hot new fund run by an ex-buddy from the Street. In turn, Richemont would never have known about it either had it not been for the fact that Cavendish mentioned it on the golf course at La Manja.

'Alpha will be okay. They're always hedged,' Cavendish assured him.

They sat in the shade, knowing that all work and no play did not make for a successful long weekend. Max suddenly appeared from the villa, wearing a dark suit which seemed unnecessary for the climate and occasion.

'Let's go. Here's our driver. No pun intended.'

'What are the plans for this afternoon?' asked Cavendish as he stood up and executed a mock swing.

'I'm going to lie in the sun here and watch Carla do her lengths,' observed Richemont, safe in the knowledge that the swing was all wrong, both the stance and grip being terminally beyond correction without a dedicated coaching session from a patient pro.

'And tonight?'

Richemont stood closer to his golfing buddy of ten years or more.

'What happens tonight is purely between yourself and Pamela in the privacy of the guest room.'

CHAPTER TEN

Jonathon knew that Nikki was right. He had to call. He took out Lauren's business card, ran his hand slowly over the embossed letters and remembered sitting close beside her. She would still be at work in her faraway time zone. He dialled Mitchell's Hong Kong. An American voice answered.

'Is Lauren there?'

'Who's calling?'

'Jonathon. From London.'

'That Jonathon?'

He deduced he was speaking to the other guy, Brad.

'Yeah. The same.'

'I hate to break the news to you but Lauren ain't here.'

'When's she due back?'

'Never. Mac just fired her. She left in tears a few hours ago.'

Jonathon froze and held the handset numbly for a moment while the news sank in.

'Do you know why?' he asked eventually.

'Lauren fucked up. She screwed up the Alpha account. That's why. You wanna talk to Mac?'

'No. 'Bye.'

He sat there and wondered about the real cause of her sudden fall from grace. He feared worse and passed the rest of the morning deep in uneasy thought, until Nikki came in with the first draft of the Mitchell's report.

'How does it look?' he asked.

'Chapman was guilty as hell. Alpha has had it.' She paused. 'Lauren sounds interesting, though.'

Jonathon proofed the report until his eyes grew tired late in the afternoon. He glanced at the clock on his PC. Eva would be at home until seven. Jack and Imogen were in good hands. Nikki had reminded him earlier about Richemont's big pronouncement at the staff meeting he'd missed, when he had decreed that henceforth all directors should set an example. 'Your expert advice again?' he asked.

'Get three cotton Oxford shirts in blue, green and lilac, and three pairs of chinos in khaki, blue and black.'

Richemont et Cie's official dress policy was now smart casual. Nikki had been dressing this way for years, but others took longer to decipher the policy. No sneakers, trainers or runners. No denim even if it was disguised as cotton twill. No round-neck T-shirts. No pseudo combat trousers. Most of the early offenders were male. Cord trousers were sighted. Bulging beer bellies were noticeable. A shirt straight from the *Hawaii Five-O* set was banned.

Leaving the office, Jonathon turned left on to the late-opening shopping pleasures of Lower Regent Street, avoiding his usual foray in to the Austin Reed store despite the sale flags outside. Store detectives in free gear who doubled as a welcoming committee guarded the entrance to Gap between the Warner store and Hamley's.

'And how are you this evening, sir?'

Hassled. Shopping with Rebecca by his side had been a breeze. They would take weekend walks up Sloane Street, past the temptations of the Italian boutiques and up the four floors of fashions in Harvey Nicks on Knightsbridge. Rebecca would tell him what to buy, miraculously producing perfect garments from racks and shelves in the men's department on LG. She spotted minor flaws and loose threads, handed her choice to him to try on, provided instant feedback on co-ordination, marvelled at how well the clothes looked and fitted. She found bargains when he didn't even know there was a sale. She voluntarily engaged pushy shop assistants in conversation, turned the tables on them, forced them to dig out new stock from the back of the shop, got him to try on three different sizes and colours merely to annoy them.

The Oxford shirts and chinos were piled high in Gap. There was every known colour in the spectrum, as long as it was khaki. He had forgotten his waist and leg measurements, having put on a few inches of late. The queues for the changing rooms were horrendous. The shop assistants chased him around the store. The place was full of couples, offering each other advice, choosing and shopping effortlessly. After ten minutes he panicked, but knew he couldn't leave empty handed. He had to buy something, to get a Gap carrier bag, to wear something tomorrow for Nikki to review. Finally he selected a sky-blue medium Oxford shirt, a navy sweatshirt and a 34-32 pair of trademark khakis. To hell with three of each. He'd try them on at home and come back next Thursday. If he had the energy. The security guard bade him farewell at 6.40 p.m.

'Have a nice day, sir.'

Walter Sayers walked briskly uphill and eastward to 33 Liberty Street. The distinctive Italian Renaissance-style stone edifice of the New York Federal Reserve stood at the corner of Liberty and Nassau, cloaked in a century of urban grime. Walking past the street-level windows with their thick iron bars, he could see why some tourists thought this place was a prison. For once, he empathised with them.

He had convened the meeting for 8 a.m. No one would see the main players arriving. The street was deserted save for a few hobos with bad hangovers who stumbled along the opposite sidewalk. Then he saw two investment bankers in dark suits alight from a black stretch limo at the arched main door. Sayers couldn't identify them from a distance but he knew the type from a hundred yards away. He went through the wrought-iron gates and stopped in the marble lobby.

'Whoa, buddy! Hang on there.'

A security guard approached him. Sayers took out his ID card. The guard scanned it, recognised the Fed logo but evidently didn't read the small print.

'You gotta put your briefcase through the X-ray

machine. We got the entire city's gold stored five storeys below us. Can't take no chances here, ya know.'

Sayers confronted the scruffy Latino in the peaked cap.

'Do you know who I am?'

'Don't matter if you're the Chairman from Washington, DC. Rules is rules.'

Walters held out the ID card again at eye level and brushed past the guard.

'I am the Chairman from Washington, DC. I make the rules.'

He took the elevator to the largest conference room on the fifth floor and pushed open the heavy doors. Approximately twenty middle-aged, suited men turned towards him. There were no women present, an indictment of the conservatism and inherent sexism of the banking industry. Some wore worried expressions. Others had been caught in mid-anecdote with industry peers. The conversations died.

'Gentlemen, take a seat, and let's begin.'

Sayers looked around at the faces before him, wondering how the past Fed presidents pictured on the wall would view current events. His PA had done well. The élite of Wall Street had answered the call.

'Most of you know each other, so let's skip the introductions.'

They looked around in awe at the heavyweight attendance. Last time they were all gathered together here was at the Christmas black-tie bash. They wondered about the purpose of this sudden meeting. Was any banker missing from this élite group? Was there a crisis out there?

Sayers continued, 'Apologies for the short notice. You will see that we have no assistants or minute-takers present – this is all off the record. What we discuss here stays within these four walls, okay?'

They all nodded in unison. He hoped they meant it. A leak would be fatal, potentially globally catastrophic. He paused, evaluating the best way to break the worst news.

'You may have read that last week a trader fell to his death from a Battery Park apartment.'

One of the guys from Goldman's cut in. Strong personalities always strive to speak first in meetings.

'I saw it on the news wires. Most think he jumped.'

'He did. He worked for Alpha Beta Capital. Art Greenbaum runs it with a bunch of former traders from Salomon's and other firms. They've a good track record, they produce superior returns. Heck, I even believe some of you guys have invested in a personal capacity in Alpha. Done well, I expect?'

More nods from around the table, particularly the CSFB duo and the guy from Deutsche.

'Is that why we're here, Walt?'

'The dead guy was a rogue trader who had built up huge unauthorised positions in Hang Seng index futures in the Far East. The index, like all others out there in the past few weeks, has plummeted since the assassination of the Chinese premier, and the civil unrest. Yesterday morning I met with Greenbaum, who advised me of significant losses. Alpha is now completely bankrupt and insolvent. Without a dime. Flat broke.'

'Shit!'

'Bad luck.'

'*Scheisse.*'

'What was Greenbaum thinking . . . ?'

Sayers leaned forward, elbows resting on the long table.

'Alpha have billions of dollars of derivatives, swaps, futures, foreign exchange and bond positions. Their gross balance sheet size is approaching fifty billion. As a hedge fund, they should have both long and short positions that minimise their risk, but many of these are outright positions in collapsing markets. Your banks are now asking Alpha to pay huge margin and collateral calls. The only alternative for Greenbaum is to sell his investments to generate cash. I fear that if he does that it will destabilise markets further. I am greatly concerned by this prospect given the current turbulence, so I need your help.'

The CEO of Chase put up a hand.

'Hey, we can help, Walt. We can hold off on the margin calls for a few days.'

'You're not getting my drift. We need to assist Alpha.'

The Chase man narrowed his eyes.

'Whaddya mean, assist?'

Sayers sighed. Trust a banker to turn shifty when it came to a direct request.

'Money.'

'How much we talking here, Walt?'

'There are ten banks represented this morning. I believe that Alpha needs term financing of ten billion dollars for approximately one year. I am asking for a billion dollars from each of you.'

In the stunned silence that followed another of the American bankers spoke up.

'Why should we be the ones who help Alpha?'

'Art gave me a list of the top ten banks with the biggest exposure to Alpha. Gentlemen, those ten banks are yours. That's why you're here.'

There were a few stifled gasps around the table. One of the European bankers saw a way out.

'Why have I been invited? We don't deal with Alpha.'

Sayers was as well briefed as ever.

'Really? Ask your risk management department in Frankfurt. You're in deep like the rest here, friend.'

The startled German rose to his feet and grabbed his papers.

'I must make a telephone call to head office immediately.'

Sayers rapped on the table. He called the shots here.

'Sit down! No one leaves this room until we have an agreement. No phone calls either.'

Questions from the increasingly concerned bankers came fast and furious.

'How do we know the numbers at Alpha are right?'

'That's all we have to work on to date. It's a guesstimate.'

'Do we get to see the books before we lend money?'

'A team of experts from the Fed and the SEC are in Alpha now reporting to me directly. You must trust me. Is that a problem for anyone here?' The bankers looked away and deliberated further. 'The choice is simple,' Sayers urged. 'You either put up a billion now with the likelihood of getting it back in a year's time, or we let Alpha go under, the markets plunge, and in such a scenario your institutions lose considerably more than a billion dollars each.'

'What if we don't get the money back in a year?'

'That's a risk. There is no guarantee here. But you guys can easily find a billion each.'

'It's a lot of money, Walt,' observed a British banker.

'Gentlemen, I could make a long impassioned speech to you, but you know that the right thing to do is to help Alpha. Their downfall has been due to a single rogue trader. It could happen to any of you tomorrow.' Sayers sensed the time was right to force a decision. 'So let's see a show of hands. All those who agree with my proposal? And remember that if this proposal doesn't proceed, only a few of us will get to the exit before the roof falls in.'

He knew as he glanced around the table that peer pressure was paramount in any vote. Five or six hands went up almost immediately. Then another. The sullen German was the last to agree. Within sixty seconds he had a unanimous vote in favour. Done deal.

'We'll advise you later of the bank account details we'll use for this support operation,' he announced, getting to his feet. 'We all know that this industry is about confidence. If you stick by me, we can pull this rescue off and no one need know about it until much later. The Fed will issue a press release when appropriate.'

'And you will take all the credit for this,' someone murmured from behind their hand.

Sayers was already basking in the limelight of the next

House testimony. He let it pass. The meeting broke up. The chairman of one of the largest US investment banks stopped him by the door.

'Walt, what's gonna happen to the poor investors in Alpha?'

Sayers received the implicit message loud and clear.

'How much are you in for?'

'About seven million bucks at last year end.'

'If this rescue works, you'll get it all back.'

'And what do you think that it's worth now?'

'You might get five cents on the dollar.'

Sayers left, wondering why he had invested most of his own life savings in Alpha four years ago, and considering how many of his closest friends had done so too based upon his personal recommendation. Sometimes he wished Art Greenbaum had been that jumper in Battery Park.

Lauren stood, unemployed and alone, in the drizzle outside Sogo's monster department store, looking for a taxi. The taxi-drivers and their red Toyota Crowns were running scared, like the rest of the general public in this angry suburb of China. Soldiers walked along the streets in groups. Army trucks passed by at irregular intervals. The odour of burning tyres hung in the air. She needed to be at home.

There was a queue of expectant punters ahead of her at the taxi rank. The drizzle steadily turned to a persistent shower, then something heavier. She eyed a row of filthy advert-ridden Citybus double-decker buses stalled in choking traffic in Exchange Square. They were heading for a variety of outlying destinations. She hadn't been on a bus for years, and already missed the Golf.

A number six proclaimed that it was heading towards Repulse Bay. Gratefully, she ran across the greasy tarmac and oily pools and clambered aboard. The Chinese driver shouted a fare and she paid with a hundred-dollar bill. Sitting at the back amidst the condensation, she inhaled the diesel fumes of the tired engine wheezing below. An old woman with emergency food supplies pushed her way alongside. Lauren looked around. Every other passenger was local Chinese and fifty-plus. She sensed a few staring back at her.

The journey took twice as long as usual. They stopped at two checkpoints. Soldiers walked along the interior of the bus, looking for troublemakers. Eventually the bus climbed high into the rain-clouds and mist as they crossed the island through a vertical tropical downpour. Lauren didn't know the nearest bus stop to her home. She hesitated, then waited too long. The bus sped by her apartment block. Belatedly she rang the bell and alighted at the next stop. It was too far by miles. She ran back in the rain.

She looked in the hall mirror at her mud-spattered suit, dense, matted hair and running mascara. After ten minutes spent under the hot shower jet, she enveloped herself in a fresh bath towel, wrapped another around her hair like a turban and collapsed into the three-seater sofa. Phat Cat was pleased to see her so early in the working day. He jumped up beside her and huddled close for some badly needed TLC. She faced towards the bay window and the deserted beach below. The sheets of rain punched against the full-length panes of glass.

The shower couldn't erase the grime, sweat and guilt after her worst day ever at Mitchell's. She had left home this morning with everything in life: apartment, job, car, future, the works. All she had now was a multimillion Honkie dollar mortgage, a pink slip, a bus ticket and a cat. She watched the rain in silence. The bulk of Middle Island to the left and the belching smokestacks of the power stations on Lamma Island to the right marred today's view. Her career at Mitchell's was finished. Mac would ensure she'd never work again at any sales desk in Hong Kong. The markets were in terminal decline. She had served her time here. There had to be more to life than a solo existence in an apartment in Repulse Bay.

The remote control for the CD player was lying beside her. She pressed 'Play' and tried to recall what she had last been listening to. Some smooth sounds of the mid-sixties emanated from the two Sony speakers on the bookshelves. Something uplifting from Motown to drag her out of this depression. Lauren tried not to think about home in Manhattan. Eight years of independence had done much to erase the bad memories.

It was all her father's fault. He was a fifty-eight-year-old CPA, Certified Public Accountant. Or Car Park Attendant, as he told his senior colleagues at Citibank. He'd wanted her to stay at home and be near him every day, wanted her to take a job in the bank. His bank, her mother always called it. Lauren had refused. If she'd given in she'd be a senior teller back in the States by now. He never called or corresponded. Her mother still called at weekends and during holidays.

Lauren got up and selected her newest CD. She fast-forwarded to track ten, played it over and over, but this time it was personal. Finally she felt the first traces of adrenaline coursing through her veins, turned the speaker volume up to full, walked to the window and looked out across the desolate beach. Hong Kong truly sucked. Bono was speaking to her about home. About being in New York, about losing it all, about staying on to figure out your mid-life crisis. New York.

Picking up her baseball cap from the window ledge, she ran her fingers over the white embossed Yankee letters, over and over again, until she could do it with her eyes closed, wondering what to do and where to go, and whether Jonathon Maynard was the visitor who had been the cause of her downfall.

The two investment bankers sat back against the plush leather interior of their black stretch limo. The chairman looked into the smoked-glass partition and carefully checked his side parting and the knot in his tie. The CEO undid the remaining buttons of his suit jacket and leaned forward to the chauffeur.

'Broad Street. Fast.'

The Slav driver cursed silently as he pulled away from the kerb. Two hours parked outside in a tow-away zone, avoiding the attentions of eager Brownies with their ticket books. Then a hot dog on the trunk and a leak into a stinking Gatorade bottle kept under his seat while he waited for the duo to reappear. All for a ten-minute drive of a few blocks to Liberty. These guys took limos everywhere. If there was a free sedan to take them to the executive restaurant down the hallway on the twenty-third floor, there'd be a queue for it. He could make out their conversation in the rear, but they remembered his presence and raised the partition.

'That's bad luck for Art.'

'Bullshit! Greenbaum has fucked up big time. First he leaves Salomon's four years ago, takes their best traders with him and some of our top guys like that German Dieter somebody or other. He opens up right across the street from us in some flea-ridden shop, takes some of our wealthiest investors, produces superior returns to everyone else and now he's bust. And we have to bail the bastard out.'

'You sore because you invested in Alpha too?'

'Losing seven mil is annoying but it isn't gonna bankrupt me. It's only a bad year's bonus.'

Gloomily they watched the heavy traffic ahead.

'It's like Sayers said. Alpha today, could be us next week.'

The chairman shook his head and fumed at the gridlock.

'We're better than Alpha. We have controls in place. This could never happen at our firm.'

The CEO ran his hand over the veneer panelling along one of the doors. Still superstitious.

'No good debating it now. We just agreed to stump up a billion. It's a done deal.'

The chairman shook his head stubbornly.

'Sure we got a billion on call at BONY. No problem with the cash. But what if this bail-out doesn't work? What if more cash is needed? What if panic spreads? We've gotta protect the firm, that's where our ultimate loyalty lies. We have thirty-thousand-plus staff worldwide to look after. They gotta put bread on the table for their families. Precautionary measures are called for here.'

The CEO caught his drift.

'Sayers says we can't tell anyone else about Alpha . . .'

'Sayers doesn't run this firm. I do. We can compromise.' The chairman grabbed the limo's cellular telephone and dialled his PA back at base. 'Convene a meeting of the Executive Management Committee in fifteen minutes' time. Tell everyone they must attend.' He hung up and stared out at the huge office building as they drew nearer. 'The others don't need to know the full story yet but we must limit the downside.'

The limo ride took twelve minutes through almost stationary traffic. They pulled up at Broad Street and took the private elevator, entering the chairman's office together. They had a full attendance as requested. The chairman stood by the window and faced the élite of the firm. All multimillionaires.

'The markets are hurting bad. I believe this bearish tone will prevail. Pre-emptive action is required. Accordingly you will reduce your proprietary positions in your respective business units, effective today.' He pointed to several of the firm's executive directors in turn. 'Ted, sell

European equities and bonds. Jerry, same for US bonds and stocks. Kate, same for options and futures. Bob, likewise for commodities, except gold and silver. Marc, convert all our FX currency positions into the greenback. No new risk positions to be taken. We will review this strategy in a week's time. Any questions?'

One of the more recent appointees stated the obvious.

'That's not a strategy. It's called doing nothing.'

'It's called minimising risk.'

'This firm thrives on risk. That's how we made four billion bucks last year.'

'I don't want to lose four billion this year.'

Another, younger executive director chipped in too.

'If you're so convinced, why don't we make some serious money? Let's short the market.'

The chairman gave him the thumbs-up, and said dryly, 'I couldn't possibly comment.'

'What's brought about this change?' asked a more senior EVP.

'Just a hunch I have,' the chairman lied. The others left in single file. Alone again with his CEO, he chuckled. 'Sayers thinks he can run the show and that he's smarter than the rest of us. But when the shit hits the fan, we look after numero uno first and foremost. There's no point in pleading the general good. The only thing that matters in this world is the interests of this firm.'

CHAPTER ELEVEN

VIGO STREET, LONDON, W1 –
10.50 A.M.

Nikki stuck her head into Jonathon's office mid-morning.

'Nice shirt! I've never seen you casual before. It works. You're more approachable.'

Jonathon was feeling distinctly uncasual. His work was suffering. He already missed the suit and tie. There were too many other things to think about at 7 a.m., with Jack and Imogen in attendance.

'How's the Mitchell's report?'

'All done.' Nikki handed over a bound copy with the prominent blue-and-gold Richemont logo.

He scanned it in a few minutes. His final changes had been made. Nikki was a real star.

'Publish and be damned,' he advised.

'I already did. I sent a copy upstairs earlier, FedEx'ed five to Mitchell's in New York.'

'And their fee invoice?'

Nikki laughed. 'I'll send it in a week. Let them read

the report before we fleece them.'

Richemont suddenly appeared in the doorway.

'Fleece who? What's so amusing?'

She clammed up. Jonathon obliged.

'Nothing.'

Nikki melted away and Richemont closed the door, hypocrisy personified in a stiffly starched shirt and silk tie. He saw Jonathon's hard stare.

'I have a meeting later with clients,' he advised. Jonathon recognised the bound report in his hand, saw that his boss had his thumb inserted halfway through. He seemed more tanned, yet less relaxed, than on their last encounter. Jonathon wondered whether Nikki had missed a typo somewhere. 'I told you to let me see a draft of this report first.'

'I forgot.'

Richemont sat down and flicked through the pages one by one, his mind seemingly elsewhere.

'When I sent you there, I didn't care who the client of Mitchell's was. Now I see that it's Alpha.'

Jonathon nodded. 'Is that a problem?'

'If I am reading this report correctly, Alpha have lost a huge amount of money dealing in Hong Kong.'

'You're reading it correctly.' Jonathon saw the worried frown and spelled it out. 'Alpha have been over-trading. One trader passed the HSI orders to Mitchell's, kept buying and lost big time. It was a recipe for disaster.'

'Have you the facts to back up that assertion?'

'It was all on the deal tickets in Hong Kong. Alpha used no other banks there. I'm sure.'

'Have Mitchells talked to the trader at Alpha?'

'Not possible. He died last week.'

'An accident?'

'No, suicide. A jumper.'

Richemont remembered reading the newspaper by the pool in Nerja.

'You mean, he was the guy in New York? He was trading that account?'

'Sure was. Common knowledge now. So what's the problem?'

Richemont ran his hand several times along his immaculate moisturised jawline, searching for non-existent stubble. This was worrying. Todd Liebowitz would be straight on his case when word of losses at Alpha broke in Geneva banking circles. He'd better call Cavendish. Cavendish knew Sayers. Sayers knew Greenbaum. He needed more information. He got to his feet with alacrity.

'Nothing. The only problem is for the investors in Alpha,' he told Jonathon, and left without a word of congratulation on a job well done.

Sir Charles Cavendish sat in the conference room next door to his plush office on the fifth floor, toying with the cold coffee and stale Danish pastries. His appetite had deserted him ages ago. Expert advisers from key departments sat alongside him with sombre faces. Pamela, his long-serving special adviser with the wonderfully high sex drive, was ready to take copious notes on an A4 pad.

He looked at his watch for the last time. Midday in London, 1 p.m. in Frankfurt, 7 p.m. in Hong Kong, 9 p.m. in Tokyo, 7 a.m. in Washington. It was the only possible time for an international conference call on a secure ISDN line. All the required parties had dialled in. Time to start. He took the telephone off mute and nodded to his colleagues. He was the convenor of the meeting and spoke first.

'I don't know why but we're seeing a major collapse in the FTSE, it's down six per cent today, and gilts and sterling have plummeted. We lowered interest rates today to help the clearing banks but it's not working. Deposits are flowing out of the banking system in billions. Our sources close to the market here say that US banks in London started the selling. We're hearing rumours about some major problem with a large fund in the US.'

Cavendish paused, implicitly inviting others to join in the call. Walter Sayers spoke next from DC.

'Shit. There's been a leak. The word is out, even in London. There is a problem with a hedge fund. We planned to bail out Alpha Corp., but it's not working. The big commercial banks are calling in the loans they made to other hedge funds. They are selling their positions to generate cash to pay back the banks. Meanwhile some of the investment banks have shut up shop, and I don't know which. They used the confidential knowledge we gave them to get ahead of the game. The bastards have stiffed us. I called the chairmen who I suspect but they denied it, of course.'

Cavendish, stunned by the news about Alpha, tried to set it aside and seize back the initiative.

'How are your markets looking today, Walt?'

'Can't be any worse than yesterday. We had the three guys on CNBC's squawk box on-screen all day wearing battered tin helmets from World War Two. These traders watch to see what Maria Bartiromo wears on the floor of the NYSE. Yesterday she was in black. We think the Dow will lose 950 points in the first hour and so trigger the circuit breaker on the NYSE. We're having discussions with the White House and the SEC. We may close the market if it gets too bad.'

Having said his piece, Sayers leaned back, looked at his executive staff and prayed that he could still get away for a few hours of privacy later that day. Cavendish invited the next participant to join in.

'Kenneth, are you on the line?'

Six thousand miles away, a team of depressed central bankers sat in the Central offices of the Hong Kong Monetary Authority. Kenneth Lam stood up, hands in pockets, walked to the windows and looked out on the smoking imported cars, the clusters of aggressive riot police, the passing clouds of CS gas and the tanks parked upon hard shoulders. He was the forty-one-year-old Stanford-educated Chief Executive of the HKMA, a career civil servant in the Chinese administration, if that in itself wasn't a contradiction in terms. The civil unrest on the streets was worsening. The police had advised that the safety of civil servants could not be guaranteed. The bankers would sleep in their offices overnight.

'The Hang Seng was down eight per cent today. The Exchange is almost bankrupt, definitely illiquid. They are owed millions by hedge funds in unpaid margin calls. They started closing out hedge funds' futures positions, have trebled margin requirements on futures trading to discourage the speculators. Some US investment banks refused to pay up, saying the Exchange can't change the rules at a day's notice. We had a knock-on effect on the cash market which is only exacerbating the crisis. We even have the Chinese Navy intensifying war games opposite Taiwan. It's all on a knife-edge.'

Next in line were the dulcet tones of Vera Engels from the boardroom of the European Central Bank.

'There is no confidence in Frankfurt. EUREX is at an all-time low, and the same for other continental exchanges. We are hearing rumours that many of the German banks are very exposed to US hedge funds. Deutsche, Commerzbank, Hypo, Dresdner and the other universal banks have lent billions. Interbank markets are dead. There were reports today on breakfast TV that widows and pensioners are queuing at some of the rural bank branches in Bavaria to withdraw their deposits in Euro cash. There could be a run on some of our AAA-rated institutions. We need to restore confidence quickly.'

Another pause, and then some staccato English from Masa Nakamura at the Bank of Japan.

'Tokyo here. We agree. We see widespread selling. It's a vicious circle. Panic leads to more panic.'

The greatest financial minds in government were

stumped. Only Kenneth Lam dared to be optimistic.

'World economies were in great shape before this. GDP growth is healthy. Inflation is under control. Exchange rates were stable. There is no fundamental reason for a crash. It's all down to an elderly assassin in Hong Kong, a dead rogue trader in New York and an insolvent hedge fund. Surely two people and one fund can't topple the global markets? That's insane. We need to seize back the initiative from these greedy investment banks, hedge funds and other speculators. It's been done before.'

Cavendish spoke on behalf of the world's central bankers.

'What do you suggest, Kenneth?'

'I have an idea. I'll call you on your private line. It may be our only hope.'

Lauren's cordless telephone rang in her living room. She stirred in bed. Phat Cat stirred too, alongside her on the sheets. It was close to midday. Such was life for the newly unemployed. Going through to the living room, she picked up the handset and looked out of the window at the new day, one eye on the deserted beach and one on the vacant carpark. Everyone else was gainfully employed.

'Hi, Lauren, how are you doing?'

She heard the distant noise of the sales floor. McFarland was calling her from the office. To gloat?

'What do you think? Not great.'

'Yeah, I'm sorry.'

'Are you?'

'Well, you know, the COO insisted. There was no choice. You broke the rules.'

She thought about hanging up and going back to bed.

'Why are you ringing me, Mac?'

'You're in danger.'

'We're all in danger right now. This country's gone mad. And you sent me home without my car.'

'Not that sort of danger. I want to warn you about Alpha.'

'I know all about Alpha.'

'People will be after you soon.'

'Which people?'

'The big guns. The SEC in New York. The Bank of England. The regulators won't let this lie. They love a good post-mortem, bayoneting the wounded. They're going to investigate everything and everyone. We're expecting the Securities and Futures Commission guys in Mitchell's any moment.'

Lauren let the handset drop to her waist, waited a while and reluctantly continued the conversation.

'You forgot, I don't work for Mitchell's any more.'

'Doesn't matter. The regulators will grill everyone who was connected to Alpha. There's a Fed team investigating them in New York. The SFC will want to talk to you here about your role.'

'I'll tell them to talk to you. You ran the FF&O desk.'

'They'll want you too. You took Chapman's orders each day. You took the telephone calls. You were the

one servicing that bloody dealer when he was over here.'
Lauren ignored the loaded innuendo. McFarland stalled
for a few seconds then persevered. 'I'm serious. They'll
hang you out to dry.'

'I can handle it.'

'I'm talking about a witch hunt. The SFC will need a
scapegoat. It's always the way. Like Leeson in Singapore
and that Daiwa Japanese guy in New York, they'll be
looking for someone to show the media, to lock up before
they throw away the key. The SFC could be on their way
to you as we speak.'

Lauren cast a glance outside but couldn't see anyone
loitering with intent.

'Why are you telling me all this?'

'Because we were close colleagues. I'm stuck running
this desk in the biggest crisis in my life, but if I could
I'd get on a plane and get the heck out of here. Take a
lesson from Leeson. Do a runner. Get a flight. Cathay is
still flying some overseas routes . . .'

Lauren pondered the advice and debated her choices.

'I have commitments here.'

'What is it that you can't leave behind?'

Phat Cat chose that moment to pass by, his smooth fur
brushing against Lauren's bare leg.

'Where should I go?'

'Anywhere. Take a holiday. Get out of Hong Kong.
Don't tell anyone, even me, where you are. If you want
my advice, I'd rather be in the States with a good securities
lawyer than stuck here in a cell with the SFC. Don't say
I didn't warn you.'

'How do I get to the airport? You going to return my car?'

'No can do. I can get you a company limo, though. We have ways and means. Let me know what time.'

He hung up. Lauren sat down and pondered her life. No job. No friends at Mitchell's. No salary. No car. Only a cat. She needed a respite from the uncertainty and the violence on the streets. She made a telephone call to Cathay. There was a flight to LA departing in a mere six hours, with onward connections to NYC. She read out her credit card number and expiry date and was booked on CX 455. She called her mother and gave her the news, noting the surprise in her voice.

She took down the two large suitcases from the wardrobe, unused since her arrival as a wandering graduate looking to escape to a new life. She packed the barest essentials and switched off the utilities in the apartment. Then she changed the message on her answering machine to tell callers she'd be away for a while and to instead use her hotmail e-mail address. She dropped a short note, keys and a few hundred bucks in a crisp envelope into the expat next door. Phat Cat would get his daily food until her return and the neighbour would keep an eye on her place. A car arrived and the gates closed behind them.

They drove past Central and Mitchell's. Inside, McFarland wandered into the COO's office.

'I scared her shitless. Told her that the SFC would chuck her in jail. She fell for it. She's on her way to the airport now. The farther she is from this office and you and me, the better. No one will find her for weeks overseas. By then we'll have shredded the incriminating evidence, got expert legal advice and briefed everyone else on the desk on what to say. We'll put the entire blame for the Alpha screw-up on one silly bitch of a woman. I always said they were bad news on any sales desk, except to look at. Next time we hire a guy.'

Walter Sayers left his prestigious DC office by the more discreet rear entrance and hailed a cab.

'Hilton Hotel, please.'

He sat in the back seat and contemplated the next two hours of ecstasy. Maybe three if he had the stamina. He went directly to the gift shop near reception, which mostly sold tacky tourist crap, and bought six red roses. Riding up to the twentieth floor, he wondered whether this was the same elevator in which they had first met a month ago. It had been the highlight of yet another international economic conference before all this market turmoil. The speakers had debated fiscal versus monetary policy that evening while Sayers had climaxed just before going downstairs to make his pre-dinner speech.

Alicia was wonderful. Thirty years younger than he was and of mixed race. Incredible sultry looks, big rouged lips, a willowy body with a narrow waist, a great ass and accommodating breasts. So much more receptive than his wife. This was the fast lane indeed, the secret life of the world's most powerful central banker who deserved some R&R in between hours spent saving the world. He knocked on the door of room 2015, just like the last time. It opened smoothly. He entered. The lights were all off. Some game? Where was Alicia?

'Take a seat.'

He heard a man's voice. The door closed in one smooth movement. A low-wattage table lamp was switched on. Sayers turned around and slowly adjusted to the poor light. A tall bulky Afro-American stood with arms folded, staring at him. He was wearing a dark two-piece suit, a gleaming white shirt, a neat bow tie and a pair of sunglasses. Sayers reckoned he was six three and maybe 240 pounds. He looked like he pumped iron on a regular basis. The body-builder stood in his way. Sayers forced a smile and made to leave.

'Looks like I'm in the wrong room.'

The adjoining door to the en suite bathroom opened and another man appeared. Same sort of intense expression as the big guy but with smaller, meaner features. Same suit and white shirt and stupid bow tie too.

'Take a seat by the desk.'

Sayers motioned to step between the two men. A firm hand was placed upon his shoulder.

'Take a seat, like my brother said.'

He sat down by the desk and the dim lamp. The two approached him, the room darkening and closing in as they came closer. He noticed their expensive-looking jewellery, solid gold rings and chunky silver watches. The body-builder's pair of wicked sunglasses was totally unnecessary in the subdued light. The smaller of the two sat down on the edge of the bed and spoke softly.

'Mr Sayers.'

So they knew his name. Maybe they'd seen him on TV. It was a small world and he was a celebrity of sorts. Sayers stared back at them, still focused on the perfectly horizontal bow ties.

'Maybe,' he conceded.

'You will answer yes or no. Do not utter any untruths.'

Sayers instantly felt at a disadvantage.

'Yes,' he muttered.

His inquisitor smiled approvingly. 'Do you know who we are?' Sayers shook his head. 'We are the Brothers of Righteousness.' He was still puzzled. 'We come in the name of Allah. Today is your chance for atonement and reconciliation with the beneficent and merciful Allah.' Sayers relaxed. They were two religious nuts, probably come to put a freebie Bible of sorts in the bedside cabinet. 'Do you know that adultery is a grave sin?'

He decided to humour them until he got a chance to leave.

'Yeah.'

'Do you know a lady named Alicia?'

'No.'

The guy leaned closer. 'I told you, no untruths today.' Sayers still said nothing.

The guy pointed. 'What's with the red roses?'

Sayers wished he'd never bought them.

'Nothing.'

'We are Alicia's brothers.'

Sayers couldn't see any immediate family resemblance.

'Seriously?'

'We care for her. Make sure people treat her right. Someday we're gonna save her soul.'

Sayers was thinking that this guy was a crackhead. High as a kite and never coming down.

'I didn't mean to get involved . . . she came on to me.'

'The time for confession has passed. It is the day of atonement.'

The small guy took out some gum and started to chew methodically before grabbing the red roses and throwing them down on the carpet. He sat nearer Sayers on the bed, flexed scarred hands together, examined his various rings one by one and ran one finger over the duvet.

'You were gonna violate our sister on this bed?' Sayers said nothing. He tried to look away but the room was too small for any other distractions.

'There's been some mistake here, gentlemen . . .'

'There's no mistake and we ain't gentlemen. You've been in this hotel room every second Thursday at six o'clock for the past few months. You tainted our sister on each occasion with your vile semen. You're getting demanding. You know what happens then?'

'No.'

'People get hurt.' Sayers said nothing. His accuser looked around the room. 'You wanna know why our sister used this room? It's got a big balcony outside. Right next to room 2016. Easy access. No problem to put a Nikon on the edge and focus it right inside the room. You get good-quality black-and-white shots these days even with poor interior light and a net curtain.' He took a manila envelope from the desk and handed it to Sayers, who was slowly getting the picture. Literally. 'Open the envelope, sinner.'

Sayers did as directed. As promised the shots were good quality. Two naked bodies, one ugly and bloated, one willowy and lithe. His ecstatic face was clearly recognisable. One shot showed him head down on her breasts, eagerly sucking her erect left nipple. Alicia looked great if somewhat uninterested when looking away from Sayers. Great mammaries. Bad memories.

'So what happens next?'

'After confession comes the penance. Your chance for redemption.'

Sayers thought he could see the endgame.

'What do you want?'

'A charitable donation from you. It's all in a good cause. Usually we ask for a modest amount but in your case we'll make a special exception. We know who you are. We even saw you on CNN and NBC this week, making you so much more marketable. These negatives are gold dust. We need a hundred grand in cash from you by next week. As an act of humble contrition.'

Sayers made to get up and then thought better of it.

'I haven't got that sort of money. I work for the government.'

'Another untruth. You got investments and cash, I'm sure.'

'I lost a lot of money in the market crash.'

'Me and my brother and our little sis find that everyone eventually pays up. Or else . . .'

'Or else what?'

'Usually we send the photos to the deceived wife, but not in your case. The *Inquirer* would love this. The *New York Post* might even go for it. These photos could be front-page news by next week. Your call.'

Sayers needed time to think.

'Let's say I have the cash. What happens next?'

'You got a private line at work?' He nodded. 'Give me the number. We'll call you next week. Have the cash ready in used hundreds. Pay up and you won't see us again. We don't even live in DC. We don't live anywhere. We go to a different city every month. Next month, who knows? Tampa? Pittsburgh? LA? Boston? Hard to say. We'll check what major conferences are on. Like we always do.'

'How do I contact you?'

'I'll give you my home number.' The man grinned. 'Just kidding. You don't contact us. We contact you.'

He stood up and ground the red roses into the carpet with one well-polished toe.

'And a friendly warning, Mr Sayers. Don't mess with us. Don't call the cops or some fancy Fed department. The consequences could be real bad. You ever had a serious auto accident? Ever had a house fire? Your wife ever been mugged? Ever lost a kid of a weekend? Think about it. Don't be clever. Be contrite.'

The Brothers of Righteousness stood by the door.

'May Allah bless you.'

The body-builder grinned at Sayers from behind the heavyweight sunglasses and finally spoke.

'Know what this is? Blackmail. Geddit?'

CHAPTER TWELVE

Jonathon's telephone rang. He looked at the LCD screen display. It was an overseas call, and he immediately recognised the country and city prefix. Switzerland. Geneva. Head office. It must be the boss. He hit the speakerphone button.

'Jonathon Maynard.'

A seductive French female accent replied.

'Hold for Mr Richemont.'

He waited.

'Jonathon, still impressing the right people.' He picked up his handset, not daring to talk to Richemont on the speaker. 'I received a telephone call today from a very prestigious client of the firm, a personal friend of mine for many years. He speaks very highly of your work for his bank.'

Richemont had too many contacts.

'Who is it? Which bank?'

'The only one that matters, the Bank of England. Sir

Charles Cavendish is enquiring about your availability for an assignment.'

'What's up?'

'He wouldn't, or couldn't, tell me. Whatever it is, I'll make sure we charge the Bank for the maximum amount of billable time. Cavendish has bottomless pockets when it comes to work like this.'

'So we have a mandate?'

'No. First, we have to go through the formality of a pitch. There are a few others on the short list, some other so-called banking experts, a girl from McKinsey and another from Cap Gemini. A civil servant and a UK Treasury official, I think. But Sir Charles advises me that you're the frontrunner. That's the very word he used. I need a copy of your CV today with details of your recent assignments.'

'It's not up to date.'

Richemont knew better, knew his business too well.

'Every management consultant worth his salt has a CV ready to go if an eager headhunter's in the offing. Tart up yours a bit. Expand on the prior assignments for the Bank of England. Send it to me this afternoon as an e-mail attachment. My secretary will send it to Sir Charles's confidential fax machine in his private office. That's the way he wants it. And we do what he wants.'

'And then what?'

'The candidates will have to meet with an interview panel. Cavendish is taking this very seriously. Remember, this is not a two-way process. You don't interview him.

Whatever the assignment is, you take it. Otherwise McKinsey or whoever will get it instead and steal our glory. We'll accept this assignment even if it is to clean all the executive toilets in the Bank's head office with a single toothbrush.'

Jonathon was beginning to have his doubts about what sort of job was coming his way.

'So I wait to hear more?'

'Cavendish wants to see you first. On Sunday. For a few hours.'

Jonathon realised that this was a problem. It was Eva's long-awaited day off.

'I can't do it. I need to be at home for the children.'

'You can do it. Sort out your domestic arrangements.'

Jonathon mutely acquiesced. He'd manage. Somehow. He'd offer Eva a large bribe.

'Where do we meet? At the Bank?'

'Sir Charles wants to meet you at a private location. I've been there once before and it's impressive. Well worth the trip. The Bank is couriering the tickets and a road map to you today.'

Alarm bells sounded more loudly. The weekend was rapidly disappearing out of view.

'We had an agreement — no more travel for me for a few weeks. I need to spend some time at home.'

Richemont sighed and then spoke clearly and firmly.

'All prior agreements are null and void. We want this assignment. Understood?' Jonathon resigned himself to the prospect of begging Eva on bended knee to stay over the weekend and keep the domestic peace. 'It's not too far to go for a day.'

'But the assignment itself will be in London?'

'That's all.'

Richemont hung up, without answering the question.

Jonathon sat and thought about the uncertainty of life as a management consultant, and whether it was a career that excluded family life. He was still taking orders from someone else. One day he'd be his own boss and make the decisions that were right for Jack and Imogen, he promised himself.

He looked at the handset and knew there was one more call to make before he went home today. He had the residential number from international directory enquiries. It was well before midnight in Hong Kong. He dialled Lauren, at the same time rehearsing his words carefully. He'd ask her what had happened at work. The phone rang and rang. He'd ask her whether she was safe. The phone rang on. He'd let her talk and talk if she wanted, just to hear the sound of her voice.

'Hi, this is Lauren. I'm away for a while. Please drop me an e-mail to my hotmail address. Thanks. 'Bye.'

He didn't have her hotmail address. He wondered where she had gone and why it had all happened so suddenly, praying it wasn't his fault. He hit redial and listened to her voice again. And again. Then one more time on the speakerphone, trying to deduce how she had felt when she made the tape recording.

* * *

Sir Charles Cavendish advised Pamela of his desired travel itinerary for the forthcoming weekend. He did not want to take the HEX to Heathrow, to walk around T2 or T3, or to sit in Club Europe. Someone in the business would be bound to recognise him, ask questions or else tell the media hacks that he was out of the country at a time of national crisis. He changed out of his dark suit and club tie into a casual jacket in his private dressing room at the Bank. Pamela kissed him goodbye several times.

The bank car collected him outside at Bank junction and set off eastward down Bishopsgate to Liverpool Street station. He had timed the ten-minute journey perfectly and clambered aboard the 6 p.m. Stansted Express. Eschewing the first-class compartment, he paid his ten-pound fare and buried himself anonymously behind a copy of the *Evening Standard* with bold headlines about global financial meltdown, always guaranteed to sell maximum copies of the paper.

He checked in at the Ryanair desk an hour later, safe in the knowledge that his peer group would never use this bargain-basement discount airline. Taking his boarding card, he asked naively what seat he was in, to be told that all seats were unreserved. Much like Aeroflot, he thought. He boarded with the scrum of holidaymakers and students and selected a rear aisle seat. They took off fifty-five minutes after the scheduled departure time. Not bad for Ryanair, apparently. The complimentary black Alfa Romeo with a driver who usually worked for the Governor of the Banca d'Italia was awaiting his arrival.

He knew the route well from prior trips. They stayed on the AI autostrada south, past Bargino, Tavernelle and San Donato. Then they took the S333 minor road, which meandered through picturesque turreted hilltop villages that tourists would clamour to see. The Chianti Classico district in the heart of Tuscany unfolded between Florence and Siena. He knew most of the communes well: Gaiole, Greve, San Casciano, Radda, Poggibonsi and others, and his own personal favourite, Castellina.

There were ten thousand hectares of south-facing vineyards in this region, all nurturing the Sangiovese grape. The stony shallow soil of sandstone and calcareous clay, and the favourable continental climate, where temperatures rarely fluctuated abruptly or substantially, were perfect conditions for the production of premium wine. Cavendish favoured his own Reserva. He saw the signs for Castellina, the nearest village to his private estate, and his spirits, sapped by recent events, rose. They drove into the cherished holiday retreat that he and Marjorie had purchased many years before. She loved the place but hadn't visited in years. Now she'd want half of this place in any settlement, as well as the house in London.

The dirt track was riddled with vicious potholes. Others called this avenue a driver's nightmare; Cavendish thought it lent character to the estate. As they turned the first blind corner, several hundred yards into the heart of the vineyard, a carabiniere stepped into his path with his left hand raised. He looked at the driver, spoke briefly in the local dialect, and stood back to wave the car past. Another police officer sat on one of a pair of gleaming Ducati motorcycles discreetly pulled under the shade of the trees. Cavendish saw him draw on a cigarette and run a hand through his long black oily locks while simultaneously maintaining an air of dignified vigilance, as only the carabinieri can do. Cavendish appreciated the discreet security for his exclusive weekend rendezvous, which came courtesy of the Governor of the Banca d'Italia, who, regrettably, was too insignificant to attend.

He stepped out of the car and admired his sanctuary: a cluster of single-storey stone buildings built on a slope, with steps winding down to a grassy area, a patio and a modest swimming pool. A few half-sized old wine casks and clay urns were strategically placed, brimming with flowers and a few weeds. The square canvas parasols were already raised. Rosa, his local cook and housemaid, was expecting him. It was another world here, far from the pressures of the City of London. The ideal location.

Walter Sayers lied to his PA that he was off to another late night Fed meeting downtown. In fact Art Greenbaum was sorely trying their 'friendship' by requesting another talk. Fuming, he walked across Water Street and Fulton Market and ascended through a tourist shopping hell to the Harbours restaurant on the top floor of Seaport Plaza. It was 9 p.m. All the depressed and manic Wall Street types had left for home. The Dow was down six hundred points plus.

Greenbaum was already sitting at an open-air table perched on wooden decking between rows of plants. As

Sayers approached, his attention was diverted to the views of the Brooklyn and Manhattan bridges. A neon sign across the river announced that it was 72 degrees. Sayers sat down, mopping his brow in the high humidity.

'This is a crazy idea. If the two of us are seen together in public, it ain't gonna look good for either of us. Just what has come over you? You losing it?' he growled.

'Maybe. I'm talking to lawyers, cops, the SEC, the Feds and other assorted greaseballs. The media are after me. I'm the centre of attention and I don't like it. Haven't slept in days. Haven't been home. They have me by the balls. I can't deal via Alpha. I can't earn a living. I miss the markets, Walt.'

'Are you liquid?'

'Nope.'

Pity. Sayers was still looking to make up the hundred K cash 'contribution' at short notice for the Brothers.

'Me neither. Can you afford to pay for this meal?'

'I'll use plastic. Live now, pay later.'

'Is Victoria okay?'

'Yes. Mainly because she hasn't got a clue what's going on.'

'You still got the apartment on the Upper East Side?'

'Signed it over to her just in time. They can't fuck with that, it's legit.'

Distant live jazz emanated from a band down on Pier 19. Pleasure boats passed below with honking horns. Strobe lighting pulsed on floating discos. The lively ambience seemed wrong for the tone of their conversation. A waiter handed them two menus, bread and water and left them in peace. Sayers made sure no one else was within earshot.

'Alpha's collapse has been a worldwide disaster. Confidence is shot to hell.'

'Ain't my fault. It was Chapman, to begin with. And now the investment banks are shorting the market.'

'Same difference as far as I'm concerned.' Sayers threw the menu down on the table. 'You know how much I had in Alpha? My pension and bonus monies from Salomon's straight down the pan. Why didn't you warn me, Art?'

'It happened so fast. One day we were making money, the next I had two homicide cops in my office.'

'You really screwed up bigtime. Now I'm working day and night with other bankers around the globe to scoop up the shit you left us. Only there ain't a bag big enough and we're all running out of time to fix this.'

Greenbaum looked suddenly more animated.

'So that's it!'

'What?'

'There's going to be intervention in the markets, isn't there?' Sayers said nothing, his expression stony. 'I knew it,' Greenbaum crowed. 'Walt, I want to make it all back for you. That's why I asked you here. I want to recoup your losses. I want you to make a profit amidst all this gloom and doom.'

Sayers thumped the table, rocking cutlery and glasses. Other diners looked over.

'Do you think I would ever again be remotely interested in trusting you with a single cent?'

Greenbaum shrugged his shoulders, put down his menu and lowered his voice farther.

'Hear me out. There's no harm in that.'

The waiter arrived, took an order for surf and turf for two and a bottle of overpriced Merlot and left them alone. Sayers was interested but needed to remain in control.

'I will listen to whatever you have to say. That's all.'

Greenbaum pulled apart a bread roll, stuffed half in his mouth hungrily yet still managed to keep on talking.

'The markets around the world are at all-time lows, but the fundamentals haven't changed. You and I know what happens eventually after every crisis — recovery. As the great Nathan Rothschild said, "The time to buy is when there is blood on the streets." Isn't it a safe bet that in a year's time they'll be higher than they are today?'

Sayers had no doubt. Short term was a big problem. Medium term was hazy. Long term was different.

'Markets will improve. But then I have to hold that view. It's the compulsory view for the Chairman.'

Greenbaum downed the rest of his bread roll.

'Does anyone really think that Microsoft, Dell, AT&T or Cisco, for example, are in worse shape than they were a few months ago just because Chapman jumps and Alpha unwinds? Now is the time to start a recovery fund. I'm gonna hire a few good people who know this business inside out. It shouldn't be too hard to get them with all the lay-offs on the Street. I'm gonna invest in quality cheaply. Gonna leverage up and trade options and futures, not underlying stocks. That's where the big profits are. Are you in?'

They waited while freshly milled black pepper was liberally dispensed over their lobster and steaks, then resumed talking.

'No, I'm not.'

'You must have cash to spend. Just a few hundred K to play with.'

'I wish I did. Count me out.' Sayers made a mental note to call his bank again. That encounter in the hotel room had left a bitter aftertaste. The risk of public disclosure remained.

'We go back a long way. If you can't invest, at least help me out.'

'How?'

'When do you think government intervention will occur?'

'There won't be any intervention?' Sayers's voice was still shrill with indignation at being caught out like this. He should have remembered of old how quick on the uptake Greenbaum was.

'You just admitted as much.'

'I didn't. And anyway I can't talk about that, Art.'

'Off the record. For a friend. It would make the timing of my investments so much easier.'

'It's also called inside knowledge, and that's illegal.'

'All I need is a phone call when we hit bottom, just before the intervention kicks in.'

'Out of the question.' Sayers ripped his prime rib and lobster apart angrily.

'We just need one spark to ignite this market. It could come from anywhere. The President or the British PM says a few words. Some big investors buy into the market. Some investment banks turn bullish. But government intervention would certainly send the right signal to the world at large. Then the markets will turn. Shit, if you got up and said a few words then we could turn this whole thing around.'

'Art, it ain't that easy. If it was, I'd have done it already.'

The two men fell silent. Sayers swallowed his final mouthful and looked out at the trains rattling over the bridges to Brooklyn Heights and the cars barrelling along the FDR. The markets would turn in time. He needed to recoup his own losses, maybe even a bit more, and make some money fast. He needed hard cash for Alicia's alleged Brothers. An opportunity did exist but he had said enough. Too much if the truth be told. Greenbaum had planted the germ of an idea. The waiter removed their plates. Coffee arrived, followed by the bill. Greenbaum felt sufficiently guilty to inspect the damage first.

'They forgot to charge us for the Merlot. That's eighty bucks. Do we tell 'em?'

'No,' advised Sayers, deciding to live on the edge. 'It's survival of the fittest.'

He took out a cigar and lit it skilfully first time. Greenbaum wanted one too.

'You got a real Cuban? How did you get that?' He winked at Sayers. 'A Federal employee with forbidden contraband. You're supporting Castro and his regime?'

Sayers inhaled long and slow on a fine piece of weed.

'I'm not supporting the Cuban regime, I'm merely burning their crops.'

'You see, Walt? Rules can be broken.'

Kenneth Lam had a Cathay Pacific Marco Polo card, and if he maximised his accumulated miles he and his wife could take that wedding anniversary trip to Bali later in the year. He determined to brazen it out in Marco Polo club class and take his chances on any attendant publicity. The government car left the Hong Kong Monetary Authority in Central and took forty minutes to get to Chep Lap Kok. The four outriders were a nice touch courtesy of the Chief Executive of the Special Administrative Region. The armed police also ensured his personal safety among the roaming gangs with air pistols who were taking pot shots at slow-moving traffic along the highways. The CE knew how much this trip meant to a former colony in South-East Asia facing the onslaught of global speculators in capitals far away. The airport interior was manic, so many desperate to leave this former Asian tiger now mired in economic and social chaos. Lam ensured that the check-in staff swiped his air miles card, and enjoyed a G&T as he sat in the safety of the club lounge. He recognised a senior American corporate banker from ING in seat 10C of the Airbus A-330 but fortunately there was no mutual acknowledgment. CX177 left HKG before midnight and arrived at Fiumincino in the early morning. He met the driver with 'Bank' written on a small placard in the arrivals lounge and slept all the way on the drive north.

Masa Nakamura took a lift with his wife from home to Tokyo station at midday. He would claim the cost of a private taxi service from home to Narita and make another few thousand yen profit in the process. He used local knowledge and an elevator to get to the lowest underground platforms, thereby avoiding the heaving masses on the move. He was confident that even such a high-ranking civil servant as he would pass unrecognised, since he never courted media attention. He stood anonymously on platform twelve, the floor markings indicating where the first-class carriage would stop. Eight minutes later the 12.15 Narita Express halted beside his diminutive size-six shoes. The train sped non-stop through undulating countryside and tiny suburban residences, often overtaking lines of stationary traffic on the parallel motorways. Nakamura had tired long ago of JAL, All Nippon, ANA and the others. He checked in at the Club World desk in the old BA terminal, a relic of the late 1970s and surely a deliberate move by the domestic airlines to stifle foreign competition. He appreciated the fact that the route via Heathrow was somewhat circuitous, arriving in the early afternoon of the next day, but London's international connections were the best. He hopped on to the first Alitalia flight to Milan and caught a few more hours of disturbed sleep. Next stop was a welcoming chauffeur and the breathtaking views of the hillside vineyards.

Vera Engels rose at 5.30 a.m. and gently kissed her

sleeping other half goodbye. She silently closed the hall
door of the Sachsenhausen home that came courtesy of
the taxpayers of western Europe, walked to the carport
and threw her overnight Samsonite bag on to the cream
leather rear seat of the metallic-painted BMW 520i.
Her ultrasonic key ring opened the metal gates on to
a deserted street. She took the A3 to the south. Off to
the rear she could see downtown Bankfurt, as the expat
bankers and journalists called it. The European Central
Bank, her own glorious personal fiefdom, was prominent
among the towers of tinted glass and burnished steel
while the drab Bundesbank building could hardly be
seen, in keeping with its present role in German monetary
and fiscal policy. The fast left lane of the autobahn was
her choice. Engels cruised effortlessly towards the Swiss
border, paying the required exorbitant road tolls and
flashing slow traffic ahead with her full beams. The
speedometer touched 160 kmph at times. She stopped
at a Mobil service station for a lead-free top-up after
the long tunnels through the Alps. A glance at the
morning IHT, a solitary walk by the forecourt and a
strong double espresso and a warm croissant revived her
for the remainder of the journey. She crossed the Italian
border and stayed on the autostrada all the way down
to Firenze. She bypassed this urban mass and took the
S222 for the hills of central Tuscany, pulling over twice
to examine the A4 map that had been faxed to her office
yesterday evening. It was shortly after two o'clock when
she left a side road near Castellini and arrived at the
agreed rendezvous.

Walter Sayers switched off the desk light in his wood-panelled office on the second floor of the Fed's marble monument to monetary stability. He descended in his private elevator and walked through the lobby, acknowledging in turn various members of his staff who knew how to defer to the Chairman. His regular driver placed his flight bag in the boot. Sayers used the in-car telephone to make a series of short, precise telephone calls and advise his deputies that he would be out of town until next Tuesday. Make no announcements, make no sudden policy changes, stall the media, batten down the hatches and tough this one out, he ordered. The car sped through the darkened suburbs of Washington, DC, and drew near to Dulles International Airport just after 7 p.m. They skirted around the main terminal buildings to the discreet VIP centre. The attendant recognised her guest and took Sayers directly to the no-frills Learjet adjacent to the building. The engines were already running. The pilot received immediate ATC clearance from the tower and VIP1 jumped a long row of Delta and United jumbos in the take-off queue. They banked east and headed out across the Atlantic at 26,000 feet on full throttle. Eight hours later the Lear skidded down on to the hot asphalt of Florence's Amerigo Vespucci airport and stopped near a hangar away from the hordes of tourists arriving for their big culture fix. Spotting a waiting driver, compliments of the Italian government, Sayers sat in the back of the air-conditioned Alfa Romeo and adjusted his watch to Central European Time – 9 a.m. local. Perfect.

CHAPTER THIRTEEN

CHESTER ROW, LONDON, SW1 –
1.50 P.M.

All was going well in the Maynard household until Jack ran into the kitchen. Jonathon was bent over almost out of sight, transferring the pile of dirty plates, Barney mugs and Sunny Delight-stained glasses from the various worktops and into the welcoming Zanussi. Jack prodded him.

'Dad, there's a man at the door.'

Jonathon had told him never to answer the door on his own. Abandoning the contents of the dishwasher, as leading international management consultants sometimes have to do, he walked into the hall and saw that the door had been left open. Another piece of advice forgotten by Jack. He was greeted by a pimply ginger youth in a yellow fluorescent sponsored top, pink-tinted curved shades, a crash helmet and bulging cycling shorts that left nothing to the imagination. The courier chewed gum as he handed over an envelope.

'Maynard?'

He nodded and signed the proffered clipboard. The rear view of the courier was equally unappealing as he sped off bare legged to dice with death in the lead oxide of London's rat-runs. As Jonathon knew it would, the envelope contained an air ticket and instructions. He saw Florence in the itinerary, a Hertz car rental coupon, a photocopied map and the flight departure details – 5.30 p.m. Today. Only a few hours away. Damn Richemont and his sudden assignments! This would be tight.

Imogen was first. They wasted ten minutes looking for the present Jonathon had carefully wrapped in Bob the Builder paper, then sped off to her long-awaited birthday party in Battersea. Once again, he watched lucky couples and their children and realised that Imogen was being deprived of something fundamental. He worried about her fifth birthday next month and how he was going to organise her party. Peer pressure demanded that it be a success, even at such a tender age. On the return journey he used the mobile in the glove compartment to call Eva at home. He was about to put her in an impossible position. Again.

'Eva, bit of an emergency. I need to go away for the rest of the weekend.'

He didn't dare specify his request precisely, but she knew what he meant. She'd had these calls before at all hours.

'Same arrangement, Jon?'

He knew what she meant. Double time. Sometimes he felt like billing Richemont in person.

'Thanks. See you by four?'

Jack watched him pack fast, running up and down the stairs, and offered some advice to his father.

'Don't forget my present at the airport. More games, please.'

By ten past four Jonathon was ready to go, but there was still no sign of Eva. He was thinking about Plan B, who would look after Jack, and whether in fact there even was a Plan B, when at last there was the familiar welcome sound of Eva using her keys to let herself in. As he passed her in the doorway, he gave her instructions on how to collect Imogen from her party at five: to look for the red balloons by the front door. There were no black cabs in sight outside. He lugged his flight bag to the corner of Holbein Place. Still no joy. He glanced at his watch. No choice now. Back to the Freelander with his luggage thrown in the back. He made for the A4.

He checked in late and was forced to carry his own luggage to the departure gate by a combative BA check-in girl who was having an equally bad day. Jonathon sat alone with beads of sweat running down inside his shirt and collecting at his waistband. The flight was delayed by forty minutes. He was so sick of this lifestyle. Sick of the uncertainty of never knowing where he was going to be. Sick of not being at home with Jack and Imogen. Sick of the way the firm ran his life. Richemont had once again robbed him of his weekend.

*　　*　　*

Engels was the first to join Cavendish as she continued the tradition of Germanic punctuality in the face of all adversity. Nakamura appeared soon afterwards, bowing politely to his English host. Sayers arrived after a forty-minute phone call to his deputies in the Fed, who were still fending off eager pressmen wondering exactly where the Chairman was. Lam was last to appear, blaming his tardiness on severe jet-lag and the lack of a wake-up call. The élite guests sat outside on the flagstone patio in the cool of the early evening. Lam felt obliged to speak on behalf of them all.

'Nice place. Tell us about it.'

They sat in a suntrap, backs to a stone wall built centuries ago, facing the swimming pool, surrounded by rustic wooden fencing and watching the sun slowly set beyond a ridge of low hills topped by the castellated turrets of an old town. South-facing terraces of wizened vines and angular olive trees absorbed the last weak rays. Dense forests of pine and oak bordered the cultivated vineyard, almost threatening to invade beyond the wire-mesh fences that kept the wild boar, rodents and other predators at bay. Solo poplars broke up the endless horizontals of the landscape. Cavendish savoured the tranquil moment. Sayers had other ideas.

'No time for a history lesson. We've all come a long way and time is precious. Why exactly are we here, Charles?'

The others frowned at his impatience. Cavendish cleared his throat imperturbably and began.

'Do any of you recall what exactly spooked the international capital markets a few years ago? Perhaps they were oversold. Perhaps Russian bond defaults started the malaise. Perhaps it was the introduction of foreign exchange controls in Malaysia. Personally, I think events can be traced back to the late July when there was a speculative attack by US hedge funds on the Thai baht.'

The central bankers nodded as they recalled the chaos. Bad, but not as manic as right now. Lam spoke up.

'There was instant global turmoil. Markets fell twenty per cent in days. The emerging ones like Hong Kong were the hardest hit. Overnight interbank rates shot up. Does all this sound familiar?' Lam turned to face the Chairman of the Federal Reserve Board. 'Do you recall what we did in Hong Kong?'

Sayers's reaction was not instantaneous but when it came it was precisely what Lam had expected. He rose to his feet.

'Jeez, no! You can't be serious.' He turned to his host. 'Chuck, tell me this is not on the agenda?'

Cavendish motioned for his guest to resume his seat. He hated being called Chuck.

'Give Kenneth a chance. Let him speak.'

'Is this what you guys discussed after that conference call we had?'

'Wait and see. Then we can judge, Walter.'

Sayers sat back down, crossed his arms, shrugged his shoulders and radiated as much negative body language as he could. The others watched, unimpressed, and allowed Lam to continue.

'I once shared some of Walter's concerns. I too was a sceptic. We had never intervened in the Hong Kong market before, but that time was different. All of us here daily take crucial decisions in the public interest. We must make those decisions with courage and execute them with real commitment.'

'Cut the crap, please.' The others glared over at Sayers. Lam persevered.

'We in Hong Kong were trying to deter market manipulation, which all of us know contravenes the antitrust laws in the US. Some might say that it was arbitrage or speculation, but I call it manipulation.'

Sayers shrugged again and then countered, 'You guys bought tons of shares and stock index futures. You spent billions in days. You were deliberately ramping up the market. It's never right to intervene in a free economy.'

Lam moved closer to his international peer.

'Foreign speculators held short positions of thousands of Hang Seng index futures. For every thousand-point fall in our index, the speculators stood to make four billion Hong Kong dollars.'

Sayers remained unimpressed.

'That's capitalism. It's a zero-sum game. There is always a winner, always a loser. That's life. Take it or leave it.'

'Nothing wrong with capitalism provided it's fair as well.'

Cavendish was impressed so far. His German counterpart was keen to hear more.

'So how did you beat the speculators, Ken?'

Lam had done the necessary research before he left the HKMA.

'Our economists said that nothing had changed. The blue-chip companies were still the same blue-chip companies but now their share prices had halved. We got immediate approval from the Chief Executive and went into the market in size, buying stocks and futures.'

The lone voice of dissent continued to object.

'It wasn't right . . .'

'The facts proved otherwise, Walter. The stock market recovered. Interest rates were unchanged. The speculators lost in unwinding their short currency and future positions. The stock market was up sixty per cent one year later.'

Lam sat down and Cavendish took the floor.

'Any questions, gentlemen? Excuse me, Vera too.'

Sayers needed no second invitation.

'Do you agree that you jacked up the market?'

Lam was almost enjoying the sparring now.

'I recall those were the emotive words used when testifying to your House Banking Committee. Actually I don't agree. We do not mind what the level of the market is, if that is what the adjustment process demands. There can never be any official view on the "right" market level. But I am against manipulation by those sending our stock market into a nosedive with no regard for the economic fundamentals. We beat them at their own game. We deterred manipulation, but we never jacked up the market.'

Sayers was now pacing up and down on the flagstones.

'You lost the plot. You're supposed to be a central

banker, but you became a goddamn investor overnight, one of the biggest in the market. Now you're a fund manager.'

'Not so. We held our investments in a separate company. HKMA staff did not get involved in the day-to-day buying. Other civil servants did that.'

Cavendish raised his hand, signalling an end to the disagreement.

'I'm impressed by what the HKMA achieved in the last crisis. There are many parallels to the current situation, which is one not of our making, I might add, but rather one generated by a group of American investment banks taking a speculative punt against global markets.'

The attack on his homeland was too much. Sayers turned away, shoulders hunched in tiredness and frustration.

'I'm off to bed.'

'It'll make more sense in the morning, Walt.'

'I doubt it.'

Cavendish stopped his guests by the door while all of them were still within earshot.

'This is the sweetener. The HKMA invested fifteen billion US dollars. A year later their investments were worth twenty-four billion. Nine billion bucks of profit, more than the number-one US investment bank made last year. If we pull this off we might even make some sizeable money at the expense of the investment banks and the herd of speculators. Poetic justice.'

Sayers, as always, needed to have the last word.

'And who the hell is going to pull this off? You, me, Ken, Vera? A bunch of civil servants?'

Cavendish placed his hand on Sayers's back reassuringly.

'I already have somebody in mind. You will meet him tomorrow.'

The connecting UA flight arrived at JFK in the late afternoon. Lauren looked for a familiar face in arrivals.

'Hi, Mom.'

'Welcome home.' They embraced. Her mother was ageless, her figure carefully honed, pepper-and-salt hair tinted ash blond. Today she had dressed casually in a pair of crisp chinos and a blue blouse, sunglasses perched on top of her head. Lauren hoped that longevity was hereditary. She looked around, partly to avoid the embarrassment of the embrace but also to see if there was a larger welcoming committee. Her mother told her intuitively, 'Dad couldn't make it. Busy at work. Citibank is frenetic, he says.'

They packed Lauren's two dusty suitcases into the boot of the Ford Taurus in the huge parking lot.

'I remember buying you those two cases. Seems a long time ago,' said her mother.

Lauren let it pass. They took all the right exits out of JFK.

'How long are you home for, darling?'

'Dunno. I can't go back until Hong Kong is safe.'

'Stay a while this time. We so like having you here.

The apartment is too quiet. Your father misses you, you know.'

Lauren wondered how it could be possible that her mother had closed her eyes to the truth for so many years. They drove at speed towards the skyline of uptown Manhattan as her mother changed lanes effortlessly and injected gas when required. Forty minutes later they left the car in a parking lot which offered the best monthly deals within walking distance of Columbus Circle. A youth with snow-bleached hair, bandanna and baggy trousers took the keys and gave Lauren a long lingering look, wondering who she was and whether he might have a chance with her. Dream on.

'Is he at home?'

'Dad works real late these days. Often weekends too.'

The sixth-floor apartment was just as it had been last Thanksgiving, minus the turkey. Low ceilings, heavy carpets, dusty curtains, faded elegance. Many would yearn to live in such a central location. Lauren already missed Repulse Bay and Phat Cat.

'Leave your cases in your room, dear.'

They still called it 'her' room. Everything had been left unchanged – embarrassing high-school photos on the windowsill, awful Laura Ashley floral bed-linen last in fashion in the mid-eighties, clothes that should have been given to charity shops years ago. Lauren didn't know how long she could stay here. The embarrassment of living with your parents at the age of thirty-two was too much to bear.

'You want to call anyone, dear?'

'Maybe later.'

She knew no one in NYC. Her friends had moved away upstate, got married, had three kids or else had cut her off socially. Hong Kong was too far away to keep in touch. Her Palm Pilot's store of local numbers was past its best-by date. She knew only a few clients in Manhattan and one of them was recently deceased.

'You want to eat, dear? Then we can talk some. Catch up on the past six months.'

'I need some rest first. The jet-lag is hitting me bad.'

The ancient elevator outside rattled into life. It rose several floors then halted.

'That'll be your father. Excellent timing, George.'

Lauren looked round as her father entered the living room, briefcase in his hand. He seemed more diminished every time they met, more stooped and wizened, and this time the bags under his eyes were heavy with age. He looked tired after the recent late nights. He was approaching compulsory retirement age at Citibank and her mother had no idea how he would fill his days after that. He brushed back some wisps of grey hair too long in truth for a man of his age and nodded to his only child.

'Lauren.'

He didn't know what to do. At first he stood awkwardly as if he were going to shake hands with a corporate client. Then he obviously changed his mind, drew closer and gave her the lightest peck on her left cheek. She made a reciprocal effort in her mother's presence.

'Dad, good to see you.'

He said nothing more. Her mother broke the awkward silence as she made for the door.

'I'll start the meal. Pot roast okay for you both?'

'Sure,' interjected Lauren's father before any contrary view could be proffered. And they were alone. The silence was unbearable, each struggling to find something positive to say just as they had done last Thanksgiving. Neither of them wished to stray on to any avenues of conversation that might in turn lead down the darker alleys of the past. She had hoped he might have mellowed in the past six months. He broke the ice.

'So, Hong Kong didn't work out, then?'

'Of course it did, Dad. I've been there eight years.'

'But you've come home with barely a day's notice to your mother.'

'Would you rather I was still over there with the rioters and looters?'

He evaded the question.

'What about your job?'

'I've left Mitchell's.'

'What the hell did you do that for? They're a great name.'

The less her father knew about the precise manner of her departure the better.

'They let me go because of the market turmoil.'

'I didn't read about that. Did many others go?'

Lauren nodded, almost glad to be talking about work instead of something more personal.

'Yes. They're keeping it quiet. You know how obsessed Mitchell's are with their public image.'

'What are you going to do here?'

'Maybe get a job on the Street.'

'No one's hiring in this market.'

'I have good experience and I have the Mitchell's name on my CV.'

'Had the Mitchell's name. You'll probably end up back part-time at that Gap store on Fifth.'

'Hardly!'

Her father got up out of his seat, apparently suddenly inspired.

'I can get you a job interview.'

'I don't want to work for Citibank. I told you that eight years ago.'

'Don't knock Citibank. It paid for your education. It made you what you are today.'

Lauren got up, ready to help her mother in the traditional refuge of the kitchen.

'No, Dad. Citibank didn't make me what I am today. You did.'

The unseen international players watched the recent arrival from afar with curiosity and then moved inside to avoid the impending chill of the late evening. Hands in pockets, Jonathon and Cavendish ambled along an undulating dusty track and turned away from the converted farmhouse. A single hawk hovered in the breeze over the hedgerows. Lizards scurried ahead of them along the sun-baked stones. The landscape up close was barren in the absence of any recent irrigation. Jonathon said nothing until they were out of sight and earshot.

'Nice place. I envy you.'

Cavendish had heard it all before. He had defended his private retreat on many prior occasions.

'It doesn't come with the job. I was a managing director at a UK merchant bank and spent my entire annual bonus years ago on buying a ruin with collapsed outbuildings and a vineyard in a state of total neglect. Turning this place around became an obsession. We sunk all our money into it. Now I don't know which one of us will keep it.' He saw Jonathon's reaction. 'There's a divorce on the way.'

'Sorry to hear it.'

'Marjorie and I bought this in the midst of a property collapse. Now every English tourist wants a piece of Tuscany for themselves, but at least it proves markets do turn. And the wine makes it worthwhile.'

Jonathon examined the rows of gnarled vines clinging to wooden trellises, all connected with yards of taut rusted wire, the grapes every colour between purple and green. He stopped and reached out to try one. Cavendish smiled wryly.

'I wouldn't, Jonathon. These aren't like grapes you pick up at Tesco. Their skin is tough, twice the thickness of an eating variety. They're regularly sprayed with insecticide, and under-ripe. You'd be sick as a dog tomorrow morning and we need you in good health for the job interview. Believe me, the wine is more rewarding than the grape.'

Jonathon was somehow relieved to hear that serious work would wait until tomorrow.

'I know nothing about wine-making.'

'We harvest in October, only use about thirty per cent of the grapes for wine. The rest we bin. We separate fruit from stalks in the winery. The tannin in the skin preserves the wine but the tannin in the stalk is too harsh for fine Chianti. We ferment the grapes for about fifteen days, circulating everything with pumps to extract the best flavour and colour. That softens the wine. Afterwards, we drain it from the fermentation tanks and store it in wooden casks to mature in our cellars. Then we bottle.'

Jonathon was reluctantly impressed.

'You know a lot about wine-making.'

'I don't. Wine-making is an art, oenology they call it, and I have absolutely no skill in that. But I know people who know a lot about wine-making. I ask them questions. I seek their advice. I rely on their expertise. They do the real work. It's sort of like banking.' They stopped by the winery, all locked up until harvest time, and sat on a low stone wall. The subject of assignment had at last been broached. The time was right. Cavendish spoke. 'You come very highly recommended. Are you ready for a challenge?'

Jonathon obliged with the answer Richemont would expect of him.

'I always have been in the past.'

'You'll meet some important people tomorrow morning. I'd like you to impress them. We have a major assignment in a worsening global situation. We don't expect you to make a decision about it right here and now, there are others on our short list who we will also see this week, but you're the one I want. You're our frontrunner.'

Olivier Richemont travelled to Amsterdam only on those rare occasions when it was worth his while. Max sat in his battered suit four rows behind in economy class, keeping a watchful eye on his boss in club. The Swissair flight from Geneva landed at Schipol in the late afternoon. They walked briskly through the concourse mêlée, knowing the location of the Hertz desk from prior visits. They carried only hand luggage.

Richemont watched from afar as his bodyguard hired a modest Opel, his own heartbeat rising steadily. Once in the car, Max removed a fat envelope from a strap around his lower leg and placed it inside his jacket. He drove with his usual expertise, first on the northbound A4 and then east on the A10 ring road. Richemont sat in the rear and used the nail-file on his penknife to push back his cuticles.

Forty-five minutes later they reached the tranquil residential suburb of Laren, five kilometres from the stench of the canals and the teeming tourists in Dam Square. Richemont liked the wealthy homes here – the double garages, high walls and dense trees, and most of all the darkness. Max had found this place. His contacts were unrivalled. The bodyguard spoke into a video intercom set into a wall and a pair of high metal gates opened. They parked on the loose gravel drive and the heavy front door opened. Max entered first, Richemont next, safe in the knowledge that he was under escort. He would never dare come here alone. The bulky doorman with no English recognised him from his last visit.

'*Wilkommen*, Herr Smitt.'

It was infinitely preferable to use an assumed name in houses like this one. Richemont sat in the spacious lounge for five minutes, imbibing a complimentary fine cognac, his heart beating faster by the minute. Max melted into the background, leaned on a wall and lit a Camel. Their middle-aged host, a fixer from eastern Europe, appeared from upstairs. He wore a black polo neck and black denim jeans, grey, youthfully cropped hair, a fake tan and a gleaming gold chain so heavy he could hardly hold his head up.

'Have I got someone special for you this time!'

Richemont hadn't travelled all day for social chitchat. His appetite was already whetted by the coded telephone call Max had received at home in Geneva.

'Show me.'

'Let's sort out the business side first.'

'You know I'm good for it.'

'We have our procedure and we don't depart from it. It's best for all concerned.'

Richemont nodded and Max reappeared from the shadows, reached inside his jacket and extracted the envelope. He placed the bundle of used hundred-dollar bills on the table and watched the pleased reaction of his host. Richemont stated the obvious.

'There's three thousand there. Trust me.'

His host insisted on counting the notes, then leaned forward and topped up his customer's cognac.

'Shall I tell you about her?' he asked in a broken accent. Richemont nodded. 'She arrived in Rotterdam on a container ship six days ago. Her family paid big money to a bent freight company in Jakarta to get all six of them over here. The father is deep in debt and needs to pay off the locals, who are leaning on him. He, the mother and the other children are in a safe house near Utrecht. They know that illegal immigration involves sacrifice. Someone must pay. That someone is called Leela.'

Richemont felt his pulse quicken to a drumbeat.

'What's she like?' he asked hoarsely.

'Slim, jet-black long hair, maybe five four in height, soft spoken, big dark eyes, lovely face.'

'Is she okay after the trip?'

'We took good care of her the last few days. Decent meals. IV fluids. Enough drugs.'

'And?'

His host sat back in his chair, savouring the evident interest of his high-paying customer.

'It's her first time.'

'Sure?' Richemont exclaimed. His palms were wet, his shirt collar tightening.

'Sure. Cherry time. Ripe for the picking.' His host pointed upstairs. 'Be easy with her now. No damage.'

Richemont stood up.

'I'll do what I want. I've paid my money.'

He and Max climbed the stairs together and walked down a quiet corridor to a set of locked double doors at the end. Richemont knew the master bedroom from last month's endeavours with a waifish Czech, all dyed blond hair, thin bones, pitifully small breasts, an annoying sniffle and, on occasion, a high pitched scream. Max unlocked the door and looked in.

'I'll be near by. If you get any trouble from her, call down. I'll sort her out.'

Max knew when to disappear. Richemont fingered the penknife inside his pocket. The plastic surface was warm and wet to his touch. He entered the room alone.

Two hours later the bedroom door was thrown open and he yelled down. Max bounded upstairs, finding his boss pale and wide eyed. His hair was standing on end and his shirt was open, the tails hanging low. Max had never seen his employer look less than immaculate before.

'I had some trouble. She wasn't well. It's not my fault. What's going to happen?'

Max looked in and saw the prone body, completely still, face down in the pillows.

'It's okay. I'll look after this. That's what I'm here for.'

'What about the guys downstairs?'

'I'll sort them. Tell them what happened. I'll keep them sweet.'

'How?'

'Same as ever. Money.' Max took his boss back inside the room and shut the door. 'Money talks.'

CHAPTER FOURTEEN
CASTELLINA IN CHIANTI, TUSCANY –
9.40 A.M.

Jonathon was ushered to the shaded patio area, where five affluent-looking middle-aged people sat in easy canvas chairs, finishing breakfast. He recognised Sayers from TV news clips and the stylish German blonde in her late forties from the recent ECB press conferences. Sitting down in the one vacant chair left, he faced down the mother of all interview panels. Cavendish introduced him to everyone present, and issued a brief warning.

'If anyone asks where you were this weekend, Jonathon, you will be suitably vague. Tell no one about our meeting. Not family. Not friends. Not colleagues at Richemont. Not even Olivier Richemont. Especially Olivier.'

Jonathon nodded in agreement, wondering what all this was about and whether Richemont would let him turn down the assignment. The others eyed the candidate. Cavendish opened a thin manila file. Jonathon recognised the pages inside. It was the up-to-date version of his CV which he had e-mailed to Richemont. The others had identical files. Cavendish addressed the panel.

'Any questions for Mr Maynard?'

Sayers had evidently read his copy of the CV carefully. He kicked off.

'So you're not a high-flier and you didn't go to Cambridge or Oxford?'

'I went to Durham instead.'

'Couldn't get into a good college, eh?'

'Durham was nearest to home. Closer to my parents and family and friends. It ranks with Oxbridge.'

Sayers turned a page.

'Your CV has a few gaping holes in it. Tell us exactly why you left Mitchell's.'

'I had a disagreement with a managing director.'

'My sources tell me they fired you. Norman Newman himself told me that. Is he right?'

'That's the official line. In fact Mitchell's asked me to park stock. It's illegal. I resigned.'

Sayers nodded reluctantly. 'So you hate them? Perhaps hate all US investment banks?'

'I don't. It was a good job.'

'Why didn't you get a job in another investment bank?'

'I don't like the culture. I prefer consultancy and so joined Richemont instead. I still get to see investment banking from the inside but it's not in my face twenty-four hours a day.'

Sayers raised his eyebrows.

'You couldn't find a real job.'

'I have a real job. Otherwise you wouldn't have invited me here today.'

'Ever run a large investment fund?' Jonathon shook his head. Sayers glanced around at the others. 'I rest my case. Next.'

Jonathon wondered whether they were all going to beat him up in a similar fashion. His chances were visibly diminishing. The German banker used her feminine intuition to address more practical issues.

'Do you have commitments at home?'

'I have two young children.'

'And your wife . . . ?'

'Lost a battle with ovarian cancer.'

'I'm sorry. Would you be able to work on this assignment for an indeterminate period of time?'

Jonathon had no immediate answer. He'd have to clear that with Eva. He couldn't say no.

'Maybe. In London?'

'We don't know yet.'

She looked away and made some notes. The Japanese banker was next.

'Why do you think there is a financial crisis?'

'There are no buyers. When there are no buyers, prices fall. When prices fall, buyers disappear, prices fall farther and you get a vicious circle. It's the worst case I have ever seen.'

'How would you address this?'

'Restore confidence.'

'How would you do that?'

'I wouldn't dare tell you your job. Maybe big speeches, maybe intervention, maybe monetary policy changes.'

Lam then took his cue from Cavendish.

'Do you recall how the HKMA fought the speculators in Hong Kong a few years ago?'

Jonathon did.

'You supported the market against speculators and the hedge funds. Rode out the eye of the storm and made some huge profits in the process, if rumour is to be believed.'

Lam sat back contented and smiled over at Sayers, who fumed silently. Cavendish pushed harder.

'Do you think that a similar strategy might work now?'

Jonathon was growing more interested. He paused politely for a moment before he answered.

'This time it's different. It's not Hong Kong, or Tokyo, or London, or Frankfurt, or New York. It's everywhere. It would have to be a massive concerted effort. It would be like swimming against a huge tidal wave. You'd need billions of dollars to have any hope of succeeding. Only a buyer of tremendous size could turn the markets.'

Cavendish leaned closer.

'What if you were that large buyer?'

'I don't have that sort of cash to hand.'

Every member of the panel smiled except Sayers. Jonathon was seeing some of the game plan now. They needed a few ex-dealers to do some dirty work, maybe people who had no vested interest and no current bank employer. He'd be one of many doing some lowly job best suited to a civil servant with no imagination. This sort of grandiose scheme would never work. The wealth of nations was much too important to gamble on a punt in the bond or equity markets. Cavendish posed the final question of the interview.

'Do you know who the five richest people in the world are?' Jonathon was thinking Gates, Dell, Eisner, Forbes, Hughes, Buffet, the Japanese Softbank guy with the unpronounceable surname, the Sultan of Brunei, the Duke of Westminster and the like. 'Jonathon, the five of us here have control of the reserves of the five largest economies of the Western world. You're looking at the richest people in the world.'

He suddenly realised that this was for real. They were contemplating massive global intervention and they had a blank cheque book at the ready. The scary part was that they seemed to want him to sign the cheques.

The five bankers adjourned to the pool in the late afternoon, with various international newspapers sourced by Rosa in town strewn around. Cavendish and Sayers sat alone in a shaded corner on the upper stone level, watching the other three in the small yet adequate pool. Cavendish thought Nakamura looked like a racing whippet in a bathing cap. Sayers thought Engels looked remarkably good in a red one-piece for a woman of forty something. Cavendish saw his stare.

'Forget it, Walt. She's not interested in the male of the species.'

'Maybe. Why aren't you in your pool? Sick of it by now?' he asked Cavendish.

'My parents sent me to a prep school where we swam each morning at seven-thirty a.m., even in winter. Up and down, doing lengths in a vat of chlorine until your eyes felt raw. Character-building, they called it. That was enough for me. This pool here is like many things in life – it's something people expect to find.'

'Much like confidence in the markets?'

Cavendish picked up the bundle of papers, consciously trying to avoid the business review with its shock-horror headlines and bold black ink. Both men knew they were skirting the real issue. Cavendish needed to know more.

'Walt, are you with us on this intervention plan?'

Sayers put down a copy of the *International Herald Tribune*, an idea already formulating in his mind.

'Intervention goes against everything I have said publicly to the press and to the House Banking Committee. I don't think I could sell it back home to the powers that be. I'd be seen as a hypocrite.'

'Walt, if you're not with us on this plan, it won't work. We need the US on board.'

'Too true. We have the billions in reserves. The others have zilch. Maybe we can work something out.'

Cavendish sensed the political animal in Sayers coming to the fore.

'Like what?'

Sayers judged the moment was now right with the others underwater and out of earshot.

'I lost millions in Alpha's collapse.' Cavendish nodded reluctantly. 'How much did you lose, Chuck?'

'Three million or thereabouts. Everything I had, almost. And don't call me Chuck.'

'How's Marjorie these days?' asked Sayers as he steered the conversation in the desired direction.

'I haven't seen her in months. Suits me. The lawyers are dragging it out.'

'Could be expensive. You'll need all the cash you can find, Charles. Pity about Alpha.' Sayers paused, choosing his next words carefully. 'I feel real bad about that. You only invested on my personal recommendation. I thought I could trust Greenbaum! I met him last week in New York.'

'He's a loser. Stay clear of him.'

Sayers swivelled around on his sunlounger and leaned closer.

'Greenbaum has a sure-fire plan to make all our money back.'

'Forget it! I don't throw good money after bad. I wouldn't trust him ever again.'

'I agree, we can lose him, but his plan might work. Poetic justice, wouldn't you say?'

Cavendish put down the recently imported *Sunday Times* review supplement.

'What's his plan?'

'The plan is to pile into the markets just before any intervention and ride the wave.'

Cavendish laughed.

'Greenbaum hasn't a clue when any intervention will happen or what form precisely it will take.'

'No, but we do. Whoever we get to run this operation will know exactly how and when. Let's say, hypothetically speaking, we had that Brit from this morning working for us. We would have oversight responsibility. He'd tell us in advance what he was going to do. We get there first. Easy or what?'

Cavendish eyed Sayers for a lingering moment, holding his hand to his eyes to shield them from the sun.

'That's called frontrunning, Walt.'

'No one will ever know, not even the Brit. It'll be you and me in this together to recoup our losses.'

'We'd be ruined if word leaked out . . .'

'We can deal through some anonymous offshore shelf company or trust.'

'And who would organise that?'

Sayers scratched his head and looked around for inspiration. In vain it seemed.

'I don't know. We need to find someone who needs cash, is prepared to cross the line and knows enough about the markets. Maybe someone who lost money on Alpha too and knows how pissed we feel.' Sayers watched his peer's facial expression, knowing that the proposal was generating momentum. 'We might need some insurance as well.'

'Like what?'

'We'd be too dependent on this one guy, Maynard.

I don't know him as well as you do. I'd need someone else to work with him. To give me some comfort.'

'No. One's enough.'

'I disagree. I'll try to find someone else we can use. Hey, we don't need to decide everything now. Just tell me you'll consider it further?'

'And if I do, you'll support the market intervention plan tonight?'

'Of course. Without the market intervention, nothing else will work.'

Cavendish looked at the busy scene in the pool. 'What about the others?'

'Fuck 'em.'

Jonathon was thinking about global game plans but still had hours to spare before BA's departure for LHR. Fortunately he had the hire car. The sight of Florence, with its Duomo dominating the skyline, stirred something deep inside him. Instead of driving directly to the airport west of the city, he turned off the searing autostrada and headed for the historic centre, fighting the snarled traffic and the lane-hopping Vespas. He found the correct one-way streets and followed the 'P' signs to a three-storey municipal carpark. Looking at his watch, he saw he had two hours maximum.

From memory he walked towards the bridges over the Arno, following hordes of American and Japanese tour parties. Guides with stupid signs and open umbrellas shouted in assorted foreign languages at the elderly slackers. He crossed over using the Ponte Vecchio, fighting both the oncoming tide and others who stood in the narrow confines of the bridge. The pavements to either side were lined with cramped shops selling dazzling gold and flashy jewellery. Everyone looked but few dared to buy.

He took a sharp right along the riverbank and came to the best photo opportunities. He stood and watched loved ones smiling back at husbands and boyfriends, wives and mistresses, with the Ponte as their picture-book backdrop. He gazed at the ochre walls, the canopies and precarious balconies of the most romantic bridge in the world. He thought about the photo in the kitchen at home and imagined Rebecca sitting in the sunshine here and smiling back at his Nikon as he captured her face for eternity.

He walked through the classical façade, along the cobbled pedestrian avenue and past the Uffizi Gallery, where they had spent a long afternoon admiring the Botticellis, the Michelangelos and da Vincis. Rebecca had always had an eye for the finer things in life. They each had their favourites but agreed that *The Birth of Venus* was second only to great sex. Jonathon wasn't going inside today.

He saw La Dispensa, her very favourite shop, entered the small delicatessen devoid of tourists and repeated almost the same order: rainbow-striped pasta, fresh pesto sauce, olive pâté, balsamic vinegar and Parmegiano Reggiano. The hardest decision was what not to buy.

The Piazza della Signoria was somewhere he felt he could spend his entire life and never grow tired of the vista. Heading for the relative sanctuary of the Logie dei Lanzi, with its unrivalled view, he passed the copy of David outside the Palazzo Vecchio, the waterworks of the Neptune fountain and Grand Duke Cosimo standing proud. Gallons of liquid sunshine splashed around in the basins of the stone fountains.

He sat on a stone seat, near enough to the heraldic rampant lions and a writhing statue of the *Rape of the Sabine Women* carved from a single block of flawed marble, yet far enough away from the omnipresent postcard and souvenir vendors. He remembered that Rebecca had bought Christmas gifts of Florentine writing paper with its distinctive swirling design. They were still somewhere at home upstairs in a wardrobe, he remembered, never wrapped, never given, never received but never forgotten.

He crossed the piazza. The open-air Bargello café, named after the nearby sixteenth-century town hall, was unchanged. The attentive staff welcomed him. He thought he recognised one of the elderly waiters in the blue waistcoats from last time. Table for one? He nodded. He sat at the best corner table at the very front and ordered a cold Peroni draught beer, just as he had before.

He remembered their last conversation here, in which she had used her vivid imagination to dream up fanciful life stories for those who passed by. Eccentric Germans in lederhosen. Japanese ladies terrified of the sun damaging their alabaster skins. American couples in loud his-and-hers matching NBA T-shirts. Eastern Europeans in drab stone-washed denim and sneakers.

The locals today were different. Pairs of Florentine lovers with Gucci sunglasses. Kindly fathers with curly grey hair and brown suede shoes. Youths with the latest cut: subtle spikes and a modest amount of gel. Slim girls with snakeskin boots and dramatically made-up eyes. People as beautiful as the churches and edifices that surrounded them daily. The overriding impression was of a population squeezing love and life of everything they had to offer. He wished he could share that emotion.

Florence had been Rebecca's last trip overseas. It was her surprise to him on his thirty-sixth birthday. She'd produced the Alitalia flight tickets and Radisson hotel vouchers out of a Kellogg's cornflakes box over breakfast one Friday morning. He stared at the single empty wrought-iron chair opposite, realising that coming here had been a mistake.

Dinner for the select group of house guests was at 8 p.m. sharp. Most of them held a glass of chilled sparkling Spumante in a thin-stemmed crystal flute. Sayers, who'd arrived last and insisted instead on a Campari and soda, surveyed the outdoor scene.

'I guess this is the Last Supper?'

Moving indoors to the open-plan dining area, Cavendish took his rightful place at the head of the table. First course was traditional antipasto: finely sliced Salame di Cinghiale, marinated green and red peppers, weird varieties of wild mushrooms and softened aubergines, wafer-thin Parma ham and solid chunks of Parmesan cheese. It was complemented by bruschetta, pieces of toasted home-made bread rubbed with garlic and olive oil, and spread with anchovy, tomato and liver paste. Cavendish bided his time. Engles dived in. Lam and Nakamura sampled the food selectively. Sayers took what was left.

'Great feed, Chuck.'

Several musty bottles of an identical red were opened. Sayers clearly wasn't happy.

'Don't we get a choice? Red or white?'

Cavendish barely restrained himself.

'Unfortunately not, Walt. This is all we have tonight.'

Sayers examined a label but found his language skills somewhat limited.

'Is this stuff any good?'

'I pressed it myself four years ago in our winery. It's a Reserva. Our best year.'

The others enjoyed seeing Sayers lapse into bashful silence. Engels nodded approvingly as the oaky red wine slipped down the back of her throat. A subtle peach sorbet with a single mint leaf arrived to cleanse the palate. They wondered how Cavendish had found such a magnificent cook in rural Italy. Rosa should be in a venue with a few Michelin stars. Main course was Bistecca alla Fiorentina: tender steaks on the bone, grilled over an open fire and seasoned with oil and herbs. Cavendish forestalled Sayers's reaction.

'Walt, I know it's not the same as a sixteen-ounce blue rib-eye in Smith & Wollensky's, but give it your best shot, there's a good fellow. Squeeze some lemon juice over it. And before you ask, there are no french fries.'

Sayers acknowledged the advice and looked at his watch.

'Let's get down to business. I fly outta here in a few hours.'

Cavendish held up a hand.

'All in good time.'

Dessert was almost neat alcohol, a communal Tiramisu in a deep liqueur-sodden dish. They finished every last morsel. Cavendish motioned to Rosa, who cleared the table and dispensed the Cantucci, small almond biscuits that they dipped into Vin Santo, a local dessert wine. Afterwards Cavendish folded his napkin neatly, eased his chair back from the table and exhaled.

'I have taken soundings from each of you privately this weekend. We share the same ultimate goal. I believe that the best solution is government intervention in the markets to restore confidence. I therefore propose we immediately organise a rescue fund to be managed by Jonathon Maynard and put significant funds at his disposal. He was the last of the candidates. We will run this fund in a covert manner away from troublesome civil servants and government officials. I propose we take a show of hands now.'

They looked at each other. Cavendish raised his right hand and waited to see who would be next. Engels was quick off the mark. Then Lam. Then Nakamura. Sayers remained still.

'The vote needs to be unanimous, Walt.'

'This guy Maynard, it has to be him? Don't we get a choice of the other candidates?'

'The others believe Maynard has the best experience and credentials.'

More nodding around the table.

'You know Maynard well?'

'I know of him and his prior work, and I know his boss very well. I trust Maynard.'

'You think he'll do what we tell him?'

'I believe so.'

'It's a hell of a risk. Big bucks.' Sayers stared over at Cavendish, recalling their poolside conversation. The eye contact was intense. 'And are we going to make some money out of this?'

'We may dispose of the investments at a higher price and realise a profit,' acknowledged Cavendish.

Sayers stared back and repeated his question in a slow, pronounced drawl.

'I mean, are we going to make some money?'

Cavendish took the hint and nodded.

'We are going to make some money, Walt.'

Sayers slowly raised his right hand and smiled back at his host.

'Good. Then I'm in. Let's make as much as we can, Chuck.'

CHAPTER FIFTEEN

Jonathon's display on the telephone console confirmed that the call was a local 207 central London number. A soft female voice greeted him.

'Pamela speaking, from the Bank of England. The Governor would like to meet you today.'

There was one way to prove this was a genuine call.

'Regarding what?'

'Regarding your visit to Tuscany. Four o'clock would suit the Governor.'

Jonathon was undecided. The assignment was too vague and open ended. He didn't want to be away from Jack and Imogen any more. He wished he hadn't made the short list. This was all happening too fast, events rapidly moving beyond his control. He needed time to think.

'I have another meeting at four.'

'I'm sure you can reschedule it.'

Pamela wasn't budging. He acquiesced.

'Four it is, then. Shall I call around to the Bank?'

'The Governor prefers a more discreet location. He will meet you at Brown's on Albermarle Street. I've booked a corner table in the drawing room in the name of Banks.'

That afternoon, Jonathon walked south towards Piccadilly. He soon caught sight of the distinctive row of international flags hanging over the main entrance to Brown's. A smart top-hatted doorman ushered him into the cosy wood-panelled lounge to the right of the lobby. He was glad to be first. He sat alone near an unplayed grand piano adjacent to a set of eighteenth-century prints of Westminster Bridge and Lambeth Palace yet far enough away from the heat of a wholly unnecessary coal fire which blazed in an open grate.

This was a previously unseen side of London for Jonathon. Afternoon tea was all the rage, evidently. Mature ladies with silver hair sat in huddles of twos and threes on plump gold-braided chairs, all wearing black or navy cashmere, holding teacups in elegant fingers. Shopping bags from nearby New Bond Street lay alongside the tables. Conversation tinkled around the room like spoons on bone china. Curious glances were thrown at the one eligible gentleman in the room. The regulars here knew Jonathon was in uncharted territory. He waited.

'The menu, sir?'

A waiter thrust a card at him. Jonathon balked at the variety available. Scotch smoked salmon, cream cheese, glazed York ham and cucumber, egg and cress bridge finger sandwiches. Freshly baked scones with clotted cream and home-made strawberry preserves. Assorted French pastries. This wasn't afternoon tea, this was an art form. Cavendish arrived and clearly didn't feel the need to apologise for being twenty minutes late.

'Afternoon, Jonathon. I've got thirty minutes before I see the Chancellor.'

He rose to greet his host. More curious glances were thrown at the pair, but there was no sign of recognition from the female of the species. Pamela had made an astute choice. No chance of meeting a City speculator or an FT journalist here in mid-afternoon.

'Great place for a meeting.'

'They know me here. Small tables. Private. Ideal. It's all the rage in London for the fortunate idle rich. Lunch is for two hours. Tea never ends.'

'It seems we're among the famous "ladies who lunch".'

'These are ladies who lunch, charge, plunder, pillage, dine and go back for seconds.'

Cavendish looked tired. No more relaxed Tuscan mood. Here was a man putting in sixteen-hour days and trying to turn market sentiment over afternoon tea. The waiter returned.

'Same pot as usual, Sir Charles? A mixed selection also?'

Cavendish nodded and explained to his guest, 'I always go for the Lapsang Souchong to oil the palate. It's a large-leafed tea from China with a deliciously smoky flavour. You'll like it. You can only truly understand tea if you've had an empire, don't you think?'

Cavendish evidently took his tea as seriously as his Chianti. Jonathon was out of his depth.

'Fine by me.'

The service was impeccable, and soon they had a steaming pot and cups and a four-tiered silver cake stand weighed down with food. Cavendish kicked off.

'We took a vote at the end of the weekend in Tuscany. We will proceed with significant market intervention funded by the central banks and we want you to manage this rescue, Jonathon.'

He had thought about nothing else for the past few days.

'Do I have a choice in the matter?'

'Richemont told me in principle you are always available for any job for the Bank.'

Jonathon thought about life at home and the upcoming birthday party for Imogen.

'I have logistical problems. I need to know the duration of the assignment.'

'No one knows how long this will take. That's the way it is.'

'And where will I be working?'

'I'll decide that this week.'

'London?' he pressed hopefully.

Cavendish looked regretful.

'Unlikely.'

'UK?'

'Also unlikely.'

'Can I ask a few questions first?'

'Like what?'

Jonathon put down his cup and instinctively lowered his voice. 'Surely there's an easier way to spark the markets back into life than investing your reserves. Why don't you and the other central bankers merely announce to the world that you intend to intervene? You don't actually have to do anything. Speaking out will send the right signal and won't cost you a single cent.'

Cavendish put down his teacup.

'That would have an impact in the short term, true. People would think that the bottom of the trough had been reached and that the only way was up. Markets would rise. But if we didn't then invest our cash, the markets would soon know that it was an empty gesture and call our bluff. They would plunge further. We would be seen as liars. No one would ever believe us again. We can't take that chance.'

'I did some research on that HKMA experience in Hong Kong. Why don't you take the same approach and allow civil servants to do the work? Why do you need someone like me to run this rescue?'

This time it was Cavendish who lowered his voice.

'Civil servants spend their lives cocooned from the real world. Most of them have never held a job in the private sector and wouldn't know how to work past five o'clock. They leak like sieves too.'

'Meaning?'

'Lam told me in confidence about the Hong Kong operation. It was meant to be kept a secret within the

HKMA but word spread rapidly. Those Chinese guys are so greedy! The HKMA staff piled into the market before the big investments were made, and so did their family and friends. Even the cleaning staff, canteen cooks and mail clerks joined in. Many of them were fired afterwards. It was an utter abuse of their position. But most importantly no civil servant knows what you do about the markets and the way investment banks and hedge funds think. Believe me, we looked. The people aren't out there.'

'Then why not get an investment banker to run it?'

'I don't trust them – their ultimate loyalty is to their employer. And the guys in the hedge funds are worse. You don't really think we'd entrust this rescue to a chancer like Art Greenbaum, do you?'

'I suppose not.'

'Secrecy is paramount. Only five central bankers and you know exactly what we are about to do. That's why even Richemont can't know. Think what a speculator or a hedge fund would do if they learned when this sort of intervention was to happen. It's a sure thing.'

Cavendish seemed to have an answer to everything. The two men sat in silence, eyeing the last remaining pastry, and both decided to leave it. Only savages devour every last morsel of food. Cavendish called for the bill.

'I don't want to have to tell Richemont that you're having second thoughts, now, do I?'

Jonathon stared into the leaves at the bottom of his cup and found no inspiration there.

'Nope,' he admitted glumly, knowing that he was trapped.

Cavendish smiled.

'I knew you were the right man for the job.'

'When do I start?'

'Next Monday. I'll be in touch later this week. And remember, tell absolutely no one.'

Cavendish settled the bill with an élite Bank of England Visa credit card. Forty-two pounds. An expensive tea for two but a small enough price to save the world from financial collapse.

Lauren wasted two days making telephone calls. She tried the big Street names first. Some of her calls didn't get past the switchboard. Others went unreturned. Some said they were firing heads, not hiring. A few were polite enough to confirm that they had a recruitment freeze in place. She discarded the top-tier names, acknowledging that she'd take any job with anyone in the industry.

She called some old contacts at Mitchell's. Some of the conversations were amiable, and one even led to a next-day appointment with a Head of Institutional Sales. Half an hour later, however, Lauren got a call from a woman in the human resources department to advise her that she was on a company hire blacklist and the interview wasn't going to happen. Worth a try anyway, Lauren responded. HR didn't seem amused.

She sat at home alone and repeatedly scrolled down the contacts in her Palm Pilot. She recognised some names from the client list at the FF&O desk, then saw Scott Chapman's name. She made to delete it, then decided that she might need it some time, and so left it intact. Her list was arranged in alphabetical order. Alpha was top, one of the many reasons that Greenbaum had so named his start-up venture.

The name under Alpha was Greenbaum's own. She'd met him once before in New York and once in Hong Kong last year. She wondered whether she dared call him. Greenbaum wasn't hiring but he was well connected and might put the word out on the Street. Every avenue had to be explored. The worst he could do was tell her to get lost and hang up on her. Nothing to lose but her pride, and she was long past caring about that. She called his direct 212 area code work number. The phone went on call-forward.

'Hello.'

'Mr Greenbaum?'

'Mr Greenbaum no longer works here. This is Joshua Markus from the SEC. May I help you?'

'It's okay. I'll get him at home.'

Lauren took a NYNEX directory and looked through the few Greenbaums listed. She found an Arthur with a good address off Fifth, the sort of place where a fallen player like Greenbaum might hang out. She dialled, then put the handset down and inwardly debated. It wasn't far. Probably better to turn up in person and make a real impact. All he could do was slam the door on her. She checked her make-up, put on a better suit from her still largely unpacked suitcases and took a cab for ten blocks. The doorman stopped her.

'I'm here to see Mr Greenbaum.' She gave her name.

He wrote her into a visitors' book and dialled upstairs. 'I got a visitor here, a Lauren Trent.'

'Never heard of her. Is she media? Is this a ruse?'

Lauren grabbed the handset before he could hang up.

'I'm not media. You remember me. I worked for Mitchell's on the Hong Kong FF&O desk.'

A pause while the inhabitant above deliberated.

'Jeez, that Lauren?'

'Can I come up, Mr Greenbaum?'

'Yeah, I guess. Fifth floor.'

She rode the elevator and greeted Greenbaum in the hall. He looked much older than last time. She was about to go into her sales pitch mode but Greenbaum had other ideas. He half blocked the door.

'You've got some nerve coming here. You took those fucking orders from Chapman. Why didn't you warn me about the size of them? Guess you wanted the commission, huh?'

As a potential job interview, this was not promising. He didn't actually invite her in but there was space to squeeze past him, and she did.

'I'd no idea what Chapman was doing. Did you? I doubt it. He duped us all for too long.'

The living room was huge and museum-like. Greenbaum clearly wasn't down on his luck entirely.

'Nice home,' she said, glancing around and taking

in the Old Master canvases, priceless rugs and French Empire furniture.

'You can compliment my wife when she gets back from the nail place. She owns all this now.'

Lauren sat down. Greenbaum stood over her as if she might do something rash at any minute.

'So what do you want?' he asked, narrowing his eyes. She had the look of desperation. He knew the signs.

'I won't waste your time, I'm sure you're a busy man . . .'

He laughed hollowly. 'Me? Sure I am. I'm wearing my ass to the bone sitting around here all day.'

'Me too.'

'What are you doing back here anyway? What happened at Mitchell's?'

'They let a few of us go. Cutbacks after the slump in business.'

'Guess you were at the top of the queue after Alpha. That guy McFarland glad to see you go?'

'Whatever. I'm back in town and looking for a new job in the business. IBK. M&A. Futures. Sales. Do you know of any job opportunities in New York?'

He looked like a shark when he smiled. She had never seen the resemblance before.

'If I did, I'd take them myself.'

Lauren was beginning to wish she had stayed uptown. She persevered, noting that no offer of hospitality was forthcoming.

'What about you, Art? You're not a worker. You're an

entrepreneur, an organiser, a major player. What's next up for you?'

'Maybe start a new fund, to invest in recovery stocks. The recovery will come, it's just a matter of time.'

'Do you need someone to work with you? I'm desperate.'

'Evidently. This venture will take a while to get off the ground. I ain't hiring yet.'

'You think a recovery will come?'

'Sure. Even Sayers is convinced.'

So Lauren had been right all along. Greenbaum was still well connected.

'You know Walter Sayers?'

Greenbaum enjoyed flexing his financial muscle.

'Had dinner with him last week. He and I go back a long way on the Street.'

She produced a few sheets of paper and stood up to leave.

'Here're a few copies of my CV. Put the word out for me. Maybe you can tell people like Sayers.'

'Sure. I'll tell Walter Sayers next time I see him. I'm sure he could do with a good laugh. He don't get many laughs these days.'

'I'm staying at my folks' place. Thanks.'

Greenbaum held the pages limply and looked her over from head to toe.

'Listen, sweetheart, no one's going hire you, no matter how good you look. Not once they know you were on the other end of the line with Chapman. Forget about a career in finance, Lauren. Maybe try the Mark up the street. They always need waiting staff. Good hourly rate, tips as well maybe. With your rep, that's all you're good for. See ya.'

Olivier Richemont rose from his sunlounger, picked up the mobile and dialled a direct telephone line that was known to only a select few. He was, after all, a personal acquaintance and golf buddy.

'Can you talk, Charles?'

Cavendish glanced at an antique wall clock that had ticked away the centuries.

'I've got ten minutes before a briefing.' He heard a distant splash of water. 'Where are you?'

'I'm back in Nerja by the pool. You and Pamela had a good time here?'

'Sure did. And the fewer who know about it the better.'

'Are you coming out for some more golf soon?' Despite his best efforts, Richemont had won their last game by four and three. Cavendish had lost three balls.

'Not for a while. Got to work.' More splashes audible on the line. 'Is Carla there with you?'

Richemont watched her come up for air. Her thrusting breaststroke was awesome to see.

'Work first, pleasure later. Listen, I have a problem. I spoke with Maynard today. He says the Bank's assignment is ready to roll, but I don't know the mandate or what the fee is.'

'No problem. The mandate is to work directly for me. The fee will be Maynard's daily charge-out rate plus expenses. Get your PA in Geneva to fax something very brief to me today and I'll sign it.'

Richemont was having trouble concentrating. He turned away from the view.

'But I need to know the nature of the assignment.'

'You don't need to know. Only Maynard does. I told him to keep it that way.'

'But how can I judge whether the assignment is a success or not?'

'If it isn't a success, you'll be the first to hear about it,' advised Cavendish.

'You'll never keep this confidential.'

'I'm doing rather well so far. There are very few who know about this and I plan to keep it that way. I've got five minutes left. Is that it? You're really on holiday while the rest of us work?' There was a pause and a crackle on the line. More splashing sounds as Carla cavorted in the pool. Richemont sighed.

'I'm here merely avoiding the Mitchell's bankers in Geneva. Did you lose much in the Alpha collapse?'

'We all did. You, me, Walter Sayers, Art Greenbaum. My heart bleeds for him.'

'I lost millions and I'm losing more each day on falling stocks and bonds. Those fucking leeches at Mitchell Leonberg Suisse are bleeding me dry. They want me to pay back some loans immediately. It's bizarre. I find I'm completely illiquid. I need help.'

'Are you asking me for a loan?'

'I have plenty of those already. No, I merely want you to exercise some influence on my behalf. Everything was fine at Mitchell's under my previous account manager. Now they've sent some over-eager young hotshot from the States and he's a problem.'

'So you want him eliminated?'

Cavendish laughed. Richemont took the question as a serious proposal.

'If it were easy as that, I'd get Max on to it tonight. No, I need someone senior in Mitchell's to lean on this Geneva guy and get him to back off. You know Norman Newman from meetings and the like?'

'You know him too.'

'Yeah, but I need his business. I can't go to him. But you could call him.'

Cavendish had a few minutes left. His door opened and Pamela demanded his undivided attention.

'I could call Newman, but I won't abuse that relationship. I suggest you find some other way to make the millions Mitchell's need. Let me know when you get an answer. I could do with making some money myself.'

Richemont was growing impatient. He hadn't spent years cultivating a stuffed shirt like Cavendish purely for the pleasure of his rather dry company. There had to be a means to an end.

'We both know that the best way to make some money is in the markets. Is it a buy yet? Is something about to happen? Is Maynard involved? Will my investments recover? Can you and I make a profit here?'

Pamela waved again from the door.

'Olivier, I've said too much. I have to go.'

'You know a hell of a lot more, Charles. Just tell me!

Tell me when it's going to happen. I need to know. Don't hang up ... we can work something out.'

But Cavendish was gone. Something big was obviously in the offing and there was only one other person who might know the details. Richemont had the required leverage to extract that information. He shouted into the shaded hallway of the sun-drenched villa. A bulky outline emerged immediately, still clad in a warm woollen suit.

'Max, call the London office. Tell them I want to see Jonathon Maynard here in person tomorrow.'

Sayers got the call on his direct line late at the Fed one evening. They told him they were in New York and had to meet. He said he'd be in Manhattan on business the next day. They asked for the name of his hotel. He had no choice. They still held the originals and the negatives. All the cards.

He'd assembled the cash with difficulty. Sold some NYSE stocks at knock-down prices, stock that he had been holding in an on-line account his wife never knew about. He also cleaned out a savings account he had used for his children's education over the years. Just scraped a hundred K together.

Their word-processed unsigned note was folded under his hotel room door in the early evening, giving explicit instructions for a few hours later. Go to Cortland Street subway station. Stand on the northbound platform near the vending machine. Be there at 11 p.m. and wait. Bring the cash in a McDonald's paper bag. Come alone. No calls to anyone. Nothing smart.

Sayers walked into the late night McDonald's branch off Broadway shortly after ten. He ordered a coffee and doughnut. The doe-eyed girl handed him his food on a tray. He belatedly said it was to take away. She glared at him and put it in a brown paper bag. He sat down alone near the door in full view, stared her down, drank half the coffee, threw away the stale doughnut and folded the bag into his pocket. He went into the washroom, passing some homeless guy on his way out, chose the first disgusting cubicle, undid the belt of his trousers, produced the cash from a money belt and placed it inside the bag.

He pushed past the subway turnstiles ten minutes before the appointed hour. The heat below ground was intense, the air clammy. The dirty platform was almost deserted. At the far end a couple of hostile-looking lanky youths in basketball gear hung out. Sayers wondered whether they were part of the set-up. He felt the breeze of an oncoming train, then saw the dot of light become a beam. He wondered whether this was his train. A number three train arrived at five minutes to the hour. The youths bounded on board and steamed their way down to the next car. He moved nearer the only vending machine.

A black girl with dyed blond hair and clumpy trainers stood alone at the other end of the platform, more interested in a muted conversation on her cellphone than in watching the chairman of the Federal Reserve Board pay off a couple of divinely directed pimps. Sayers heard the distant scream down the tunnels, saw the piercing lights of another train drawing closer. He momentarily enjoyed the rush of stale air against his face, the dust and grime commingling with the beads of sweat on his forehead. It took some minutes for the lights on the tiled walls to catch up with the screaming sound of metal on metal. The paper bag felt heavy and damp in his hands.

The fourth car stopped exactly where it always did. Sayers saw them standing by the door, the same men, in bow ties. The self-styled Brothers of Righteousness. The body-builder put his oversized shoes to either side of the open door. The other guy jumped off, holding an open cellphone in his hand.

'Penance time. You got it?'

Sayers held the bag out. The doors moved to close, then jammed halfway.

'It's all in there.'

The Brother took the bag, looked inside and grinned through his gold fillings.

'Allah thanks you.'

'You got the photos?'

'Next time we want two hundred. You got a month. We'll be in touch.'

'Wait! . . . That's not what you fucking said . . .'

'No blasphemy, please.'

The Brother jumped back on board. The feet were removed and the door slid closed. The train moved off into the tunnel, more raw metal on metal. Sayers watched the two men smile and make off to his left towards the rear of the train. He looked in desperation down the platform for some sort of assistance. There was no one to help. Even the girl with the cellphone had at last boarded a train. He couldn't deliver any more cash. That hundred K was a one-off. He had no more assets to liquidate. He'd be publicly ruined.

The lights and windows flashed past Sayers. He saw the girl walking through the cars towards the Brothers with the cash. He made eye contact and watched her stare back. He thought he recognised her from somewhere. She closed her cellphone, placed her left hand on her head and yanked off a blond wig. Then leaned against the glass of the empty carriage, ran her hand down to pull up her T-shirt, slowly fingered her left nipple. He recognised her then. Alicia, his former squeeze, honey-trap *par excellence* for the blackmailing Brothers of Righteousness, smiled back.

CHAPTER SIXTEEN

MALAGA AIRPORT, SPAIN – 12.20 P.M.

Jonathon was unimpressed with the short notice but couldn't ignore the summons. He'd be there and back in a day, so told Jack and Imogen he was going to the office but flew BA to Malaga. He eschewed a Seat Marbella at the Avis desk, it being the sort of car you needed a tin-opener to get into. Instead he hired a red Seat Ibiza cabriolet, heading north-east towards Motril along the Highway of Death.

One hour later Nerja hove into view after a suicidal hairpin bend. He had expected a Costa del Nightmare with banks of high-rise hotels left over from the 1970s. Instead he found a small historic town straggling along the coast off to his right. A single church spire and a few trees indicated the location of the old town square. Up on the hillside to his left were tasteful villa developments, all optimally arranged to catch el Sol. Jonathon guessed a player like Richemont would reside here, and hung a left.

The map faxed to Nikki was useless. It took an eternity to find the villa. Jonathon sought help from two locals using his pidgin Spanish. They eventually showed him the exclusive Calle de los Habiscos, evidently so named after the abundance of lush plants that hung down from the whitewashed walls and terraces. Otherwise known as Millionaires' Row, in Jonathon's humble opinion. Number seven was at the very end of the road behind imposing wooden gates. Richemont clearly liked his privacy. Jonathon rang the bell tentatively, knowing just enough Spanish to be able to decipher a Beware of the Dog sign. An elderly maid in a starched uniform answered his call immediately and led him through the cool whitewashed rooms of the villa.

'*Hola.* Señor Richemont is expecting you.'

He walked through the silent house, wondering whether anyone else was staying here. Richemont stood up courteously.

'Please sit down, Jon.'

They sat in the shade. Richemont poured him a glass of iced tea with lemon. Jonathon was beginning to see how his consultancy fees were spent.

'Nice home.'

'It's not home, that's in Geneva. This is called a change of scenery.'

If this was Richemont's holiday home then his permanent residence must be a palace. Richemont sipped his drink and looked out over the still water of the azure pool. He was about to speak when a patio door opened behind them. A girl in a white towelling robe ambled towards them, so drop-dead beautiful she looked as if she had just stepped out of a double-page spread in *Vogue*.

'I didn't know we had visitors today, Olivier,' she observed.

'Carla, I thought you were taking a siesta. I told you stay inside, remember.'

'It's too hot. I need to swim,' she answered. Jonathon deduced she was at most twenty. She had almond-shaped eyes and a perfect complexion. Her bronzed skin confirmed that she too was a dedicated sunworshipper. She had a distinctly Italian accent. It worked for him.

Richemont felt the need to explain her presence.

'This is Carla, a friend of the family. She likes the sun.'

Jonathon shook hands with her. Family friend indeed. Unfortunately Richemont dismissed her.

'We're talking business here. Have your swim and leave us in peace.'

Carla gathered up her long black hair and dropped her robe at the poolside to reveal long arms, undulating yet accentuated curves and exquisite exposed shoulders. Her one-piece swimsuit might have been painted on to her, possibly at birth. She ran her fingers along the inside of the crotch, stretched her square shoulders back in an arch, looked around once at Richemont, knowing he liked to watch, and then slipped into the water. Jonathon broke the lingering silence in error.

'Is your wife here also?'

Richemont stared at him. Jonathon wished the ground would open up.

'She doesn't like the sun. She's in Geneva.'

The two men watched Carla do the breaststroke. Jonathon thought he could be watching a former Eastern Bloc swimming champion. Richemont was some lucky bastard. The men waited until the fourth length. Carla's style remained flawless. Richemont turned at last to the matter in hand.

'You know why I asked you over here?'

'It was more of an instruction than a request. Wouldn't a phone call have sufficed?'

He wondered how his boss would react to such plain speaking. Richemont appeared unruffled by it.

'This had to be done in person. You are about to start another lucrative Bank assignment. I want to know what that is.'

'You'd better call Cavendish.'

'I tried yesterday. He won't tell me. You must.'

Jonathon shifted uneasily.

'I can't. The Governor made it a condition.'

Richemont rocked forward in his chair.

'I'm your boss. I run this firm.'

'Cavendish explicitly told me to tell no one. He mentioned you specifically.'

'Did he? Then it has to be something to do with the global markets. He can't be working on anything else right now.' Jonathon said nothing. Richemont was growing visibly excited. 'Jesus, tell me!'

Jonathon debated his choices. Maybe he should tell Richemont about the rescue, let word trickle back to Cavendish, watch the assignment die a death and avoid weeks spent working on this somewhere godforsaken.

But he'd stood by his principles before and he'd do so again.

'If I do then the whole assignment is off. The fee income will be forfeited, and you don't want that.'

'I didn't ask you all the way out here to be dismissed like some trainee. Tell me or else . . .'

'Or else what? What can you do? Fire me? Then lose the assignment.' Jonathon felt the need to defend himself. 'You know the Governor better than I do. Ask him again.'

Carla had finished her lengths. She swam to the edge of the pool beside them, placed two tanned arms on the tiles and hauled herself out of the water.

Richemont gave up. 'It's absurd. I run the company yet I don't know what my own staff are doing.' Neither of the two gentlemen moved to help Carla. Chlorinated water ran down her black one-piece in glittering rivulets. She bent to pick up a towel. Richemont wasn't finished. He tried a different approach.

'If you need any help then let me know Jon.'

Carla undid her hair and ran her hands through the dripping strands. It was like something out of a Bond flick or a Cosmo mag, thought Jonathon. She spoke to him, delivering a long, lingering look with her big brown eyes.

''Bye, Jon.'

He'd love to have stayed but Richemont's body language forbade it and he had a return flight to catch in less than two hours. He rose to leave. Richemont said nothing further but sulked behind a newspaper. Jonathon wondered whether he should have yielded as the maid reappeared on cue to lead him outside. As soon as he had gone, Richemont moved over to Carla, removed the towel and slid his hand inside her swimsuit.

'You fancy that guy?'

'Who wouldn't?'

'You think he fancies you?'

'Who wouldn't?'

He moved closer and found the object of his desire. She gasped and stood, her legs farther apart.

'I have a job for you, Carla. There's some cash in it too.'

'What do you want me do?'

'Get some information out of that guy. Any way you know how. Fuck him if you have to.'

Charles Cavendish's special adviser entered his office exactly on cue and sat down opposite him.

'Governor, here's my paper on the various options.'

His adviser was forever preparing papers on selected esoteric topics. Such were the fruits of a fine education, assorted research jobs in the Fiscal Studies Institute and the CBI, followed by rapid internal promotion within the Bank. Cavendish had chosen well.

'I have fifteen minutes maximum before a conference call with the PM on the worsening international crisis. Time is money, as you and I both know. Maximum confidentiality too.'

His adviser took the cue, walked to the door and turned the lock. They retired to the couch in the corner and sat close together. His adviser crossed her legs and performed a perfect introduction.

'You asked me to identify the optimal offshore tax-advantageous investment-friendly location in which to base a special-purpose vehicle company.' His adviser liked to use adjectives and hyphens. 'It would help if I knew exactly what type of investment was being proposed.'

'Let me worry about that. So what are the best tax havens in the world?'

His adviser glanced down at the papers in hand.

'We want to avoid anywhere on the OECD blacklist. Aruba, Belize, Liberia, Liechtenstein, Maldives, Montserrat, Panama, Turks and Caicos and Vanuatu.' Cavendish nodded. 'The first possible location for an offshore SPV is the Isle of Man. Top personal tax rate of fifteen per cent and no capital taxes at all. Good established banking infrastructure. English mother tongue.'

Cavendish grimaced visibly. He had been to Douglas on some regulatory banking conference junket a few years ago out of season. Had thought the island looked like Clacton on a bad day in the mid-sixties. He wasn't sure about the mother tongue either. He had needed an interpreter in the hotel lobby. The only social event taking place at the time was a talk on fossils and dinosaurs by some aged BBC B-list personality.

'Any other advantages in locating a Special Purpose Vehicle there?'

'It has some of the best motorcycle road racing in the world.'

'How exciting. It's too near London. I need somewhere farther afield. Next.'

'There are the Channel Islands, Governor. Jersey,

Guernsey, Alderney, Sark and a few others. Personal tax rate goes up to twenty per cent, though. No capital gains tax. Lots of offshore SPVs.'

Cavendish was worried. There were too many regulatory authorities in the Channel Islands monitoring banking and finance. He didn't need others delving into these particular SPVs.

'I'm still not convinced. Any other advantages?'

'Jersey has the sunniest climate in the British Isles . . .'

'That's not saying much. Next.'

The papers were shuffled in her hand. Cavendish eyed her wonderful form.

'There's our little bit of Spain we're still hanging on to: Gibraltar. No capital gains taxes. Many British banks there. Only the one scandal with Barlow Clowes. Easy access from the UK via the Costa del Sol.'

Cavendish was thinking of one person he knew with a nearby residence.

'One scandal is one too many. We don't need to follow those criminals to the sun. Anything else I should know about it? And I don't mean the apes on the Rock.'

'There are excellent golf courses in nearby Spain.'

His adviser saw his reaction. What was the Governor's objective here? Was it tax efficiency or eighteen holes in some exotic location?

'Next.'

'Barbados. No capital gains tax. Income tax top rate of forty per cent. Lots of reliable Canadian banks in Bridgetown. Lots of hungry lawyers looking for fees. Great climate. English and Bajan spoken widely. Only downside is that the occasional hurricane passes close by.'

No reaction from the Governor.

'Excellent cricket too. Plenty of West Indies Test matches against visiting teams.'

Cavendish leaned forward. His adviser was pressing all the right buttons as usual.

'We're getting closer to the optimal location, I think.'

His adviser came to the penultimate page.

'How about a radical choice, Governor? Somewhere where there are no taxes whatsoever.'

'Does such a place exist?'

'I'm talking about the Cook Islands in the Pacific Ocean.'

Cavendish wasn't convinced. He sat back and shrugged his shoulders.

'We can't use the place if we don't even know where it is on a map. I've heard stories. Flights there are bloody impossible. They don't use a timetable, they use a calendar. You might be hard pressed to find a flight this side of Christmas. Too remote. What else?'

'I've saved the best till last.'

He hoped so.

'How about somewhere between the UK and the US? No income, capital gains, transfer, wealth or gift taxes. The third-highest living standard on earth per the OECD. There is a well-established English legal and banking system. English mother tongue too. A year-round semi-tropical climate. Daily BA flights from London Gatwick.' She paused. 'Bermuda, Governor.'

Cavendish was almost salivating, thinking of moving there himself on a permanent basis.

'Sounds perfect. Any downside?'

'Too many celebrities perhaps. A Hollywood star owns one of the biggest hotels. NBA pros and former US presidents play golf, although not at the same time. Pop stars and tennis tour pros have holiday homes. Former Conservative party leaders stay at the Cambridge Beach Hotel in Somerset. The pink sands are decorated with gorgeous unattached women per my sources, since Bermuda is the air stewardesses' favourite destination. The island is also widely regarded by ageing millionaires as the best source of trophy wives, and vice versa. Romantic weddings and honeymoons can be booked in a matter of days at the Coral Beach Club but apparently divorces take a little longer.'

Cavendish resisted the implied hint at his own personal circumstances.

'So privacy could be a problem. Are there paparazzi everywhere?'

'I checked. There are only two resident photographers on the island. If anyone else shows up with a motorised camera and zoom lens, you call the Governor and he sends round a bobby in shorts on a bicycle and the issue is resolved. Snappers have been taken to the airport and deported for working without a permit. Trust me, this is the one place you will never see in the *Sun*.'

It was perfect. Cavendish was already thinking of the full ramifications.

'Do you know the size of Bermuda?'

His adviser didn't even need to consult her file.

'It's about two miles across and ten miles long. Claustrophobic, I'd say.'

'How many daily flights are there from the airport?'

'Four to New York and Canada. One to London. That's all. Tiny airport too.'

He was more convinced than ever.

'What about getting there by boat?'

'Some American cruise liners dock there. It's too far to make it to land by small craft.'

Perfect for his needs. He took one last admiring look at his adviser as she uncrossed her legs.

'Let's go there. We'll need twenty locally incorporated shell companies in Hamilton. Call the Governor of the Bank of Bermuda and get him to recommend a law firm there. Use some off-the-shelf company names that have no connection to us.'

'Might I ask what this is all about?'

'Unfortunately, no.'

'What's the time line?'

'I need this done by the end of the week.'

'Consider it done, Governor.'

She rose to leave, straightening her skirt and glancing at her reflection in the glass of the antique clock.

'See you tomorrow evening, Pamela. My place this time?'

'Most definitely, Governor.'

Lauren retrieved Scott Chapman's residential number from her Palm Pilot and called ahead. She took a yellow cab downtown at midday and stopped near Hudson

Tower. There was a short delay as she stood facing an anonymous CCTV security camera. She wondered whether perhaps Kim was having second thoughts. Finally the lobby door buzzed as required. She rode the elevator to twenty-eight. The door to apartment 2802 was already half ajar. Kim wore holed black leggings which had seen better days and a tired grey Russell Athletic sweatshirt. Her hair was uncombed and unwashed. She held out her hand.

'Hi, I'm Kim.'

They sat uncomfortably together on a sofa.

'I used to call here from Hong Kong,' observed Lauren, looking around.

'I remember. When Scott was here.'

Kim fell silent. The living room looked as if burglars had just departed. A PC glowed on a chaotic corner desk. The windows were closed, the air stale. The cream curtains were drawn unnecessarily, shielding them from a view of the river and the New Jersey side.

'Why did you want to come by?' enquired Kim.

'I felt I had to. To wrap up the loose ends.' Lauren paused, looking for the right words. 'To express my condolences. Say how sorry I am about Scott.'

'Thanks.' Kim was also looking for words. 'What are you doing back in New York?'

'Leave of absence from work. You okay?'

Another silence. Coming here had been a bad idea. Lauren wondered about leaving.

'You wanna coffee?'

Definitely an invitation to stay a while.

'Sure.'

Kim left for the kitchen. Lauren was irresistibly drawn to the window. She tried the door to the outside world and it eased open to her touch. She stepped out on to the balcony and felt the heat and the soft breeze of NYC. She held the metal handrail and suddenly realised where she was. Scott had stood here on his very last day. She looked downward, leaned out a bit farther and thought she recognised the clump of bushes below from photos she had seen on the CNBC screen weeks ago in Hong Kong.

'Don't do that! Come back inside.'

Her hostess had almost dropped two mugs of coffee. Lauren stepped back and closed the door.

'What's wrong?'

The mugs were slammed down on a low table.

'No one goes out there again. Not me, not anyone. Not after what happened.'

'You should lock the door.'

'We don't have a key. I don't have a key. We lost it. Scott said no one would get in on the twenty-eighth floor. He said no harm would ever come to us up here. Those were his very words.'

They sat back down and struggled to drink the steaming coffee.

'Good coffee, Kim.'

'Never as good as Starbucks on the next block. I'd go downstairs for one but I haven't the energy. I want to stay inside. What's the point of going out any more? Scott's gone. Did you know him well?'

'We met a few times. I guess we spoke a lot too.'

A pause as they realised this was dangerous territory. Kim broke the ice.

'I never understood exactly what he did.'

'I used to think I did.'

'I read in the press about his trading. They say he was a criminal.'

Lauren hadn't read the New York press recently, except for the 'help wanted' columns, but she knew that Kim needed reassurance, however phoney.

'He was as honest as the rest of us.'

'The press says that he was the one who caused this financial turmoil. I can't believe it. You ever have anyone you loved, who changed so much that you just wondered if you ever knew the real person inside?'

Lauren recalled growing up.

'It happens.'

'I haven't spoken about this to anyone else.'

'It's always better to talk.'

Kim put down the mug and ran a finger under her eyes. Tears were welling up.

'These past few weeks have been hell. I was a prisoner here for days with all those journalists camped downstairs. I even had the newscopters hovering out front, trying to zoom into my living room. It got so bad I escaped to my parents out west for a few weeks. I gave up doing my yoga classes at the club. I even put on a few pounds. First time ever. I only came back here last weekend.'

Lauren cast a polite look at the discarded clothes, the remnants of takeaways and TV listings magazines.

'It's a nice apartment.'

'I'm going to sell it. It holds such bad memories. I just came here to get Scott's things. It's all I have of him now.' She fingered her sweatshirt. 'This is his. He wore it when we last went jogging together along the Battery. I can still smell him from it. I'll never wash it. Never.'

'I understand.'

'Maybe you do.'

Lauren looked around, unsure of Kim's receptivity, and spied a photo of the couple on the side table.

'Scott was a good-looking guy. That's a nice photo.'

'It's my favourite. We were on vacation in Mexico a few years ago. He was happier then.' Kim pointed at the desk. 'You know why I have that PC on all the time?'

Lauren looked over. Netscape was open and some basic website was up on screen. She made a guess.

'For e-mails?'

'So I can look at our photos. My parents live in California so we didn't get to see them much. Scott did what all the Wall Street types are doing these days. He built his own website called kimandscott.com. He put digital pics up on the site so my folks could see us together.'

Lauren walked over to the PC. Kim followed her, picked up the mouse and scrolled down the screen.

'That's us on vacation in Europe. We did Paris on a long July fourth weekend. Had to rush back, I remember, as Scott had to be at work on Tuesday. That's our engagement party in the Hamptons. That's us on the beach on Long Island . . .'

Lauren looked at the photographs of happier times, lingering to show Kim she was genuinely interested.

'Scott did all this work himself?'

'He didn't trust anyone else. He used some software package.' Kim pointed at a discarded box called FrontPage and some old disks. She clicked on the top right-hand corner icon and closed the screen. 'Scott was a clever guy. He could do anything. Except survive.'

Lauren left after another hour of meaningful yet guarded conversation. Kim stood by the door.

'Thanks for coming by. You seem to understand. Maybe you could call again?'

Cavendish left a voice mail for Pamela to say he was ill. The taxi collected him from the Barbican at 6.45 a.m. The City roads were utterly deserted. He arrived at City Airport in Docklands half an hour later. He checked in at the Crossair Executive desk in the tiny yet efficient departures area on the ground floor. Flight CR 841 left on schedule at 7.55 a.m. There were few delays at such a small airport.

He sat in seat IA, as was his custom, and pondered what they were about to do. Sayers had sown the seeds of the idea by the pool in Tuscany. They both had to make some money fast. His own divorce was only a matter of time. Sayers hadn't said why he was so desperate for cash but Alpha had patently ruined them both. They needed a plan and someone to carry out that plan on their behalf. The phone call from Nerja had revealed that there was such a person, who was also under financial pressure and was well connected. Their Alpha investments could be recouped.

The landing ninety minutes later was bad but he'd endured worse. His taxi hogged the fast lane and sped along the banks of Lac Leman, set against the impressive backdrop of the Alps and Jura mountains. Cavendish knew they were drawing near when he spied the impressive Jet d'Eau, 500 litres of water per second thrust 140 metres into the air by incessantly labouring hydraulic pumps. They headed towards the right bank of the lake, with its luxury hotels and commercial heart. The city centre was chic and compact, criss-crossed by bridges and bustling tramlines. It was clean, precise, organised and reliable. Everything he expected of Geneva.

The Hotel du Rhone was unchanged from his one prior visit for a World Bank economic gathering. The lobby was quiet, refined, elegant and discreet, qualities one would expect of any five-star place with a prominent Leading Hotels of the World brass plate outside. It was preferable to meeting in the Richemont office. This was unofficial business after all. As he waited, Cavendish read more depressing market news in the IHT. The NYSE had closed early yesterday when the circuit breakers kicked in.

At 11 a.m. the doorman rushed to the revolving doors at the lobby entrance. He nodded in deference to the more regular guest at this clandestine meeting. Richemont strode up to Cavendish, followed by the usual brute in a suit. He wore a navy K-Swiss tracksuit and gleaming white Nikes. Had casual day gone that far in Geneva? Cavendish let it pass without comment.

'What's the plan? Do you have a meeting room booked here?'

Richemont shook his head.

'I come here at this time every week. Follow me.'

They strode past the ground-floor designer boutiques and empty brasserie, up a staircase and through a set of oak double doors marked 'Members and Residents Only', to end up by the front desk of a plush leisure club. Cavendish had found the stairs an effort. He was puffing.

'Looks like you could do with some exercise other than a round of golf. How about a swim?' asked Richemont. Cavendish hesitated. Richemont saw it. 'You can swim, Charles, can't you?'

He had to bluff it out.

'Love it. Did a lot of it at school.' He sucked in his stomach. 'I didn't pack my kit, though.'

Richemont nodded to the male attendant seated behind the counter.

'A spare pair of trunks for my guest. Large, please.'

A lurid pair of swimming trunks was instantly produced. The two disrobed in the changing room, with its cold, wet floor tiles. Richemont revealed a lean, fit body with a six-pack stomach that belied his age, while Cavendish avoided looking in the wall mirrors. He remained unconvinced about swimming.

'We can't discuss this in the pool. What if someone overhears us?'

'They won't. It's empty.'

They walked through to the twenty-five-metre pool, which was indeed devoid of other swimmers.

'What if other guests arrive?'

'The pool is closed. Maintenance, officially. I called the manager an hour ago. He knows me well.'

'I'd be unhappy about that if I were another guest.'

'Who cares? Fuck them. Survival of the fittest, I say.'

Richemont walked past the Jacuzzi and hot tub to the deep end. His tanned body silhouetted against the brilliant white tiles, he made a perfect dive, hardly disturbing the still water, and reappeared way down at the far end. Cavendish walked gingerly to the shallow end, clambered down the metal rungs and bellied in, causing a minor tidal wave. He watched Richemont do ten or more effortless lengths, hardly coming up for air at all. Cavendish needed an excuse for standing about doing nothing.

'What's the latest, Olivier?' he shouted.

Richemont came to a sudden halt. 'You tell me.'

'We have the approval of the central bank boards. Offshore shell companies have been formed, trading accounts have been opened. The bank lines are in place. Maynard flies out at the weekend.'

The two set off in tandem in a slow front crawl. At the side of the pool, Richemont ran his hands through his wet hair.

'This is a gem of plan. As long as I know in advance what Maynard intends to do, and the information is passed to me, then I'm certain I can invest ahead of him and make good profits for us. But the central bank intervention must work. Will it?'

'Who knows? I hope so. It's a hell of a gamble. What if it goes wrong? What if you forgot something?'

Richemont swivelled round in the water in one smooth movement.

'Charles, do you think I'm out of my depth?'

'Of course not.'

Richemont stood up.

'You're quite right. It's only a metre deep here.'

'We'll be ruined if someone leaks the details of the plan,' pressed Cavendish.

'If that happens, then Max will drown that person here in this very pool. Who actually knows about our plan?'

'You, me, Sayers. Pamela set the companies up with a local law firm but she doesn't know about our one special trust fund. Not even the lawyer we used knows what that fund is for.'

'What does Sayers think?'

'I'll see him this weekend at the G7 in Tokyo. I'll check then.'

'So we're fine, then. We'll make so much money out of this, there'll be more than enough for all three of us. I'm seeing my banker at Mitchell's tomorrow, then we're ready for next Monday.'

Richemont swam to the other side and made for the changing rooms. Cavendish had other ideas, easing himself out in several clumsy movements. Richemont directed him to a wooden slatted door.

'In here. It's the best place to talk.'

Cavendish felt an enormous blast of heat. The thermometer in the sauna showed 110 degrees on the Tylo dial. They sat on towels. The wood of the seats would have seared them like two chargrilled steaks on a barbecue. Mingled water and perspiration ran down Richemont's chiselled torso.

'What's the problem, Charles?'

Cavendish was distracted by the signs that warned against spending more than ten minutes in the sauna, thinking back to his last medical with the Bank's doctor in Harley Street.

'You know this guy Maynard much better than I do. Can we trust him to get this job done?'

'He told me nothing in Nerja and I really pulled rank. Shortly he will undergo another test, one of his discretion, now that I have all the information I require. In any case, Maynard will never be a problem.'

Cavendish winced visibly.

'What do you mean by that?'

'We can remove him from the scene if he gets wise. Terminate him.'

'You mean, fire him from your firm?'

'I mean terminate him.'

Cavendish was inwardly appalled but tried not to show it.

'Who's going to do that?'

'Max will be looking after Maynard on-site.' Cavendish swallowed nervously. Richemont saw the reaction. 'You can take the heat? If not, you'd better say so now.'

The thermo showed dead on 120 Fahrenheit.

'No problem, I can take it,' he gulped.

'Then we are done. Time to cool down.'

The two men exited and fell into the plunge pool to close their open pores. It was like knocking a hole in an Arctic icecap. Richemont enjoyed the frisson, Cavendish less so. He got out, showered and met Richemont back at the front desk. He was famished, his plastic airline breakfast a mere memory.

'What now? Lunch?'

'I have another appointment. Next time perhaps, Charles.'

The door opened and a girl entered: eighteen or nineteen years old, tall and well muscled. In all probability not a genuine blonde. She was in danger of either exploding out of a crisp tight white uniform that was too short or falling off a pair of teetering heels that were too white and too high.

'Are you ready, Olivier?'

She spoke in a heavy Teutonic accent and maintained steady eye contact with her next client.

Richemont grinned at Cavendish's expression.

'Ingrid has such great hands. She does a wonderful job with hot oil. You must try her some time.'

He bade farewell to Cavendish before following Ingrid into a private side room, saying over his shoulder, 'You know that if you exercise regularly, Charles, you'll live on average ten years longer.'

Cavendish wasn't going to let him get away with any more put-downs.

'Yes, but they'll be your last ten years when you're old, senile and incontinent. Then you'll want to die.'

CHAPTER SEVENTEEN

VIGO STREET, LONDON, W1 – 7.25 P.M.

As Jonathon exited the lift on the ground floor of Richemont's office, his gaze was drawn to a young woman sitting on the seat in reception. He could see only her profile, but it was enough. A ribbed white top hugged her form, slim black leather trousers rustled as she shifted position. There was enough classy gold jewellery on her elegant hands to open a shop in Hatton Garden; long black hair, professionally cut and carefully combed; a pair of bronze sunglasses resting upon her high cheekbones. She carried off the ensemble effortlessly. He thought he might know her, hoped he might know her, but he was running late tonight and needed to get home so Eva could leave. He was almost through the revolving doors, heading towards the grime of the Tube, when she spoke.

'Jonathon?' He turned to view the vision. He couldn't quite place her. 'It is you, isn't it?'

That Italian accent. Unique. He would have recognised her earlier if she had still been wearing the black one-piece swimsuit with the crossover straps and high-cut legline. He was good with names.

'Carla.'

She stood up amid a collection of designer shopping bags. Max Mara. Emporio Armani. Harvey Nicks. The tough life of a serial shopper. They shook hands. She felt warm to his touch.

'What brings you to London?'

'I'm spending Olivier's hard-earned money.'

Jonathon didn't think Richemont had ever earned money the hard way. He had everything in life. The Nerja pad and Carla herself proved that. Jonathon didn't know how to handle this gorgeous freeloader. An awkward silence prevailed. Carla pushed her sunglasses atop her head and ran a hand through her hair.

'I am waiting for Olivier. He is meeting me here,' she announced.

The omniscient receptionist knew how to eavesdrop. It killed the boredom of handing out visitor passes and stalling courier guys. She stood up with a smile as genuine as her interest in working the late shift.

'You're Carla? Mr Richemont left about an hour ago for a meeting in the City. He sends his apologies.'

Carla feigned a look of disappointment and looked at Jonathon long and hard.

'I'm on my own tonight, then. It will be room service for one in the hotel. What's the point of coming all this way and being abandoned like excess baggage?'

She smiled. Jonathon had a choice. Eva could see to Jack and Imogen tonight. He called home. All was well. If he didn't at least make the offer then word would filter back to Richemont. But maybe she would turn him down.

'Let's eat. Leave your bags here. We can have them delivered to your hotel in a cab.'

The receptionist gave him a scathing look.

'No trouble at all. Have a nice evening.' Not.

They walked off along bustling Piccadilly, past Eros and into the warren of Soho. Trying to offer his unlikely guest the most favourable impression of the capital by night, Jonathon kept her away from the seedier dens, though without a reservation there was zero chance of finding a good table in any decent restaurant. They were surely destined for some tacky Chinese off Gerrard Street with stained pink tablecloths, over-attentive waiters, nasty white wine and wind-tunnel air-conditioning. Carla stopped outside the windows of the Soho Brasserie.

'Let's eat in here.'

Some chance. This wasn't Geneva, where they ate at seven o'clock and were back home in bed by ten with a cup of cocoa. This was peak dining time in one of the busiest London hot spots. They went inside. Before Jonathon could speak, Carla confronted the maître d'.

'We don't have a reservation but we want a table for two.'

Even less chance now. The maître d' chewed an old pencil, looked down a list, shook his head and mumbled something. Italian. Carla stood her ground, speaking softly to him in their native tongue. She leaned closer and utilised her full battery of charms. He stared back at her, almost stunned, like a rabbit caught in the oncoming headlights. He wilted and scribbled with the stub of the pencil.

'One table has come free.'

Jonathon saw the instant effect Carla had on the mostly male diners who followed her passage through the restaurant, like a magnet slowly drawn through iron filings. There was no competition here tonight. Carla ordered moules and pommes frites for two with strong Belgian beers, followed by rotisserie chicken with herbs and two chocolate alcohol-laced desserts in tall glasses. He drank the beer. She drank a bottle of Perrier. His head was spinning by ten o'clock.

'You're much better company than Olivier has been of late, Jonathon.'

The beer brewed by the Belgian monks had taken its toll. Any inhibitions had evaporated.

'What's wrong with him?'

Carla leaned forward across the narrow table and fingered the gold on her hands.

'It must be all this money trouble that I read about in the papers. I have a high sex drive. I need intercourse every few days to maintain my hormonal balance. The more often I have sex, the more enjoyable it is, and we haven't done it for weeks,' she said, pouting.

Jonathon almost directly inhaled the last drops of his cold cappuccino. Richemont was mad to ignore someone like Carla. She breezed on to other matters. 'So what sort of work do you do?'

'Assignments.'

'What's your next one?'

Jonathon thought about the Tuscany meetings, Nerja, Brown's Hotel and the agreement he had made.

'It's confidential.'

She took his hand in hers. She was so warm, her fingers perfect, her nails long and shaped like daggers.

'You can tell me. I won't tell anyone else.'

'Carla, no can do.'

'It sounds important. Secret too. Tell me.'

'Absolutely not.'

'Is there anything I could do to make you tell me?'

She still held his hand across the narrow table and leaned forward so that her breasts just brushed his outstretched fingers.

'What about you? What do you do?' he asked, fighting to bring his voice under control.

'I walk down catwalks in foreign cities in other people's clothes for about one hour a week. It's sooooo boring.' She leaned back in her chair and stretched provocatively. 'Are you starting to feel tired, Jonathon?' she asked. 'I think maybe I am.'

He gestured for the bill and tried to keep his eyes off her top button which had mysteriously come undone.

'Where do you live, Jonathon?' Carla asked.

'Not too far away.'

'Is your home big?'

'Big enough.'

She leaned closer and he inhaled her wonderful scent.

'Big enough for me? Tonight?'

'Big enough for my two children and me.'

'What about me?'

'I'll take you back to your hotel.'

He paid the bill, ignoring her protestations, and they took a taxi along Piccadilly and into Old Park Lane. When they reached her hotel, there was a queue outside a roped-off area by the main door. Jonathon was puzzled.

'Why the queue?'

'It's the Met Bar. They say it's the hottest place in the coolest city in the world. Wanna come in?'

'It's going to be members only, isn't it? Full of celebrities, I suppose?'

'It's open to residents of the hotel. Come on in with me. Take a chance.'

Jonathon eyed up the wannabe trendies blagging their way past a pair of six-foot bouncers in parkas.

'I'm about twenty years too old for the place and I'm not dressed in black. Look at those fashion clones going in. There must be a funeral going on inside.'

She leaned against him, gazing imploringly into his face.

'Funny guy. Come upstairs with me.'

'No. Richemont is inside, remember.'

'I can get another room. C'mon. Women like sex too.'

'Sorry, Carla. It wouldn't be a good idea.' Sternly he resisted temptation. He watched her enter the lobby and speak to a receptionist before blowing a kiss back to him.

There were no cabs in sight. He walked off towards Green Park Tube station alone, knowing he had made the right choice. Carla went up in the lift, feeling puzzled. She was losing her touch. In their room she saw Richemont lying on the bed in a loose bathrobe, reading a newspaper.

He removed his spectacles, conscious that they added years to his appearance.

'What happened?'

She frowned, still piqued by her failure with a man who had obviously been attracted to her.

'He told me nothing.'

'Did you come on strong to him like I said?'

'I know what to do, Olivier.'

'Are you sure?'

'It worked on you, didn't it?'

Carla gave him one last withering look as she entered the bathroom.

'So you think I can trust him to keep his mouth shut?' he called after her.

She didn't bother to reply.

Richemont was pleased with the evening's outcome but he needed to remind her who paid the nightly ransom for an eighth-floor corner penthouse at the Metropolitan Hotel. He waited for her to start running the free-standing bath with views over the rooftops of Knightsbridge. She didn't even notice the gentle curves of the Helen Yardley rug, the sculpted pear-wood screen, the clean lines, subtle colours and understated use of natural light. Luxury hotels were nothing new to her. He had seen the shopping bags earlier in the hallway.

'How much did you spend today?' he called out.

'A thousand, like you said. Fair payment for what I had to do. Anyway, you're loaded.'

He wasn't. Extracting the penknife from his suit pocket, he barged into the bathroom, where she stood naked, examining her cupped breasts in the mirror. He dropped his own robe to the tiled floor and stood close behind her, holding her tight as they both faced the steamy glass.

'So you do sex with strangers for a thousand?' he asked her. She nodded slowly. He grasped her left breast in his clenched hand and produced the gleaming knife. He placed the side of the cold blade against her skin, held it close and examined the slight indentation it made in her skin. 'Would you have done it for a hundred, I wonder?'

She paused, considering the monetary compensation. 'Probably. He was nice.'

He waited until they were both sufficiently aroused. 'Would you have done it for ten?'

Carla leaned forward against the washbasin, grasping the sides with her hands.

'No way. What do you think I am?'

The bath taps continued to run in the background, the water almost overflowing to the floor.

'Carla, I know what you are. Only the price is under discussion here.'

They ignored the steam. Richemont took his cue and proved to her that he still called the shots.

Lauren wondered whether the telephone call from Art Greenbaum was genuine. Her CV, mentioned almost in jest in conversation over a beer, had in fact been well received, he said. The interview opportunity for the unspecified vacancy was immediate. She walked the short distance down Park Avenue, hung a left on 48th and went into the Inter-Continental Hotel. She was ten minutes early and sat in the lobby by the gilded cage with the penitential parrots serving a life sentence, watching the money walk in and out of the swing-doors. At nine, she rode the elevator to sixteen.

She knocked on the door to suite 1630. A handsome black guy in a smart tan suit opened it. She could see an earpiece in his ear, the wire disappearing inside the collar of his white button-down shirt.

'Can I help you, ma'am?'

'Lauren Trent,' she said more in hope than expectation.

He nodded and pointed to a pair of double doors inside the suite.

'You're expected.'

There was no sign of anyone else inside. One of the doors leading off the room was half ajar.

'Come on in.' The disembodied voice then spoke to the Suit. 'That's all until I call you.'

Walter Sayers stood in the master bedroom before a full-length mirror. He wore a buttoned shirt and held one navy-patterned and one gold-striped tie in his hands.

'What do you think?'

'Gold,' she advised.

Lauren thought he looked different from his carefully constructed media image. He was older, greyer, fatter and smaller in reality. His half-eaten breakfast lay on the bed, crumbs and plates discarded on the folds of sheets and plump pillows.

Sayers was impressed by the girl's appearance. There was one chair near the window. He stood in the way of it and gestured. 'Take a seat.' He saw her puzzled expression. 'Anywhere you like. On the bed is fine.'

She sat carefully on one corner of the covers, crossed her legs and wished that she had worn trousers instead of her interview best, a sharp two-piece suit with white linen blouse and elegant jewellery.

'I can call you Lauren?'

'Yes.' The next words came out involuntarily. 'Mr Chairman.'

'Call me Walter.'

She wasn't sure she wanted to be on first-name terms. 'Chairman' would have been a more preferable compromise. He expertly knotted the gold tie, buttoned down the collar of the shirt and then took the only chair.

'Art tells me that you need a job. What are your qualifications?'

'You have my CV. It's all there.'

'I prefer to hear it face to face. You tell me. Sell yourself.'

Lauren didn't know how to take the last comment. His gaze wandered all over her.

'I know about the stock markets, hedge funds, futures trading and the Far East.'

Sayers sat back in the chair and stared at her. He was thinking that maybe she was a C cup.

'You worked for Mitchell's?' She nodded. 'Yet you didn't mention it now. Art told me you took the orders from that rogue trader who checked out in Battery Park?'

'Yeah.'

'Why did you leave Mitchell's Hong Kong?'

'They let me go. The markets are dead. There was no business. They had to cut costs.'

'What's the real reason you left Mitchell's?' Sayers was enjoying this interview. He held all the cards. He wondered how she'd look in a pair of stockings and a garter belt and not much else. He shifted in his seat to regain some semblance of dignity. 'I called Norman Newman. You know him?'

Lauren fidgeted on the edge of the bed.

'I never got to meet the CEO. I know of him.'

Sayers was convinced that he could see some cleavage.

'He told me off the record that Mitchell's fired you for frontrunning client orders.'

Lauren nodded reluctantly and got up to go.

'This has been a waste of time for both of us.'

'Sit down. Art says you're back with your parents.'

'What's that got to do with anything?'

'Your mom and pop know about the frontrunning?'

'They don't need to know.'

Sayers could see he was wearing her down.

'Does Pop know that you're up to your neck in debt? You lost a fortune on the condo you bought in Repulse Bay. In deep with a mortgage at HSBC, I understand.'

Lauren looked outraged.

'How do you know that?'

'My friends at the Agency did a credit check on you in Hong Kong through their local contacts. I have a file on you. It doesn't make pretty reading. So you frontrun to make money. Means you can lie whenever you feel like it. I wonder, am I still interested in hiring you?'

'There really is a job, then?'

'Sure. It's an investment management job. Buying stocks and managing a portfolio.'

'And selling the stocks too?'

Sayers stifled a smile as he continued to mentally undress his interviewee.

'There will only be buying, no selling.'

'Sounds like a strange investment strategy.'

'It's a rather unique fund.'

'Who owns it?'

'I do, I guess. And a few very select associates.'

Lauren struggled to keep the conversation businesslike though she was intrigued.

'What's the size of the fund?'

'Minimum fifty.'

'Million?'

'Billion.' He enjoyed the way her eyes widened and

that she only just stifled a gasp. 'There's one English guy going to run it but there's too much at stake to rely on him alone. I need someone on my side, someone else to help run it, just in case.'

'So ... so am I on the short list?' faltered Lauren, almost unbelieving. Last week Greenbaum had told her to go wait tables. Now he'd given her a steer towards the biggest investment fund she had ever heard of.

Sayers decided he was tired of teasing her. It was time to be more authoritative.

'Let's cut to the chase. You're not any candidate, you're the only candidate for the job. I have no time to look around. I'm under pressure to find someone for next week. You meet all the criteria. You will report to me and to me alone. I will tell you the information that I will require on a daily basis.'

Lauren stood up.

'I'll let you know if I'm interested.'

He quelled her with a single look from his mean little eyes.

'Sit down. This isn't an offer. I'm telling you, you will do this job.' He produced an envelope. Lauren could see that it contained some tickets and some typed papers. 'This is an offer you can't refuse, Ms Trent. You know who I am and what I can do to anyone in the business who pisses me off. You start on Monday. Questions?'

Lauren was wondering just how desperate she had become.

'I'll take it if I'm going to be adequately rewarded.'

'How much is your property debt?'

'You know how much.'

'So I do. It's about half a million bucks. That's your remuneration. If all goes well.'

Lauren could clear the burden of the mortgage with one pay cheque. Yes, she decided, she could work for this slimeball.

'The job is here in New York?'

Sayers leaned even closer and fixed his eyes on the V of her linen blouse.

'No. You'll be able to stop living with your folks. Now won't that be nice?'

On shaking legs, she made her way out of the suite, glad to be employed again but uneasy that her new boss knew every single detail about her background and wouldn't hesitate to use the information as and how he saw fit if she screwed up this job.

An indeterminate number of weeks in a warmer climate required one immediate course of action. Nikki made the call in the early morning. Becky had gone to Australia for the summer. Angie was having her second baby. Carole had left an entire year ago. Jonathon got a half-hour appointment with an unknown. Once again it was a lottery for a single male in that most alien of West End environments, the salon.

The optimistically named Headlines Hair Emporium was the nearest to the Richemont office. Nikki had recommended it ages ago. She practically lived there, leaving work early every Friday to drop by for a consultation and a vegetable tint. The glitzy writing in the windows proclaimed 'Unisex Salon', but Jonathon could see no other male customer among the clientèle. Five o'clock was not a firm appointment, more an aspiration. They made him wait on a row of uncomfortable seats.

'Mary's running late. Paper? Cappuccino?'

The *Sun's* headlines joyfully proclaimed 'Crash!' He doubted whether they had today's FT and he hadn't come here for caffeine. Just a trim. Eventually he leaned his head back into a curved basin, like a disloyal subject greeting the guillotine. Doused in aromatic shampoo and conditioner, he sat in a gown, feeling like a glove puppet. It was impossible not to stare around him. The lithe ones in black scurried from client to client, wheeling driers about, sweeping up remnants and constantly checking their own looks in the mirrored walls. At 5.20, his designated nemesis approached wearing a pair of combat trousers and matching T-shirt.

'How are ye keeping?' His hopes were raised. Nikki had advised that dyed blondness in a stylist was usually in inverse proportion to their talents with scissors and cut-throat razor. Mary was a natural redhead. No gelled spikes. No dyed purple streaks. No navel piercings. Not even an exposed midriff. Irish, too, judging by her soft accent. 'What are ye havin' done today, love?'

'Just a tidy-up. Nothing radical. Conservative, you know.'

The story of his life. Someday he'd ask for the number-one blade, get a goatee and vicious pointed sideburns, but not while he was working at Richemont and not when he was about to save the world.

'I'll only take off a bit off then, love.'

Said with the absolute conviction that a 'bit' was a technical term. He nodded and moved over to the chair.

'Any grey hairs you see, rip 'em out.'

'Sure, you're too young to have grey hairs.'

He saw the heads of other clients turn away from the pages of *Hello!* and *OK*. They stopped pointing at pictures in *Cosmo* or asking for more of what Jennifer or Giselle did with their own abundant manes. All eyes turned to the solitary man. Jonathon felt like the last male left on the planet.

First impressions were encouraging. Mary plied the scissors with natural confidence, only taking her eyes off the job to establish eye contact in the mirror, checking the length precisely, running her hands through his hair repeatedly. He thought she might even be enjoying it. Minutes dragged by with no conversation. Jonathon could never find the right topic at moments like these. At last Mary made the effort.

'So are you working today?'

'Yeah.'

'What do ye do?'

He was always hard pressed to describe his job, so he kept it simple.

'Banking mostly.'

His mind drifted. He sat alone thinking about the FTSE, the Dow, what he had to do next week, where he was going, how Eva would manage Imogen's birthday party, and how much he'd miss Jack and Imogen. Mary was in her own world of MTV – Travis, Moby, Limp Bizkit, Dido and the rest. She made the effort again.

'Been on holiday yet?'

Nerja and Tuscany were excellent holiday destinations but day trips on business were a different matter.

'Not really.'

'They're working ye too hard at that bank.'

She probably thought he usually stood behind a bullet-proof screen at a cash counter at NatWest or Lloyds TSB. Suddenly he found salvation. 'I'm off to the sun on Sunday.'

'Where're ye going, love?'

'Bermuda.'

Mary evidently had no idea where it was but seemed impressed.

'Posh. Near the Canaries, isn't it? Ye got kids?'

'Yes. Two.'

'They'll love it.'

'They're not going.'

'Your wife's going?'

'I'm a widower.'

She was momentarily stalled in mid-conversation, scissors poised over his head.

'You'll have the time of your life,' she rallied. 'You'll be out all night. You must be excited?'

Terrified, in truth. Mary finished in twenty minutes, running her hands through his hair for ages as she blow-dried the result. She leaned over him just inches away and he averted his eyes from the swaying, unbridled contents of her V-neck. As he left the salon, significantly poorer, he looked in the mirror and gazed in awe. Quite a feat for anyone to snip away for thirty minutes and still not take anything off.

Cavendish opened the door of the Barbican flat and immediately knew that he was not the first home. He could sense a presence. She duly appeared, took his pin-stripe suit jacket and kissed him.

'Working late, Governor?'

'Too much to do. Too many worries. I need to relax.'

Pamela recognised the vibes. She disappeared into the bedroom and returned five minutes later, wearing the same suit jacket with the sleeves rolled up to her elbows, heels and stockings. She had knotted his Old Etonian silk tie loosely around her neck. He was certain from prior experience that she wore nothing else underneath.

'A pity you can never wear that to work in the Bank.'

They retired to the master bedroom. Cavendish undressed entirely. Pamela sat back on the bed, left her heels on, slowly undid the buttons of the jacket and further loosened the knotted tie.

'The only way to truly unwind is with a man of power.'

'That's what got the Deputy Governor fired a few years ago. He was caught *in flagrante* in his office.'

'It could easily have been us.'

His earlier assumption proved to be somewhat wide of the mark. Pamela had found his favourite striped braces in the wardrobe, slipped them on underneath the jacket and clipped them on to the top of her stockings. The taut braces stretched from her shoulders over her breasts, brushing against the edges of her nipples. She placed her thumbs under the red silk and collapsed back on to the pillows.

'Evening, Governor.'

She lay up against the wooden headboard as he slowly undid the tie, gathered her hands together and used the tie to make a simple yet effective knot securing her to the wooden spar. She heaved up and down and exhaled deeply. The telephone in the hall rang.

'Who's that at this hour?'

'Leave it, Governor.'

The answering machine cut in. They both listened to the transatlantic drawl.

'Chuck, it's Walter here. This is important. If you're there, pick up.' Cavendish deliberated between discussing global finance and reaching a rapid climax. Sayers was insistent. 'C'mon, Chuck. It's vital.'

Cavendish wandered naked into the hall and picked up the telephone.

'Walt, do you know what time it is here?'

'This plan of yours just got better.'

'Walt, it's not my plan. It's our plan.'.

'You know, I have my doubts about your guy Maynard . . .'

'Not my guy. Our guy.'

'What if he doesn't deliver? What if he goes down? What if he falls ill? We're so dependent on him.'

'He's one of the best, according to all my sources. Richemont rates him highly. Relax.'

'This is too big. I need this money badly, got some

commitments that are kinda open-ended. I'm gonna hire someone else to help Maynard.'

Cavendish turned away from the distracting view of Pamela through the open door and focused on the conversation with difficulty. He lowered his voice and spoke closer to the mouthpiece.

'This is going live next Monday. You'll never find someone else at such short notice.'

'I already got someone. A girl, ex-Mitchell's. She knows futures. She's fucking perfect, in every way.'

'Don't speak to her until we've thought it through and told Richemont. We don't want to cut anyone else in.' Cavendish lowered his voice. 'Even Pamela doesn't know what's happening.'

'Is she there now?'

'Yes.'

A slight pause at the other end of the line.

'Gee, am I keeping you from something? Anyhow, it's too late. I met with this girl today. She's on board. It's a done deal. I cut her in for half a million.'

'Jesus. It could jeopardise the whole plan ...'

'You got your limey on the deal. I got my own person on it now. One each. Sounds fair to me. Safer than relying on one Brit to get a big job done. See you in Tokyo. Have a good climax.'

Cavendish slumped into the easy chair in the hallway and sighed. Pamela called to him from the bedroom. His attention drifted to the day's unread post on the hall table. The top envelope was from Speake Windsor & Co., a big law firm in the City. He wandered back into the bedroom and opened the bulky legal envelope. Pamela was still keen.

'Come on, Governor. This tie is hurting my hands. I'm losing circulation. It's tight.'

He read the first few lines of the letter and swore.

Pamela tried to sit up in the bed but failed dismally. 'What now?'

'Marjorie's gunning for me. It's all going to get ugly very soon.' Cavendish read the long preamble, but something didn't seem right. No mention of a separation due to irreconcilable differences. The dreaded word appeared on page three: infidelity. There was mention of evidence of a young woman witnessed leaving his Barbican apartment on a number of days. Marjorie had someone watching his apartment.

'She knows about you! She has witness statements taken by some private eye. Christ, she'll bleed me dry.'

'I'm so sorry. Untie me and let's talk about it. I understand how you feel.' Cavendish stood beside her, then thought about the following week and tore the letter into small pieces. Pamela watched them fall on to the bedcovers. 'It's so awful. Marjorie will take you for all the money she knows you have.'

He slid back her braces, took her firmly around the waist and pulled her towards him.

'That's the beautiful part. It's bloody perfect. Now lie back and think of the Bank of England.'

CHAPTER EIGHTEEN

Jonathon awoke in the early hours yet arrived late at Richemont. He went straight over to Nikki.

'There's been a change of plan for Monday next. I won't be going away anywhere.'

'You said this mystery assignment was important.'

'It is. But Jack's gone down with some sort of viral infection. I'm not leaving him in this state.'

'Have you cleared this with the boss?'

'Eva agrees, I have to stay in London.'

'I meant with Richemont.'

'I'll sort him out now.'

He felt his adrenaline levels rising as he went up to the top floor, walked past Jackie, ignoring her objections and into the boss's office. Richemont was alone on the telephone and still apparently wearing a suit to work each day. Jonathon stood over him, immune to the negative hand signals, partly distracted by the sound of some escalating street noise outside. His boss hung up the handset.

'What?'

'Jack's ill.'

'Who?'

'My son.'

Richemont hardly looked up as he shrugged. 'So why bother telling me?'

'So I can't leave him next week.'

Richemont contemplated the perfectly organised off-shore dealing structure that was now in place. The absence of the leading player would jeopardise their entire plan. He had never bothered to start a family. He tried to sound sympathetic and reassuring but only managed to seem peevish.

'Surely that Swedish girl can cope with any little problem of that sort?'

But Jack's raging temperature and stomach cramps were not so easily dismissed by Jonathon.

'She has a name. Eva. I can't leave her alone either. I cannot start the Bank assignment yet.'

Richemont looked out the window at the park, also now aware of noise below. He didn't know much about the American girl Sayers had hired, but she wasn't as highly qualified as Jonathon.

'Forget it. We have a mandate from the Bank. You're going on Sunday afternoon.'

'Impossible.'

Richemont stood up, steadily turning red with rising anger.

'I cannot allow any employee to challenge my authority. If you want to keep your job with this firm, then you will do this assignment. If you are not on that plane out of Heathrow on Sunday afternoon, then don't come into this office on Monday morning. Or ever again. Keep your troubled domestic life separate from the affairs of this company. Don't bother me with trivia like this again. That is all.'

Jonathon seriously thought about doing an about face and walking out, never to return. He thought logically, wondered whether he still wanted this job, remembered his mortgage, the annual school fees, his pension plan, his commitments, Eva's wages. He glared back.

'I'll make the final call on Sunday. You'd better hope that Jack recovers.'

He went back downstairs and uncharacteristically slammed his door in a rage. Nikki came into his office and saw his dark mood.

'You have to go?' He nodded. 'Jack will be okay. I'll call Eva at home. Maybe I can help her.'

'Thanks but I can't afford two nannies.'

'It's okay, I don't mind.' Nikki tried to change the mood. She walked to the window and looked below. 'See that? Do you hear the noise? All those whistles and that chanting? Sounds like a big crowd.'

He could hear it too. Much clearer. 'What is it?'

'They're marching down Piccadilly, according to Eddie. I promised them I'd go down. They need some support. You wanna come too? We'll only be five minutes.'

Jonathon looked out at the sunshine, then down at the

long list of unread e-mails on his PC, and thought about
the manner in which his boss had handled his request
for personal space. No contest. They left.

Nikki led him through Burlington Arcade.

'Remind me again what Eddie does,' he said.

'Nothing now. He's an activist. He used to be in
the army.'

'Did he ever kill anyone?'

'He was a chef. Probably.'

They saw the crowd of several thousand passing
along Piccadilly Circus. The average age was early twen-
ties, Jonathon reckoned. He felt old in comparison.
Many wore rainbow colours. Some shouted slogans and
soundbites into megaphones. Edgy police in fluorescent
jackets walked alongside. Other officers sat atop throbbing motorcycles or nervous chestnut mares. The media
followed, goading the players, looking for their photo
opportunity for the front page.

'Where are they going?' he asked.

'They're going to make a stand at the Bank of
England.'

'They'll be killed by the traffic. What's the point of
the march, Nikki?'

'They're celebrating the end of capitalism. They say
it's all over, the collapse of the stock markets proves it.'
Nikki grabbed his hand and insisted they moved forward
together, stopping on the pavement by a silversmith's
window. Their fellow onlookers were tourists, shop
workers and equally bemused office workers in suits.
'Aren't they wonderful?'

'I think that you're in the wrong job at Richemont?'

'I've been telling you that for years.' Nikki suddenly shouted out and pointed. 'There's Eddie. Hiya, love!' A pasty-faced guy with dank dreadlocks and hollow eyes waved back at her. This was her boyfriend? 'Isn't he cool?' she said proudly. Jonathon bit his lip. Nikki joined the crowd.

The hard core passed him by. The banners were uncompromising. Money Down the Drain. Fuck the Capitalists. Revenge Now. British Communist Party. Marx Got It Right. Reclaim the Streets. Anti-Globalisation. Anti-Everything. Jonathon feared for the safety of all McDonald's branches on their route. A few breakaway marchers pointed at the onlookers and shouted in his direction.

'Fucking suits! Fucking suits!'

Jonathon looked around the crowded pavement at the others, glad for once not to be in a suit. Some prat on the pavement made a bravado remark behind the safety of a sturdy policewoman. They heard his right-wing jibe. Some pushing and shoving at the edges. A can of Coke was hurled towards the prat. Evidently the anarchists still supported international corporates selling branded beverages to the world. The can was full and was aimed high. A plate-glass window shattered behind them. Other marchers farther back took the cue. Stones started to fly in the air. Jonathon's favourite Merc showroom by Green Park tube station bore the full brunt of their anger as the CLK 320 took a direct hit. Jonathon turned and went back up the Arcade, the marchers' roars still audible from Piccadilly.

'Eat the rich! Eat the rich!'

Olivier Richemont sat in the office and waited for the Mitchell's account manager to make the first move. Liebowitz looked up from the pile of loan account statements on his desk.

'You're early, Mr Richemont,' observed the Toddler.

Richemont didn't even need to look at his Rolex. Max had done a steady fifty kilometres per hour on the outskirts of Geneva in the Audi A8. Once again they had deliberately arrived late.

'I'm not early.'

'I gave you six weeks to repay the loans. You're back here after only three weeks. That's what I call being early.'

'I'm not here to repay the loans.'

'So what are you here for? Do you want another loan from us? If so, forget it.'

'I wish to open a new private client account with you to trade securities, index futures and stock options.'

Liebowitz almost smiled.

'You want to open a new account to trade securities during the biggest financial collapse in recent history? You know, you're a funny guy.'

'I'm serious. The markets are at an all-time low. Now is the best time to buy.'

'If I had a buck for every time someone said that to me in the past few weeks I could retire. I've had hardened clients and old widows in here in tears in the past few weeks as they watch their life savings go down the pan. The markets are at an all-time low until next week. That too will be an all-time low.'

Richemont threw a bulky half-open envelope on the desk as a demonstration of intent.

'I'm not here to discuss market sentiment. I can get that elsewhere. Everything you need is in here. Trust deeds. Power of attorney form. Lawyer's letter. Get me an account opening form to sign.'

Liebowitz hesitated, then pulled an ominous looking form out of a drawer. He opened the envelope and glanced over the papers with an expert eye as he began to fill in some basic details.

'This is an offshore trust domiciled in Bermuda. Called Horseshoe Trust. You gonna be lucky?'

'I expect so.'

'Who owns this trust?'

'Myself and a few of my personal acquaintances. There are no know your client issues here. Your bank has known me for many years. You can't have any of those Swiss money-laundering concerns.'

Liebowitz could tell that Richemont was one step ahead of his own thought processes. He still wasn't sure how the more urgent matter of loan repayments had been so easily circumvented.

'Let me tell you how Mitchell's will operate your account,' he began, trying to wrest back control.

'No. Let me tell you how I will operate this account. I will decide what to buy and sell. No one else will trade. I will be overseas for a period so I will telephone you with the orders. Can you handle that?'

Liebowitz examined the POA, checked the lawyers' signatures of the notarised forms and saw that Richemont was authorised by them to act on behalf of the trust.

'Sure. We offer Martini finance.' Richemont didn't react. 'Access any time, anywhere in the world.'

'My orders must be acted on immediately. How fast is your execution time?'

'It depends on the product. We pass UK orders to Mitchell's London, US orders to Mitchell's New York, Far East orders to Mitchell's Hong Kong, and so on. That's the way it works.'

'You got an account number for me?'

'We always have accounts ready to activate at short notice.' Liebowitz handed over a card with an alphanumeric account identity and then the form for signature. 'Where do I mail the account statements?'

'I don't want any statements. Hold on to them here.'

'I'll need to see some funds in this new account before Horseshoe Trust can trade.'

Richemont was still one step ahead.

'I have arranged to deposit a few hundred thousand dollars by same-day wire transfer today.'

'Where are you getting that sort of money from?'

'I've got friends in all the right places.'

Richemont rose to leave, the sole purpose of his visit completed. Liebowitz rose too.

'What about repaying the loans? I heard about Alpha. You must have lost a lot. We're getting worried.'

Richemont liked the thought that he worried his bankers.

'I've still got three weeks left. Plenty of time to come good. Sweat it out till then.'

Liebowitz stopped him by the door.

'And the credit card bills are still enormous. That Carla Gambino visits designer shops all over Europe. If the spending stops I'm going to report her as a missing person.'

'She has good taste.'

Lauren had one day left in Manhattan. Her mother was out at the florist shop uptown arranging the flora for a charity bash. Her father was at work at Citibank. She had avoided a confrontation and told neither of them that she was leaving JFK on an AA flight that day. She'd leave her mother a carefully worded handwritten note sealed in an envelope and call her later. Her father could work it out for himself. She located her two suitcases, still largely unpacked, discarded some older clothes and realised there was space for more. She exited into the teeming streets of the Upper East Side.

First stop was an Internet café, where she paid a few bucks to log on for an hour when she needed only ten minutes. There were no e-mails in her hotmail inbox. She had evidently been struck off the social register in Hong Kong and Mitchell's worldwide. She took out the travel documents couriered from the Fed, read the small print and did a search in Google for her destination.

Her hopes were confirmed on the home page.

www.surfway.bm was a vacation resort, not some grey anonymous corporate hotel in the city centre. Great shots of manicured lawns and distant beaches dominated the gallery page. The location page confirmed that the resort was on the south coast of Bermuda. The accommodations page showed tiered rows of pastel single storey bungalows perched among palm trees. The directions page stated that it was only twenty minutes from the airport. She ignored the USD room rates page. The federal government was paying the tab. She logged out.

Subconsciously finding her way to her favourite Gap store on Fifth, she shopped accordingly for the right clothes for a hot climate, racking up a few hundred easy bucks on her HSBC plastic. Cool chinos, athletic tops, cotton and linen shirts, faded denims, canvas deck shoes and enough underwear for the indeterminate number of weeks away. She dared to select some aquamarine swimwear too in the hope that it wouldn't be all work and no play with this unknown guy accompanying her.

Her last stop was vaguely ironic. She entered the nearest branch of Citibank and asked the jaded teller to change a few hundred bucks into Bermudan cash. She watched his puzzled expression as he looked up a computer listing of the more obscure forex rates. This could have been her if she had taken her father's advice, perched on a stool behind glass in some lonely retail outlet instead of jetting off to a glamorous new job for the Chairman. The teller advised her that the US dollar was the currency of choice on Bermuda. He knew more than she did about global foreign exchange. Lauren left feeling chastened.

Half an hour later, she was sitting on the edge of a suitcase in her bedroom, cramming the last of the Gap gear inside, when the hall door opened. It must be her mother home for lunch. Perhaps this was an opportunity to tell her in person of her plans. Her father looked in on her room from the hall.

'Going somewhere?'

Lauren's heart thumped. Just the two of them.

'What are you doing here, Dad?'

'I live here.'

'It's midday.'

'I gotta fly on business tonight. I came home for my overnight bag.' He stepped into the bedroom, his presence an odious reminder of times past. 'So what's with the suitcases?'

'I got a job.'

'Packing suitcases?'

'I got a banking job.'

He didn't seem impressed.

'Really? With who?'

'I can't say.'

'So you haven't got a job at all?'

'I have. It's confidential.'

'Says who?'

'Says the guy who hired me. You'll get to hear about it eventually, I guess. Maybe in the newspapers.'

Her father sat down on the edge of her bed, resting on the soft mattress. He was much too close.

'Don't get smart with me. I know what's going down. You got a crap job and some money on the way, so now you're moving out to an apartment over the West Side, to get away from me and your mother.'

'That's not true.'

His bunched fists lay on the Laura Ashley duvet cover. The very same duvet cover.

'Jesus. First we give you a damn good education and you immediately disappear to the other side of the world and cut us off. You only come back for a few days every Thanksgiving. Now, when your poor mother thinks you're back for good, you're suddenly off again. Were you even going to tell us?'

'I was.'

'I don't know why we bother.'

Time for Lauren to speak her mind. She stood up and dared to mention the unmentionable.

'Do you remember the last time you sat on this bed?'

'What do you mean?'

'Answer the question.'

'It was a few weeks ago, I suppose.'

'I mean the last time when I was in the room too.'

He stood up immediately, his evasive eyes unable to meet hers.

'What . . . ? I don't know what you're talking about.'

Lauren knew that it was a lie. They both remembered only too well what she was referring to, but the thought of it left her breathless and disoriented, unable to voice the horror of it coherently.

'When Mom went out to set up the flowers at those charity functions . . . You knew she'd be gone for hours. I dreaded those nights alone. You came in here ...'

Her father moved away from the bed, as if his mere presence beside it was incriminating.

'You're all mixed up, Lauren. You don't know what you're saying.'

She brushed tears of anger from her eyes.

'You touched me! You lay on this bed with me. And much more. Don't you dare deny it. Why the hell should I stay here if I have a choice now? You poisoned home for me a long time ago.'

He pointed to the hall door. His face was animated, red with fury and denial.

'I don't ever want to hear you utter such lies in my home. If you're going, then get out now.'

Lauren picked up the two suitcases and her backpack with the tickets and cash.

'That's what you really want, isn't it? You can't stand having me around here in case I talk about it to Mom. Well, don't worry, I'm going. And this time you're free from me for good. I won't ever be back. And if Mom asks why I've gone, I'll leave it to you to explain it to her. That's if you've got the guts to admit to her and to yourself what a lying hypocritical child-abuser you really are!'

Five minutes later she sat in the back of a lurching yellow cab on the Van Wyck to JFK, wiping away the last tears out of sight of the driver's rear-view mirror, forgetting about the turbulent past and her excessive mortgage, looking forward to life on a paradise island

and the best job opportunity any futures sales executive could hope for in these troubled times.

The party of five sat at a corner window table on the fifty-first floor of the Park Hyatt Hotel. Subtle jazz played in the background. Conversation was limited. Four of the diners were distracted by the panoramic view way below. Incessant commercial traffic weaved through the monotonous array of grey 1970s buildings. The bright lights of Roppongii's neon sex strip stretched off to the left; the cavernous Shinjuku train terminal was to the right, visited by two-million-plus weary commuters every day. The Tokyo Tower held centre stage, a smaller version of the Eiffel Tower, brightly lit against the night sky. Their host sat at the head of the table and showed off his excellent command of the English language.

'An impressive vista?' encouraged Nakamura.

'Not compared to Manhattan. This is a tiddler of a building,' sneered Sayers, ever the diplomat.

'Look at the wonderful décor here and the colour murals of Manhattan life. Like a real New York grill,' Nakamura persevered. 'You must feel at home here, Walter?'

Sayers shifted in his seat and surveyed the interior of the restaurant. He took a jaundiced glance at the giant picture of a Yankee pitcher against a clichéd skyline.

'Takes more than décor to make a New York grill. It looks like Disneyland in here. The place needs some real atmosphere. I need a beer. Which one is our waiter? All these guys look the same to me.'

'The menu is good though? American steaks and French wines?' inquired their host.

Sayers studied the menu and was appalled. 'I didn't travel ten thousand miles through twelve time zones to eat like at home. I love Jap food. Sushi with hot wasabi, miso soup, raw ginger, Soba noodles, sticky rice, Junsai vegetables, pickles, yakatori and all that stuff. If I want a real New York grill, I'll go home. And look at the goddamn prices here.' Sayers rambled on. 'Seven thousand yen for a steak. Seventy bucks! Nine hundred yen for a coffee. Nine bucks for a shot of caffeine? Get real. How does anyone live here? Just as well we're only five or we might bust the BoJ expense account. Who else wants a Kirin? I'm dying of thirst. All that endless talk today.'

Cavendish looked around at the adjacent empty tables and cut in to stall the developing international hostilities. 'Is this place safe? Can we talk freely?'

The BoJ Governor perused his oversized menu inscrutably, wishing he had booked somewhere traditional.

'No one else will be here tonight.'

'Is that because of the crash? Are all the bankers broke? Can't they afford to dine out?' asked Lam.

'I told the hotel to leave the other tables vacant. Nothing but the best for the G7,' advised Nakamura.

'But we're not G7 tonight. We are G5. I wouldn't trust the Russkie at all and the Canadian woman is too boring for words,' Cavendish added. The others concentrated on making their choices in silence. 'Let's use this opportunity wisely. Our lords and masters, the PMs and finance ministers, are off chatting among themselves, dining at the Imperial Palace with the other top brass. It's not often we governors get a chance to talk off the record on a matter close to all our hearts. Not since Tuscany.'

The waiter appeared and the order was taken. Beer arrived. Sayers shut up. A hush descended as they got down to the serious business. Cavendish spoke quietly as he briefed them on recent developments.

'We go live next week in Hamilton. Jonathon Maynard and Lauren Trent will be ready to start as soon as the markets open. We have located an ideal office for them. Huge credit lines are in place. We have incorporated the local investment trusts in Bermuda. New accounts are open at major overseas brokers and banks. The world recovery is about to commence.' He looked over at Sayers. 'We hope.'

'Let's have a toast to good luck,' urged Nakamura.

Sayers nodded towards Cavendish, maintaining steady eye contact. Sayers put down his beer.

'Chuck and I want this to be a success. Let me tell you what we will do.' Cavendish froze. 'Chuck is gonna help me to choose a good red from the cellar. He's the wine expert.'

Cavendish relaxed and rose. The two men stood in the narrow confines of the visible and voluminous wine cellar that ran along the inner well of the restaurant. Cavendish made straight for a few bottles of South African but Sayers caught his sleeve.

'So is our own plan ready to roll, Chuck?'

'Don't call me Chuck. Richemont assures me that all is ready. There's only one outstanding matter, Walt. We need to decide how much we want to make.'

'What's your gut feeling.'

'I say five million each?'

'Let's aim for more. This is one of those rare chances in life to really think big, Chuck. What about ten million each?'

Cavendish paused, contemplating the enormity of what they were about to do. In for a penny, in for ten million.

'Ten it is. Let's go for it. And the same for Richemont?'

'I guess so. You trust him?'

'As much as I trust you. I called him in Geneva today. I got some extra assurance.'

'I don't follow.'

'Richemont is going to take a golfing holiday next week.'

'You gotta be fucking joking. At a critical time like this? The guy's an asshole to do that.'

'He's going golfing in Bermuda. He'll be on the ground in person.'

Sayers seemed relieved. They returned to the waiting table, a few bottles in hand. Cavendish gave the nod to a distant waiter to get to work with a corkscrew. Engels examined the suitably dusty labels, took the first measured taste of the choice red and was instantly impressed.

'Seems like the two of you know exactly what you're doing. *Prost!*'

CHAPTER NINETEEN

From the air the island looked like one lush golf course, with verdant hillsides punctuated by shoreline sandy bunkers and azure water hazards. The BA flight touched down at the international airport on schedule. The Boeing was the only commercial aeroplane on the apron, the terminal parochial but suitable for a mere sixty thousand inhabitants. A welcoming steel band played for the beaming tourists. Jonathon wished he was one of them and that Eva and the children were here, or that he was at home in Chester Square. Jack was making a good recovery. He'd call first thing from the resort.

He realised that this was an assignment to die for. Others at Richemont, if they knew, would be madly jealous. Especially Nikki. Several weeks in paradise with someone else paying the bill and an unknown American girl about to join him tomorrow. He boarded a Toyota

357

Hi-Ace cab at the rank and gave directions to the Surfway resort on the South Road, as advised by Cavendish's helpful assistant.

First impressions from the side window were good. They passed luxuriant golf courses, the becalmed waters of Harrington Sound, a perfume factory and the Rum Swizzle Inn. There were pastel shades, winding roads, wooden bridges and tempting glimpses of water. The wealth all around was evident. Here was the third-richest country per capita in the world, with zero unemployment and no illiteracy. The government had long ago abolished income tax. Countless British, American and Canadian firms had set up offshore brass nameplate headquarters on law firms' front doors in their constant quest for minimal corporation tax in their P&L. Banking, insurance and reinsurance business soared. Servicing international business was the island's main industry. This global recovery, if and when it happened, would be tax-free.

Jonathon made an effort at small talk as they drove along the coastal road at a ridiculously slow speed.

'Why is all the traffic going so slowly?'

The middle-aged cabbie sporting two days' worth of grey stubble turned down the soothing jazz.

'It's the speed limit. Twenty miles an hour. There's no hurry, mon. Welcome to Bermuda.'

Jonathon wound his watch back by four hours as the taxi approached Paget parish. He had done the basic research. He was now six hundred miles off the coast of North Carolina. In 1503 a wandering Spanish navigator had come across an uninhabited archipelago of 180 islands between Europe and the Americas. Apparently unimpressed by this semi-tropical discovery basking in the Gulf Stream, he'd left immediately. His name was Juan de Bermudez. The rest, as they say, was history.

A century later another mariner lost his ship, the *Sea Venture*, in a hurricane off these shores. Admiral Sir George Somers was seemingly also disenchanted by his surroundings. He stayed on Bermuda only long enough to build two aptly named ships, the *Deliverance* and the *Patience*, from the remains of his previous one, a prodigious feat of carpentry. Somers' crew had other ideas, and sixty of them returned to the newfound paradise to settle in St George, the first capital of the fledgling colony. The island had thrived ever since.

Jonathon tried again.

'The airport's quiet today.'

'It's like that all the time. We prefer it that way.'

The locals always did things their own way. They had found economic salvation during Prohibition when the first American tourists came to the colony not for the sun, beaches or other leisure pursuits but to escape the Volstead Act and to down fine whiskey. They were ideally located to survive the Second World War intact, but nevertheless did their bit. British experts sat out the war in the cellars of the Princess Hotel, Hamilton, using significant amounts of steam and glue, covertly intercepting mail sent to Europe by German spies in the USA. In 1940 the United States requisitioned two square miles to build a military airbase, as they are wont to do on foreign soil – not a big space in itself but nevertheless representing one-tenth of the entire island's landmass.

He tried a further conversational gambit.

'Do you have any local airlines here?'

'Like what?' pondered the cabbie, swaying his head from side to side to the easy rhythm on the radio.

Jonathon shrugged, finding this conversation increasingly hard work.

'Like Bermuda Air?'

The driver gave him a big grin in the rear-view mirror, displaying his gold molars.

'Sure, mon. We have Bermuda Air. You're breathin' it.'

Jonathon awoke at 6 a.m. local time – 10 a.m. in London. His first thoughts were of Jack and Imogen. He stretched over to the bedside table and dialled. Eva answered on only the second ring. Jack was improving. Imogen was fine. In the warm Bermuda dawn, he felt less guilty, even less hostile towards Richemont. He gave Eva the local number and extension and said he'd call every morning at this time.

His ride to Hamilton was scheduled for 8 a.m. He waited on his veranda and watched the surf breaking over the pink sand of the narrow beach below. He could make out the reef offshore, separating the dark blue of the Atlantic from the light blue of the shallows. There was real heat in the sun even at this early hour. Sunburned lizards climbed nearby trees and red crustaceans burrowed in the sandy soil. A silver BMW

3-series Compact pulled up near reception at 8.20. A bulky guy in a dark suit, square-shouldered and sporting a crew cut, sat inside. Removing his shades, he leaned out of the window.

'You Maynard?' Jonathon nodded, picking up a European accent. 'You ready?'

'Been ready for twenty minutes.'

He got into the car. The driver was holding a Camel in his right hand. Jonathon stared at him. The driver stared back, drew on the cigarette, ignored the glare, and drove off at excessive speed.

'I'm Max.'

No further information was forthcoming.

'What do you do, Max?'

'I handle the arrangements.' He paused and remembered his lines. 'For Mr Cavendish.'

'He's a Sir, isn't he?'

'That's right. Sir Cavendish.'

Jonathon wasn't convinced. He had now placed the accent.

'Are you German?'

'Is that a problem?'

'Not for me.' Jonathon eyed the speedo on the first tight bend – 45 mph. 'The speed limit here is twenty, isn't it?'

Max took both hands off the steering wheel, then flung his cigarette butt out of the window into dry foliage.

'That's fucking crazy!'

'It's the law, so I'm told.'

Max stared back, remembered his role as welcoming host, and hit the brakes immediately.

'Remind me if I forget again.'

Jonathon already had other ideas.

'It won't be necessary. I'm going to hire a car.'

'Visitors can't hire cars here. That's the law too. You can hire a fifty-cc scooter, but who wants one of those things dangling between your legs? Crazy place, eh?'

'So you don't live here?'

'No chance.'

Jonathon thought about the full ramifications of this.

'Whose car is this?'

Max shrugged and took his eye off the hilly road for too long to be safe.

'I borrowed it from a friend. Don't worry about it. You're only here to work. I got some office space for you in Hamilton. I don't know what's the plan but the office is kitted out with the best hardware.'

They sat in silence as they approached the harbourside city of Hamilton at 19 mph. Max stopped in a pay-and-display public carpark along Front Street. Jonathon followed him into a narrow pedestrian alley called Chancery Lane and up a series of steps. They stopped by a door decorated with rows of polished nameplates by the entrance, mostly lawyers, accountants, tax advisers and offshore company formation offices. Max produced a set of keys and handed it to Jonathon.

'You'll need these. You're on the third floor. Another firm uses the rest of the floor but your space is totally secure and separate. It's got everything you requested. I hope it all works.'

They rode the elevator and walked into a low-ceilinged room with a limited yet attractive view of the harbour. Jonathon was satisfied. It was almost an authentic dealing room with enough IT hardware to trade anywhere in the world any time. Two Bloomberg terminals. Two Reuters terminals. Two PCs. Two faxes. Two telephones. Two TV's. Two of everything. There were even wall clocks showing various times around the globe and a microwave, presumably for those inevitable late night shifts. He felt almost reborn as a dealer, like the old days at Mitchell's bond desk before his working life became so complex and varied. Max stood in the doorway, apparently also content with his initial inspection.

'Anything you need, call me. I'll always be near by. That's my job. Here's my mobile number and a map of the town and island. So you don't get lost and go missing on me.'

'Anything I need?' Max nodded. 'Then fill up my fridge. I need fruit, veg, pasta, eggs, milk and beer.'

The burly man balked at this request.

'I don't do groceries.'

'Then find someone who does. That's your job, isn't it? You handle the arrangements?'

'I'm only here for the important stuff.'

Jonathon's curiosity was aroused.

'Like what?'

'Like if you think someone is following you, or if you ever feel threatened, in any danger.'

'You think that's going to happen?'

'Security and confidentiality in this operation are paramount, so Sir Cavendish told me.'

Jonathon was more certain than ever that Max had never met the Governor. He was about to leave. Jonathon tested him one more time.

'What do you know about this American girl?'

'She used to be with some big-name investment bank and knows about the markets, like you.'

Jonathon couldn't argue with his partner's apparent credentials. Max looked over at him.

'You ain't wearing a ring. You married? Hooked up with someone?'

'I'm not married. Or hooked up.'

'Then the two of you should get on fine. I heard about her. She's hot, apparently. Single too. I'm looking forward to meeting her. I'll drop her round later as soon as she arrives. You want a lift back to Surfway today?'

Jonathon had already seen the ample supply of taxis at the rank outside. He wanted his independence.

'I'll take a cab.'

'Suit yourself.' Max hesitated, then remembered something. He took out a slim manila envelope and handed it over to Jonathon. 'This is for your expenses, eating out and the like. Maybe groceries too if you lower yourself to go shopping. Let me know if you need more. There's a thousand bucks. Money's no object here.'

The morning was a disaster. The dealing screens didn't work. The user IDs were inactive. There were no live price feeds, no Web or e-mail access on the PCs. Jonathon called Max. Max wasn't happy. Jonathon killed time reading the latest meltdown news in the WSJ and the FT, but old news was no news in this business. Max returned late morning with two brain-donor electrical guys who got the show on the road by midday. Bloomberg lived. Reuters lived. The PCs lived. He was ready to trade.

He scribbled some notes. The task was simple yet there were myriad ways to produce the desired outcome. Did he buy stocks or bonds? Did he buy in the US, Europe, Japan or the Far East, or all of the markets? Did he buy in the cash markets or did he buy options, futures and other derivatives? Did he play the currency and metals market? Did he dare trade before his partner arrived? No. He waited.

He took lunch at Kearney's bar but stayed off the alcohol, preferring a Diet Coke and BLT with fries. He walked the town in five minutes. Two enormous cruise ships were docked along the main street, so huge it almost looked as if Hamilton were moored to the ships rather than vice versa. He people-watched as large parties of larger tourists disembarked to scour the souvenir shops for pieces of pink coral, fridge magnets, model lighthouses, painted seashells, loud T-shirts and plastic goods manufactured in China.

Passing the carpark in the town centre, he noticed that the silver Compact BMW was still there. There was no one inside. Jonathon wondered what Max did during the day and where he was now. Returning to the office, he saw that the Dow had opened down four hundred points and was glad he had waited to buy.

At four o'clock he heard the sound of keys and voices on the third floor and knew that the American must have arrived. The door opened. Max smirked as he introduced the girl with a briefcase in her hand.

'This is Lauren Trent.'

Jonathon, momentarily stunned, thought she looked even better than in Hong Kong. Involuntarily, he said, 'You look great.'

She stood rooted to the spot. Max butted in.

'This is . . .'

'Jonathon. I know. We already met.'

There were no other words, each of them wondering who was the most embarrassed. Max looked bemused.

'You guys know each other?'

Their vocal cords were simply not functioning, Jonathon thinking of that meal in the Ritz Carlton and what had happened, or hadn't happened, afterwards, Lauren thinking that the job was already going wrong but she couldn't go back home. They nodded, speechlessly.

'That's great. I'll leave the rest to you.'

Max was gone. Handshakes were deemed unnecessary. Jonathon recovered first.

'There must be a mistake. You can't be working here.'

Lauren placed her briefcase on the dealing desk, folded her arms and established her territory.

'I got a job offer from the Chairman of the Federal Reserve Board in DC. He told me exactly what has to be done here. Job offers don't come more solid than that.'

Jonathon sat at a dealing desk.

'Mine came from the Governor of the Bank of England. We should have been told about this.'

Lauren sat down and looked at the screens. Her dealing position felt good. It felt like home. She scowled across at her new colleague and recalled her last day at work in Hong Kong.

'I can't work with someone who had me fired from Mitchell's.'

'And I can't work with someone who breaks the rules and frontruns client orders.'

He instantly regretted his words. He wanted her to stay, and not just because she was the only familiar face on the island. She looked amazing in a pair of jeans and a cropped T-shirt. But now he knew he'd had her fired. This would never work out. Lauren's body language was defiant as she pulled her chair nearer the screens.

'You bought anything yet?'

'No,' he replied. He should have dealt earlier, established his credentials.

'Leave it that way. I'm going to freshen up.'

'Wait, we need to sort this out.'

'I'm hungry. Sort out something for later.'

'I don't know anywhere to eat.'

'If you're going to save the world, you should at least be able to find a table in a restaurant.' Lauren picked up her briefcase, took a last look at the Bloomberg screen and made for the door. 'Looks like the Far East is still the cheapest of all the markets. That's where I'd start buying. I'm outta here.'

'How do I contact you?'

'At Surfway. Max knows where it is. Ask him.'

So they were going to be neighbours as well. Lauren left. Jonathon did what he was supposed to do in any emergency. He called Max.

'Book me a table for two at a good restaurant tonight. I fancy an Italian.'

In truth he fancied an American. He wondered if the American in turn fancied an Englishman.

Max didn't balk at this request.

'Great to see the two of you getting on so well.'

Lauren took the best seat in La Venezia off Reid Street. Jonathon didn't object. The table was too near the main door and too near the kitchen, almost an impossibility in any decent restaurant. The fake brick walls were festooned with fake posters of Italian cities. Waiters with fake accents offered laminated menus. A fake pergola served only to reduce still further the limited space in the restaurant. The red-check tablecloths looked like rejects from a Wild West saloon. The bread on the side was stale. The pitted olives were pitiful. The antipasto for two had come straight out of a supermarket jar. Lauren was distinctly unimpressed.

'Disgusting! Rubbery salami, sodden red peppers and this mozzarella is gross.'

'I could do better myself at home.'

'You cook?'

'When I'm in the mood.'

There was too much pasta, too much Parmesan and way too much black pepper. The house red was chilled by the air-con. Two wandering minstrels arrived, playing ear-aching music on a violin and guitar, crooning away as if in some cheap ice-cream advertisement, before moving off to the next restaurant, a few dollars richer but not enough to retire on. Lauren had waited just long enough to raise the sole topic of their evening out together.

'One of us has to quit. We can't work together. I think it should be you who leaves.'

Wild thoughts of that evening out in Hong Kong came flooding back to him. He was here to stay and see the job through. He wanted to get to know her too. But it didn't look promising.

'Why me?' he replied mildly.

'Sayers says this job could last for weeks, maybe even months. You told me you've got two children. Think of them sitting at home, wondering where you are and when you're coming back.'

She wore a pink linen shirt that was buttoned low down, her freshly washed hair gathered back and tied with a silk band. Alluring yet lethal. She was obviously going to try everything tonight. Even below the belt. He countered, swiftly.

'I call Jack and Imogen each morning. Wouldn't you prefer to be back in the States with your folks?'

'Last week in New York was enough for me. It's gotta be you.'

'My boss made me take this assignment. The Bank of England is a mega-client of ours. If I quit, he'll fire me.'

'Then you'll know what it feels like.'

Jonathon took the hint. He knew he'd have to choose his next words carefully. 'It wasn't like that, you know. You had the screens open on your PC. I assumed that everyone on the desk was frontrunning when I saw you were doing it. Even Mac.'

'You knew nothing about the FF&O desk! You knew nothing about what happened at the Ritz Carlton ...'

'What did happen?'

Lauren kicked herself mentally. Shamefaced, she admitted, 'McFarland told me to take you out for that meal. He paid the maître d' to slip you a kir royale doctored with some powder he got from a Chinese medicine shop. That's why you were ill all night and the next day. McFarland was happy to see you lose valuable working hours. It was a dirty trick.'

'I forgive you.'

'I wasn't looking for forgiveness.'

Jonathon thought back to that grim night spent retching in the bathroom. He remembered Lauren close by; visions of her tending to him were still haunting his dreams.

'What happened between us in the hotel room afterwards?'

'Nothing happened. You're imagining things.'

The same things she'd imagined, if the truth be told. But he'd been way too ill. The desserts were a modest improvement on the main course, but that wasn't difficult.

'This is a once-in-a-lifetime opportunity. It could make or break us, set us up for life if we pull it off,' said Lauren, suddenly enthusiastic and not looking to score any points. 'It's bizarre. If you hadn't got me fired from Mitchell's, then I wouldn't have gone to New York and I wouldn't be here now. I suppose I have something to thank you for.'

'So what's it to be?'

'We both made mistakes. Let's forget about the past. Let's stay and get the job done. We leave it at that.'

He was relieved, even pleased at this diplomatic outcome. They smiled and then shook hands. The waiter, coming over with the coffees, wondered what sort of date this was. The bill arrived soon afterwards. They both winced at the cost of living in Hamilton. Lauren didn't offer to split it.

'I assume I'm paying?' queried Jonathon.

He placed two of Max's crisp hundred-buck bills on the tablecloth. She shook her head.

'Not really. Sayers is paying. And Cavendish. And whoever else is with them.'

CHAPTER TWENTY

HAMILTON, BERMUDA – 9.10 A.M.

Jonathon and Lauren sat at the bank of virginal screens, ready to make their first move. They had billions burning a hole in their bottomless pockets. The markets were lower in Europe. The Dow was yet to open. Nervously, they wondered whether two people could really stem the awesome tide. Lauren spoke first.

'Okay, let's start the ball-game.'

Jonathon had already given the matter much thought over a sleepless night spent alone. They'd discovered at the reception desk at Surfway that they were in adjoining bungalows, sharing the same veranda even. He was glad she sat beside him now and not on a seat on the next flight back to New York.

'Let's do what the HKMA did a few years ago. Buy stocks in leading companies,' he proposed.

'That's a bit obvious, isn't it?'

'It worked for the HKMA. Kenneth Lam told me so.'

'You move in all the right circles. We should be more

373

imaginative on our first trade,' Lauren countered. 'This is the best buying opportunity we'll ever have if this strategy works and the markets recover. We need the maximum return for minimum outlay. We need leverage. We need to buy futures or options.'

She had all the right ideas. 'You're only saying that because you work at an FF&O sales desk.'

'Used to work. Remember? Let's target the only five stock markets in the world that matter: US, UK, Germany, Japan and Hong Kong. We buy near-month call options on five large-cap stocks in each market. If we can kick-start the prices of leading benchmark stocks, we may drag the rest of the markets up in their wake.'

Jonathon added a dose of realism.

'If that doesn't work, the options will expire worthless and we'll lose all the up-front margin.'

'That's a risk we have to take. Anyway, it's taxpayers' money.'

'We're taxpayers.'

'Only those with permanent salaried jobs are tax-payers,' Lauren said darkly.

She started scribbling down some stock names and offered the page to him.

'GE, Microsoft, Cisco, Ford, AT&T in the US. Vodafone, BP, Shell, AstraZeneca, Glaxo SmithKline in the UK. Deutsche Bank, Deutsche Telekom, Deutsche Post, and Deutsche anything in Frankfurt. NTT, Japan Tobacco, Japan Rail, Softbank, Sony in Japan. HSBC, China Light, Cheung Kong, Cathay, Hutchinson in

Hong Kong. That's my hit list, my top twenty-five call options.'

Jonathon couldn't disagree.

'How much do we buy?'

'A thousand calls in each. Only size will move a market. Per day.'

'Per day? Why not do it all today?'

'We need a sustained recovery. No point spiking the market today and watching it slide tomorrow.'

Jonathon knew that made sense. He would have worked with her on any trading desk.

'Let's spread the orders around these offshore trusts as much as possible.'

Bermuda was optimally placed in relation to most international time zones. Jonathon placed the US orders with Goldman's in Broad Street, Manhattan, once the salesman confirmed that the trust accounts were open. Lauren placed the UK orders with a guy she knew vaguely from his days in Hong Kong, but who had moved back to HSBC Securities in Thames Exchange, London. Jonathon placed the German orders with some zealous salesman at Hypo Bank, Munich. Should have been Hyper Bank.

Within minutes they received return telephone calls confirming the executions, followed by execution faxes with the call prices in black and white. They watched the Bloomberg screens. The option prices moved up but there were still too many sellers out there. The upward tick wasn't convincing.

'Maybe we'll see more recovery tomorrow. What about the Far East?' he asked.

'It's eight p.m. in Hong Kong and nine p.m. in Tokyo. We can leave overnight orders at the desks for execution tomorrow.

'There'll be no one there now.'

'They'll have twenty-four-hour service in a fast market like this.' Lauren grinned. 'You call MSDW in Tokyo. I'll do Mitchell's in Hong Kong. I might even enjoy this call.'

Jonathon called some unfortunate insomniac salesgirl in Tokyo who had drawn the short straw and hadn't enjoyed a decent social life in weeks. He watched Lauren dial her old number in Hong Kong. It rang and then went on call forward to another extension. A familiar tired voice answered.

'Big Mac, Lauren here.'

She smiled at Jonathon and put the telephone on speaker to share the moment, knowing that Jonathon shared her feelings towards McFarland.

'Don't call me Big Mac. What do you want, Lauren?'

'Any news there?'

'Would I tell you if there was? You don't work here any more, okay? Where are you?'

'You don't need to know. Any messages for me?'

'Nope. Oh, hang on. Brad says that English guy called for you. Sounds like he misses you dearly.'

Jonathon froze as he remembered his telephone call. He wondered what Mac would say next.

'What English guy?' Lauren looked over at Jonathon with raised eyebrows. She almost smiled.

'You know – Maynard. That bloody consultant.'

'What did he say exactly?'

'Love and kisses. Shit, I don't know. Who cares? The guy was a pain in the backside. What do you want?'

'I want to give you an order for tomorrow, Mac.'

'I thought you preferred using the Web to dealing with an investment bank.'

'Maybe, Mac, but this is a big order.'

'You come into some big redundancy pay of late?'

'I want you to buy a thousand call options in five stocks. Same order for each of the next five days. Fill the order over the course of each day, not all at the opening. Interested at all, Mac?'

The audible gasp emanating from the speakerphone confirmed that a faraway salesman at an FF&O sales desk was slowly waking up.

'Is this some sort of wind-up? Should I hang up?'

'Only if you want to forgo the huge commissions. I got a new job. I'm a buyer of this market.'

Lauren let Mac stew on the other end of the line until his curiosity got the better of him.

'Who are you working for now?'

'These orders are on behalf of some trusts – Coral, Elbow, Chaplin, Devonshire, Jobson and the like. They're all live accounts that were opened last week. Check them on the client system.'

'Damn right I will.'

They were left on mute for a few minutes until the doubting Thomas returned to the line.

'You're bloody right! The accounts are open. They look legit and your name shows up as a contact. You're talking a thousand lots a pop per day? That's huge. You'll need millions of margin.'

'It's all sorted. Check the credit screen. We have a large credit line in place for all the trusts. We've deposited significant holdings of US T-bonds and T-bills. And some other triple-A supra-national bonds.'

A second pause while another Mitchell's in-house computer screen was viewed.

'Jeez! Your collateral is fucking huge. Hundred of millions per trust. Who owns these accounts?'

'They belong to some very influential friends of mine.'

'That's one hell of a job you got.'

Lauren gave Mac the five stock names. He'd fax the trade confirmation so they'd have it first thing the next morning. The day's dealing was done. They had taken their first gamble. Jonathon stood up.

'I'll call Cavendish later on to brief him. There's nothing more we can do today. We've rolled the dice and won't know until tomorrow if it's working. I'm going to get a sandwich.'

Lauren didn't react. He wanted her to come too but didn't dare ask her along and risk immediate rejection on day one. He made for the door. She spoke just in time.

'I'll brief Sayers. I wanna check my hotmail. I'll follow you down in five. Wait for me.'

Jonathon left. Lauren logged into hotmail. There was still no new mail from anyone. She typed up the summary details of the stock options. Sayers had advised her not to use his official Federal Reserve address because his PA and staff accessed his work e-mails. Instead she typed in the recipient address that he had given her in New York: chairman@msn.com. She hit 'Send', logged out, powered down and left for lunch with the most eligible dealer on the island.

Olivier Richemont threw aside his half-read copy of the *Royal Gazette*. The newspaper was tangible proof that nothing of any significance ever happened in Bermuda. The lead story in the sports section concerned a disaffected local soccer fan who had switched off the stadium floodlights at a cup final because he didn't like the half-time score. The round of golf could wait. His phone was ringing.

He opened his Nokia 7110 WAP-compatible mobile, specially bought from the Bermuda Telephone Company. He looked at the state-of-the-art LCD screen. The message wasn't a telephone call. It was a forwarded e-mail, routed automatically by a mail rule in Sayers's Outlook system – the message he had been expecting. The sender was chairman@msn.com.

He held the mobile in his right hand, a chilled piña colada in his left. He moved under the protection of a canvas parasol, somewhat larger than the fake pink one planted in his cocktail, and scrolled down the e-mail, ignoring the names of the US and European stocks. They were past their best-by date, being in the same time zone as Richemont's select party by the pool. The midday sun had yet to clear the tops of the precise row of palm trees, and lunch was not yet on the horizon. The Asian and Far East stocks were of much greater interest. He scribbled down the details in the ample margin of the pathetic business section of the *Gazette* and dialled the European telephone number in his pre-programmed address book.

'Todd Liebowitz.'

Richemont averted his eyes from Carla, who was enjoying one of the two natural saltwater lap pools at Blushing Sands. It was difficult to tell where the pool ended and the sea began. She was alone in the water. His eyes were fixed on her svelte form as she powered from end to end. When she came out to dive off the board in the deep end, all male conversation around the pool dried up while wives glared.

'I have the first orders for you for the Horseshoe Trust account.'

His attention was momentarily distracted by a muscled poser in wine-coloured Gant shorts who walked to the deep end and crashed into the pool, surfacing dangerously close to Carla.

'Are you in Nerja again, Mr Richemont?'

He looked around the luxury colony. Forty deluxe rooms, suites and cottages bathed in pastel colours. Private terraces all with ocean views. Caliban's Restaurant on the edge of the sea. The bar with photographs of celebrity friends of the Hollywood movie star part-owner. The Nirvana Day Spa with Tisserand aromatherapy, where Carla unwound before lengthy bouts of pre-dinner sex. The tennis courts, the massage treatments, the putting greens. No need to tell the Toddler where he was. Let him imagine all he wanted. That was the beauty and the anonymity of a mobile telephone.

'I want to buy a thousand near-month call options in NTT, Japan Tobacco, Japan Rail, Softbank and Sony in Japan. And I want to buy the same dated options in HSBC, China Light, Cheung Kong, Cathay and Hutchinson in Hong Kong.'

There was a pause far away in Mitchell's Geneva

'That's a big order.'

Richemont watched the twentysomething Gant guy do four perfect lengths. He sported a stupid gold neck chain that glistened in the sun, a few days' designer stubble on a square jawline and a chest wig that looked more genuine than most of the battered toupees lazing around the poolside.

'Is there a problem?'

'No. I'll pass the orders on to our affiliate companies in Tokyo and Hong Kong.'

The Gant guy passed Carla in the shallow end. He smiled over at her. Richemont refocused.

'I want an immediate fill of the entire order at the market opening. That's very important.'

'I will advise the respective sales desks. What about the execution confirmation?'

'Don't send it anywhere. Remember what I told you. I'll call you tomorrow.'

Liebowitz immediately filled out two standard client order forms for his PA to fax. One would go to the FF&O desk of Mitchell Leonberg Japan Inc. in Maranouchi, Tokyo. The other would go to the FF&O desk of Mitchell Leonberg Asia Pacific Inc. in Central, Hong Kong.

'What if I need to contact you?'

'You don't.'

Richemont put the telephone down and returned to his sunlounger. He continued to watch Carla, who now stood with the Gant guy in the shallow end, running her hands through her long dark hair. The sun glinted off her bare shoulders and arms. Richemont could see her erect nipples through the black swimsuit. He turned around and gave a nod to Max, who emerged from the shaded bar nearby.

'What's up, boss?'

'What's the news on Maynard and Trent so far?'

'Looks okay. He walked around the town yesterday after lunch at Kearney's. Yesterday afternoon they were together for a while at the office. She took a taxi to Surfway at four-fifty. He took one at five-forty-five. They shared a taxi from Surfway at seven-forty to La Venezia. They left there at ten-thirty, slept in their own bungalows. He made some early morning calls to the UK, according to the manageress. She didn't call New York at all. They shared a taxi to work today at seven-thirty. They're still there. Looks like they're keen.'

'No unaccounted time? No conversations with anyone else?'

'None that I saw.'

The Gant guy was still monopolising Carla. Richemont gave another nod. Max walked over to him as he towelled down his six-pack torso in the tiled shower area. Richemont repeatedly opened and closed the blade of his penknife. Max spoke to the guy, pointed at Carla, then faced him off, patting the bulky breast pocket of his suit. Carla pouted. The Gant guy sped off and wasn't seen outdoors for the remainder of his holiday.

Jonathon was puzzled by the overnight confirmation fax from the FF&Q sales desk in Hong Kong. The names of the trusts were down the left-hand side and the execution prices for a thousand call options in the correct stocks were down the right-hand side, but there was something wrong.

'A screw-up by your former colleagues,' he said with some glee.

Lauren looked over from her Bloomberg screen, which showed some promise of rising prices.

'That wouldn't surprise me. Let's see.'

He handed her the single-page fax on Mitchell's headed paper.

'The trust names are all the same as those I was given by Cavendish. Marley Trust, Coral, Elbow, Chaplin, Devonshire, Jobson, Whitney, Clearwater, Gunner, Achilles, Jennings and the like. But there's one trust on this fax that isn't on my list. Horseshoe Trust bought the same stock options as us but it isn't ours. Where the hell has that come from all of a sudden? You wanna call Mac?'

Lauren already had her hand on the speakerphone, fingers tapping out the direct number she knew so well.

'Nothing would give me greater pleasure.'

'Isn't it gonna be late out there?'

'Who cares? He'll be there. Otherwise I got his home number.' The phone rang. Mac was there. 'We got a problem with your confirmation fax. Horseshoe Trust isn't one of ours. We DK it.'

'You must know it!'

'Nope. Don't Know. DK.'

Jonathon heard the buzz of the dealing floor far away. McFarland came back on the line.

'We made a mistake. It's another new client we have. Ignore it. Sorry.' Lauren liked to hear Mac apologise. It hadn't happened often enough in the past. 'Hang on, Lauren. We did another thousand today. You're moving this market. Any other orders? Don't hold one little mistake against us.'

She kept Mac on tenterhooks, making him sweat even more than usual.

'What if you sent our confirmations to someone else in error? Our orders are huge. The consequences could be disastrous. No new orders for you today, Mac, sorry. Stick with the daily option order. Guess next time we might use Goldman or Deutsche instead. 'Bye.' She hung up.

Jonathon circled the word 'Horseshoe' and the order on the fax and looked at the list again. 'It's weird, though.'

'What is?'

'Another trust bought the same five stock options as we did on the same day. What are the odds on that?'

'Another speculative investor somewhere else in the world. Hong Kong is a huge market.'

'It's like this is one of our own trust accounts.'

'But it's not. McFarland told us that.'

'Only you and I know what we decide to buy each day. No one else.' Jonathon had a terrible thought. He dared to speak it aloud. 'It's not you? You're not Horseshoe? You're not frontrunning again?'

Lauren looked at him, clearly outraged. He regretted the allegation. They had agreed to forget the past.

'Of course not. No one else knows what we buy except our masters.'

'What do you mean?'

'Sayers and Cavendish. That's who.'

'Don't be ridiculous. They don't know.'

'But you talk to Cavendish each day.'

'He asked me to call him. I give him general information. I don't tell him any more.'

'Doesn't he ask you what stocks we buy?' she asked.

'No.' He looked at Lauren again. 'What are you saying? Are you telling Cavendish?'

'Not him. I'm telling Sayers what we're about to buy each day. I e-mail him the details.'

'Whatever possessed you to do that?'

'He asked me to. I assumed Cavendish had asked you the same. We work directly for them.'

He stared at her blankly, his mind racing over what was possible and whether Lauren was part of it. Suddenly he didn't know whether he could trust her. Was she here to help him or to keep an eye on him? Did she work for Sayers, Cavendish, Max or who? Was her apparent interest in him real or was it an act? Impossible to tell.

Lauren wasn't satisfied yet. She got up and walked over to the window, gazing out at the view of the harbour. She was reminded of her days overlooking Victoria Harbour.

'Let's tackle this another way. I've seen that name somewhere recently. Horseshoe. What is that, Jon?'

'Something a blacksmith hammers out on an anvil.'

Lauren paced the small room, fax still in hand. He was impressed by her energy.

'I mean ... where did all the names of our trusts come from?'

'They came from whomever Cavendish and Sayers used to set up the Bermudan trusts. Lawyers?'

Lauren glanced out at the view again.

'Horseshoe has something to do with Bermuda.' She racked her brains and then recalled the *Destinations* magazine she had browsed through during the flight from JFK. 'Have we got a map of Bermuda here?'

Jonathon pointed over to the corner of the office.

'Max left me a map.'

Lauren opened the map on the dealing desk, obscuring the screens, and eyed up all twenty square miles of the island. She looked it over several times and suddenly pointed to a spot at the left end of the south coast.

'Horseshoe Bay! I knew I remembered it from somewhere.'

Jonathon peered at the fine print but was lost.

'It's a beach. So what?'

All the beaches on the map were coloured pink. Lauren's index finger was running along the coastline.

'Horseshoe Bay. Jobson Cove. Whitney Bay. Elbow Beach. Coral Beach. They're all here. That's where they got the trust names from. They used a map of Bermuda.'

Jonathon was still lost in this seemingly dead-end local geography tour.

'So some lawyer takes trust names from a map?'

'Not just some lawyer. The same lawyer set up all the trusts. Horseshoe is connected to our trusts but it's not on our list. It's playing the market with us in size, but someone else runs it.'

'How do we find out more?'

'I'll call Mac again. Spin him a line.'

Lauren hit auto redial on the speakerphone and heard the familiar din again.

'Mac, the mistake was on our part. Horseshoe is one of our trusts. Can you confirm that?'

'Gimme a moment.' They waited while he dug out the evidence. 'Definitely not. We get the orders from somewhere else. What are you trying to pull?'

'Okay. No problem. 'Bye.'

Jonathon looked sympathetic.

'Nice try. Shame about the dead end.'

But Lauren was thinking back to her days at Mitchell's. She knew the names in Ops. It was worth a try.

'Not quite dead yet.'

She dialled Mitchell's switchboard and was put through to the documentation department.

'Lauren here from FF&O on eight. I need some info on one of the desk clients. It's pretty urgent.'

Some junior Ops grunt mumbled down the line.

'Wha' name?'

'Horseshoe Trust.'

Another pause while some papers shuffled in the background.

'Wha' ya want to know?'

'Who owns the account?'

'The trustees.'

'Which names?'

'I don't know. No names are shown. Guess that's the point of a trust.'

'Who formed the trust? Is there a name of a law firm on the file?'

'I'll look for the file.'

Another interminable pause. The Ops back office was all over the place. Nothing had changed.

'Can't find the file.'

Lauren wondered whether it had been removed. Horseshoe was becoming more intriguing by the minute.

'You can't open a new client account without a file.'

'A new account? You shoulda said. Must be in the in-tray.' More shuffling. So much for the paperless office. 'Here's the file. The name of the law firm who set up the trust was Cranley Adams & Co.'

'In London? New York?'

'No. Hamilton, Bermuda.'

Lauren gave Jonathon the thumbs-up. She was making more deductions than the average payslip.

'Is there anything else on the file?'

Another pause.

'You said you work on the sales floor upstairs?'

'Yeah.'

'Sounds awful quiet up there.' She'd been rumbled. 'I'll call you back on your internal line.'

She slammed the telephone down.

'Damn! That's the end of any info from client accounts. Pity.'

Jonathon already had the local telephone book in his hands, going straight for the Cs. Lauren was ahead of the game. She stood up and grabbed him as she made for the door. He liked decisive women.

'Forget the phone book. Follow me.'

They went down to the shared entrance in Chancery Lane. She searched the numerous brass nameplates and pointed at the brick wall.

'Cranley Adams & Co. We share the third floor with them. They set all the trusts up. Everything we need to know about the Horseshoe Trust is in this very building. What do we next?'

Jonathon watched some other workers departing the offices after their working day.

'We'll visit the firm of Cranley Adams & Co. at a more opportune time.'

They exhausted the supply of local restaurants in less than a week. Jonathon felt the need to be culinarily creative. He imagined that he was back in Chester Row, cooking for Eva and the children again. Lauren arrived, as invited, precisely at eight. Hardly a surprise since Jonathon had seen her leave next door twenty seconds earlier and appear from the far side of the low brick wall that divided their joint veranda.

'Smells good. Can I look?'

'The unwritten rule is that the guest never witnesses the disasters that occur in the kitchen. You'll appreciate that rule when we dine sumptuously at the Michelin-starred Chez Lauren tomorrow.'

'In your dreams.'

He poured two glasses of Chablis.

'Are we celebrating something?'

'The fact that we can work well together. And the Nikkei and Hang Seng rose today.'

They sat on the warm veranda on nasty yet functional plastic chairs. Jonathon looked out at the palm fronds and breaking waves and then back at Lauren. She wore the same pink shirt, evidently travelling light, as he always did. Her skin looked moist in the humid air. Her hair blew in the soft onshore breeze. She looked better every time. He wasn't sure he would be able to restrain himself if they had to spend several more weeks together in that tiny dealing room.

'Let's eat.'

The best food was flown in from the States. It cost a fortune but was worth it. The mozzarella-and-tomato salad was as good as at home. The seafood tagliatelle was better than at Chester Row, with fresh local shrimps and clams. Lauren savoured it.

'Best meal I've had all week. Where did you get the provisions?'

'I gave Max a list. He was livid. I told him I'd call Cavendish if he didn't find me some basil.'

'What do you make of Max?'

'I don't trust him. I think he's been told to watch us.'

'Me too.'

'I don't even think he works for Cavendish.'

Lauren looked thoughtful.

'He never mentions Sayers.'

They ate ice cream and assorted fruits as the sun slowly set on the horizon and the air turned chill. Lauren rolled down her shirtsleeves and buttoned her shirt up fully. Pity.

'You cold? Want a loan of a jumper?' Jonathon suggested.

She nodded. He went inside and reappeared with a new navy sweatshirt. Lauren saw the label.

'Gap?'

'So?'

'Nothing.'

They sat in comfortable silence until the kettle whistled. Time for coffee. Lauren sat up.

'You got some music?'

'There's a CD player but I only brought one disc with me. It was in my luggage from Hong Kong.'

'I got a good CD inside.'

She disappeared behind the low wall and emerged wearing her Yankees baseball cap, jumping up and down with a single CD behind her back, hidden like a gift about to be presented to a loved one.

'I'll play you my favourite track.'

Jonathon produced the pot of steaming coffee as the first strains emanated from the Panasonic. He recognised the gravelly voice. Track ten, no doubt about it. He loved the intro. Lauren saw him smiling.

'You know it.' She drew closer and poured the coffees. 'What did you bring with you?'

'Same one. The best track is "New York". I like Bono's lyrics.'

The chorus broke in the background. Jonathon thought of Rebecca, about losing your wife in the queue for the lifeboats. Lauren thought of home, about finding your space and figuring our your mid-life crisis.

'Me too. I guess every song means something different to everyone.'

She crossed her legs as she sat on the edge of the wall. Jonathon admired the way her thin belt accentuated her narrow waist. He liked the way she smiled, the way her eyes sparkled under the peak of the baseball cap and strands of auburn hair hung below her earlobes with their tasteful diamond studs. Her profile reminded him vaguely of times past, perhaps time spent with Rebecca.

He hadn't felt these deep emotions in an age. He was close enough to Lauren to lean over to her, hold her tightly, run his hands over her perfect skin, inhale her wonderful aroma and kiss her. But he dared not make the first move. There was too much at stake here.

CHAPTER TWENTY-ONE
HAMILTON, BERMUDA – 1.20 P.M.

Jonathon and Lauren sat on Kearney's balcony over-looking the bustle of Front Street. It should have been an idyllic moment but the reality was somewhat different, with incessant street noise, gridlocked traffic, rows of buses, plumes of exhaust fumes from cars and the revving engines of scooters. Businessmen scurried about in Bermuda shorts and matching knee-length socks. The solo cop in the birdcage to the right had his work cut out. The view of one of the most beautiful harbours in the world was obscured by another giant Celebrity Cruises liner moored by passenger terminals one and six, bastions of American capitalistic pleasure yet registered in the wonderfully lax port of Monrovia, Liberia.

It had been a long week with a few surprises, but the markets were definitely improving. They spent billions. The HSI rose for the first time in almost two months. The Nikkei was up. The FTSE was down only a fraction at the close. Confidence was clearly returning. So much so that, instead of a quick sandwich at their desk, they took a long lunch. They picked their way through the dry house burgers, lukewarm fries and stringy coleslaw served on off-white plates. Jonathon left half his food untouched and downed the pint of cold Fosters. Lauren was seemingly of the same opinion.

'You'd better cook something wonderful tonight.'

'Are we celebrating?'

'Sure we are. Some commentators have been saying that selective buying by big buyers in the options market has positively impacted the cash market. That's gotta be us. CNBC say there is a flight to quality and that institutional investors are returning to blue-chips with substantial revenue, good earnings and positive cash flow. Some of the smaller stock markets are up today, an event unparalleled in recent weeks. A few optimists are speaking about the trough bottoming out. We might pull this off yet.'

He was impressed. Lauren certainly knew her stuff. He looked around, considering ordering another cold beer. The tourists poured on and off the ships through the restricted customs area, mostly huge middle-aged men in baseball caps and their trophy wives in glitzy T-shirts and cut-away denim shorts. Oriental crew members in virgin white alighted for some well-earned R&R. Jonathon wished that he, like the tourists, didn't have a care in the world. He wondered how long these days with Lauren would last and what he would do when he found himself alone again.

'This street is misnamed. It should be Affront Street,' he observed.

His gaze wandered up and down the road below and settled on a vision approaching him. She was very young, immaculately dressed, tanned and wearing cool Police shades. She was the only woman he'd seen in a week on the island dressed all in black, and it worked. Here was money on two elegant legs. He looked hard, then suddenly pulled back from the railing.

'Look at that woman in black!'

Lauren turned for a better view of the street but was not impressed.

'Jon, I don't go around here getting excited about every handsome man I see. There's no need for you to let your male hormones run wild just because you see a girl like that. Anyway, she can't be more than eighteen or nineteen. Far too young for you. Forget about her.'

'What the hell is she doing here? We need to leave. Now.'

Jonathon left a twenty-dollar bill on the table, grabbed Lauren, ignored the waitress in the safe knowledge that he wouldn't be back again, and ran downstairs to street level.

'Are you crazy?'

'I know her. Stick with me. Let's see what she's up to.'

Lauren reluctantly followed.

'Who is she?'

'Carla somebody or other. She's my boss's other half. Apart from his wife, that is.'

They followed Carla at a safe distance, stopping only occasionally to stare into some grim shop window display as she did the same a few stores ahead. She paused in front of a Marks & Spencer's.

'She's hardly going in there,' remarked Jonathon. Carla moved on almost immediately. 'I didn't think so.'

She disappeared into Trimingham's, the largest department store on the island – Harrods, Selfridges, Harvey Nicks, Macy's, Saks and Barney's all rolled into one but without the merchandise, staff, selection, kudos or floor space. They trailed her up to the ladieswear floor, where Jonathon took fright.

'She knows me. I can't risk it. You get closer. See what she's doing.'

'What else can she be doing? She's shopping, dummy.'

He lurked behind a row of oversized maternity clothes. Lauren reappeared five minutes later.

'She's bought two swimming costumes that leave nothing to the imagination. More like sun thongs.'

'I know the sort.'

'What?'

'I've seen her in them. In a pool in Spain.'

'There's more to you than meets the eye.'

'Anything else?'

'She paid with a gold credit card from Mitchell's Suisse.'

'She loves spending Richemont's money but she'd hardly come here just for the shopping. Quick! She's on the move.'

They followed Carla downstairs, outside and towards the taxi rank. She took the first available cab. Jonathon and Lauren waited one minute and jumped into the back of the next. He pointed ahead.

'Follow that cab.' The bemused driver looked around. Jonathon grinned. 'I can't believe I said that.'

It was never going to be one of those classic high-speed pursuits with screeching tyres and burned rubber along winding roads and hairpin bends. The line of traffic ahead, the single-lane roads, sets of rigorously observed traffic lights and the speed limit of 20 mph saw to that. They were in more danger of rear-ending their quarry than of losing sight of the cab. They crawled along the South Road in Devonshire Parish, stopping every few minutes as a pink municipal bus ahead dropped off passengers.

'I wonder if she's alone? Last time I saw them together they looked inseparable.'

The other cab made a left turn between some impressive entrance gates and rows of mature palm trees. 'Blushing Sands Beach & Golf Club,' announced the stone sign. It looked like the sort of place that Carla and maybe Richemont would choose to frequent. They stopped a safe distance from the main reception area and watched her pay the fare and go inside. She re-emerged shortly afterwards jangling a set of keys in her hand, and made her way towards some low bungalows nearer the sea. Jonathon slid open the door of the cab.

'Wait here.'

He stood before the reception desk and bluffed.

'I've a delivery for Mr Richemont.'

The duty manageress looked at him, examined a print-out hidden under the wooden counter, held out her open palm, smiled pleasantly, as was to be expected of Blushing Sands, and countered effectively.

'Where is it?'

He bluffed again. 'Outside.'

'I'll make sure Mr Richemont gets it immediately.'

So he was here.

'They're confidential business papers. What bungalow is he in?'

She was having none of it.

'We only allow residents and club members to go any farther.'

He left, knowing for definite that Richemont was near by. What had possessed him to take a holiday in the midst of a global crisis, why had he come here and at the same time as Jonathon? Richemont wasn't supposed to know where the assignment was based. Cavendish had insisted. But it was too much of a coincidence. Jonathon jumped into the idling taxi and told the driver to head back into Hamilton.

As they left the hotel a solitary figure emerged from the shade of some nearby trees and stubbed out a Camel cigarette on the warm tarmac. Max scratched his shaven head and pondered recent events for a moment. He was undecided as to the relative merits of following the couple in his BMW or warning his boss in the beachside bungalow that the two hired hands now knew about his presence on the island.

* * *

Jonathon had definite plans for Saturday morning – to
see the island and catch some rays. Instead he woke
to the sound of rain pummelling the roof, and the
occasional clap of thunder far overhead. He pulled back
the edge of a curtain and saw torrents spitting from the
skies. The water splashed on to the concrete paths like
golf balls pitched into sandy bunkers. His enthusiasm
to get up and send some postcards instantly disappeared. He called home, spoke to Eva and Jack and
told them all was well. He lied, in truth. He lay alone
on the creased sheets, still half awake yet unable to
get back to sleep, thinking about what it was that he
and Lauren were part of and who else might be on
the island.

He wondered what Lauren had planned on her first
day off work. She'd expressed no desire to return to
New York for the weekend. She was only feet away
from him on the other side of the wall, her bedroom
backing on to his. He thought about what she might
be doing right now. Staring out of the rear window
at the same dismal scene? He thought about what she
might wear in bed in this sticky climate and why the
two of them stayed resolutely chaste, denying their basic
instincts in deference to professional integrity. Most of
all he wondered whether she was as interested as he was.
When the hunger pangs became too much, he got up,
brewed some coffee and opened the door to the veranda.
The air was humid and crackling with electric energy,
the skies heavy with more laden storm clouds about to
unleash their contents.

'Good morning.'

Lauren sat on the edge of her adjoining veranda. She was holding out her hand, trying to catch the rivulets running down from the tiled roof overhead.

'Not quite.'

The water splashed on to the oversized plain white T-shirt which came down to her thighs. Jonathon didn't think she was wearing anything else underneath. He wished he hadn't worn his oldest and shabbiest pair of boxers. He sat beside her, out of the rain.

'Wish you were working today?' she asked.

He threw a despairing glance at the skies. This rain would last the entire day and they both knew it.

'Guess we gotta stay indoors today.'

He hadn't meant it to sound that way. She ran her hands through her wet hair.

'It's warm enough to take a shower out here in the open.'

'You wouldn't dare.'

They both knew that the rear of the bungalows facing the sea was not overlooked.

'Watch me.'

She stepped off the veranda and faced up to the sheeting rain. Jonathon watched her dance solo for a few moments, saw the open invitation in her eyes and knew he had to join her. They stood in the deluge, moving closer together as their clothes became saturated. He was suddenly aware of the unmistakable signs of his arousal. It had been a long time. Too long. He moved away.

'Let's get inside and dry off.'

She followed him into his bungalow and headed towards the en suite bathroom. He handed her the largest bath towel and watched her dry her hair. She tilted her head to left and right, yet her eyes never left his. She eyed the few raindrops trapped in his chest hairs, couldn't resist and rubbed him down with the same wet towel. Thunder clapped directly overhead. It was getting louder.

He had never been this close to her. Her T-shirt left nothing to the imagination. She saw him looking and moved nearer. It was the most natural thing in the world. He kissed her and forgot about the overnight stubble. She responded and didn't seem to object to the bristles. He tried to peel off the T-shirt; she helped him. He stepped out of his boxers and moved even closer. More thunder above.

'I've been waiting a week for you to make the first move,' she breathed.

'Me too. I'm glad you did.'

They stayed indoors all Saturday, alternating between bungalows sixteen and seventeen.

The storm had cleared by Sunday. Max called around with the BMW as a rainbow appeared at sea.

'Thought you might want a lift, maybe to a beach?'

Jonathon was thinking about asking him for a ride to Horseshoe Bay, just for the hell of it. Just to watch Max's facial reaction and see whether he knew anything about the other trust. Maybe not. The sun wasn't that convincing, though, and beaches were easy places at which to keep an eye on people. Lots of open space and uninterrupted views. No crowds to mingle with. Jonathon had decided on their preferred destination.

'We'll take a ride into town.'

'Where are you going?'

'Here and there,' answered Lauren.

Max drove them in silence into Hamilton. He parked. They went their separate ways. Max was watchful under his false smile. Lauren carried a camera to make it look like a sightseeing trip as they walked towards the Perot post office on Queen Street.

'Let's be tourists first. Then we'll lose him.'

Lauren took Jonathon's hand as they walked on the shaded side of the street, each of them knowing it wasn't merely for effect. Occasionally their shoulders brushed together. Visitors from the cruise ship hovered in search of postcards for the folks back home. Jonathon looked back but could see nothing suspicious. They walked up to Church Street, ducking into shops and dodging into narrow alleys; back down the slopes of Burnaby Street, more narrow streets, stopping and turning frequently.

Jonathon had decided that Sunday would be the best day. Working days with office workers were an impossibility. There were too many revellers at nearby restaurants and bars at night-time. They reached the top of Chancery Lane. Still no sign of Max.

'We need to make sure the coast is clear.'

They waited in the shadows, one eye on the passing traffic, but their real attention was directed towards the office doors opposite the steps. After fifteen minutes, Jonathon was convinced it was now or never.

'No one's there. Let's do it.'

He produced the keys that Max had given him on day one and tried the lock. It didn't have the desired effect. He tried the door again, then pushed it open. They walked inside.

'Sorry, no visitors in here.'

An elderly security guard with mutton-chop whiskers and a navy uniform that had seen better days appeared from behind the reception desk. Jonathon didn't recognise him.

'We work on the third floor.'

'I ain't seen you two before.'

'We only work weekdays usually. We're new.' Jonathon showed him the keys and took his silence for agreement. 'We've got some work to do this afternoon. We won't be long.'

'First you gotta sign the book.'

They scribbled their names down before riding the tiny elevator together to the third floor.

'I never thought there'd be a security guard here on a Sunday. And I wish we didn't have to sign in.'

'He's harmless.'

'Until he goes walkabout upstairs or tells Max we are here.'

Jonathon unlocked the door to their office. He ignored the dealing screens today.

'I examined the building from the outside on Friday. There's a central core, with an elevator, stairs and communal facilities like washrooms and storage rooms. We have one washroom here, which is adjacent to the central core. I'm sure there's only one centrally plumbed area in a building like this. Our washroom must back on to another used by Cranley Adams. They have the same small windows at the rear. I saw a ledge which isn't overlooked. It's the only way in, short of breaking down the main door, and that might give the game away on Monday morning.'

'What if there are alarms?'

'There are no alarm boxes or wiring on the outside of the building. Anyway, who needs alarms here in Hamilton? The only crime on this island is what some of the tourists wear when they come off the ships.'

They went into the washroom. Jonathon stood up on the toilet seat and locked the cubicle door.

'If you hear anyone else, then slam the door hard.'

He opened the small window and climbed out on to the ledge, crawling along until he came to a set of three identical windows. He tried all three and decided the middle window was the least secure. He leaned against it, grasped the wooden frame with both hands and rocked it back and forth. There was some play in it. He heard something give. Finally, the latch snapped. He climbed into the washroom and then the office area. The interior looked like any lawyer's office. Chaotic. Empty too, thankfully.

A legal job from a bunch of central banks would have been a major coup for a small law firm such as this. He was sure that one of the senior partners would have handled the job personally. The more senior the partner, the bigger the office. They'd want a harbour view. Jonathon made an educated guess and headed for the largest corner office. The sign on the door said 'Andrew Cranley'. He examined the lever-arch files on the shelves but didn't recognise the company names. Some files at the bottom looked new. He found one labelled 'BoE'.

He sat at the walnut desk. The file had alphabetical tabs with identical documents at each separate tab. He recognised the names of the trusts listed, went straight to H. Horseshoe Trust was there, and it contained more paperwork than the others. There was a letter from a Todd Liebowitz in Mitchell's Geneva office confirming some payment instructions. Also a fax confirming that Olivier Richemont was the individual who had opened the account. Jonathon sat back in the chair and exhaled. The last page contained scribbled comments about a conference call. The trust's three beneficial trustees were listed as Richemont, Cavendish and Sayers. He heard a door slam loudly.

Gathering the contents of the file together, he slipped under the desk. He heard someone enter the outer office then push open the door six feet away from him. He peered out and recognised the white socks of the security guard. The door to the washroom was still half open. So was the middle window with the smashed fixture. He crouched there, wishing he were somewhere else. A second set of shoes appeared, topped by what looked like a dusty black suit. The two men stood together. There was a short conversation.

'Look normal to you?'

Jonathon froze as he heard the accent. Max was in the room.

'Yes, sir.'

The two men walked around for a few moments but didn't enter the corner office. They left and locked the outer door from the outside. Jonathon waited a while, then got up, powered up the photocopier and waited a further two minutes while it came to life after a weekend on power-save economy mode. He copied the entire Horseshoe file as quickly as he could.

Twenty pages later, he replaced the file on the bottom shelf, looked around the office, closed the washroom door behind him and clambered back through the window. It wouldn't close. He knew that a close inspection from the inside would reveal the damage, but they'd never prove that it was anything to do with him or Lauren, or even when the damage had occurred. He crawled along the ledge, one hand still clutching the bundle of papers.

'Did they see you? I slammed the door as hard as I could,' Lauren told him anxiously.

'No. You did well. Did Max come in?'

'Yeah. He asked where you were. I said you were in the washroom. Did you find anything next door?'

'Maybe too much.'

Jonathon sat alone on the veranda in the gathering dusk until Lauren appeared. He had told her nothing more. Didn't want to worry her until he had thought through the full implications of his discovery.

'Are you cooking for me tonight?'

'I don't much feel like it. Let's spend the last of our dollars in the restaurant by the pool.'

She stood beside him, rested her head against his bare shoulders.

'You're not your usual self, Jon. What did you find in the lawyer's office?'

He stood up and grabbed his sweatshirt.

'We're going out.'

First he went into the kitchen, took down the coffee jar and emptied the entire contents into a spare mug. He put the twenty pages from the lawyer's office inside, plus the faxed confirmations from their own office, and screwed the lid tight. He hid the jar in the sweatshirt he carried, and rejoined Lauren.

'Where to?' she enquired, content to let him make all the running for once.

'We're going for a walk down by the cliffs to the beach.'

'At this hour? It'll be deserted down there.'

'Precisely.'

'What happened today, Jon? I can tell it's serious.'

'Let's wait until we're out of sight.'

The beach was small and devoid of other guests. They walked in silence to the very farthest part, past gnarled driftwood and domestic refuse, until Jonathon stopped and looked around him.

'You lost something?' Lauren asked.

'I need to bury this jar somewhere.'

'What's in it?'

'Our insurance policy.'

'Bury it behind this outcrop of rock. It's distinctive enough.' She pointed.

He looked around one last time, then dug out a sandy hollow with his hands and buried the jar.

'What now?' she asked.

'We take a romantic walk for two on the beach at dusk. That's the reason we came down here.'

'I wondered when you were going to get romantic.'

'Max may be watching us. Or that manageress at the front desk. I don't trust her either.'

They walked back hand in hand, their bare feet splashing in the water. Burying the evidence was a weight off his mind, as if he had somehow distanced himself from the problem. Lauren was still inquisitive.

'What's in the jar?'

'Proof that my boss is behind Horseshoe. Proof that he's the one who bought the same options.'

'Jeez! A frontrunner in our midst. How does Richemont know what we traded?'

There was no easy way to tell her.

'Others are involved too.'

'Then I'd better tell Sayers.'

'No point. He's in it up to his neck.'

Lauren caught her breath. 'The Fed Chairman? For God's sake, you better tell Cavendish.'

'No point.'

She stopped, caught his glum expression and knew what it meant.

'You mean they're all in it? We're working for pillars of the establishment on one gigantic scam?'

'That's exactly what I mean.'

'Is that why Max follows us? And why your boss is here? Jeez, we're in danger. Jon, what do we do?'

'I don't know.'

Lauren became very silent as they climbed the steps. Surfway didn't look so homely now. She stopped.

'We got to make it look like it's business as usual until we find a way out. Like we don't know anything.'

She pulled him towards the outdoor hot tub, surrounded by low hedges and lit only by a low-voltage night-light. A few tree frogs croaked in the background. Otherwise the night was still.

'No one can see us here. If anyone approaches, we'll hear their footsteps on the gravel path. Let's relax for a while, recharge our batteries. Tomorrow is a fresh start.'

She pulled off her T-shirt, turned on full power and slipped into the bubbles in her bikini. Jonathon threw off his polo shirt and joined her. He felt the wonderful sensation as jets of hot water massaged his tired body, yet he wished he were somewhere else. With Jack and Imogen in Chester Row. Anywhere else on this planet as long as Lauren was there too. She watched him in the dim light, his profile outlined in shadow, and moved much closer, then undid the strings on her bikini.

'Gotta make everything seem like normal. Pretend you're enjoying this. And think.'

CHAPTER TWENTY-TWO
HAMILTON, BERMUDA – 9.15 A.M.

After a weekend without work, Jonathon hated this surrogate dealing room already. He'd rather be outside. He was certain Lauren would too. He knew her so much better than the last time they had pulled up their chairs at this desk. They had spent two days together, and bungalow number sixteen was now surplus to requirements. It was difficult to concentrate on work-related matters, but they managed to spend billions in the early hours buying major stocks in Europe and the US. Markets were visibly rising. He pulled his swivel chair closer and kissed her.

'You okay?'

'Sure. Great weekend. Except for Horseshoe.'

'We won't be here for ever. This assignment will finish. I don't know what Richemont and the governors plan, but we must take every precaution possible before we leave.'

'You think they'll let us leave?'

'Why not? They don't know we know. Let's keep it that way. But remember, our only chance to avoid being incriminated along with them is to get as much evidence about Horseshoe as we can.'

'What sort of evidence?'

'We know from that fax that Horseshoe traded the same five Far East call options as we did, but one trade isn't enough to prove a pattern. We need to know everything about Horseshoe's trading. That information must be somewhere in Mitchell's. How do we get hold of it? You know the bank.'

'You worked there too.' He gave her a withering look. 'We could call Mac again and dig deeper?' suggested Lauren.

'It might set off alarm bells. We need some other source in Mitchell's.'

Lauren thought back to her days in Hong Kong and how she'd handled client enquiries.

'Client Services have client account statements.'

'Give them a call.'

'They won't talk to me,' she protested. 'I'm history in that firm.'

'They mightn't know you've left. Bluff it out. All they can do is hang up.'

'Let's not make the same mistake twice.'

Lauren went to the pile of office junk on a nearby table, most of it still shrouded in bubble wrap and never to be opened. She ignored the calculators and staplers and selected a new Phillips Dictaphone. It already contained batteries and operated to her touch. She set it down on the desk and dialled. Jonathon saw the Hong Kong number flash up and recognised the extension. He put his hand over the handset, about to cut her off before she uttered a word.

'I said not to call McFarland.'

Lauren put her elegant fingers to her full lips and hushed him. McFarland answered with a grunt.

'Mac, Lauren here. We may have a big market order for you. Hang on a moment.'

She put the telephone on mute, smiled and hit the record button on the Dictaphone, holding it close to the handset. The only audible sound was the incessant background hum of the sales floor. Nothing happened for several minutes until Mac broke the interminable silence.

'You still there, Lauren?'

She stopped the recording and frowned.

'We'll call you back.' She hung up. 'That's all he's good for. Background effects.'

She rewound instantly, checked the recording and redialled Mitchell's switchboard on the speakerphone.

'Client Services, please.'

A girl answered. Jonathon could hear it all. The tape was playing. It sounded real enough to him.

'Lauren from the sales floor here. I got a client giving me some serious grief.'

'Who?'

'Horseshoe Trust. They haven't got a mailed statement yet and they want one.'

They heard a keyboard being hammered as the required information was located.

'That account is handled by the Geneva office.'

'Meaning?'

The background tape played on. Jonathon wondered how many seconds were left.

'Meaning that we pass the executions to Geneva and they send a statement to the client.'

'Who's the AE in Geneva?'

Another pause on the line. The tape must be near the end. They waited an eternity.

'A guy called Todd Liebowitz.'

Lauren took his telephone number and hung up.

'That's bad news and good news. The bad news is we gotta call Liebowitz. The good news is if we can get that statement, it will show all Horseshoe's trades, not only those in the Far East stocks. If all of Horseshoe's trades go through this account then we can work out how much they've made. Or lost.'

Jonathon was impressed.

'I don't think they've lost anything. What are you going to say to Liebowitz?'

'Nothing. You're gonna call him. Tell him you work in Bermuda with Cranley Adams & Co. Speak with that nice accent. Say Richemont is coming to the office later, needs a statement faxed over right away to you.' Jonathon wasn't convinced. She persevered. 'As you say, all he can do is hang up.'

'And tell Richemont perhaps?'

'But he won't know who you really are.'

'Okay, I'll call him at the end of his working day. He'll be hassled. Let's rehearse how we do this over an early lunch.'

First thing in the afternoon, Jonathon dialled Geneva and got through to Liebowitz's direct line.

'It's Andrew Cranley here from Cranley Adams in Bermuda.'

'Evening, what can I do for you?' answered the American, five hours ahead in the working day.

'We handled all the paperwork for Olivier Richemont's Horseshoe Trust. You probably know that Mr Richemont, his friend Carla and business associate Max are holidaying on our island at present.' Liebowitz was thinking that it explained the sound of poolside splashes during Richemont's daily calls. 'Mr Richemont is coming into my office later to discuss some financial matters. He asked me to call you for the latest account statement. Says he hasn't received one yet.'

Jonathon waited a few moments while the AE assimilated the information. Then Liebowitz balked.

'Of course he won't get a statement. He asked for a hold mail facility.'

'Nevertheless, Mr Richemont would like a copy sent today by fax.'

'That's somewhat irregular. I need to receive the instruction directly from him.'

'I am advised that Mr Richemont is probably on the eighteenth hole of the Southampton Princess golf course at present. I dare not disturb him on his mobile at a time like this. You know what he's like. He has no private fax machine at his own resort so he wants you to fax the latest statement to our office.'

'That's still irregular.' Liebowitz was playing hardball.

'I can't see what the problem is. We both work for Mr Richemont and we both know he's a pushy Swiss bastard who likes to jerk our strings, but the client is always right, and he pays the bills. You know who I am and you know I'm in Bermuda. I'll give you the fax number here.'

Another long pause. Jonathon hoped he had sounded confident enough.

'What's your number?' Lauren scribbled down the number of the office fax machine. Jonathon called it out, preceded by the local 441 area code.

'I'll see what I can do.'

Liebowitz hung up, but wasn't sure what to do next. Richemont was always so bloody difficult. He went into the enquiry screen and printed off the Horseshoe statement. One more check was needed. He went to his file and took out the Cranley Adams & Co. letters. He compared the fax number on the letterhead to the fax number he had been given by Cranley. They were not the same.

Jonathon and Lauren sat in silence, watching the lights on their fax machine still glowing red. After ten minutes, Lauren checked that the machine was working and had paper while Jonathon paced the room.

'It's not going to work. Liebowitz smells a rat. He'll wait to talk to Richemont.'

'Patience. It takes time to get a statement printed and faxed,' advised Lauren.

In Switzerland Liebowitz was still puzzled. Perhaps he should call Cranley back to check whether he'd made an error. On second thoughts, the numbers were quite similar. Same area code and first three digits. Only two digits different in the last four. It was probably another fax machine on the same office floor. The call seemed genuine and the caller certainly knew Richemont well. He faxed away.

In Hamilton the fax machine sprang into life. Several pages appeared bearing the Mitchell's letterhead. Jonathon smiled.

'Bloody hell! It worked.'

They sat at the desk and examined the three pages of almost illegible small print made worse by the long-haul fax transmission. Jonathon recognised the trading pattern first.

'Horseshoe is trading identically to us. They bought call options on the first day. They bought options in the same five Tokyo stocks as we did last Tuesday, and S&P futures on Wednesday, and HSI futures on Thursday, and the exact same US and European stocks on Friday. That is a million-to-one shot. The execution times are all at the opening bell. Horseshoe is placing its order before we do. In fact, I think you know what we call this, Lauren?'

She grinned.

'Frontrunning.'

Jonathon took out a pen and started number-crunching.

'Let's mark these positions to market. See if they're making as much as we are.'

Lauren called out the live prices from Bloomberg. Jonathon scribbled down figures to the nearest million and totted them up without the aid of a calculator. He sat back finally and threw the pen on the desk.

'I reckon they've made about seven and a half million dollars in five days. They're on to a sure thing.'

'This account statement is dynamite. What do we do with it?' she asked.

'Looks like we're going for another long moonlit walk on the beach this evening.'

'You're such a romantic.'

Max approached the poolside in his trusty suit, daring to interrupt his employer as he lounged in the sun.

'Excuse me, sir. We've got a problem.'

Richemont opened one eye lazily and avoided the glare of the sun directly overhead.

'What sort of problem?'

Max lowered his voice, although there was no one within earshot.

'The senior partner at Cranley's called me. He was looking at his trust files today. One of his files is in the wrong order, he says. It's as if the pages have been taken out and then replaced in a hurry.'

'So one of his staff made an error. Why tell us?'

'His staff know how Cranley likes things. They don't make that mistake twice.'

Richemont raised himself off the sunlounger and slowly focused.

'Which trust is it?'

'The one you said mattered most. Horseshoe.'

'And all the papers on it are in that file?'

'Yes.' Max crouched down lower for maximum eye contact. 'There's more. There's a sequential counter on the only office photocopier. They use it to charge large photocopying jobs to the clients at a few cents a page. The copier was used over the weekend.'

'Any staff in Cranley's office then?'

'We checked the lobby book. The only two visitors were on Sunday. Our couple, Maynard and Trent.'

'They're not a couple.'

'They are from what I can see. Very friendly these days. Hand in hand all the time.'

Richemont was wondering whether perhaps someone else was trying to muscle in on his operation. He looked around the poolside, apparently deep in contemplation. 'You sure it really was them in person?'

Max nodded. 'I drove them into Hamilton myself that afternoon.'

'Jesus! How the hell did they get into Cranley's office?'

'Cranley found a busted window in their washroom. It could have happened any time but the splinters look pretty fresh. The window gives access from the dealing room into Cranley's office.'

Max recognised the ominous signs. Richemont was now examining his cuticles minutely.

'How many pages were photocopied?'

'Twenty. The exact same number of pages as in the Horseshoe Trust file.'

'Highly regrettable. And I assume my name is in that file as a trustee? As are Cavendish's and Sayers's?'

Max nodded affirmatively and waited for his boss to spell out the options. Carla chose that moment to emerge from the shaded bar, carrying two tall iced teas. She stopped by the two men.

'You look hot and bothered, Olivier.'

'I am. Where have you been all morning?'

She pulled a face.

'I went into town. I'm bored here. There's nothing to do.'

'I told you to stay away from town. Max, see that she stays in the resort.' Carla sat down and began to massage his limbs, running beads of perspiration and oil together. He wasn't interested. 'Go for a swim. Find that guy in the Gant shorts again if you dare, so Max can break his legs later. I could use a laugh.'

She left them alone. Richemont had come to a decision.

'Those two have confidential papers that must not fall into the wrong hands. Search the dealing room when they're not there, then go through their bungalows. Just get everything back and shred it. Tell Cranley to arrange for someone to be in his office twenty-four/seven, and that I'll pay for it.' Max rose, glad to have his instructions. 'We also need to take some preventative measures. While you're in Surfway, take whatever else we night need as insurance should the need arise. You know what I mean, Max.'

Jonathon and Lauren returned early to Surfway after another successful day's trading. The markets were up all around the globe. Confidence was palpable. The downside was that as markets recovered they themselves became less significant. Expendable even. As they walked towards bungalow seventeen, they noticed that the front door stood slightly ajar. Jonathon was the first to see movement inside.

'Someone's there.'

'It's probably the maid service.'

'Not this late, not even in Bermuda.'

He pushed the door with his right hand, remained outside and watched it creak open. He saw a dark outline inside in the shuttered half-light. Before he could react further, he realised that he recognised the man who stood in his living room.

'What's going on, Max?'

Max's reply was almost a stutter.

'You're back early.'

'What are you doing?'

Jonathon waited for Max to come up with something.

'I was just passing by. Thought I'd check on your groceries.'

Jonathon couldn't help but be sceptical about this sudden desire to ensure that his larder was well stocked. Max looked around the sparse living room for inspiration and came to his senses.

'There's been a burglary, I'd say. Someone broke in.'

Jonathon gazed around the interior of his apartment. The TV was still there. So was his Nikon. So was the CD player and one CD. And the portable clock radio. His Ray-Bans were on the table.

'Nothing's been taken.'

Max pointed to the bedroom.

'The safe-deposit box in the wardrobe is busted open. It's empty. Was there anything valuable in there?'

Jonathon bent down and examined the barren safe-deposit box.

'Just the rest of the cash you gave me, my passport, credit cards and open return ticket. That's all.'

'They obviously knew what they were coming for when they did the bungalows.'

Lauren picked up on the nuance.

'Bungalows?'

Max regained his usual composure but was perspiring heavily. Maybe it was the suit. He came closer.

'They did next door. Similar MO. Safe-deposit box was jemmied open. It's empty.'

'My ticket and passport. Bastards!'

Jonathon was still evaluating the implications.

'So all the bungalows have been burgled?'

Max shook his head.

'Just your two. Guess they knew you weren't average tourists. You've clearly got money.'

'Had money. It wasn't even ours.' Jonathon went for the obvious option. 'Have you called the police?'

Max grabbed his jacket from the bed and began to ease his way towards the door.

'I told the manageress. She'll report it. But there's no point calling the police out for this. I know the island and I know how these types work. They'll want the cash but not the rest. There's a chance I can get your passports and tickets back. It might cost me, but it's worth a try. Leave it to me, that's what I'm here for. I never thought we'd have people like this targeting you.'

He passed them in the hallway, his sagging jacket carried over his left arm. Jonathon stopped him.

'We're down to our last few bucks.'

Max took out a single hundred-dollar bill.

'That's all I got on me. Spend it wisely.'

Jonathon and Lauren sat on the veranda, beer bottles in hand. The beer was flat. The night air was chill, the sky heavy with another approaching storm. Jonathon wished he were somewhere else.

'I know now why Cavendish chose Bermuda. It was never purely for tax reasons. Lauren, we're marooned. We're on this tiny island with its one airport, hundreds of miles from anywhere. Our passports are gone so we can't travel. Our flight tickets are gone. Our credit cards are gone so we're being drip-fed cash. We can't hire a car, and even if we could there's nowhere to drive to. We are either chauffeured or watched wherever we go.'

'Hey, it's not that bad.'

'Isn't it? My boss is staying a mile down the road, which must be one of the all-time greatest coincidences.

Max clearly doesn't work for Cavendish because he doesn't even know how to address him, so he must work for Richemont or Sayers. They must know that we know something. Three very powerful men have made millions of dollars in the past few weeks through frontrunning and they have everything to lose. We're the only two who know what has happened. We're way out of our depth.'

Lauren gave up on the beer and placed the bottle on the ledge.

'We need help. We should call someone. Like the local police.'

'I don't trust anyone on an island this size. It wouldn't surprise me if Richemont and the others had bought up the entire place. A few hundred thousand dollars here could go a long way to buying someone off. It obviously worked on the manageress. She's always watching us come and go, don't you think?'

'Yeah, I noticed that too. We could go to the Governor of the island and ask for help.'

'That guy regularly wears a ceremonial white uniform with pith helmet and plume of ostrich feathers. He lives in another world. He wouldn't even know what we were talking about.'

'Let's go to the financial authorities, then. What about the central bank?'

'Cavendish and Sayers are the sort who have contacts. The governor here would do whatever a Fed Chairman asked. Once we start looking for help here, we run the risk of discovery and retribution.'

'We could go to the consulate or embassy. British or American? Both?' Lauren suggested.

'Cavendish will have contacts in the British embassy. Likewise Sayers with the US. All we need is for word to get back to them that we're fleeing the island and it could be the end of us.'

'What do you mean?'

'There's so much at stake, millions. I don't like the look of Max. He's a heavy, and dumb men like that do as they're told for money.'

'Can we call anyone else?'

'Who else is there? I'm not going to call Eva. She has enough to worry about with Jack and Imogen. I don't think Nikki could do much either. I'm not going to call anyone else at the firm. I don't know who else there may be tied in with Richemont. Is there anyone you can call?'

Lauren was thinking of her diminishing list of contacts. She wasn't going to call home and give her dad the satisfaction of yet another failure. She could call Art Greenbaum, but he was the one who'd put Sayers on to her. Some favour, in hindsight.

'We need to get the hell out of here,' she declared. 'Then tell as many people as possible.' They sat in silence for a few minutes, listening to the repetitive strains of the tree frogs in the foliage. This is a huge scandal. Let's tell the media, then run for cover somewhere on the island.'

'You mean, meet a local reporter in a darkened underground carpark and hand over our evidence? A small-time guy like him wouldn't have a clue about frontrunning. I doubt the *Royal Gazette* has the international clout to break this story, and Bermuda hasn't a single underground carpark.'

'Looks like we're in a dead end.' Lauren looked thoughtful. 'I'm not giving in yet. There has to be a way to break this news to the world from here. Gimme time.'

'That's the one thing we haven't got.'

CHAPTER TWENTY-THREE

SURFWAY BEACH CLUB, BERMUDA –
9.10 P.M.

It had been another very successful day. The Dow posted its biggest one-day gain of all time. The FTSE broke out of a tight trading range. Tokyo had one of its highest-ever volume trading days. The billions they had invested had turned into many more billions. Jonathon and Lauren were not celebrating. They knew their vital role was coming to an end, and wondered how they would get off the island. Or whether they would at all. They sat in the late evening on the veranda and heard footsteps approaching along the gravel path.

'Max?' enquired Lauren.

Jonathon wasn't so sure. 'Sounds like more than one person.'

They saw Max first, then a smaller figure behind him. It was dark but not that dark. Olivier Richemont appeared on the bungalow steps, wearing a stupid floral shirt. Jonathon stood up immediately.

'Sit down,' instructed Max. He did as directed.

'You don't seem that surprised to see me,' said his boss.

'I'm not. I heard you were here.'

'From whom?'

'Just heard. It's a small island, you know. How's Carla's suntan?'

'Improving. Everything go okay today?' enquired Richemont.

'With what?'

'The markets.'

'I can't talk to you about that. Cavendish told me so. I talk only to his staff.' Jonathon turned to Max. 'Markets are up again. The recovery is under way. We bought more S & P, NASDAQ, FTSE, DAX and CAC futures to help things along.' As if Max knew what they were. 'Any sign of our passports or tickets yet?'

The minder sat on the edge of the low wall, where they couldn't see his face. Richemont cut in again. 'You're talking to me from now on. Don't forget, you still work for me.' Jonathon wondered for how much longer. 'I was sorry to hear about the theft. You'll need to reapply to get new passports issued. Fortunately Max has good contacts in the embassies here so it's just a matter of time. But there is another, more urgent matter. You need to do us a favour, then we can sort out the passports.'

'What sort of favour?'

Richemont nodded to Max, looked out to sea and let Max spell it out.

'There was a break in at Cranley Adams.' They said nothing. 'It happened last Sunday when you were in your office. Some photocopies of documents were removed from the premises. The lawyers want them back. You know anything about it?' They both shook their heads. The less said the better. 'Pity. I told them you would help. If the papers were to be left in an envelope with the security guard in the lobby tomorrow, that'd be fine. Then you might get your passports.'

'I don't know what you're talking about,' insisted Jonathon.

'You ever telephone a guy called Todd Liebowitz? He works at a bank called Mitchell's in Geneva.'

'Nope.'

'Received many faxes on your fax machine this week?'

'Nope.'

Richemont nodded again for Max to proceed. The minder stood up, his neck muscles bulging over his shirt collar. Lauren saw the beads of sweat running down his forehead and on to his white shirt. Max flexed his fists several times. Jonathon wondered about the apparent bulge underneath the left-hand side of his suit jacket. Max turned to him.

'You and me do the same sort of job.'

'I don't think so.'

'We solve other people's problems.'

Jonathon shrugged. 'Maybe.' He thought he could see the brown leather of a shoulder holster.

'No maybe about it. This is one of those problems I gotta sort. And I will. Like the others.'

Max looked for guidance. Richemont nodded to him to continue.

'I worked for someone else a few months ago. My boss had a problem so I sorted it. He had this girl's body. I took her in a hire car to a place I know near Amsterdam, called Loosdrecht. It's about ten kilometres from Laren. You know what's so good about Loosdrecht? It's got a yachting marina with big boats and deep water. The Dutch made the lake from the polders they built in the lowlands. They have dykes there.' Max turned to Lauren. 'You know what a dyke is, lady?' She nodded silently. 'It's quiet at night there. I didn't know how I was going to weigh her down until I opened the boot of the car. The spare tyre and a heavy jack worked fine. The fuckers back at the airport charged us for the missing items but there's been no sign of that kid since. Problem sorted. That's what I do, you know?'

Jonathon and Lauren prayed he would go now, but he didn't seem to want to leave. Richemont stood up.

'Jon, the time for games is over. You're out of your depth here. Find those documents or else . . .'

'Or else what?'

'Max is a family man.' Jonathon was lost. 'He has relations everywhere. His brother was in the French Foreign Legion, but now lives in London where he does odd jobs. Very odd jobs, occasionally. Sometimes he drives near Chester Row in a van. He might call in on Eva. There are a lot of children around there. A speeding van could easily hurt one of them. Or maybe they would accept a lift to school or wherever. You hear terrible stories about strange men enticing vulnerable children into their cars, don't you? Think about it. Work it out. Which matters more? Jack and Imogen, or some papers from a lawyer's office.'

Jonathon jumped up from his seat and lunged at him, grabbing Richemont.

'Seems like the papers matter more to you. Fuck you, you bastard!'

Max intervened just in time and pushed Jonathon back against the low wall, balancing him on the edge, sorely tempted to do some real and permanent damage. Jonathon could now see the contents of the shoulder holster. Richemont straightened his appalling shirt and smirked down at his ex-employee.

'Be in touch about those missing papers. Or you'll lose more of your family. That's a promise.'

The idea came to Lauren later that evening. She walked alone along the winding paths back up to the main buildings of Surfway, and approached the manageress in reception.

'What can I do for you?'

She was sure that the manageress was on the take from Max, that she reported back on their daily movements, maybe listened in to their telephone calls, and that her friendly manner was a front for something more sinister. Lauren chose her words with some care.

'I saw your website when I was in New York. Was

your site built here?' The manageress nodded. 'So you're an expert?'

'Not me. I paid someone else to build the Surfway site. One hundred dollars a page it cost.'

Lauren was thinking that if she and Jonathon didn't eat for a day, they could maybe scrape a hundred bucks together.

'Is the PC here?'

'Sure can't do without a PC these days. We get vacation enquiries by e-mail and we check our site on the Internet.'

'Who built the site?'

'Brett built it. He's a local university student, a clever guy.'

'Can you contact him?'

The manageress shook her head.

'He goes travelling every summer. California, Sydney, Thailand. He won't be back until October.'

Lauren's initial enthusiasm was waning. This was going to require some effort.

'Could I use your PC to check my personal hotmail? It's so much easier than going back into town.'

The manageress shrugged.

'Anything for one of my guests.' She pointed to a door behind the counter. 'This way.' The office was tiny. The Dell PC and other hardware looked antique. There was a newer Oki laser printer and a scanner. 'I'll log you in first. You can access your e-mail.'

Lauren stood while the manageress sat at the keyboard. There was no chance of being left alone. The manageress watched the empty hotmail inbox message appear.

'Looks like no one knows you're here.'

True enough. Lauren spied a book on a nearby shelf. *Getting Started with Microsoft FrontPage.* It struck a chord in her subconscious. Somewhere back in an apartment in Battery Park. Kim's place.

'Did Brett use FrontPage to build the website?'

'Yeah. He made us buy it. It cost us extra money. But well worth it in the end.'

If Scott Chapman had built a website with his family photos for people far away, perhaps she and Jonathon could do something similar. Lauren picked up the user manual and held it close to her chest.

'Can I borrow this?'

'You must be running out of vacation reading material.'

They went back into reception together. Lauren pushed her luck further.

'Jonathon's two children back in London miss him terribly. We'd like to surprise them. Do you think he could scan some vacation photographs here and e-mail them back to London?'

The manageress shrugged again, then nodded.

'Why not? If he knows how to do that.'

Lauren walked back down to bungalow seventeen, slid open the glass door to the veranda, turned off the cable television and threw the user manual into Jonathon's lap.

'Read this.'

He looked at the cover, entirely bemused. 'You gotta

be joking. I know nothing about building websites.'

'Neither do I. Just read it. I got an idea.'

The spotlights installed by the news crews competed for space with the grand chandeliers in the biggest function room of the Midtown Sheraton. Expectations were high as the two men made their way to the main podium. They had tossed a dime in the anteroom with some PR advisers. Cavendish had won.

'I shall read a prepared text. Walter will take any questions.' The latecomers took their seats. Others crouched on the floor in the front row. 'The collapse in stock markets was of grave concern to governments and central bankers. We had to act and we have done so. I am pleased to confirm rumours that the recent recovery, while primarily attributable to concerted buying by large institutional investors, was prefaced by sustained and unprecedented market intervention by the world's central banks.'

There was a gasp, then a ripple of mild applause. Cavendish gestured to Sayers in mutual recognition, but he was miles away. First, he knew this text verbatim, having worked on the final draft in the bath this morning. Second, he was to hand over hundred K in cash to the Brothers in a Times Square diner in three hours. Cavendish waited for silence, wishing the others were here. A full attendance would have eased the burden. But Engels was ill in Frankfurt and Lam and Nakamura couldn't make the long-haul trip at such short notice. Cavendish finally got the silence he desired.

'The five leading central banks invested tens of billions

of dollars in blue-chip stocks, options and index futures over the past two weeks. I am pleased to say that the value of these investments has grown by twenty per cent plus, in line with the overall market recovery in the United States, Europe and Asia.'

Then it was Sayers's turn. He sensed his adrenaline rising as he stood up to field the questions. This was like any regular House hearing and was no trouble for a pro like him. Hands went up in the audience. He heard the shouts of TV reporters and journalists, each wanting to be the first to the microphone ahead of their peer group. His eyes adjusted to the arc-lights. He could see the eager faces staring back. He grazed the sea, looking for a familiar face from CNBC, CNN or CBS. They were all Caucasian faces. Just like the giant trading floors downtown. Diversity had yet to reach Wall Street.

'Mr Sayers, how much of the taxpayers' money has been wasted?'

Then he saw two faces that definitely didn't fit.

'Walter, what's gonna happen when you guys stop buying and the market crashes again?'

Suddenly he was sitting on a well-sprung bed in the DC Hilton with a voluptuous girl.

'Mr Sayers, who's running the show here? Is it the Fed or is it the Brits and the Europeans?'

He was on a deserted subway platform with a McDonald's bag and a hundred K in cash.

'What are ya goin' do with all the money you've made?'

He answered the questions mechanically, sounding unconvincing. No money had been wasted, only invested. They had stopped buying and the market was still on an up tick today. It was a joint effort by the central bankers, the profits as yet unrealised. Cavendish stared over at Sayers, baffled by the dire quality of his answers. Sayers, however, was focused on the two men with the gleaming white shirts and neat bow ties sitting at the back of the room. The smaller of the two slowly raised his left hand. Sayers wondered what sort of question he could possibly have. There was too much to lose. He ended the session prematurely, a bundle of nerves. After they'd exited the room, Cavendish cornered him alone in the executive washroom. He checked the empty cubicles first.

'What the hell happened there, Walt? You were useless.'

'I lost my train of thought.'

'You need to hold your nerve at a time like this. Especially with what's happening in Bermuda.'

'What's happening? I thought we were all done.' Sayers approached the urinals.

'Richemont called me last night. He says Maynard and the girl know.'

'Know what?' Sayers unzipped.

'About Horseshoe. They broke into the lawyer's office and found the files. Photocopied the trust papers. Those papers list our names as the trustees. They know Horseshoe was trading in the same products as they were, they got a statement from Mitchell's in Geneva, and they know how much money we've made to the nearest cent.'

Sayers almost wet his pants. 'Shit! How the hell did they do that? We gotta do something.'

'Richemont says he'll take care of it,' Cavendish soothed him 'That's why he's there on-site. That's why we gave him his share. To take care of unpleasant business like this.'

'So what's the endgame?' enquired the Chairman as he made for the perfumed soap and warm towels.

'Richemont has a bodyguard out there. He says Maynard and Trent won't be coming home. There's gonna be an accident.'

'And what about us?' Sayers mopped his sweaty face with a towel.

'We're gonna wash our hands of the whole affair,' Cavendish assured him.

Jonathon and Lauren spent the day at work without dealing, just planning a way out. They finally did as Lauren suggested and searched on their PCs under Yahoo! for media organisations. They went into each site and looked for the best contact e-mail address. They wrote down twenty, including Reuters, Dow Jones, WSJ, CNN, CBS, NBC, BBC, ITN and Associated Press. It was a start. They left the office early and ate in a down-market diner, a feat of discovery in Hamilton, before taking a cab back to Surfway and collecting their keys from the dim relief receptionist.

'Where's the manageress tonight?'

'It's her evening off.'

They walked back to their bungalows. Lauren took Jonathon's arm, held him close and kissed him.

'You gotta do it now.'

He wasn't so sure. He had spent hours reading the riveting publication that was *Getting Started with Microsoft FrontPage* and thought he had understood most of it, but time would tell.

'I'll need the photocopies and the account statement.'

Lauren disappeared down the steps to the deserted beach. She found the coffee jar without any difficulty in the shimmering moonlight. Bounding back, she thrust the rolled pages into Jonathon's hands and kissed him again.

'I know you can do it. Good luck!'

He nodded to the receptionist on his return to the deserted reception area.

'The manageress said I could e-mail some photos to my kids in London.'

The relief manager was more interested in the sports newspaper on the counter. The lights were on but there was no one at home apparently.

'I don't know nothin' about that, mon.'

'Didn't she mention it to you?'

'No. Doesn't bother me. You know what to do?'

'Yes,' he lied.

Jonathon closed the door to the back office and powered up the PC. He was bewildered by the array of icons before him and selected FrontPage but the screen instantly went blank with menus at the top. This

Web lark was beyond him. Everything he had read in bungalow seventeen seemed a lifetime away. He thought about the student who worked on the Surfway website, then went to the file option and saw recent Web files. He chose the most recent. The contents of surfway.bin opened up on the screen. It was all here. He was in.

'You okay in there?'

The receptionist stood framed outside the doorway.

'Yes, fine so far.'

He was left alone again. That guy Brett had designed the default template. Jonathon saw the Surfway logo and the navigation bar leading to the other pages. He typed a few words of rubbish and saw it appear on the new page. He needed to be sure his efforts would be saved correctly. He selected 'File', then the save option. He hadn't thought of a page name, but what else? He typed in horsehoe.html and hit 'Save'.

The Oki 96 Elite scanner sat beside the PC with a mass of grey spaghetti wires hanging out of the back. He ran his fingers over the dust on the cables and figured it hadn't been touched in months. There was an icon called Photosuite. This had to be the way Brett had scanned in the photos of Surfway. If a photograph worked, then a photocopy would also work. He double-clicked.

The Photosuite application powered up. He selected the obvious option, 'Get Photos'. It gave him a bewildering choice of hard disk, floppy disk, photo CD, photonet, scanner and digital camera. He went for the scanner choice. A dialogue box opened up and said 'Connecting Scanner'. He sat back and waited. 'Error code 2: Scanner r/w test failed.' He clicked 'OK' in vain. Another dialogue box opened. 'Unable to enable Twain source.' What the hell did that mean? He was finished. These error codes were beyond him.

He sat alone under the revolving overhead fan, leaned back and stared up at the ceiling for some inspiration. He could type up text for the Web, but without the documentation there would be no hard evidence. He glanced down at the floor. He saw a twin plug socket in the wall. One socket was in use, the other was not. A plug on the end of a grey cable lay on the floor. He picked it up and followed it to the back of the scanner. He plugged it in and tried again. It worked.

He took the first page from the trust files, unrolled it, placed it face down on the clear glass, closed the cover, hit 'Preview' and watched the band of white light move along the glass like the copier at Cranley's. He saw a weak image of the page slowly appear on the PC screen. He hit 'Scan' and saw the picture quality improve significantly. The incriminating text and handwritten comments were clearly legible. He hit 'Save'.

'You still okay? What's the noise?' yelled the receptionist from outside.

'It's the scanner. I'm loading the photos for the kids,' he lied.

He prayed the door wouldn't open. He had to get the page from the scanner to the Web page. He thought back to how, in the London office, he would watch Nikki work her magic as she typed reports in Word or added up trades in Excel. Copy and paste always worked. He clicked on the document, copied it, went back to the new Web page and pasted it. He scanned in the documents one by one until all twenty pages from the trust files were on the Horseshoe page. He scrolled down to make sure they were in the correct order. The page featuring the names of Cavendish, Sayers and Richemont was perfect. Then he did the execution faxes from Mitchell's Hong Kong and lastly the account statement from Mitchell's Geneva. He saved the page.

The explanatory text was the easy part. He wrote about the trust deed from the lawyer's office, the names of the three trustees, the trades done in Bermuda at the request of the governors, the e-mails of trades to Sayers, the fax confirmations, the account statements. It was surely enough to interest any newspaper sub-editor.

The last obstacle was to get the Horseshoe page on to the website. The manual mentioned a file transfer process. He saw an icon called FTP. The initials looked promising. He clicked and the website pages came up. A dial up connection dialogue box opened with a user name and a password. The user name was Surfway but the password was blank. He was lost. He thought about trying different passwords but knew that sometimes you got locked out of applications after three erroneous attempts.

He wondered what Brett would have done when he built the original website. He must have written down the password somewhere. Jonathon looked around the office. He paged through the user manual again, then went to the index at the back and looked up passwords. There was some scribbling on the inside back page. Some telephone numbers, file names and then the word Harvard. Was that where the student went to college? Worth a try. He typed in the name of the college and hit 'Return'. It worked. He dragged his new page from the left to the right and watched it upload to the website. He closed all applications and opened up the Internet. He typed in www.surfway.bm/horsehoe.html and saw his new page. It was a URL to die for.

His last task was to ensure that the page would not be found accidentally or deleted easily by anyone at this PC. He deleted FTP. He deleted the FrontPage hard disk files. He deleted the Horseshoe page, safe in the knowledge that it was already posted to the World Wide Web. Then he looked around the office, took the FrontPage installation CD and snapped it in two. The door opened as he powered down.

'You finished? Did it work?' asked the reception-ist.

'I got some great pictures.'

Jonathon walked back and let himself into Lauren's apartment, slipped off his shorts and T-shirt and crawled naked into her bed. He moved nearer and cradled her from behind. The air-con was off and she was hot to his touch. She turned around and kissed him, her tongue exploring his teeth.

'Well, Mr Webmaster?'

'I feel an irresistible urge to make love to you tonight.'

She ran her hands down to his midriff, and then farther down. He was aroused already.

'But first I need to know what happened, Jon.'

He kissed her again, lingeringly, and spoke softly into her left ear.

'We're on-line.'

CHAPTER TWENTY-FOUR
SURFWAY BEACH CLUB, BERMUDA –
1.03 P.M.

Jonathon took the only decision possible after another long walk on the beach.

'We're getting off this island today. The best way out of here has been staring us in the face for weeks.'

'We've got no passports, no tickets, no money and Max is watching us all the time.'

'Trust me. I gotta make a call first.'

'To who?'

'Home.' He dialled London, let the phone ring for a few seconds, but there was no reply. 'Damn. Maybe they got to Eva and the kids already.' He thought about the other options, dialled again and then spoke urgently.

'Nikki, Jon here. Listen, I haven't much time. Leave work right now. Say you're ill. Go over to my house. Find Eva. Take her, Jack and Imogen back to your place immediately and stay there. Don't let any of them return to Chester Row, don't let them go to school or go anywhere alone. Stay indoors if you can. Don't talk to anyone else from Richemont. I'll call you again very soon. Thanks.'

Lauren's hopes were raised. She sensed he knew what to do.

'Pack some things as if we're going back to the beach today,' he told her. 'Dress like a tourist with a backpack. Take your Yankees baseball cap. Pack some overnight stuff, a change of warmer clothes, toiletries and whatever food is left in my fridge.'

They were packed in minutes. Lauren gathered some toiletries which she'd left in his bathroom over the past few days, always a good sign in a developing relationship. Jonathon squeezed some clothes inside the backpack and counted out eighty bucks in cash, the last of their money.

'We gotta save these dollars or we don't eat tonight.'

'And where exactly will we be eating tonight?'

'Time will tell.'

'What about the rest of our gear?'

'There are Gap stores in Manhattan but not in Bermuda.'

She liked the sound of Manhattan. He knotted the backpack shut before slinging it over his left shoulder.

'It's customary for the guy to carry everything for his girl on the way to the beach.'

She nodded in agreement, enthused by the possibility of escape.

'What's the plan?'

'We get to Hamilton first. Max is probably parked

somewhere out on the South Road, waiting for us to appear in a cab. Maybe he's watching us this very moment. So we're going to our beach for a lazy afternoon.'

They closed the door of the bungalow behind them. The manageress waved back from a nearby veranda.

'Don't worry about her. She'll tell him we're going to the beach.'

They descended the tiered steps. Jonathon pointed to the rocks to their left.

'The next beach down is Elbow. It's low tide right now. We can walk directly there along the beach like we're regular guests. Then we hit the South Road.'

The water lapped against their legs as they clambered over the rocks and on to the residents-only pink sands of Elbow. This resort looked even more affluent than Blushing Sands. Rows of blue parasols with pairs of loungers for couples with cash. They climbed more steps and walked through some of the five acres of landscaped gardens. As they emerged on to South Road, Jonathon pointed at the nearby sign.

'We'll catch the bus from here.'

Lauren looked at the bus stop. She knew the markings. Blue at the top meant the bus was outbound.

'That's going the wrong way, away from Hamilton.'

'That's why it's such a good choice.'

They stood hidden under the trees until the number seven municipal bus arrived as per the timetable. Jonathon handed over eight bucks' worth of the required bus tokens, purchased earlier in town.

'Dockyard. For two.'

The bus took them past the main entrance to Surfway, stopping to pick up a couple they recognised from the pool. They sank back in their seats. Lauren pointed to the right. They saw the BMW Compact parked on a side road. There was no sign of its driver.

'Good call, Jon.'

The journey along the western spine of the island through Southampton, Sandy's and Somerset took thirty slow minutes. They were running out of land as the water came closer on both sides of the road.

'What's next, Jon?'

'We take the ferry.'

They alighted at Dockyard, an old naval port that had been converted into a tourist, arts-and-crafts centre selling prints, ceramics, posters, glass and souvenirs to the coachloads. There was no time to see the sights: the Clocktower mall, the Bermuda Arts Centre or the Dolphin Sea Quest in the Keep. The 2.30 Sea Venture ferry stopped on cue by the pier. Jonathon first eyed the passengers from the safety of the slipway. There were no solo Europeans with fair complexions and out-of-season clothes. Lauren made for the best seat on the upper deck above the bow of the ferry. He pulled her back. He had noticed the attention she received from other men.

'Let's sit below and keep a low profile. Be as anonymous as you can. Hard for you, I know.'

She tucked her auburn locks under her baseball cap and pulled the peak down lower. They almost enjoyed the picturesque trip across the bay. Jonathon surveyed every other passenger who boarded whenever the ferry came to the jetties at Boaz Island, Watford Bridge, Cavello Bay and Somerset Bridge. Hamilton harbour soon came into view. They recognised the *Horizon*, the giant navy-and-white Celebrity Cruises ship, which dominated the skyline. Her sister liner had evidently left for other climes.

'What next, Jon?'

'Merge with that party of American tourists ahead. Stay close to them as we disembark. Don't turn right down Front Street like everyone else will when we get ashore, but walk off to the left.'

They passed through turnstiles, depositing their four-buck tokens in the machines to exit. Lauren stopped.

'But how are we going to get off this damn island?'

Jonathon pointed to the harbour. Lauren followed the direction of his finger to the huge ship moored near by.

'That's our way out of here.'

'You can't be serious.'

'You got a better idea?'

'That ship is for vacationers going back to the States.'

'Don't you want to go home?'

Lauren had no wish to return to her folks uptown but preferred to focus on more practical issues.

'We don't have any passports.'

'They only check for passports when everyone first boards a cruise. I asked the Kearney's barman yesterday.'

'What happens when we get to our destination? We'll need passports then.'

He nodded reluctantly.

'If we get on board, then we get off the island and tackle that problem later. I'd rather talk to some US immigration officer about a missing passport than argue with Max here.'

Lauren could see more problems.

'We can't afford two one-way tickets with less than eighty bucks.'

'We're not going to be paying.'

'If we do get on board, we won't have a cabin.'

'We can sit in the bar, find a communal area, eat something, sit up on deck. No one need know that we're temporarily homeless. We just gotta get on that boat and blend in. That's the part I'm still working on.'

Lauren could see it was their only chance. They walked towards the ship, their hands inter-clasped for mutual support, two holidaymakers on a dream vacation. If only. Jonathon saw it first. He pointed to the public carpark along Front Street.

'There's Max's BMW. Shit! He's in town. He must know we left the resort.'

They stopped in the shadow of the huge hull and saw the sign displayed prominently for all lucky vacationers. 'Departure to New York today at 5 p.m. sharp.' Jonathon looked at his watch.

'We have two hours to get on board. Let's do some reconnaissance.'

A white awning covered the street-level access to the *Horizon*. It shaded crew and passengers alike from the beating sun but made closer inspection impossible. Twenty or so sweating tourists stood in an orderly line. They carried shopping bags, cameras and camcorders, but nothing to show how they would reboard. Jonathon and Lauren joined the line.

'What happens when we get to the top of the queue?'

Jonathon lowered his voice as they hunched up along the suspended gangway.

'When we're a few feet away, you say you forgot something back in a shop and we'll leave. We just need to see how they check the passengers.'

They drew nearer to a uniformed Filipino officer with gold braid who stood at the head of the queue. A young couple stopped ahead of them and held out two orange cards with bold print on them. The officer eyed the cards lazily and nodded. They passed inside. Lauren spoke in her best native accent.

'Oh my lord, Harry. I left the bag in the store.'

Jonathon joined her in a sharp about-turn. Going back down the gangway, he raised his eyes to heaven.

'What's with this Harry stuff?'

'It just came to me. Overacting, I guess.'

'You did well. You get a good look at the cards?'

Lauren nodded.

'It's an ID with their name. No photographs. One for each of them.'

'We want two of those cards. We need to borrow them from a couple still in Hamilton.'

'But they'll know the cards were stolen and will report it. Then the crew will know they have stowaways.'

'Not necessarily. They might think the cards were just lost. If we get on board first, what are the crew going to do? Check the ID cards of every passenger on board before they depart? I doubt it. Let's go looking for two unfortunates. The best place to start is in Trimingham's.'

They walked the few hundred feet to the main entrance of the town's flagship store.

'Look for a couple of obvious passengers who have just one bag with them. There's a chance that any ID cards will be in there.'

'And if not?'

'We put it back and look for another.'

They wandered around the floors of the store with zero interest in the merchandise. Lauren stopped before they got to the top.

'We need to find a lady's purse.'

'Where do we find one?'

'On the floor of a changing room. Let's go to the rear,' she advised.

She spotted the likely victims within five minutes. She was sixty-plus, popping in and out of the curtained changing room in a violently patterned sweater. He was seventy-plus and stood uninterestedly near by in a pair of conservative shorts and a Detroit Lions T-shirt. Lauren saw the patent clutch purse on the floor of the changing room. There was a corner of orange card visible from an unzipped side pocket. It was well past four. They were running out of time. She picked the nearest garment from a rail.

'Distract her, Jon.' He looked blank. 'Ask her something.'

Jonathon stood close to their victim. 'Did I see you on the ship?' The woman nodded and looked vacant. Lauren darted behind them into the changing room and pulled the curtains. 'What time does it depart today?' The victim mumbled something about five o'clock. Jonathon heard nothing. Lauren bent down, grabbed the two ID cards and slipped them into the waistband of her shorts. The curtain suddenly opened.

'I'm in here,' announced the victim.

'My mistake. Sorry.'

'Got everything, dear?' Jonathon asked her.

Lauren gave him a look that told him the mission was accomplished. 'Sure thing, Harry.'

They stopped near the main exit to the store on Front Street. Just in front of them, a bulky man with a blond crew cut lazily lit a Camel, drew on it and looked up and down the busy street.

'Shit! Back up.'

They stood behind the gents' casual wear. Max inhaled again, looking uncertain as to which way to go.

'C'mon, you bastard. Move off. The clock's ticking.'

'What if that couple find they're missing the ID cards?' asked Lauren. 'We gotta get back to the ship before they do. Otherwise these two cards are useless.'

'They're still here.' Jonathon turned around. 'Shit! Here they come now. They're on the move.'

The victims passed them by, another local shopping bag in hand. A booming ship's foghorn sounded close by, an advance notice to all of imminent departure. Jonathon looked at his watch again. Lauren stared at the only obstacle between them and the ship. Then a slight, tanned, grey-haired man in a floral shirt approached Max.

'Richemont ... This gets worse.'

Having given Max some sort of instruction, Richemont walked off to the left alone. Max stubbed out the cigarette and moved off to the right, towards the Birdcage and away from the *Horizon*.

'Let's go.'

They lost sight of their victims ahead. The queue by the gangway was much longer than before. They were grateful for the awning this time as they joined the slow-moving line. Jonathon threw cautious glances around but couldn't see their victims in the vicinity. Departure time drew nearer. Lauren tugged at his arm.

'There's no sign of that other couple yet?'

'Correct.'

'So they're doing more shopping?'

'Probably. They've got thirty minutes.'

'Let's do the rest now. Give me five minutes. That's all I'll need.'

'No. It's too risky. Wait.'

Lauren ran towards Chancery Lane and disappeared up the side alley. She reached their office building. The same security officer was downstairs, dozing over his afternoon coffee.

'Anyone upstairs today?'

'No,' he mumbled.

She went up to the third floor. The dealing room was empty. She powered up the PC and chose the hotmail option. She wrote a short attention-grabbing three-liner with the URL for Horseshoe, cut and pasted it into twenty different e-mails and hit 'Send'. Each editor would think he had a world exclusive. She ran back down the stairs and out of the building, just as the security guard put down the telephone after a short yet informative call to Max's mobile. Max was on his way. Easiest fifty bucks ever.

Lauren ran between the Front Street traffic into Jonathon's welcoming arms.

'It's done, Jon.'

The same ship's officer stood at the head of the sweltering queue. Jonathon wondered how diligent he was over this daily routine. Their turn finally came. Jonathon held out two ID cards. He glanced at them.

'Welcome aboard. Had a good day?'

Jonathon didn't want to say anything too English. Lauren obliged.

'Fantastic! Swell place.'

They were on board.

'Where do we go now?'

'We do what everyone does when a liner leaves a port. We go to the top deck, but we won't be waving.'

They took a swish elevator up as far as possible and exited. A high-pitched voice came from behind them.

'One moment, please.'

A pale junior rating with significantly less gold braid on his uniform stood before them.

'Do you have your passes?'

Jonathon tentatively held them out. Had they been rumbled so easily?

'This is the Marina deck. First class. Orange is Florida deck below.'

Lauren obliged on Jonathon's behalf again.

'Gee, guess we hit the wrong button in the elevator.'

They took sanctuary on less salubrious Florida deck and carefully watched the tiny waterfront buildings way below, suddenly appreciating how small Hamilton was. Lauren had better eyesight.

'That's the couple from the shop, isn't it?'

The Detroit Lions couple was remonstrating with the top-tier gold braid, waving their hands and shouting as only irate tourists can. After five minutes they were escorted inside and disappeared from view.

'Now I don't feel so bad about talking their IDs,' Lauren said.

'They can go to their cabin and prove they should be on board. The cards just went AWOL.'

Jonathon was looking farther away and could see the public carpark.

'Keep back from the railings. The BMW's still parked there.'

They counted the minutes towards five o'clock. The gangway was taken in. Ropes were hurled back on board from the jetty. The deafening foghorn sounded directly above them. Diesel plumes appeared.

'This is bloody well going to work!' Jonathon crowed.

'You're the best.' Lauren held him around the waist and kissed him.

Jonathon looked down at Front Street. Richemont and Max stood by the BMW, looking up at the huge ship. He could see the expressions on their faces, see the growing doubt as the ship moved off, the horrible suspicion that the couple they sought were on board. Max stubbed out a cigarette and got into the car. Richemont put his hands in his pockets and continued staring up. Jonathon pulled Lauren to his side and took a step away from the railings.

'Keep back.'

Two tugs pushed the *Horizon* and its 1,300 passengers out into the harbour. The water was still, the sun slowly setting over the island. The sky was painted in red and pink hues with every promise of a better tomorrow. Lauren was drawn back to the railings. She turned to Jonathon, moved much closer and kissed him slowly.

'Fancy leaving Bermuda on a cruise ship. So romantic.'

They avoided the Starlight restaurant and sat in a dark corner of the Martini Bar for most of the time, making their two drinks last an eternity. They never saw the Detroit Lions couple again. The *Horizon* docked at 11 a.m. at 12th Avenue and 55th Street two days later. Jonathon and Lauren were kept in an INS waiting room for three hours. She gave it her best shot with the INS officer, throwing in the tears as required. A robbery on the ship, passports, tickets and money all taken. There were checks on Federal computers. They found her NY state driver's licence record with a passable photograph and were satisfied. Jonathon was next. The INS called the British consul in Manhattan. Emergency visas appeared. They were finally waved through customs in the late afternoon.

They stood together on the sidewalk, watching the passing street life of the West Side. The heat was intense, sunlight bouncing off the asphalt, the oppressive brick-work and concrete walls. They missed the cooling sea breeze of Surfway already, feeling weak and exhausted. They had eaten only twice on board ship, surviving like castaways on stale snacks from the backpack and bottled water. Their focus had primarily been on escape, but their ultimate destination was vague.

'We need to save our cash. Let's walk,' suggested Jonathon.

'Where?' asked Lauren.

'To your parents' place.'

She recalled the precise manner of her departure from her father two weeks ago.

'I don't think so. I'm not going home begging for help. You must know someone in New York.'

'Only you.'

Lauren was under pressure. Her local contacts were limited. She pulled out her Palm Pilot from the back pack.

'You got a dime?'

Jonathon turned out his pockets.

'Just about.'

She used a telephone booth on the corner, dialled a 212 number, and a girl answered the call immediately.

'Is Art there?'

'Yes. Can I say who's calling?'

Lauren hung up and exited the booth.

'Seventy-seventh and Fifth.'

They walked the blocks east through Central Park. The same doorman got the approval from upstairs. They rode the elevator and knocked on the impressive door. Lauren introduced Jonathon as a friend without imparting much additional information. Greenbaum looked tired, drawn, no more the star of the Street. He rolled his jaded eyes to the heavens, not really interested in any conversation.

'You again. What do you want?'

'I need somewhere to stay for a few days. Somewhere people won't find us.'

'Don't tell me, you're in trouble. With the cops? The Feds?' asked Greenbaum.

'Maybe.'

'So you met with Sayers and he gave you a job? Bet you wish you hadn't taken it now. He stole my damn idea, the crook. Good riddance to him. The markets recovered and I never made a cent, but I'll get even, see if I don't. They'll be looking for witnesses to nail him and I'll be first in line.'

'Yeah. It didn't work out. The job's over,' Lauren confirmed wearily, not really following what he was saying.

'Sure is. And I ain't getting involved in serious shit like this. You're on your own. Goodbye.'

He slammed the door. Lauren wondered how much he knew. They rode the elevator down to the street and realised they had only one other person to turn to. She hailed a cab. Jonathon sat inside and hoped he had enough money for the return fare if required. Lauren leaned forward.

'Hudson Tower, Battery Park.'

Ten minutes later, Lauren rang the intercom at street level.

'Kim, it's Lauren. Can I come up?'

Kim stood by the open door, looking much happier than on Lauren's last visit. She wore well-ironed summer clothes, her shining hair was combed, her make-up subtle. She actually smiled as she held out her hand in greeting.

'Who's your new friend?'

'Jonathon. He needs a shave and a shower, but apart from that he's okay.'

The interior of the apartment looked different. The windows were open and sunlight and air streamed into the bright sitting room. There were packed storage boxes in the main room; others lay open half full. Kim explained.

'I sold the apartment. I'm moving back to my folks in California.'

'Good for you. Kim, this is going to seem kinda strange. We need somwhere to stay for a few days. Can you help?'

'Sure, I could do with the company here. Stay as long as the paperwork takes. Anything else you need?'

Lauren pushed her luck. 'We're short of cash. We might need a loan until we can get to a bank.'

'I can lend you a few hundred bucks. I got loads now.'

'You come into some money?'

'Sure did. Scott had a life policy, watertight. I got a big cheque Friday. That's why I can afford to leave my job here and go home to California. I'm gonna chill out. I won't need to work for a long while.' Kim studied the two of them and seemed to be psychic. 'You hungry?'

'Starving,' admitted Jonathon.

'Then take a seat. Let me make something for you. Pasta okay?'

Lauren stared at Jonathon. He took the hint and resisted the temptation to cook. 'Perfect.'

They sat down near the TV, which was on at low volume. Jonathon hated US TV. His and her ethnically balanced anchors sat with sculpted hair, pancake make-up and superimposed smiles. The same repetitive rolling news stories were regurgitated at the viewers hourly. The horror of a concrete slab dropped on a passing truck window. The banality of a kidnapped poodle in a Manhattan co-op. Incessant links to alleged traffic gurus. Overhead shots of the TriBoro Bridge and the Turnpike.

'Check out the news. There's some big story breaking,' shouted Kim from the kitchen.

'What?' asked Lauren. Kim didn't hear her. They were

on to five-day rolling forecasts with happy glowing suns in shades and grey sullen clouds. Thirty-second clips of home runs, the only highlight in three-hour-long Mets and Yankees games, wholly indecipherable to any Englishman. The business news had scrolling ticker prices and volume stats. Dot-coms and more dot-cons. News on the S&P and Dow Utilities. The anchor's backdrop was littered with green up arrows. Definitely no need for their continued presence in Bermuda. The programme cut to a solo guy with a mike standing outside the Federal Reserve in Washington, DC.

Leaning forward eagerly, they watched library footage of Sayers at some prior Congress testimony, standing erect with his right arm raised like a pious preacher. Kim came back from the kitchen and waved at the screen.

'Can you believe that guy? And they thought Scott was bad . . . ?'

Lauren and Jonathon exchanged eye contact. The story was out there.

'It worked!' Lauren exclaimed. 'That's what Greenbaum meant.'

Kim was puzzled.

'What worked?'

Lauren let it pass. Kim picked up a copy of that day's *Post* from the corner table and thrust it at them. 'It's in the newspaper too.' The banner headline proclaimed 'Central Bank Governors in Share Dealing Scandal' above pictures of Sayers and Cavendish. 'Where you been for the past twenty-four hours?'

'Travelling.'

Kim seemed to be enjoying the chance to talk.

'Sayers is as guilty as hell. The evidence was posted on some vacation website in Bermuda for the world to see. I had a look on the Web today on my PC. Dorky site design but unbeatable content. They got the Governor in England too, and some Swiss millionaire guy who organised it. The TV guys say that this Surfway vacation site got a million hits in the past twenty-four hours since the story broke. The owners of the resort have been flooded with enquiries about vacations. Strange about Bermuda. It's so near yet I've never been. You ever been there on vacation?'

Lauren spoke on behalf of both of them as she smiled a promise at Jonathon.

'Not yet.'

Two months later

Jonathon walked along the edge of the sublime arc, allowing the powdery grains and warm lapping water to run through his toes. There were few other footprints in the virginal sand. Waves surged repeatedly on to the reef off to his right, their regular intervals giving assurance that life would carry on here for eternity. This was a solid contender for any list of the world's most perfect beaches.

'So this is it?' Lauren stopped and looked at him from behind a pair of slimline sunglasses. 'Horseshoe Bay. What it was all about? You know, they're right. The sand actually is pink.'

He'd clearly read the fine print in the Berlitz travel guide.

'It's the crushed coral reef, eroded over millions of years.'

Small clusters of sunworshippers sat near by on beach towels placed at intervals carefully calculated to ensure complete mutual privacy along the quarter-of-a-mile stretch. A team of locals energetically played beach volleyball near the more public end of the sand. Their occasional enthusiastic yells to their team-mates were the only sound. Jonathon took Lauren's right hand in his left and drew her closer, running his hand over her bare back and down to the low-cut edge of her turquoise bikini. His fingers loitered. Her skin was wet and warm to his touch. Small droplets of salty water and grains of sand remained after their swim.

'Not here, Jon.'

'Where?'

'The other end of the beach. Past the rocks.'

He quickened his gait. Lauren caught him up and pointed to the shallows, where Jack and Imogen gambolled among the breaking waves, never out of their depth. They waved over at him.

'I should have brought them here the first time around.'

'They're good kids. You're very lucky. Will they be okay?'

'Someone has their eagle eye on these children. Always has. Always will. Especially in times of danger. She did well.'

Eva sat under an umbrella with a hamper and assorted playthings strewn near by. She wore a floppy sunhat, her snow-white legs now covered entirely by a towel. They waved over but there was no response, her attention focused on the children.

'Nikki did well too. I like her,' noted Lauren. 'I'm glad she got a good job in media with more money.'

They reached the sanctuary of the small coves at the far end and diverted into a deserted crescent almost entirely surrounded by rocks. They lay down together in the sand. Jonathon pushed back some wet strands of streaky hair from her face, took off the well-worn Yankees baseball cap and ran his fingers over her perfect features. Lauren ran her hands over his stubbled jaw and newly cropped hair, enjoying the sensation of the prickly follicles on her wet hands.

'What number blade was it?'

'Number one. Mary did a better job.'

'You've changed.'

'It's only a haircut.'

'You know what I mean.' She looked back at the picturesque cove and took her last chance to come up for air. 'I'm going to miss all this.'

He too looked around at the wide-open spaces.

'Do you miss Hong Kong? Do you want to go back there now life has returned to normal?'

'Been there. Done that. The apartment is let out to a German banker for a great monthly rental. I'll see how the property market goes. Phat Cat has moved in permanently with the Brit expat next door. I got an e-mail from Brad. Mac's apartment block was torched at the peak of the rioting, before Mitchell's fired him too over Alpha. Best to leave the past behind and look to the future.'

He didn't comment. London seemed a lifetime away. 'You'll like Chester Row.'

'I know. We've got free vacations at Surfway for life so there's no hurry.' They lay with the waves lapping around their feet. 'What about your job?'

'Richemont et Cie are under investigation by the SFO. I'm on gardening leave. This time it suits me. I won't go back to consultancy work. I want to be my own boss, and get a balance between work and time at home with Jack and Imogen. There are all sorts of interesting offers coming in at present.'

'What's your favourite?'

'London correspondent for the WSJ, syndicated columnist for the *Economist* or else some regular TV work with CNBC Europe. Maybe all three. I appear to be an expert. Famous already.'

'It's what we all desire, to discover what we really want to do in life, and then to just go out and do it. I'll love London, Jon, and I'll love living with you and the kids. Not so sure about Eva, though.' Lauren smiled, then stretched back in the pink sand and looked up at the cloudless sky. 'Tell me, how did you know that Horseshoe Bay was the best beach in Bermuda?'

Jonathon moved closer.

'It had to be. People like Richemont, Cavendish and Sayers always want the best for themselves.'

EPILOGUE

A Can of Worms

Anyone returning to work after a long summer holiday this week could be forgiven for doubting the headlines. Frontrunning share deals. Exposés on the World Wide Web. Sexual intercourse inside the Bank of England. Naked photographs of the Federal Reserve Chairman. Expenses fraud and resignations. Faked university degrees. Lesbian insider dealing. Jail-cell suicides. It's not media speculation; it's what we now know about the private lives of five former central bank governors.

Sir Charles Cavendish, the former Governor of the Bank of England, out on bail, was already embroiled in a financial scandal before the *Sun* published revelations about his private life. Cavendish's personal assistant, Pamela Gardner, 39, received a large sum to disclose

details of their three-year affair. The story broke when
a private detective confirmed he had been paid to
monitor the couple. Gardner spilled details of their
after-hours encounters in the Bank's main boardroom and nights spent in a Barbican apartment where
Cavendish liked Gardner to wear his Eton tie during
intimate encounters. Cavendish's wife of 24 years,
Marjorie, was unavailable for comment at her home
in Kensington pending divorce proceedings. Cavendish
remains at an unknown location outside London following his immediate dismissal by the Chancellor of the
Exchequer after sensational share-dealing allegations
and documentary proof were anonymously broken on
a Bermuda holiday website.

Former Federal Reserve Chairman, Walter Sayers,
went one better earlier this month when he featured
in a photo spread in the *New York Post*. Lurid pictures showed Sayers in the company of a call-girl in
the Washington, DC, Hilton Hotel. The *Post* paid a
six-figure sum to a photographer but would not reveal
their source, nor the identity of the girl. Later *Playboy*
magazine offered fifty thousand dollars to the mystery
girl for an exclusive. Sayers was being blackmailed
and apparently paid a large cash sum to two men in
a New York subway. He can now contemplate his
newfound notoriety as he waits at home behind closed
doors following his Grand Jury indictment on criminal
fraud and conspiracy charges.

Suspicions that other central bankers were involved
in the frontrunning share-dealing operation proved

unfounded, yet they have not escaped the public gaze. Japanese government officials investigated the business travel of the former Bank of Japan Governor, Masa Nakamura, and found he had defrauded the Bank over the past seven years in a large-scale expenses fraud. Kenneth Lam, formerly the Chief Executive of the Hong Kong Monetary Authority, resigned following Stanford University's confirmation that he had dropped out of college in his final year and lied about his qualifications when he joined the HKMA in 1993. Finally, Vera Engels of the European Central Bank has admitted to a long-term lesbian relationship with a leading Frankfurt business reporter and is alleged to have passed her inside information in bed on upcoming European Central Bank interest rate changes.

Swiss multimillionaire Olivier Richemont's death was as unexpected as it was bizarre. Richemont, 52, was the principal shareholder in an élite Swiss consultancy firm and was alleged to have organised the secret offshore trust account used by the Central Bank governors in their share dealing scheme. He was found dead in his cell at Geneva's Favra remand prison last Thursday, having cut his wrists with a penknife secreted from prison staff since his arrest on insider dealing and corruption charges. Richemont had earlier protested his innocence but had been refused bail. Sources in Geneva said that his suicide followed extradition proceedings against him by Dutch vice police investigating the death of a sixteen-year-old Indonesian refugee. Her bruised body was found weighed down in a polder in the residential suburb of Laren, south of Amsterdam, five days ago. Witnesses interviewed since by Dutch police allege that Richemont was seen with the dead girl in a house believed to be owned by the Russian mafia.

Dutch and Swiss police are still searching for Maximillian Arhus, 32, a former employee of Richemont. Richemont's alleged former girlfriend, up-and-coming Italian model Carla Gambino, 19, was seen this week at Paris fashion shows in the close company of a married forty-seven-year old media billionaire.

*   *   *

The Times

The author may be contacted by e-mail at
paulkilduff@eircom.net